The Cylinder Program

Die Zylinder-Programm

By Paul M. MacDonald

Hey Nat, we did it!

Table of Contents

Introduction

November 1, 1968. Pacing up and down the hospital corridor, all kinds of thoughts raced through my head. This waiting is killing me. C'mon Doc give me some news. Maybe I'm too old for this. I will be forty-eight this month. In fact, somebody just referred to me as an old guy the other day. I'm sure he said it in jest. Still, gray hair tells me, I'm not getting any younger.

A door swung open and our doctor in his scrubs came towards me.

"Mr. Baker, there is a problem with the delivery. It's what we call a breech baby."

That hit me like a slug in the gut.

"What does that mean?"

"The baby should be facing head down, but in this case it's facing the opposite way. We're attempting to turn the baby around. We're going to keep trying, but we may have to do a Caesarean delivery."

"Is there any danger?"

"I don't want to alarm you, but there are always risks either way. We'd like to see a normal birth, but we're prepared to do the Caesarean if necessary. I have to get back."

He hurried back through the door and left me in a worried state.

I began to dredge up old memories of a tragic accident that happened to me over twenty years ago. Oh, God, it would be more than I could handle.

I went down to the little chapel, sat down, bowed my head, and prayed.

My mind took me into a fog of serenity, when a gentle hand on my shoulder awakened me from my stupor and a distant voice spoke my name.

"Mr. Baker... Mr. Baker. It's a girl! They're both doing fine. We turned the baby around, and the birth was completely normal."

I stood up and instantly understood the good news.

"Thank God! And thank you doctor, I was so worried. Can I see them?"

"Absolutely, I'll bring you in."

He led me into the antiseptic smelling delivery room where I saw my Iris propped up a little in a bed looking very tired and pale. She gave me a forced smile and turned proudly to a tiny bundle next to her. Nurses congratulated me, as they went about their business. Timidly looking around, I cringed to think of what Iris had experienced in that room. I eagerly peeked in at our little angel peacefully resting after the ordeal of being born, and she took my breath away.

I bent over and kissed Iris, "She's beautiful! She looks just like you."

"Oh, Bill, I'm so happy. The doctor said she's a fine healthy baby."

I followed the two orderlies, as they wheeled her bed into a nearby room. On the way a heavy sense of responsibility came over me, as I suddenly realized that we had just become a family. Again, I thought about my age and prayed that God would let me see my daughter grow up and become a woman. But, what if something did happen to me before she could get to know me? She'd have to rely on what others told her. I'd hate that.

At last we were alone together, just the three of us.

Iris tried to talk, but exhausted and medicated, she couldn't keep her eyes open. A nurse came in to take the baby to the nursery, so they could both get their well-earned sleep. I kissed Iris and told her I would return later.

I walked down the corridor to the glass window of the nursery. As I gazed in at that wriggling little miracle, I vowed then and there to write my life's story for her sake. If I do pass from the scene, she won't have to find out about me from strangers. I especially want her to know about the last two years, how I met her mother, our underwater search for the gold coins, and how we tangled with those no good, diehard Nazis. Also, I want her to know about all our many, good friends who helped and participated in that great Key West adventure. I want her to know it all, as it really happened, in my own words

My Story

I'm Bill Baker. Since 1949, I've been a charter boat skipper here in Key West, the greatest little spot on earth. I'm originally from a little coastal town called Scituate in Massachusetts, a place I still enjoy visiting in the summer. It's an historic old town, settled by the pilgrims and incorporated in 1636. Scituate, with its cozy little harbor, proudly overlooks the Atlantic Ocean midway between Boston and Plymouth.

I was an only child and pleased to say, spoiled by my two loving parents. My father drove a semi trailer truck for a struggling trucking outfit that had been downsizing since the stock market crash in 1929. He gratefully accepted any job, even though some required him to be away for many days. Unfortunately, as the depression wore on, he found himself at home for longer stretches between jobs. Being just a youngster, I liked it when he stayed home, not realizing the hardship it caused. He always had a project around the house and would let me be his helper. He showed me how to use tools and make many of the common repairs expected of every homeowner. Improvising was like a religion to him.

"Sometimes, you just have to make do," he would say.

Now and then, he rented a rowboat and would take me fishing a little ways outside the harbor to one of his favorite spots. We just used simple drop lines made with tarred line, a hook, and a lead sinker wound up on a piece of wood. We baited the hooks with sea worms for haddock, cod, or flounder. If the mackerel were running, then we would use jigs tied to a length of line strung from the end of a bamboo pole.

"We never got skunked," as he liked to say.

We didn't know what we were going to catch, but we always came home with something. He showed me how to clean the fish before we brought it home and to never take more than I could use. My mother would always wrap some of it up in newspaper and have me bring it to a couple of elderly neighbors, a kindly lesson I never forgot.

My mother, always wearing an apron, loved cooking and gardening. One of my earliest memories is her showing me how to hoe the weeds around the corn.

I can still see her doing the laundry, in the old soapstone sink, on a washboard with a big block of my father's homemade lye soap, which we used for bathing as well. I liked to watch him make it, using the bacon fat that my mother would carefully purify through cheesecloth and save in old coffee tins. He always made me get well back, when he added the lye. After a lot of stirring, he poured the warm liquid into wooden, cheesecloth-lined trays made out of scrap wood. Then, when it set up, he cut it into blocks like my mother cut fudge. After curing for at least a month or two, it was ready to use. My mother took pride in hanging out the whitest whites, summer or winter. In addition to my father's homemade soap, she made me promise not to tell anyone about her other secret, Mrs. Stewart's bluing.

In the fall the kitchen became a canning factory. She put up all kinds of vegetables and made the best piccalilli. She bought pears, peaches and berries for canning as well.

The antique house we lived in came with the original scary root cellar, accessible through the basement. Although, complete with cobwebs and spiders, my mother took full advantage of the storage space, which kept food from freezing in the winter and cool in the summer. Her root crops, squash, and some fruits wintered well down there.

She also baked bread every week along with the occasional cake, pie and cookies.

I used to love it when she'd make us a nice cup of tea. She would take down two of her dainty flowered teacups from the top shelf, and then, preheat the teapot with boiling water. After awhile, she would empty the hot teapot water into the dishpan to use later to wash the dishes. She placed the carefully measured tea into the pot and added fresh boiling water. Waiting for the tea to steep she would tell me happy stories about things she did as a little girl and her favorite subject, history. My mother could tell the most interesting stories about the historical past of America and Scituate. She would then pour the tea putting extra milk and sugar in mine. With a couple of her cookies, I couldn't have been happier. The best part came later, when we finished the tea. She would take my cup, turn it upside down on the saucer, rotate it three times then turn it over. Peering into it, she would study the leaves; and then, in a serious voice tell me my fortune.

"You're going on a long trip someday," she would say or, "You're going to get a letter or some money."

Happily, all her predictions came true.

As I look back now, I know and appreciate how their unselfish love, hard work, and sacrifice sheltered me from the Great Depression. The first time I realized I came from a poor household became evident when I got to college. But, I also realized that I was rich in a far different and better way. Happy times of helping my father fix up around the house and the many treasured scenes and aromas in my mother's kitchen are safely stored away in my memory bank, more precious than gold.

My best friend Freddie Fineran and I spent our young summers together exploring the endless nooks and crannies of Scituate, especially the beaches and the harbor. As soon as we got out of school, down to the barbershop we would go for our annual summertime crew cuts. I still remember sitting in that big barber's chair, looking forward to the long free summer ahead, watching my neatly combed blonde hair disappear and thinking, this has got to be what heaven is like. Freddie would make fun of me and call me baldy. I did the same to him when his rusty hair joined mine on the barber shop floor.

We could be seen together all around town dressed in tee shirts, old patched trousers over our bathing suits, and Keds sneakers riding our bicycles, usually toting bamboo fishing poles. My faithful dog Laddie, our constant companion, got plenty of exercise keeping up with us.

When I'd bring home a nice cleaned cod or haddock, my mother would put on her apron and carve off two fillets for dinner. The rest of it, including the head, bones, and tail, she carefully washed and placed into a pot of water. Then after boiling it she picked out the meat and strained the broth for her delicious fish chowder the next day. Meanwhile, my father and I looked forward to a delicious fish dinner later that evening.

I have many fond memories growing up in that beautiful little seacoast town.

I went through the Scituate school system, and there, I met my first and only girlfriend Rose Smith, also an only child. Her family just became new residents in town, and she joined our senior class of 1939. Her father represented a sheet metal machinery company in Chicago, and they gave him the Southeastern Massachusetts territory, a big promotion for him. They came out here looking for a place to settle, and both fell in love with Scituate. Her parents felt bad for Rose, but they needed to move right away. She could have stayed with an aunt to finish high school, but fortunately for me she decided against it.

I had never seen such a pretty girl. All the boys thought the same way too. But she didn't seem too happy. I realized that I wouldn't be too happy either, if I suddenly found myself in a new school, surrounded by all new faces in my senior year. Being a little shy, it took me a while to get up the courage to speak to her. I needn't have waited; she was as easy to talk to, as she was pretty. I helped her break the ice by introducing her to all of my friends in the class. She thanked me and admitted how uneasy she felt being a total stranger in a new school. She also felt homesick for all her old friends in Chicago. Before long, the only thing that gave her away from being a townie was her accent. When we poked fun at it, she would smile and say, "You think my accent is funny, you should hear yours."

Her blue eyes would sparkle when she laughed at one of my silly jokes. I loved being with her, and we agreed to go steady. I knew I would marry her someday. Of course, I didn't tell her that, but I did dream that she felt the same way.

I applied to Northeastern University in Boston, and my parents were so proud of me, when the acceptance letter came in the mail. Neither one of them finished high school, so this meant so much to them. They had been putting some money away in the hopes that I would someday use it for college. It was a good start, but I still needed more money, so I applied for a job at the bank in the harbor and they hired me for the summer. Rose got a full time job with the travel agency in the harbor, so occasionally we were able to have our lunches together on the waterfront.

My friend Freddie joined the Navy, something he always talked about as far back as I could remember. I saw him off at the train station, the day he left for the Great Lakes Naval Training Center, in Illinois.

I rode my bike to that same station in North Scituate every day, rain or shine, to take the Old Colony steam train to Boston. I majored in engineering at Northeastern, and I took full advantage of that commuting time to study. Getting through that school didn't come easy. Those long lonely hours hunched over a little desk in my bedroom, ultimately paid off when I finally received that sheepskin.

On a whim, I joined a gym near the college. They had a boxing club and I gave it a try. I enjoyed sparring in the ring and after a few months, I asked an old timer if I should try to become a professional boxer. He asked me what my major was, and I told him Engineering.

"Baker," he said, "as a boxer you'd make a good Engineer."

I took his advice and stuck with the Engineering.

I continued going to the gym until I graduated, and did the training just for fun and the exercise.

The war with Japan and Germany had started, so everyone wanted to help in the war effort. My father got a job driving a fire engine at the Hingham Naval Ammunition Depot, and later, my mother started working there as well. Over three thousand civilians, sailors, and marines worked around the clock there producing a huge amount of ammunition, most of it for the Atlantic Fleet. The gravity of the war became evident and personal, when my mother told me she assembled hand grenades. The travel business slowed down, so Rose joined my mother putting together those hand grenades.

In the second semester of my senior year 1943, the recruiters of all the branches actively pursued us to sign up for Officers Training. I talked with my parents and told them that I made up my mind to do my part and chose the U.S. Navy. Although a bit apprehensive they agreed it was the right thing to do.

My mother and father got all dressed up for my graduation. Their praise and admiration made me feel a foot taller in my cap and gown. My eyes started to water up, when I saw them trying to fight back tears of joy. After the ceremony we had a marvelous dinner at a fancy restaurant in Boston. I'll never forget that day.

Like a million other GI's I put my life on hold for the duration, including wedding plans. I gave Rose an engagement ring, but we both agreed to put off getting married until I got out of the Navy. Luckily, they stationed me down in Florida, so I was able to get back home a couple of times a year.

While on deployment, Countless letters streamed back and forth between Rose and I. When I did get leave, we spent every possible minute together talking about the future. We found a little house and with the help of our parents, we were able to get a loan to buy it. Rose and both our parents spent their weekends fixing up the house for us. The next time I came home our house had a fresh coat of paint, inside and out. With the floors refinished and the walls papered, it looked like a new house. Rose had the wedding plans finalized, just waiting for the war to end, so we could set the date.

In July of 1945, I received a letter from my mom that Freddie was killed in action during the battle for Okinawa. A Kamikaze plane flew in a straight line hugging the water, somehow evading all the frantic anti-aircraft fire and slammed into Freddie's ship. The piloted flying bomb detonated the ship's magazine. The massive explosion caused the vessel to rise up amid ships out of the water and break in two, sinking in just minutes, with the loss of almost all hands.

I felt sick when I read it. I had just received a letter from him a few weeks before, telling me he had seen plenty of action. However, the scuttlebutt going around had the crew all excited that his ship would be returning to Pearl Harbor soon, ironically, to upgrade their anti-aircraft guns. They would be there for a month or more, so he looked forward to getting leave to come home and with a bit of luck might get to see me.

The next time I traveled home to Scituate, I visited his parents. Having gone down with his ship, they displayed some photos of Freddie in uniform on the mantle. We all ended up crying, as we reminisced about our childhood adventures and misadventures together. Emotions began to spiral out of control. It became a difficult moment for them and for me. Fortunately, Rose, seeing our plight, gently suggested that we leave.

V-E Day or Victory in Europe came on May 8, 1945. V-J Day or Victory over Japan came on August 14, 1945. The war finally came to an end, and a month later the Navy issued me my honorable discharge. I said goodbye to my crew and gave my sincere thanks and appreciation to my CPO, John Dollar.

I packed up my car and made a beeline for Scituate. When I arrived, the town had banners up celebrating the end of the war. My mother and Rose made a "Welcome Home Bill" sign and my father staked it out on the front lawn. It sure felt good to be home for good.

Rose and I set the date for October 27th. A more beautiful bride never walked down a church aisle. We became man and wife in a traditional Nuptial Mass ceremony in St. Mary's of the Nativity church. After the reception we drove down the Cape for our honeymoon.

At long last, we settled down to a normal life together. I started working at the local bank, where I worked all the summers during college. It wasn't engineering and I didn't care that much for the job, but they gave me a pay incentive to stay on. In time, I told myself, I could find something better and more to my liking. The Ammunition Depot downsized and my father went back to truck driving, my mom became a homemaker again, and Rose went back to the travel agency.

A year later my son Billy arrived. A handsome little guy that our parents couldn't get enough of, especially the two grandmothers who talked Rose into staying with the travel agency part time, so they could take turns minding him. I couldn't wait until he got a little bigger, so I could teach him how to fish, play baseball, and all kinds of things, and just watch him grow into manhood. Sadly, it wasn't meant to be.

It happened on a cold Saturday afternoon on January 22, 1949, a date seared into my memory. At an intersection in Scituate, the light turned green and as I accelerated, all I can remember is Rose saying, "Oh, God no!"

I woke up in a hospital bed unharmed, not knowing how I got there. My devastated parents had the sad and difficult task of breaking the terrible news to me that Rose and Billy were dead. That auto accident changed my life forever. A pickup truck ran a red light and struck us on the passenger side. My wife and our three-year-old son died instantly. Seat belts and car seats for kids didn't exist then, although they may not have helped in this case. No skid marks were left at the scene, so the other driver never touched his brakes. An open bottle of whiskey was found with the deceased driver of the truck. Even so, I blamed myself. If only I had looked before accelerating. I relived that final scene over and over in my mind, and kept hearing Rose's last words, "Oh, God no". That senseless accident took away the two souls, I cherished more than my own life. My heart still pumped blood through my body, but it was devoid of feeling. I was mad at God for letting this happen.

The wake and funeral were more than I could have ever handled on my own. My family and friends kindly ushered me through those dark days. I mindlessly navigated it like a sleepwalker. Thankfully, I don't remember very much of it.

Afterward, I fell into a deep depression, and just couldn't snap out of it. I became an uncaring, hollow man going through the motions of living. Rose's parents' felt the pain as deeply as I did, having lost their only child and grandson. They did their best to help console me, and we did commiserate together, but I needed to deal with my grief over Rose and my son in my own way. My boss, Mr. Stetson at the bank, tried to overlook the mistakes and lack of interest, but finally with apologies, let me go. I didn't blame him, and I told him so. I just didn't care anymore. I began to question the reason for living without them. I started drinking heavily. Our little home that Rose took such pride in evoked many happy memories, which now filled me with sadness. Weeds invaded Rose's manicured flowerbeds. I lost all interest in the upkeep of the place, and hired a neighbor's son to cut the lawn. The more people tried to help me, the more I withdrew from them. I didn't want to be closely attached to anyone even my own parents. I vowed that I would never be hurt like that again. I became very reclusive.

On a bright July morning, hung over as usual, I drove down to the harbor. To clear the cobwebs out of my head I bought two cups of black coffee to go and walked over to the fish pier to check on the commercial fishing activity. The peaceful ocean with a light onshore breeze, pointed to a perfect boating day, but I didn't care. I parked myself on a weathered, overturned skiff that commanded a sweeping view of the fishing fleet. For some reason it was the only thing I had any interest in.

Tied up right in front of me stood a weathered old fishing boat I'd never seen before. It was a boat you would not soon forget, a real ugly duckling. The name "Maria" was painted on the bow. She must have pulled in during the night. Just about all of her paint had been spalled away by the relentless rust. She reeked noticeably more than the other fishing boats with a generous compliment of flies. On board a clean-shaven elderly gentleman dressed in black trousers, vest, suit coat and white shirt deftly worked a shuttle mending a net. His way with the shuttle, weathered face and hands, and snowy hair flaring out from under a well-worn, black fisherman's cap, portrayed the hard life of a fisherman.

Just then, a yodeling seagull swooped down and made a chalky insult on the deck of his boat, barely missing him. He let out a litany in Portuguese, shaking his fist at the gull. Then we made eye contact.

"Do you speak Portuguese?" he asked.

I answered, "No, I don't."

That's when I noticed he chewed tobacco.

"That's good luck, you know!" he said, pointing at the deck. "I just wanted to let that seagull know, in Portuguese, how thankful I am."

I thought to myself, I can't speak Portuguese, but that sure sounded like something a bit more salty than a thank you.

I just smiled and nodded to him.

"Hey, what are you doing today? How would you like to go fishing with me? My mate didn't show up, and I can't go out alone. It will be a day of adventure for you, one you'll never forget, and I'll even share the catch."

"Sure, why not, I'll go out with you," I answered impulsively.

I walked up to the boat, and leaning over the rail, held out my hand to shake on it. He got up, and smiled revealing a fine set of teeth, but stained by the tobacco. He stood straight and taller than I expected, with broad shoulders. He motioned with his finger, excusing himself for a moment, as he spit aft out over the rail; a few drops of the brown liquid dripped down his chin and stained his clean white shirt. He didn't seem to notice it and wiped his chin with a handkerchief. He took my hand, and I had never experienced such a sandpapery and powerful handshake. This was a different man from the little old one I had just seen hunched over repairing his net. That handshake told me; he still had lots of iron in that right arm of his.

"My name is Tony, Tony Sousa," he said with pride.

"My name is Bill Baker."

"Very well then, stand by Bill, while I get the engine started, then I'll let you know when to cast off and come aboard."

As I stood by the lines, he stepped up to the controls and turned the switch to start the engine. It turned over, but wouldn't start.

"I'll just go below and see what's wrong."

He went below and I could hear more Portuguese. He came back up and said he gave it some ether. He tried it again and after a few starts and stops, coughing and wheezing, then a loud backfire with an ominous billow of black smoke, the old diesel finally started. The irregular firing of the cylinders started the vessel to vibrate noisily, causing some rust to fall here and there, but then surprisingly the engine settled down to a nice steady rhythmic chugging. All the while, Tony acted nonchalantly, as though this was a typical start up.

"Who were you thanking down there?" I asked. "I heard more Portuguese."

"Oh, I just gave my thanks to Mr. Gray who made the engine. Now, you can cast off all lines."

I looked over the big cinnamon colored hulk, and began to rethink my decision to go fishing with him on this rust bucket. However, with the stimulus of the caffeine buoying me up, I threw all caution to the wind, obeyed his command to cast off the lines, and jumped on board. He shoved it into reverse, expertly backed out, and spun her around. Then, in a cloud of black smoke and soot that began to dissipate once under way, he snaked old rusty through the forest of boats and slipped her into the outward bound channel at the proper harbor speed limit.

As the Maria kept the green buoys to her starboard, coming up on the port side our beloved town motif, the Old Scituate Lighthouse came into view. It opened for business in 1811 with Simeon Bates being the first keeper of the light. Two years after the War of 1812 started, his two daughters, Abigail and Rebecca became an Army of two.

As the story goes, a British warship the H.M.S. La Hogue sent two longboats of armed Marines into the harbor to sack the town. The two young girls, being in charge of the light while their father was away, knew exactly what to do. Unafraid, the Bates sisters playing a fife and drum marched up and down unseen behind a nearby grove of cedar trees. They put on such a grand performance playing "Yankee Doodle"; they fooled the Marines into thinking they were about to face a serious force of mustering militia. Discretion being the better part of valor, they decided to return to their ship, thus saving the town.

Just below the lighthouse, lay my favorite little beach where my freckled childhood friend, Freddie and I used to peddle our bikes out to, for a swim. Right next to it stretched the stone jetty from which, we could catch as many fish as we wanted. Those precious summer memories are warmly and vividly etched in my mind forever.

Looking astern, I could see the old one hundred and fifty foot Lawson Tower, another sailor's landmark. Back in 1902, when a huge iron water tower appeared; a wealthy Scituate resident Thomas Lawson deemed it an eyesore spoiling the view from his mansion. At great expense, he hired an architect to encase it with a wooden medieval tower patterned after one in Germany. It became the most expensive water tower in the country and has become a tourist attraction ever since. He also had a carillon installed consisting of ten bells weighing from three hundred to three thousand pounds that are still played on special occasions. It is well maintained and is an impressive and beautiful landmark.

The lighthouse marked the entrance to the harbor, and once we cruised by it we were in the open waters of the Atlantic. Tony pushed the throttle forward and the Maria obediently stepped up her speed losing the smell and all but the most tenacious flies. Soon, the Scituate Light and the Lawson Tower inched below the horizon, and Tony's boat became like a toy on that humbling expanse of sea and sky.

I had forgotten how much I loved the bracing smell of the salt air, the steady throb of an engine, and the vessel's bow parting endless water leaving a telltale milky trail. In no time at all, I had my sea legs back arousing those tucked away memories of my Navy days when stationed in Key West. Having a rolling deck beneath my feet felt good and natural to me.

A couple of pleasant hours went by, when I was awakened from my reverie by an awareness of a sluggish feeling of that deck beneath my feet. I looked around and saw Tony's concerned look, as he ran to the cabin door and looked in.

"Jesus, Mary and Joseph!" he said, quickly blessing himself, "My Maria, she is sinking!"

In just minutes the stern started to settle down, and the bow started rising up. The engine became flooded, and the Maria's heart stopped beating; leaving us with just the sounds of the indifferent wind and lapping waves. She was going down and fast.

Tony's boat, suffering from years of utter neglect, picked this moment to succumb with yours truly on board. I frantically looked around for a life raft or at least something that would float. Everything seemed to be made out of metal, rusty metal. Without even a life preserver, we were going into the water and here we were, out of sight of land and not another boat to be seen. Me, a former naval officer, I should have known better than to get on board a derelict like this. What was I thinking? That's just it, I wasn't thinking. Remember, you're the one who didn't care anymore. My poor mother and father, they won't know what happened to me. Then, I thought of the marine radio and shouted to Tony to send an SOS.

Shrugging his shoulders he said, "My radio is broken."

Well, I thought, this isn't going to end well. It's a watery grave for Bill Baker. Maybe it's just as well. If there's a heaven, I'll get to see Rose and Billy again.

Looking out at the horizon, I said aloud, "God knows, I'm ready to go!"

"Where are you going? Don't worry, look," he said, producing a little rubber lifeboat pack, imprinted with USAAF on it, "I bought this at a surplus store a couple of years ago, or so."

Standing in ankle deep water, I looked at it and chuckled, "This is it, the end of the line!"

With a lot more confidence than I had, he pulled the little red tag and to my disbelief the little yellow craft popped and puffed itself to life. We just had time to grab some fresh water and get in it. We were crammed in that little yellow life raft, up close and personal, with a thin sheet of rubber protecting us from the ocean depths. Seconds later, we watched the Maria go down and disappear into the secret world of Davey Jones' Locker. She was there, and then she was gone; the ocean quickly healed itself erasing all but her memory. With tears in his eyes, Tony solemnly blessed himself again with the little gold cross he wore around his neck and stared at the empty spot.

My watch said twelve o'clock as we drifted aimlessly. We anxiously scanned the horizon in hope of rescue. We saw a couple of boats, but they were too far off to notice our little yellow speck.

Occasionally, we saw the spray of whales in the distance.

"I know they have a blow hole on top of their heads, so they can breathe when they surface, but why do they spray water into the air, Tony?"

"When they come up, they are blowing out old moist warm air from their lungs, when it hits the outside air it turns to vapor. That's what makes the spout you see."

"There seems to be a lot of them, are they dangerous?" I asked.

"This is the Stellwagan Banks area, a popular feeding ground for them this time of year. We don't have anything to fear from them, but I guess they could overturn our little raft here without even realizing it. Now, the killer whales, they're the ones to be afraid of. They move faster and are much more vicious. I saw a pack of them attack a baby whale, and it wasn't a pretty site."

Suddenly a whale surfaced like an island just a few yards away. I moved closer to Tony as it slowly came toward us. Then a large gentle eye peered at us like a curious child seeing something unusual for the first time. Tony whispered that it was a humpback whale and to stay still.

The whale slowly descended with its great flukes rising high into the air above us so close we could almost touch them. Mercifully, they came down slowly parting the water with hardly a ripple. After that, we just heard their occasional snorting sounds and could see their white spray in the distance. Tony enjoyed the encounter; however, the sheer size of the gentle giant frightened me. As the day wore on, I came to realize how fortunate we were to have had such an experience.

Tony, seventy-six years old, with no living kin and having just lost his boat, all of his possessions, and the means of making a living took it remarkably well.

"When your boat sinks out on the ocean, what are you going to do? You can't unsink a boat. Over the years I found that at the loss of something material, when a little time went by, I was able to laugh about it. Now, I don't wait to laugh. I've learned that crying and sadness are better saved only for when you lose someone you love."

Floating in our little yellow craft, like two peas in a pod, Tony didn't wait to laugh. He revealed the marvelous sense of humor he developed over his lifetime of experiences. For the first time since my accident, even in this perilous situation, he had me laughing with his jokes and tall stories of his colorful past. Of course, sad times were no stranger in his life. Long ago, his eighteen-year-old son was caught in a net and dragged overboard. Before he could haul it back in, the boy had drowned. He had to bring the body of their only child back to his wife, Maria. It broke her heart and she never recovered. A few years later, he buried her next to his son.

The sun set in the West gently turning the day into night. Starting with one and then soaring to a million the stars flooded the clear night sky. Later, a full moon rose in the East making our miserable plight at least little brighter. The temperature dipped forcing us to huddle together to keep warm. The whales seemed to know where we were and kept their distance.

Later, I told him how I lost my wife and son. Tony caringly listened.

After a long pause, he said, "Eventually, we have to get back to the business of living. We both lost our wives and sons and know first hand that good and bad memories are being created with each tick of the clock and can never be changed. We want all our memories to be good, but in this life we know that is impossible. The next life may be different, but who's in a hurry to find that out? It is important to grieve, but we have to work our way through it, and make the most of the precious time we have left. 'Time and tide wait for no man.'"

Tony had a simple way of looking at the mysteries of life; the kind of outlook I needed to adopt to turn my life around.

"What are you going to do, Tony, if we get out of this?"

"It looks like the Old Sailors Home for me, Bill. I lied to you about my mate not showing up. I haven't had a mate in years. I've been working the boat myself, just barely getting by. I have no kin and everything I owned, even the little money I had, went down with my Maria. All I have is on my back and this gold cross and chain my Maria gave me on our wedding day. I'm sorry I got you into this."

A fishing boat, on its way back to Scituate, picked us up early the next morning. We were cold and hungry, but the crew wrapped us in blankets and plied us with coffee laced with rum. The stale leftover donuts were a most welcome treat.

I shudder to think how close to eternity we came. If it weren't for that little USAAF life raft, no one would have ever known what happened to us.

A few hours later the crew tied up to the pier in Scituate harbor. We thanked them for rescuing us and their generous hospitality. They wanted to know if we needed a ride or a place to stay. I told them I had my car nearby and would take Tony with me. I went right over to the package store and bought a jug of rum to replenish their supply, and we both thanked them again.

This adventure with Tony brought back a long forgotten dream about being a charter boat captain in Key West. When stationed there, I developed an interest in deep-sea fishing. Whenever I could, I chartered one of the local fishing boats. I tried a different one each time, and I got to know all of their captains, finding it easy to make friends with them. I was very impressed with their practical marine knowledge and the intimate bond they had with the various game fish they were hunting. I'll never forget the thrill of catching my first sailfish. It became my favorite pass time, and I started to work as a mate on my days off. Also, I couldn't help but notice and like their laid back Key West lifestyle, and I thought it would be a great way of life.

After the war however, when I came home and saw how Rose had our little house all decorated, I didn't have the heart to even mention it to her. I forgot all about that dream as we settled down in our little home. Rose and I were happily married. I loved her and I knew she loved me. With such a perfect wife, and mother to our son, I couldn't have been more content, but fate took it all away.

It started to become clear to me, why I crossed paths with Tony. That same fate or maybe even Rose, somehow, had intervened to help me get my life back on track after the accident. I had another chance to grab the brass ring and have another go around on this carousel of life. The harrowing experience with Tony and his philosophy did indeed turn me around. For the first time since the accident, I found myself looking forward to the rest of my life.

I decided at that moment, to revive the dream of being a charter boat Captain. I asked Tony if he would come with me to Key West, and join me in starting up a charter boat business?

He thought for a moment, then giving me a big smile and a little salute he said, "Aye, Aye, Captain. It'll sure beat the Old Sailors Home."

Over the next couple of months, I sold the house and traded my car in for a second hand, 1940 Chevy pick-up truck. I sold and gave away everything I wouldn't need in Key West. The rest of my belongings we stuffed into the old Chevy truck. I said my goodbyes to my parents and the few friends I had left. They made me promise to write and keep them up to date on my progress. They all let me know how happy they were for me, especially my parents, to see that I had finally snapped out of the doldrums.

I visited Rose and Billy's grave to say goodbye. I said a prayer and told her I would remain faithful to her and see her and Billy again in heaven.

Then, full of optimism, Tony and I headed south in mid September 1949.

We followed A1A all the way to its end. The trip itself turned into an adventure. We broke down several times, but Tony, being a first class mechanic, always managed to get us back up and running. However, when the transmission started acting up we had to seek help. Somehow, Tony with his affable personality turned every calamity into a welcome event, like being invited home to dinner by the mechanic who repaired that transmission and later being asked by his wife to spend the night. Tony showed himself to be a real charmer, especially with the ladies, young and old. As a result, all the way to Key West, those ladies showered us with gifts of sandwiches, coffee, lemonade and even a pie. He genuinely loved people and had a way of quickly disarming them.

The day finally came when we arrived in Key West, early in the morning. All the way down I talked about Maury's and how much fun I had there, while I was on active duty, during the war. With all my stories about the place Tony couldn't wait to see it and meet Maury and Denise, so the first thing we did was head for Maury's Bar and Grill.

Maury Greer and his wife Denise became very close friends to me. I did keep in touch with them by mail over the last few years, however that stopped after the accident, so they had no idea I had just arrived in Key West. I thought it would be fun to surprise them. When I left Key West in 1945, I told them I would return someday, but I never thought it would be to stay. Maury and his wife, Denise ran the best bar and grill in Key West.

"If it isn't Bill Baker," said Maury, giving me a big bear hug. "I said to Denise just the other day, I wonder when Bill's going to show up? It's good to see you again. Let me go tell her."

Denise came out from the kitchen all smiles and gave me a hug and a kiss.

"Oh, Bill it's so good to see you. Is it just a visit or are you going to stay?"

"I'm here to stay, Denise. Let me introduce you to my friend and partner, Tony Sousa."

It didn't take long for Tony to fit right in. Denise and Maury took to him and we had a nice long visit getting reacquainted. I told them about Rose and Billy. They offered their sympathies to me and asked if there was anything they could do. I told them the whole experience was personally tragic and nearly beat me, but with Tony's help I'm over the worst of it.

They were both delighted to hear we were going to start a charter boat business and asked if we needed to borrow some money. We thanked them for the offer, but Tony and I were financially okay for at least six months. We did need a place to stay and asked if they knew of anyone looking to rent a small house.

After a few phone calls, Maury tracked down a friend that had a furnished house he wanted to rent. He gave us the address, and we could look at it right away.

We left Maury's with a promise to return later that evening.

We found the house and while we were waiting for the owner, Tony and I took a walk around it. The location couldn't be better, within walking distance to downtown and the harbor. The well-built house sat on a corner with an adjacent vacant lot. A one-car garage set further back made enough room in the driveway for two vehicles. Overlooking the faded white paint and some needed repairs we liked what we saw.

The owner showed up and told us that his father had lived there for many years. He passed away the year before, and it has been vacant ever since, also we were welcome to use the furniture.

Three steps led up onto a nice size front porch. The entrance on the left opened into a large living room. A hallway divided the house with two bedrooms on the left. On the right a flight of stairs led up to the second floor with a third bedroom in the front and a storage room in the back. A large bathroom came next after the stairs and then the kitchen in the back. The furniture had seen better days and the whole interior needed a facelift, but it sure looked good to us. The rent was very reasonable and being able to move right in meant we wouldn't have to stay in a hotel that night. The owner said he wanted to sell it, if we were interested. I told him we might be, but for now we would just like to rent it. He agreed and I asked him if he wanted us to sign anything?

"Maury vouched for you, so that's all I need to know."

He held out his hand and said this will be our contract. The three of us shook hands on it and he handed us the keys.

"I like the way they do business here in Key West," said Tony.

I backed up the truck to the front door and it didn't take us long to move our belongings into our new home.

We went out to pick up a few things and some groceries. First though, I drove around the island showing Tony all the highlights.

We happened to drive by an old boat for sale sitting in a front yard. It looked like it hadn't seen the water for several years. I turned around and we drove by it again slowly. It looked like the kind of boat we wanted, but it also looked like it needed a complete overhaul. We debated about it and agreed that we should at least take a look at it. It belonged to an elderly woman, whose fisherman husband had died four years before. Soon after his death she had it hauled to her front yard where she put a for sale sign on it. Obviously, she hasn't had an acceptable offer.

We received her permission to go aboard to make an inspection.

She measured roughly forty-feet long with about a fifteen-foot beam and a four-foot draft. It had a spacious cockpit with a gin pole for hoisting heavy fish aboard and a single fighting chair fastened down to a sound teakwood deck. An aluminum ladder allowed access to the upper control area with a Bimini frame. Underneath, out of the weather, the main controls and wheel were thoughtfully placed for maximum visibility. A roomy cabin greeted you as you walked through the hatchway complete with a sink, stove, and icebox. Further on a sleeping area for up to six and of course the head. The cradle holding her up had deteriorated and needed immediate attention. We didn't see any signs of rot, however a couple of her planks had to be replaced, but other than that, we confidently pronounced her as sound as a silver dollar. A good stem to stern scraping, caulking, and painting would make her fit for duty again.

Whoever built her used the best materials and knew what they were doing.

After our survey, we decided that as long as she fit into our budget, we would buy her.

Tony and I went back up to the front door to start the negotiations.

"You can call me Millie. Have you had lunch yet? Are you hungry?"

We said we hadn't, and yes, we were hungry.

"You come in and I'll fix you something."

She showed us where to wash up and then sat us down at her kitchen table. I don't know how, but it almost seemed like she knew we were coming. She served up the most delicious fish chowder like my mother used to make, and I told her so. After the second helping Tony asked her how much she wanted for the boat.

Ignoring the question she brought out a Key Lime Pie and said, "I hope you have room for some dessert and coffee?"

After the pie and coffee, Tony asked her again about the boat.

"Well, I'm sick of looking at that ark in my front yard. If you think you can use it you're welcome to it. You're the first ones to inquire about buying it in four years. I just got a price to have it hauled away, so your timing is good. They wanted a tidy sum, so I figure I'm getting the best of the bargain. And, besides my late husband Barney would have been pleased to have it restored rather than broken up."

She made out a bill of sale and to make it legal she reluctantly took one dollar for it.

"I'll put it in the collection on Sunday."

We were very grateful to her and thanked her for the excellent lunch and for being so generous.

"It's been a long time since I fed a hungry man and feeding you two brought me pleasure. If you ever need a good home cooked meal, you're welcome to stop in anytime."

"You'll be seeing me again, Millie," said Tony.

We picked up some groceries and headed back to the house. We spent a couple of hours putting things away and moving furniture around to suit our needs. There were some items we would need, but they could wait for now. Our limited funds would have to last until we started to have paying customers. We could only spend money on necessary supplies to run the business and get the boat in shape. Of course, high on the list of allowable expenses was the occasional visit to Maury's. Speaking of which, when we went back there later, we could celebrate with Denise and Maury, finding a house and getting a boat on our first day in Key West.

We got cleaned up and it was nice to be able to walk over to Maury's.

We sat up at the bar, and ordered two draft beers. It felt good to be in there again after all these years. Looking around, not much had changed. Tony couldn't get over all the nautical artifacts on display. He felt right at home.

"It's a real sailor's bar," he said reverently.

"Everything's on the house tonight for you and Tony!" said Maury. "Welcome home. Don't worry it's okay, Denise suggested it."

We thanked them for their generosity and enjoyed talking about old times. We both had the peel and eat shrimp. Tony raved about how good they tasted, the best he's ever had. I told him that the locals call it Key West's pink gold.

We told Maury about the boat and thanked him for helping us find the house. We were off to a good start in our Key West adventure.

The next morning we arranged to have Barney's boat and cradle hauled to a local boat yard and the sentence meted out to us... three months of hard labor getting her shipshape.

After we made the necessary repairs to the cradle, Tony and I went back to Millie's place and cleaned up the aftermath of the four years of weed growth under where the boat sat. We raked it out and spread some fertilizer and grass seed. She was thankful for our thoughtfulness and supplied us with sandwiches and iced tea.

Those two heavy planks in the hull had to be replaced. They were a full two inches thick so to get them to conform to the contours of the boat they had to be steamed to make them pliable and then quickly bent, clamped, and fastened into place. The yard had a steam box available and on the day we started steaming, several of the local boat owners came forward to volunteer their time. One of them told us that Barney's wife Millie was well known to them, and they appreciated how we cleaned up her front yard.

They had steamed planks many times before, so they brought along plenty of extra clamps. What would have taken us a couple of days to do in stages, with their help, we accomplished in just a few hours. At noontime we were finished, so I told them the beer and sandwiches were on us. In a half hour I returned with the goods, and we all sat around in the shade of the boat and enjoyed the lunch and got to know each other. It reminded me of the old days, when they had a barn raising and neighbors gave their skills and time. We wanted them to know we were ready to reciprocate whenever needed. These Key Westers are good people.

The engine had to be rebuilt with new head gaskets, hoses, belts, plugs etc. Being an excellent mechanic, Tony took charge of that. He liked the fact that it was a gasoline engine. He claimed it would be cheaper and simpler to maintain then the diesel he had in the Maria, and he wouldn't need his Portuguese as much.

After serving our time, we finally got our reward, on that happy Christmas Eve day, when we broke a cheap bottle of champagne on her bow and christened her the Rose Maria. Then, I opened a bottle of expensive rum, and poured a cup for Tony and myself to toast her, as we rode her down the rails into the awaiting turquois water. I tossed the nearly full bottle to our new found friends who had gathered for the launching. Gratefully caught and passed around, they cheered us on and wished us luck.

She behaved like a real lady, all spruced up and happy to be set free of the land. Tony's engine eagerly started and ran like a top as we revved it up to full speed, putting the Rose Maria through her shake down cruise. We were very proud of her when we pulled into our slip on charter boat row.

Every once in a while Tony would visit Millie for the promised home cooked meal and did a few chores around the house for her. He would supply the wine, fresh fish and flowers. He told me he enjoyed her company and highly praised her cooking.

We struggled for a while, but Tony's years of experience as a fisherman began to pay off. He taught me all kinds of tricks of the trade like how to properly bait hooks, tie knots, watch the clouds and wind for the weather, spot fish oil slicks, how to read bird action, and on and on. Generations of firsthand experience were crammed into him. He could literally smell where the fish were. When he talked about fishing I listened and learned. We started bringing in trophy size fish when other charter boats were coming in empty. It didn't take long until everyone wanted to charter Bill Bakers boat.

The other charter boat captains were hesitant at first to come around and ask Tony a question or for advice. That all changed when they found out how happily he shared everything he knew. He became a very popular guy on charter boat row. Actually, he made an impression on Key West. He never had a license to drive, so anytime he wanted to go somewhere, he stood on a corner and thumbed. Whoever gave him a ride would be repaid by his jovial personality and left with their spirits uplifted. It wasn't long before, even women were happy to stop and pick him up and he liked that, especially the widows. He always carried a screwdriver with him and if someone's engine didn't sound right, he would ask him or her to pull over. He would then lift the hood and with the rough engine running, adjust the carburetor until it settled down and sounded like new. Most drivers ended up going out of their way to bring him to his destination, especially the ladies.

Thanks to Tony we started to make a real good living in Key West. We made many real friends, and best of all settled into that envied and exclusive "Key West life style."

In 1958, age finally caught up with Tony and he passed away. It was a tribute to him, to see so many people attend his funeral, including several teary eyed widows who showed up dressed in black to say goodbye. That caused quite a stir in Key West, generating hearsay about Tony's romantic prowess that elevated his likeability to a loftier level. I suppose we all would like to think it true and why not at his age. However, I knew Tony to always be a gentleman in every respect; from the first time I met him until he passed away, and I'm sure the ladies in black would attest to that. He never divulged to me very much about his visits with the ladies other than their outstanding talent for cooking. A real gentleman, Tony loved everyone.

At the end, he confessed to me that he intentionally neglected his Maria for a number of years planning to go down with her when she sank, if he could go through with it. Because, I happened to be with him on that day, he didn't have to make that fatal decision. He thanked me for taking him into my charter boat business, and he told me that these last few years were the happiest of his life. I told him I had the best part of the deal, because he saved me from myself. I sincerely thanked him for that gift. I think of him, every time I quote one of his wise sayings or use one of the Portuguese cuss words he taught me. I miss him and his fishing knowhow, the pranks along with the stains and smell of his chewing tobacco. I'll never forget that wonderful contagious laugh of his, and the never ending stories he could tell. He was a very special friend.

The following year, 1959, Jacques LaPort became a houseguest of mine due to a personal tragedy, which I helped him deal with. He struggled with the long recovery and when he felt better, I asked him to try being my part time mate, to see if he liked it. Quick to learn, he enjoyed the interaction with the diverse mix of people that made every trip different and unique. After a dozen charters, he took me up on the offer to be my full time mate. I paid him a salary equal to the going rate for mates in Key West. The tips he received from the customers supplemented it. It turned out that he had been a professional chef for a restaurant in Haiti, so we worked out a bartering deal that he would do the cooking and KP for room and board. I eventually owned up to him that I hated cooking and especially doing dishes.

The next seven years were very kind to me. I made a good living and was able to buy the house with the extra lot that Tony and I had started renting, when we first arrived in Key West. I made a small vegetable garden and did some landscaping on that adjacent lot, which then became a focal point from the new covered deck I added.

My life fell into a beautiful routine that some might call dull. The house and boat were paid for and I had money in the bank. I did a few charters every week, which I enjoyed, and I had delicious home cooked meals and no dishwashing. I found myself in hog heaven. I had it made, as the years pleasantly drifted by and my hair began to turn a distinguished gray.

Monday, January 10, 1966

Then, 1966 happened. It all began on a beautiful January Key West morning. My Haitian mate, Jacques and I left the dock with our charter for the day; then set the Rose Maria on a course for our favorite deep sea fishing grounds. We were dressed in our usual khaki shirts, trousers, and sneakers. I wore my long billed khaki fishing cap and Jacques his colorful knit watch cap. In stark contrast to his formal courtroom attire, our charter, a big shot criminal attorney from Boston, Jeremy White, sported a loud Hawaiian shirt, shorts, sneakers, and an official Boston Red Sox hat. He told us that he recently won a long and intense case in Boston and collected a very generous fee from a most happy client. He chose getting out on the ocean, behind a man sized fishing rod, as his favorite way of relieving the pent up stress. It was hard to imagine this gentle soft-spoken man, standing in the middle of a courtroom, pleading his client's innocence.

After several disappointing charters out of Miami, a friend told him about me in Key West, so he set up the charter. His expectations weren't very high so when that awesome sailfish struck, then leaped out of the water, skipping, and dancing across the waves, he went wild with excitement. For more than an hour Jacques patiently coached and rooted for him, as he struggled in the chair fighting that fish. When we brought the seventy-five pound prize aboard, he just lost it. He gave Jacques a big hug and waltzed him around the fighting chair yelling and screaming for joy, so much for the gentle soft-spoken man.

"I did it! I did it!" he said. "No more tall tales about the one that got away."

He looked up at me at the upper controls and tipped his hat. He was as happy as a clam at high tide. He called it a day and made me radio in to have a taxidermist waiting for us at the dock. He couldn't wait to get that trophy on his office wall in Boston. I can hear him describing to potential clients how he battled with that fish for hours against all odds and won, the way he will personally fight and win for them.

Jacques whispered to me, "Old Jeremy, doesn't know that you saved that fish a dozen times by maneuvering the boat."

"That's true, but that's part of our job. He doesn't ever have to know, let's not spoil his big day," I whispered back.

At the dock, I took some photos of Jeremy holding a rod in one hand and with his other, spreading out the sail of the strung up fish. Then, Will the taxidermist took a couple of shots of Jeremy, Jacques, and me with the impressive prize. I told Jeremy I would get the pictures in the mail as soon as I got them developed.

"Hey Will, don't spare anything," said Jeremy. "I want those colors perfect and that fish looking like he's going to jump off the wall. How much will it cost and when can you ship it?"

Will took out a yellow pencil and started jotting on a pad of paper, "Well, you know that's a big fish, these things take time, and I'm pretty busy right now. Let me see?"

I walked over and pulled the pencil out of Will's hand and handed it back to him, "The man wants that fish perfect and hanging on his wall in three weeks, how much?"

"Seventy dollars plus freight," he answered instantly.

"You've got a deal," said Jeremy. "Let me know what the freight is and I'll send you a check. Bill has my address."

After Will left with the fish, Jeremy asked, "Is he the right guy for the job?"

"Will is the finest artist in the Keys," I said. "You'll be very happy with his work."

I can still see Jeremy's big grin when he came up to me and shook my hand thanking me for the best fishing trip of his life.

"I'll be in touch about a charter for next year and maybe even sooner, if I get another windfall."

He then shook hands with Jacques and thanked him as well, then turned and started to walk away down the pier.

Jacques waving a twenty-dollar bill said, "That's the biggest tip I ever got!"

I looked down and opened my hand, expecting to see a matching twenty-dollar tip. Much to my surprise, I saw old Ben Franklin looking back up at me. Jeremy's generous tips amounted to double what I charged him for the charter.

He almost reached the end of the pier when I yelled to him, "Thank you for the tip, Jeremy."

"Thank you from me too, Jeremy," yelled, Jacques.

He turned, waved, and disappeared around the corner.

Jacques carefully placed the twenty into his wallet saying, "This was a profitable day."

"I couldn't agree with you more, Jacques," I said, picking up a mop. "Let's clean up the boat."

"I can read your mind, Bill," said Jacques, taking the mop from me. "You can't wait to get down to Maury's and slap that hundred on the bar. So, you go ahead, I'll finish up here. But, you owe me a cold one."

"It's scary how well you know me. You're right, I can't wait to see Maury's face when I show him and I'll have a tall cold one waiting for you. Thanks, Jacques."

Maury's Bar and Grill was like a second home to me and big Maury Greer, all six foot six of him, has been like a big brother. As a lighthouse guides sailors to safety a gaudy neon sign guides patrons to Maury's, the best bar in Key West. It sat on a corner and all the shutters and doors could be pulled back, which gave the whole place an open-air atmosphere. A guitar player sang songs about the sea, ships, islands, and Key West, tempting strollers down Duval Street to pause and come in and have a beer. Inside, the tables, chairs, booths, walls, and the longest bar in Key West were all natural wood freshly varnished. Shiny brass and copper accents everywhere made it all very inviting. And, behind the bar like the Captain of his ship, with the ever present bar towel over his left shoulder, stood the imposing Maury Greer.

Maury's evolved into the hangout for an expanding cadre of Key West fishing, shrimping, sailing, diving, and snorkeling skippers along with their crews. I was proud to say, I was a regular. Nowhere in Key West could you find a more comfortable place to have a drink and be with fellow nautical types. Maury Greer had his finger on the pulse of Key West. If you needed to know anything about anything, you asked Maury. We all relied on him to relay messages, keep track of bets, and a dozen other things. He could be a blabbermouth, in fact he loved to gossip. But, he knew when to keep his mouth shut. Not really. Whatever you did, you never asked Maury to keep a secret. Everyone in Key West knew that the three major means of communication were Telephone, Telegraph, and TellMaury.

That's Maury, but in spite of that one major fault he always told you exactly what he meant and never resorted to double talk.

Flotsam and jetsam are revered and encouraged by Maury. All kinds of souvenirs, dredged up from the ocean, are displayed here in all their grandeur. Hanging from the ceiling the walls or standing in corners, if someone took the trouble to dive for it and haul it back here, then Maury proudly displayed it. A career Navy veteran, he loved anything nautical. Maury's Bar and Grill with it's ever growing eclectic marine collection had been written up in several travel guides as a must see attraction in Key West.

"After all," he would say, "I make my living off all you men and women, so the least I can do is make you feel at home."

I remember the first time I came in here back in 1943. If only these beer soaked floors could talk, well, maybe its best they can't. After finishing a hasty three months training program at Columbia University in New York, I graduated as an Ensign in the U. S. Navy, and they gave me command of a small patrol craft with a crew of eight in Key West, Florida.

The first time one of them called me Captain I have to admit my ego elevated a couple of notches. But, I had the sense to know that I was just a big fish in a little pond and a really green Ensign. I quickly bonded with the one person that could help me, my Chief Petty Officer, John Dollar, "like the dollar bill" he would say. I privately went to him with hat in hand and asked for his help, and he did come to my aid in a big way.

"The first rule is, from now on, you never admit that to anyone ever again. Now let's get to work."

On the QT, he took me under his wing and proudly showed me the ropes. With his twenty something years of experience, asking John's help was the best thing I ever did. In private we became good friends, but there was a line that must not be crossed. At his strict insistence, in public we were always at different levels of Officer and Enlisted Man. He always called me Sir and I always called him Chief. With his able tutoring, in time I became a first rate Captain of a squared away boat with a great crew.

I picked up an old salty, tarnished officer's hat at a local pawnshop. My newly issued shiny one didn't quite fit the image of a Captain slugging it out with the enemy. I felt that I should at least look the part.

For my first Friday night in Key West, two of my newfound Officer buddies were most agreeable to show me the town. Especially, since I offered to bankroll the evening.

The Navy was proud of us as we left the base, three trim young Officers in their tropical white uniforms. We were gentlemen, by Act of Congress, going ashore to spend a dignified evening in Old Town.

Several hours later, after making all the bars up and down Duval Street, we stumbled into Maury's with three very thirsty girls who somewhere along the line attached themselves to us. Our uniforms were wrinkled, a little dirty, and gentlemen we certainly were not.

We all crowded into a booth and ordered a pitcher of beer, which the girls hastily put away. One of the Officers promptly fell asleep and the other one and myself started yawning uncontrollably. I kind of remember, big Maury escorting the girls to the door with some resistance, until he mentioned Police.

Turning to us, he said, "You young sailors ought to be ashamed of yourselves. Just look at you, need I say more? Ninety day wonders, what is this Navy coming to? Well, I wouldn't want your squashes in the morning. Come on, old Maury will get you home."

Picking us up like rag dolls, he stacked us in the back seat of his old model A Ford and drove us back to the Base.

The next morning I woke up and felt like my head had been kicked for a field goal. As I lay there I started to recall some of the events of the night before. I started to sweat, because I couldn't remember how I got back to my bunk. I just assumed the Shore Patrol nailed us and we'd have to face the Commanding Officer.

Much to my relief, I found out that Maury quietly transported us back onto the Base and to our quarters. It seemed that almost everyone in Key West knew Maury or owed him a favor.

Later that day, I went back to Maury's to apologize and to thank him for rescuing us.

He just laughed and said, "I've been there too." Then reaching under the bar he produced my salty old hat and said, "You forgot your hat last night, Captain."

From then on Maury and I have been solid friends, and like I said before he's more like a big brother to me. I can't wait to see his reaction when I show him this hundred.

"Where's the rest of the crew, Bill? Isn't it a little early?"

"Oh, I left Jacques to clean up the boat today. He'll be along in a little while."

"That's not like you, Bill, you getting lazy?"

"You know me better than that. My charter caught a beautiful sailfish and decided to call it a day, so we came in early. Take a gander at the tip he gave me."

"Holy mackerel! That's the biggest tip I've ever seen. Looks like you'll be pulling out all the stops tonight eh, Bill."

"You can bet your bar towel on it."

"Hey, speaking of big tips, did your charter wear a loud Hawaiian shirt and a Red Sox hat?"

"Yeah that was Jeremy."

"He stopped in here for a quick ball and dimey draft. I heard the whole story how he fought that fish for hours. He was on cloud nine. He left me a five dollar tip."

"He's a pretty good guy. One thing's for sure he's the most generous lawyer I ever met. He said he wants to set up another trip next year, or sooner."

"Well, Bill, we'll sure make him more than welcome, if he does come back. Now, the least I can do is share one with you on the house."

In a jiffy, he expertly drew off two draft beers and with a little more flourish reached under the bar and produced a bottle of "Old Bushmills" Irish whiskey. "This is my private stock for special occasions only and this is one."

In one of his big hands he placed two shot glasses and steadily poured them to the brim with the Irish nectar.

"Hey, what's the big celebration, you guys?" came the familiar voice of Maury's wife, Denise, just coming out of the kitchen carrying a tray of food.

Denise is a Conch, born and raised in Key West. She met Maury, on a blind date, while he was stationed here as a Navy cook back in 1938. They hit it off and got married when he retired in 1940. That's when they started the business. She's the real secret behind the success of Maury's Bar and Grill, an unsung hero. She's the one who runs the kitchen and supervises the general running of the business, especially the financial end of it. They realized early on that Maury had no head for business. Things got out of hand and they came close to going broke. Denise took charge of all the money transactions and put Maury on a short leash. He was a soft touch. No more free drinks, meals on the cuff, and loans out of the register that never got repaid. She ran a tight ship and it paid off. Maury, having learned his lesson, concentrated on running the bar and keeping the customers happy.

Anytime, someone asked for credit, a loan, or anything to do with money, he told them to see Denise, and they knew better than that. Since then, they've had "Fair Winds," as Maury liked to say.

"You should see the big tip, Bill got today," answered Maury. "We're about to splice the main brace."

"Good for you, Bill, you deserve it. Everyone knows you're the best charter boat Captain in Key West, and the best looking too."

"I thank you for the compliments, Denise, but I think you're giving me more credit than I deserve."

"You're too modest, Bill."

Nodding at the two shots and walking away, she said, "Go easy on that stuff, Maury; remember you have a bar to run tonight."

Without sincerity, Maury said in a whisper, "Women! Hey, while we're on the subject do you ever think about getting married again?"

"Not really, I'm at that stage of life where I don't have to work too hard. I own my house and boat outright and can come and go as I please. Why would I want to wreck that set up? Do you ever think about not being married?"

"Occasionally, but I'm at that stage of life where I know that I couldn't survive without her. So why would I want to wreck that set up?"

Holding out his hand to me with the two shots, he said, "Well, seeing as how we're both happy with our set ups, let's celebrate that too."

As I carefully took one of the glasses from him, he said, "Here's to your good fortune today and to our long and..."

At that point, he was rudely interrupted by several demands for service from the noisy "Happy Hour" crowd two deep at the bar.

In his booming voice, easily heard across the street, he said, "Keep your shirts on. Bill here, got a fabulous tip today, and I just wanted to congratulate him. See!"

Before I could stop him, he brandished the century note to the crowd. A cheer went up, and the bill traveled around the bar so everyone could fondle the seldom seen note. Knowing all of them; they crowded around me to shake my hand and pat me on the back.

"Quiet, please." said the big voice, silencing the bar.

Then, lifting his shot glass and nodding to me to lift mine, he proposed a toast. "To, Bill Baker, the best Charter Boat Captain in Key West!"

"What a bunch of crap, 'the best Charter Boat Captain in Key West'. I should have worn my boots in here today," bellowed the unmistakable voice of Joe Stalker.

Joe Stalker bald by choice and wearing his usual tight fitting long sleeve shirt, shorts, and sandals was the bully of Key West. A big bruiser with rippling muscles everywhere and well over six feet tall, he wasn't a bad looking guy, clean shaven in his forties, but what an attitude. He came here from Cuba with his charter boat about five years before. He had a heavy German accent, but claimed he grew up in South Africa. One by one, all who tried to befriend him over the years got stung. A loan to Joe, in money or equipment, would later be declared to have been a gift. Everyone involved declined to dispute the issue with him because of his size and demeanor. The word circulated like a bad penny to stay away from Joe Stalker.

Now, here he stood in the middle of Maury's with all eyes upon him; making a scene and basking in the attention, even though every man and woman in the place glowered at him.

And of course, in the shadow of his master, sharing the same spotlight groveled Joe's mate, Slip. A scruffy little guy a few inches below Joe's shoulder sporting a sailors hat turned down like a helmet, surplus work shirt with the sleeves torn off, long pants, and sneakers without socks. Playing his lackey role well, the sly little Slip slinked around Key West, spying, listening, and reporting back to his boss. No one knew his last name or anything about his past, although rumors abounded. Needless to say, Slip was also seen as an outcast in Key West.

Without thinking, I said, "Hey, Joe, let bygones be bygones. Let me buy you a drink."

"Oh, the best Charter Boat Captain in Key West wants to buy me a drink. Did you hear that, Slip?"

"I did, Joe. I surely did." chirped the little mascot."

"And what do you think I'm going to say to that, Slip?"

"I can only guess, Joe. I can only guess." he replied, parrot like, shrinking behind Joe.

Then, looking up and down the bar at each face, as though to remember them, he said, "I'm the best Charter Boat Captain in Key West. So, what do you think of that? Anyone here, want to say different?"

"You're out of bounds here, Joe," I said, "If you want to be the best Charter Boat Captain in Key West then go ahead. No one's going to disagree with you, okay? Now, why don't you and your pal there, leave us alone. We don't want any trouble here."

Disappointed that his provocation didn't work, Joe got into my face and started poking me on the chest.

"So, you think I'm out of bounds do you?" he said in a raised voice. "Well, let me tell you something; I think you're out of bounds. And, trouble? You don't know what trouble is. I'll show you trouble. And, another thing, you don't tell me to leave. I'll leave when I'm good and ready. I'll leave maybe, after I teach you some manners."

Before I could answer him, from behind the bar came Maury, with his lead filled baseball bat.

Maury had a few inches and at least twenty-five pounds on Joe. Even without the bat I think he was a good match for the big gorilla.

Holding the bat in his right hand and slapping it into his left, Maury stepped in between us.

"Well, Joe," said Maury, in a voice like a lion's roar, "I'm telling you that you're ready to leave, now. Get the hell out of my bar, or they'll have to scrape what's left of you off the deck. And take that little weasel with you. And, don't come back, you're not welcome here."

Joe, looking at the bat and heedful of the fierce look on Maury's face, started moving back.

"So, you're going to do Bill's fighting for him now, Maury? What's the matter, can't he do his own fighting?"

"There'll be no fighting here today, unless you're a damned fool and decide to try something. Let's just say I'm backing Bill up."

Then, from the stunned and silent crowd at the bar someone shouted in a defiant voice, "Me too, I'm backing up Bill."

Then, another bold voice sounded off and another bringing everyone to their feet with angry faces and clenched fists, including the women. They started to surround Joe and his cringing sidekick forcing the stunned pair out onto the sidewalk.

Visibly shaken by such a show of solidarity, Joe Stalker blurted out, "This ain't the end of it. I'll get you!"

As they started down the street, he yelled back defiantly, "I'll get each one of you!"

Everyone went back, feeling pretty good that they had finally stood up to Joe Stalker, after all this time. Years of frustration and anger with Joe had been simmering so this confrontation long overdue, finally boiled over.

"I could see him push one or two of us around," said Maury, "but to come in here and try and bully the whole lot of us, who does he think he is? He must have thought that we were like a herd of sheep. Joe crossed the line this time and we let him know it."

Then, Denise said somberly, "I don't like the way he threatened all of us like that."

"Don't worry about Joe," I said, "he's a paper tiger. I'm sure when he cools off he'll regret what he said."

"I don't know, Bill. He's a pretty mean guy. I think he meant what he said."

Someone yelled out, "Hey, what if he gets one of us alone?"

Maury, still holding the baseball bat in his big hands said solemnly, "Listen up, if he does something to one of us, it's as though he does it to all of us, and you all know what that means. We take care of him Key West style!"

At that, a shout of approval went up, easing the anxiety of the crowd.

Someone hollered out, "Yeah, we'll spread the word, so he'll get the message that we're like the three musketeers, one for all and all for one."

Everyone cheered in agreement and gradually things settled down somewhat to normal.

In his get attention voice, Maury said, "Hey, everybody, Bill has something to say to all of you."

All eyes turned to me as I started speaking.

"I want to thank, Maury here, and all of you for standing with me. I can't tell you how good it makes me feel, but I can certainly show you."

Holding up the hundred-dollar bill, I said, "Maury, the drinks are on me till it's gone. Ring 'Old Mariah'."

Now, "Old Mariah" is a ships bell that an old timer wheeled in here in a baby carriage during the war. He salvaged it from a ship that wrecked on a reef back in 1900. Maury fell in love with it and gave the old sailor free drinks for two whole months in payment. "MARIAH 1893" prominently embossed on the heavy brass bell identified the ship that was lost. He cleaned and polished it up like new and built a proper stand for it. Bosun Jim, a retired sailor friend, went all out and decorated the stand with beautiful and elaborate nautical fancywork.

Maury proudly took hold of the braided lanyard attached to the clapper of the grand old bell. He waited patiently until absolute silence reigned, and then he pulled the familiar four double strokes (eight bells), then after an appropriate pause, one more. That ninth bell, never heard at sea only at Maury's, warmed the cockles of the hearts of serious tipplers. It rang out loud and clear, "The drinks are on the house!"

Needless to say, it lit a fire under the gang. Everyone rushed the bar shouting their orders.

"Whoa there!" bellowed Maury. "You all know better than that. We have a procedure we follow for times like this."

He calmly commandeered two capable bartenders from the crowd and motioned them to change sides of the bar and start pouring. Then, out came the "Closed Private Party" signs, which he ordered posted. A nod to Jimmy the entertainer to get back up on his little perch and do his thing.

In his rich radio voice he made the anticipated announcement, "Happy Hour prices in effect for bottled beer, wine and hard liquor until closing, whenever that is. Draft beer only is on the house and hold onto your glasses, so you can refill them. You know the drill. Let the party begin."

Then, putting his thumbs in his belt, he surveyed the crowd to make sure everyone was happy, then nodded his approval and smiled.

"Sit back and relax, Bill," he said, "it's shaping up to be an interesting night."

"We're sure off to a good start, Maury."

"I don't think it'll beat your forty fifth birthday party last November. That set a new standard for parties in Key West."

"Don't remind me, I didn't get back to normal for two days. Hey, for a while there, I thought we were going to have an old fashioned donnybrook in here like the good old days during the war, remember?"

"I don't know how good they were, Bill, but they certainly were, let's say, exciting. It was nothing to have two or three fights in here every night, some of them real doozies."

"I got dragged into a few of them myself."

"Yeah, but I had to step in and break all of them up by myself. When I did, both sides started in on me. I felt like a piñata at a Mexican birthday party. I went through a lot of Bengay and spent a bundle on furniture repairs. They were interesting times, Bill, but I'm glad that things have settled down over the years. I couldn't handle it today; I'm too old to cut the mustard anymore."

"That's one of the reasons I'm glad you stood by me today, Maury."

"Don't mention it. Hey, where were we, before we were so rudely interrupted?"

We headed back to the two shots of Old Bushmills, amazingly, still sitting on the bar, however the two draft beers had disappeared.

Just then, Denise came by, "Oh, Bill, I'm sorry I forgot to tell you before, with all the excitement, earlier today, there were three guys in here asking for you."

"That's okay, Denise. Did they say what they wanted?"

"No, but I didn't like the looks of them. Their boss, believe it or not had on one of those old-fashioned tropical white suits, like they used to wear in the movies and before the war. He even had the Panama hat. He seemed like a gentleman, but the other two with him, wharf rats for sure."

"He's probably just looking for a charter."

"If he comes back, I'll let you know."

"I don't know about you," Bill, "but I'm going to down this shot before we get side tracked again. Here's looking at you."

We touched glasses and downed the shots and they were good.

Just then, Jacques walked in and did a double take.

Three deep at the bar, a line at the phone booth, private party signs, music and the unmistakable promise of a night to remember.

Jacques, with a 'what have you done now grin', said to me, "This has your fingerprints all over it. I let you come over here by yourself and look what happens."

Trying to keep a straight face, I said, "Whatever do you mean? This is just a typical Happy Hour crowd. It happens every night in here. Let's go over to our booth and I'll buy you that beer."

Jacques, looking around, said, "This is typical? All I can say, it looks like Key West is getting off to a slow start tomorrow morning."

Denise came by to our booth and delivered a couple of draft beers and a basket of Conch Fritters, "You two better have something to eat. You don't want to be drinking on an empty stomach, or you'll end up dancing on the tables. Hey, I heard you had a good day today."

"We caught a trophy size sailfish and our charter gave me a twenty dollar tip and you should see the tip Bill got."

"Good for you, Jacques. I heard about Bill's big tip. You guys deserve it, because you're the best."

Grinning, Jacques and I thanked Denise and clinked our glasses together.

"So, how about the special tonight, some peel and eat shrimp?"

"That sounds good to me, Denise, what do you say, Jacques are you up for a feed of shrimp?"

"That suits me, I'll go for the shrimp too. Hey, by the way, what's Bill got us into tonight?"

Denise winking at me, replied, "whatever do you mean, Jacques? This is just a typical Happy Hour crowd. Two shrimp specials coming up."

"Told you!"

Meanwhile, the Key West grapevine showed its effectiveness as the place started to fill up for the impromptu party. Maury ever vigilant scanned the bar, to spot any trouble and quash it before it got out of hand.

Denise delivered the peel and eat shrimp along with a pitcher of beer. "Are you guy's all set for now?"

Each of us gave her the thumbs up sign.

Maury made an announcement that Jimmy the singer had a new song he wrote about Key West. He wanted to try it out to see what everybody thought.

"Let's pipe down a bit and listen," he said.

All eyes turned to Jimmy as he started off with the chorus.

"Key West is Paradise to me,
That's where I always want to be,
No matter where I roam, this will always be my home,
Key West is Paradise to me."

A cheer of approval went up by all, as Jimmy continued with the refrain.

"I love those sunsets down at Old Mallory Square,
With the street entertainers and peddlers gathered there,
People come from all around, just to see the sun go down,
And, then go have a good time in Old Town."

Some of the crowd started to join him in singing the chorus. Then he continued with the second refrain.

"I love to walk up old Duval Street in the evening,
With its music, shops and bars along the way,
And, of course there's Sloppy Joe's, as everybody knows,
The great one was known to have a few."

Then, everyone in the place sang along with Jimmy in the next chorus. The final refrain got everyone's attention.

"This Caribbean Island is unique
With a climate all those Northerners do seek
We welcome every one, to this Island in the sun
But, don't try to change the way that we have fun."
The whole gang was on their feet cheering that last line.

"Jimmy summed up my feelings about Key West, Bill. I hope things never change here."

"Me too, I like it the way it is. But don't forget, Key West has a history of change. Well anyway, Jacques, I did like Jimmy's song."

"Looks like the shrimp hit the spot," said Maury. "You can't get them any fresher, they were swimming out there last night. Key West's Pink Gold."

Jacques rubbing his stomach with both hands said, "I couldn't eat another one. They sure were good."

"That goes for me too, they're the best."

Maury filled in Jacques about the confrontation with Joe Stalker and how I gave my tip in thanks for everyone backing me up.

"Well... We're off to a good start," he said. "I figure the beer should last for another couple of hours."

Jacques opened up his wallet and pulled out the twenty-dollar bill and handed it to Maury.

"I'd like to add this to the pot. It'll keep the party going a little longer."

"You're all right, Jacques. I'll let the gang know," as he headed to Old Mariah.

"Thanks, Jacques," I said. "I appreciate that."

Maury holding the clapper lanyard again," said in his big voice, "Listen up everybody, this here twenty bucks was Jacques's tip today and he's putting it in with Bill's to keep the party going."

Maury rang the eight bells plus one to the delight of the crowded bar. Then, one of the charter boat skippers slapped a sawbuck down next to Old Mariah. That started an avalanche of bills and coins piling up on the bar.

Maury shaking his head, said, "This is a first. I can't ring the bell for every one of your donations. That would be almost disrespectful. But, I will ring it once more, not only for drinks on the house, but to something much bigger than that. Here's to us, all of us, together in Key West tonight, showing the rest of the world how it's done. I'm proud of all of you. And, to boot, I'm tossing in a keg of beer on the house."

That brought everyone to their feet as Maury began the ritual ringing of the Grand Old Bell and then, with everyone holding their breath, came the hallowed ninth toll. For a few seconds, there was total and almost a reverent silence as that ninth golden peal of old Mariah ebbed away, then pandemonium.

"Just a typical Happy Hour Crowd, right Bill?"

"I keep telling you that."

A few more musicians joined Jimmy with a standup bass, drums, fiddle, and a big pair of speakers. A steady trickle of locals soon had the crowd at Maury's bulging to capacity.

Denise came by and said, "Those guys are back. They're over at the door. Do you want to see them?"

I looked over and chuckled at the white tropical suit. The two guys with him were obvious bodyguards.

"Sure, Denise, tell him to lose the two bookends and send him on over. I'm sure it's just a charter."

"Okay, Bill, let me clean up your table first."

We watched Denise go up to the man who removed his hat for her, revealing a full head of silvery blonde hair. She pointed over to our booth and he nodded. He took out his wallet and handed some cash to the two men, who grinned with delight and quickly disappeared. Denise escorted him over to us.

"Here's that man who wanted to talk to you, Bill. I'll be back in a few minutes."

I half stood up and introduced Jacques and myself to the tall handsome stranger. He reached out and gave a surprisingly firm handshake. He smiled and accepted the invitation to join us and sat down next to Jacques.

"Good evening, Bill and Jacques, my name is Erik Von Hurlich. I'm glad to meet you at last. Oh, and I apologize for intruding on the private party."

"Glad to meet you too, I'm sure," I said. "You're not intruding at all. This is just a bunch of us locals doing our thing. Welcome to Key West. Is this your first time down here?"

"Yes, it is, although I have been to Florida before."

"This isn't exactly Florida," I said. "There's a little different lifestyle going on down here. We're a little more, let's say independent."

"That's quite a suit, Erik," said Jacques. "We don't see too many of them anymore."

"My sister bought me this suit for my trip down here. From all the stares I've been getting, I feel a little out of place. Also, she heard that Key West was a rough place, so she insisted on the two body guards."

"Whoever told her that exaggerated and since the war and air conditioning, we've been dressing much more casual here," I said. "You'd probably be more comfortable if you took off that jacket and tie."

Erik stood up and removed the suit jacket and tie and opened the top button of his white short sleeve shirt. I could see the reason for the firm handshake; he obviously worked out in a gym to keep in such good physical condition.

"Thank you that does feel much better, I've been wanting to do that since I got here."

Just then, Denise came over and asked, "Is everything okay here, Bill?"

"We're good, Denise, I think Erik, here may like something to drink."

"Yes, Denise, I'd love a draft beer and another pitcher for my new found friends here. And may I say, Denise you have a lovely smile."

Denise, stunned by the compliment, spontaneously wiped her hand on her apron and put it up to her hair. Her distrust of the man vanished.

"Thank you Erik, would you like to try some of our local shrimp? It's very good. These two just polished off a pound apiece."

"That sounds wonderful, Denise. Now that I think of it, I am quite hungry."

Smiling, Denise said, "You're going to love the shrimp. I'll be right back with the beer."

As Denise headed to the bar, Erik said, "Isn't she nice!"

"She takes very good care of us. She's the best," said Jacques.

"They don't come any better than, Denise," I said. "She's more than just a friend, she's family."

"So, is it a charter you're looking for, Erik?" asked Jacques.

"Possibly, but first I have to verify one fact. Are you the Bill Baker that had the skirmish with a German U-boat off the coast here during the war?"

"Yes, I remember it very well. Why bring that up and how did you find that out?

"Well, Bill, let's just say for now, I have my sources."

Just then a group of friends came over to the booth to thank Jacques and I for the drinks and to shake hands. Some of them are fellow charter boat Captains. A few of them, received their hands-on nautical and fishing education, serving as mates on my boat years ago, after they graduated from high school.

They all felt free to come to me with fishing and boating questions and sometimes even their personal problems. I always made time for them and went out of my way to help them as best I could. In turn, over the years anytime I needed a favor, they always came through for me. That's just the way it is here in Key West.

"I'm sorry for the interruptions, these are all close friends of mine. I'm going to mingle a bit with them. Jacques can answer any questions you may have about life in Key West."

The noise level reached a higher degree than normal and required everyone who wanted to carry on a conversation to raise their voices, which of course made matters worse.

"I do have a few questions," said Erik. "And by the way, you're very fortunate to have so many good friends. We could always get together tomorrow if that would be more convenient?"

"Not at all," I said. "You've piqued my interest now. I'm very anxious to hear your story. Oh, and don't worry about Jacques here, he's like a brother to me. There are no secrets between us. I'll be back in a while."

When Bill left, Erik moved to the other side of the table, to more easily talk with Jacques.

Denise swung by with the pitcher of beer and a glass for Erik saying, "I gave Bill a glass of beer over at the bar. It looks like he'll be tied up for a while. Your shrimp is coming right up, Erik."

"Thank you, Denise. That will give Jacques time to tell me all about Key West. I want to learn all I can."

"Well, if there are any questions he can't answer, just ask me. I was born here and that makes me a Conch. I'll be back in a jiffy with that shrimp."

"Jacques, what's a Conk?"

"Conch is a shellfish found all around the Keys. Its spelled conch but we pronounce it conk down here. Tradition has it that if you're born in Key West that makes you a conk."

"Looks like I've been pronouncing it wrong all these years, thanks for telling me. I can't help but notice that this place is really jumping. Is it like this every night?"

Jacques laughed, "No this is a special night."

He went on to tell Erik of the successful charter they had and the big tips. Then, the run in with Joe Stalker and the way Maury and the gang backed up Bill. That's why Bill used his tip to get the celebration going to show his appreciation.

"Just who is this Joe Stalker?"

"Nobody really knows. Joe and his scuzzy mate Slip arrived in his boat about five years ago. Anyone that has had dealings with him has been hurt either financially or physically. Now, he's a pariah and avoided like the plague. He has a German accent, and claims to be from South Africa."

"If I heard him talk, I could tell where he's from," said Erik.

Denise delivered a big plate of peel and eat shrimp and placed it in front of Erik, "That's our homemade cocktail sauce. If it's too spicy I can get you something milder."

"I'm partial to Mexican food, so I'm sure I'll like your cocktail sauce, Denise. There's quite a bit of shrimp here. Would you like some Jacques?"

"I've had my fill, thanks anyway. You won't have any trouble finishing them. I like a little TABASCO sauce on them."

"I think I'll stick with Denise's sauce. Thank you Denise."

"Okay, I'll check back later, when I do, all I want to see are the shells."

Peeling a shrimp and dipping it into the sauce, Erik popped it into his mouth.

"Wow! This is the best shrimp I've ever tasted. They're like eating candy. You're right, Jacques, I won't need help in finishing them."

The conversation slowed down as Erik wiped out the shrimp one by one. As he was squeezing the lemon on his hands and drying them with his napkin, Bill came back to the booth.

"Hi, Bill, I must look like the proverbial fatted calf. I can't believe I ate them all."

"I've known that feeling many times, and I'm still not tired of it," I said sliding in next to Jacques. "You're going to have some entertainment in a couple of minutes."

"What are you up to now, Bill?"

"I just suggested to Maury that it's about time the Stanley twins, Christian and David get back together again.

"The Stanley twins are both charter boat Captains and protégés of mine. Because they were twins, I made an exception and had the two of them serve on my boat together while I trained them. In a public shouting match over some fishing tackle, probably worth less than ten bucks, they had a falling out and haven't spoken to each other for months.

"There goes Maury now; he's got Christian. Now, he's got David."

Maury had the two boys by their necks in each of his massive arms and went out to the middle of the bar.

"Now, I want you two to kiss and make up."

Everybody in the place stood up cheering, "Make up! Make up!"

"No, never! Let me go, Maury," shouted Christian.

David cried out, "I'll never make up with that no account brother of mine."

Maury twirled around with the two imprisoned twins, to the delight of everyone, saying, "This sounds like it's going to be a long drawn out fence-mending. This could go on all night. I might as well get comfortable. Hey, somebody get me a chair."

A chair was provided, and Maury sat down causing the two reluctant boys to end up on their knees.

"That's better," stated Maury. "Are you two comfortable? I know I am. I can easily outlast you two whippersnappers."

Meanwhile, the gang continued to chant, "Make up! Make up!"

Realizing their ridiculous situation David started to laugh. Then, Christian started laughing too.

"There could be hope for these two yet!" said Maury.

Then to the cheers of everyone, Christian spoke up, "Okay, Maury, I'll make up if David does."

Maury jiggled David a little and said, "Well?"

"Yes, yes," he spouted, "I agree. I'll make up. Just let us go, Maury."

"First I want you two to shake hands, and then I'll let you go."

The two boys managed to get their hands around to shake and then to the joyful cheers of the crowd, Maury let them go.

They got up and shook hands with Maury, thanking him. Then arms around each other and all smiles, they were absorbed back into the throng warmly received by their wives and many pats on their backs from friends celebrating their reunion.

"I've never seen anything like that before," said Erik. "What a wonderful thing to do. Maury is quite a guy to get those two boys back together again like that. I'd like to meet him."

"Maury is one of a kind," I said. "Under that big brawny chest of his, beats a heart of pure gold. He's been a positive influence on many of us here. If you ever need help, you don't have to ask Maury twice. I'll be happy to introduce you when he comes by. Now tell us what brings you to Key West?"

Erik looking around, leaned closer across the table and lowering his voice, said, "What I'm about to tell you must be kept secret."

Jacques, with a little grin, blurted out, "We better not tell, Maury."

I almost choked on my beer and managed to say, "You may as well put it on the front page of the Key West Citizen."

Jacques and I started laughing and poor Erik, unaware of the deeper humor, looked at us a little dumbfounded.

And, who happened by at that moment, of all people was Maury saying, "What's so funny. Let me in on it."

Jacques and I look at each other and burst out laughing again.

I managed to compose myself and with tears in my eyes from laughing, I changed the subject and said, "Let me introduce you to our new friend here, who is thinking of a charter. Maury Greer, meet Erik Von Hurlich."

Maury and Erik greeted each other and shook hands.

"You deserve a lot of credit getting those two boys back together again."

"Thank you, Erik, I always feel good when I can reunite two people like that. Sometimes, they both really want to make amends, but neither one wants to take the first step. I guess their pride gets in the way. It's so much easier to cajole them back together in a festive atmosphere like this. Well, I have to get back to work. Nice meeting you, Erik, we'll talk again. I still want to know, later on, what you were laughing at?"

After Maury walked away, I said, "I'm sorry, Erik about the laughing jag. When you get to know Maury you'll come to appreciate it. Now, back to that secret of yours?"

Again, he leaned closer, but because of the noise level had to raise his voice to be heard.

"What I'm about to tell you must be a closely guarded secret between us. The captain of that U-Boat jettisoned a fortune in Nazi gold that day while you were engaging him. That gold is still out there and you, Bill, are the only one who knows where it is."

"What!" I exclaimed, raising my voice, "Nazi gold from that U-Boat? And I know where it is? I don't know anything about Nazi gold. Who told you that? You've got to be kidding?"

"Bill, please keep your voice down," said Erik. "Someone may hear you."

Jacques, something catching his eye, stood up and looked out toward the street, "Too late! There goes sneaky Slip running down the street. Listening right here under our window that little creep heard every word we said, and you don't have to guess who he's running to."

"That's Joe Stalker's petty spy," I said, "Maybe he didn't hear everything. It is pretty noisy in here."

"You're kidding yourself, Bill. You can bet that little snoop Slip overheard the best part about the U-Boat, the Nazi gold, and you knowing where it is. Joe Stalker is getting an earful right now."

"So much for secrecy," said Erik mournfully.

"We'll have to assume that Jacques is right. I'm sure Joe isn't about to tell anyone else about it, so we only have to worry about him. Of course, he's going to want to know where that gold is, so we'll have company out there. Speaking of which, Erik, what makes you think that I know where all that Nazi gold is?"

"I have a cousin, Gerhard Wagner, who told me about the fortune in gold jettisoned that day. He told me that his Captain convinced of immediate capture jettisoned eight to ten wooden boxes of bronze cylinders. Each box contained nine cylinders, and this is the most exciting part, each one held seventy-two twenty dollar gold pieces. I estimate that the total could be well over six thousand coins in all. At today's gold price the melt value alone could be well over two hundred thousand dollars.

"Do you think, you could retrace the course the U-boat took that day?"

"Absolutely, we follow that same course heading out to sea on just about every charter we take. Just think, Jacques, of all those sixty dollar charters we've taken out there with all that loot just a few feet under our keel."

"Could you tell me about your encounter with the U-Boat?"

"Sure, It turned out to be the only exciting day of my whole wartime experience stationed here in Key West. I never got to fire my guns in anger again, as they say.

"A couple of hours before dawn in late 1943, we got an alert that a fisherman spotted a submarine and called it in. To this day, I can't figure out why he was in such shallow water so close to dawn. Anyway, by the time we caught up with him the stars were starting to disappear and the horizon off to the east glowed brighter. Sure enough, we could see him as big as life chugging along heading for the open sea. I can still see the number on the conning tower, 198.

"When we got in range I had my gunner, using our Browning 30 caliber machine gun, fire a couple of bursts over his bow, which of course he ignored. He partially submerged to protect his U-Boat from getting peppered with bullet holes. He couldn't go too deep because of the potential of running aground in the fairly shallow water. He still had his diesel engines running using a snorkel, but with the main body of his ship underwater his speed drastically slowed down. In spite of the foot of protective water washing over the U-Boat, a few of his crew wearing lifelines were trying to get their deck gun ready to fire. I gave my gunner the nod to open fire on them. He winged one of them and chased the others away. They could have easily blown us out of the water with that heavy gun. Then the shooting started in earnest. Using small arms, they shot at us from the shelter of the conning tower, and we returned fire with the machine gun and our small arms.

"In the early light of the dawn, we could just make out the smoke on the horizon of our destroyer coming at flank speed, maybe an hour away. My orders were to delay the sub and not to seriously damage it, until the destroyer could get there, the main objective being to capture the U-Boat intact. We were easily gaining on him, and the sound of bullets hitting us and whizzing overhead got more plentiful.

"I got this," pointing to a dime size scar, "when a bullet hit the boat near me and sent a wooden splinter into my cheek. My crew told me I should put in for a purple heart, but I saw too many vets with missing limbs to think that this scratch was worthy of such an honor.

"My chief yelled that a bullet shattered the water pump and the engine wouldn't last much longer. I told him to ignore it, and keep it at full speed. As expected, steam started pouring out of the engine compartment.

"As we watched each other through binoculars, I could see the German Captain start to smile as he saw the steam. Then, sure enough, we could hear the sound of the engine seizing up and grinding to a halt. I saw the German Captain give the cease-fire sign to his men, which at the time I thought quite decent. I immediately gave the cease-fire order to my crew as well. Our boat plowed through the water and came to a stop. Then, all that could be heard was the hissing of steam from our engine and the diminishing sound of the U-Boat's exhaust, as the distance between us rapidly increased. The whole incident didn't take more than fifteen or twenty minutes.

"Again, as we watched each other through the lenses, the U-Boat reached deeper water and started to dive. He looked off to the horizon at the oncoming destroyer and then at me. He lowered the binoculars and in a gesture of chivalry gave me a salute, which I courteously returned. He smiled and then quickly disappeared into the submerging U-Boat. As I watched it slide beneath the water, I thought, 'By God, I hope he makes it'.

"And, he did make it. The destroyer searched all over the area for the rest of the day without a sign of him. At daylight a couple of planes tried to spot him as well to no avail.

"I often wondered what became of him. I can't describe the emotions I had at that moment. Our blood was up and we were trying to kill each other and then suddenly, we were respectfully saluting each other. I always thought highly of him for his military courtesy and wondered if he survived the war.

"Did your cousin ever say what happened to the Captain?"

"Yes, my cousin liked Captain Wolfgang Krueger and served under him with pride and he did survive the war, but died a year later. The Captain signed on as an enlisted man in the German Navy in World War One. He loved submarines and worked his way up through the ranks to become a career submariner Officer. The next war gave him his own command, and he excelled at his craft to the dismay of Allied shipping. An honorable and religious man he served his country well. He temporarily lost his command because of the cylinders. However, with the shortage of experienced U-Boat Captains, he soon was given command of a newly launched submarine. Gerhard requested a transfer to serve under him again and the Captain gladly helped get it approved. They went on three more successful voyages and on the last one in late 1944, a British destroyer off the coast of Ireland disabled them. They abandoned ship and shortly afterward a preset charge detonated, sinking their sub. Gerhard, the Captain and all of the crew were picked up by the British warship, and they spent the rest of the war interned somewhere in England.

"After the war, while Gerhard served time in a German prison for a war crime, which I'll tell you about later, he wrote to the retired Captain and they corresponded with each other until the Captain passed away. The Key West adventure came up, but Gerhard never got the impression that the Captain ever knew what the cylinders contained. Before he got out of prison, he received a letter from the Captain's wife saying that she had something for him and asked Gerhard to visit her when he was released.

"Shortly after his parole, he called on the Captain's wife. She welcomed him like a son returning home. It turned out that none of the other crewmembers, of all those who served under the Captain, ever communicated with him after the war. She showed him through the small house and into the Captain's office. He enjoyed looking at the many photos proudly exhibited on all of the walls. An empty chair stood at attention behind the neatly arranged mahogany desk displaying his sextant, compass, and navigation instruments all patiently waiting for him to walk in.

'I keep everything the way he liked it,' she said, 'as though he would soon be coming home. I know it may sound silly, but I pretend he's on another voyage. It helps me weather the loneliness, and now, I don't have to fear the telegram.'

"Over her nice lunch, Gerhard couldn't get over her knowledge of the details of life aboard submarines. Feeling empathy for her, he couldn't help but wonder about all the war widows in Germany and around the world, weathering that same loneliness.

"When leaving, he thanked her for the enjoyable lunch and conversation. She handed him a small package saying that the Captain instructed her to place it into his hands. It turned out to be his personal bible."

"What I wouldn't give to have spent a couple of hours talking to the Captain," I said. "The stories he could have told."

Jacques asked, "Were you a Nazi during the war, Erik?"

"Of course not, I'm an American, and I fought on our side. In fact, being able to speak fluent German, I volunteered to join the OSS and they accepted me. "

"The OSS?" I said. "That was top secret stuff. I heard about some of their exploits. You had to be good, really good to get into that outfit. I'm impressed, Erik, and I salute you for your service."

"I appreciate your salute and return one back to you for your service. I'm glad our side won."

"Well, if we didn't win, we'd all be speaking German or Japanese. And, I don't think I'd be a charter boat Captain today."

"I don't want to think of what I'd be doing," said Jacques.

"Life sure would be different for all of us," said Erik. "But let's not dwell on that, when we've got that gold sitting out there. Tomorrow, we'll go out and get it. You do remember where it is?"

"Whoa!" I said, laughing, "that was a long time ago and that's a big area out there. From the time I first made contact with the sub and when I saw it submerge, we're talking a distance of four or five miles. I could probably bring you to where I first saw the U-Boat give or take a mile or so.

"Secondly, those wooden boxes have long ago been eaten up by shipworms, so all that's left are the cylinders. Every storm since then has moved the sand around, so there's a good chance they're covered up. You could scuba right over them without ever knowing it."

"I never realized all that," said Erik. "I can see now that this is going to take a little more time than I thought it would."

"We could use a metal detector, Bill."

"That's a good idea, Jacques. Those cylinders are heavy and are still right where they landed in a clump. All that concentrated metal is going to give off a good signal. Those ten or so clusters of cylinders are strewn out in a long straight line as they jettisoned them. When we find one batch and locate the second we can establish a straight line and find the rest, working in both directions."

Meanwhile, the party had reached a fever pitch and the noise level was such that you almost had to shout to be heard. So, I suggested we continue the discussion the next day.

"That's a good idea but first," said Erik, "we have some business to settle. I'll put up all the money to finance the search. I propose that we split the proceeds three ways, you, my cousin Gerhard and myself. Are we agreed?"

"That's more than fair, and I'm going to split my share with Jacques."

"Bill that's way too much. I'm just your mate, and I don't deserve that big a share."

"That's the way it's going to be, Jacques. First, we have to find those cylinders, and I'm afraid that's going to be easier said than done. Secondly, we know we have to worry about Joe Stalker, but how are we going to get away with searching around out there without arousing the suspicion of the rest of Key West. The last thing we need out there is more competition."

"What if you had a crackpot from New York, who charters your boat for a month to look for a sunken Spanish treasure ship? You give everyone the impression that I'm a little... eccentric!"

"Yes, I think that would work. Everyone thinks those people looking for sunken treasure are a little wacky. Also, we could move around to different sites to confuse Joe Stalker, so he won't know where the real site is. What do you think, Jacques?"

"I think Erik's plan will work. Anyone wearing a white suit like that has got to be a little, as you say eccentric."

"Then that settles it. I have a bunch of fishing charters scheduled, but I can work them in with some of the other captains. There's only one that we really have to do, so we can pretty much look for that Spanish Galleon full time at least for the next month or so. What do you say we all shake on it? Then, we can get into this party, so Jacques and I can spread the word about our peculiar charter."

The three of us stood up and shook hands, as a Police car with the siren going and lights flashing pulled up to the front door of Maury's.

"Is this a raid," asked Erik. "I hope we won't get arrested or anything?"

"No raid." I said. "This is Key West. See that empty stool over there, next to Old Mariah? That's reserved for the Chief of Police. Maury always tips off the Chief to let him know there's a time like this going on. The Chief said it's his civic duty to observe how the public behaves in situations like this. He claims it makes him a better Police Chief. He doesn't wear his uniform so he can blend in and let people relax and be themselves. Of course, then he can sample some of the free spirits solely for the purpose of professional self-improvement. He's actually a swell guy. When he gets settled I'll introduce you."

The place was really hopping. A few couples were trying to dance in a little area squeezed out of the growing happy crowd encroaching onto the dance floor. A mug of beer sat beside each player in the band, as they merrily entertained the crowd. Jimmy never sounded so good, especially after having to sing his new song several times by request. The beer performed its magic, instilling happiness into all whose lips it touched. Maury, like a proud father, surveyed the gang and displayed a smile of approval. Denise, snaked through the crowded bar carrying a full tray of food with the grace of a ballerina.

Jacques with a grin said to me, "Just a typical happy hour crowd, right?"

"That's what I keep telling you."

"I don't see anything typical about this extravaganza," said Erik. "I've seen and done quite a few things in my time, but never anything like this. I'll tell you one thing, I'm beginning to like Key West."

"What's not to love?" I said. "This is what we call a Key West Shindig. Once you've lived here for a while, you'll never want to leave. Let's hope it never changes, Erik."

"I've only been here for a day and I love it already. Key West is almost too good to be true, Bill."

"Hey Jacques, how about spreading the word about our luck in getting a live one, with big bucks, from New York. And, we're delighted to let him charter our boat for the next month or so to go roaming around the Keys looking for sunken treasure."

"I'll start with, Maury, and tell him to keep it under his hat."

"That's a great idea." I said, laughing. "That will get the word out."

"Now let's enjoy this celebration, Erik," I said. "Let's go meet the Police Chief. Don't forget to act a 'Little Eccentric'."

I introduced Erik to the Police Chief and then to a few of my friends. Erik being a charmer mixed right in; especially with the ladies and in no time at all the happy crowd accepted and swallowed him up.

The discord of all the different sounds of laughter, shouting, conversations, music, singing, dancing, clinking of glasses, and even the telephone ringing all merged together to create a pleasing symphony rising up to a beautiful star filled Key West sky.

"Just a typical Happy Hour at Maury's," sighed Jacques.

Tuesday, January 11, 1966

At ten o'clock in the morning, Jacques quietly began to raise one of the green window shades and it got away from him. It quickly recoiled itself up with a loud flapping sound, allowing the sunlight to suddenly flood the darkened room. The two of us, fully clothed, groaned at the loud noise and quick exposure to the light, like a couple of surprised salamanders under a flipped over rock. Erik stretched out on the leather couch, and me in the leather chair with my feet on an ottoman both looked like the survivalist, Joe Knowles when he came out of the woods. He was a character who entered the great north woods of Maine in 1913 naked. Two months later he emerged scruffy, bearded, and primitively clothed in deerskins, moccasins and a bearskin coat. He created a sensation, but was later called a fake.

"Sorry about that. Rise and shine you two. It's a beautiful Key West morning. I've got some juice and coffee here."

"Go away," I said.

"Where am I?" asked Erik.

"Where am I? Where am I?"

"Who said that? Is there an echo in here?"

"Ha, ha, that's Ernie, Bill's parrot. Be careful what you say around him if you don't want it repeated."

"I don't feel so good," said Erik.

"I don't feel so good," mimicked Ernie.

Jacques placed a cover over Ernie's cage.

"Why do I feel so rotten?"

"It's known as overindulging. Remember the big shindig last night at Maury's? You both went a little overboard."

"Oh yes, I remember eating shrimp."

"The shrimp you ate isn't what's troubling you this morning."

"Oh yes, It's starting to come back to me. I hope this feeling means I had a good time last night. Please tell me I did, Jacques?"

"I bear witness that you both had a good time."

"Where am I? And, how did I get here?"

"This is Bill's house. I didn't know where you were staying, so I marched you and Bill back here at three o'clock this morning. When the police came to escort the Chief home; I figured it was time for us to leave. Oh, and he had a good time too."

"What do you mean marched?"

"You both were having a little trouble walking a straight line, until I started counting cadence. You know, forward march, hup, two, three, four. Your military training came right back to you. For some reason, every streetlight inspired you both to stop and harmonize, Sweet Adeline. In spite of your unique condition it didn't sound too bad. Here, have a swig of this tomato juice, I spiked it with some TABASCO sauce, it will make you feel better. It's my secret recipe for hangovers. I perfected it on Bill."

"Unique condition, you mean we were drunk?"

"That's so blunt, I was just trying to be genteel in saying it."

Erik, sat up, took the juice and drank it down quickly.

"Whoa! Spicy hot," he gasped. "What are you trying to do to me, Jacques? Quick, get me some water."

Jacques had a glass of water ready, and Erik gulped it down.

"That certainly woke me up. I don't know which was better? The way I felt before or the way I feel now? All I can say is, Wow!"

Erik, jolted to life by Jacques cure, looked around and saw an inviting and comfortable man's living room. Wooden walls, ceiling, and floor of Dade County pine and comfortable leather furniture, no curtains, mounted fish, fishing trophies, old rods and reels, ashtrays, and a large cigar humidor. A cozy haven created by and for the two bachelors.

"I'm never going to drink again," I said.

"I've heard that before," said Jacques.

"Please, no lectures."

"No lectures. Here, have some tomato juice."

"Go easy on that juice, Bill; it will curl your hair."

"Jacques and his TABASCO sauce that's his remedy for everything."

"It works. Look at Erik there."

"Sure, look at me. I'm a new man."

"C'mon you two, have you forgotten? We've got a treasure to find. Who wants to hit the shower first?"

A couple of hours later, the three of us were sitting outside, having breakfast on a covered open deck off the kitchen with two overhead fans spinning. Erik and I felt fifty percent better after showering and shaving. I fixed him up with some of my clothing.

"This is a beautiful spot you have here, Bill. Tell me about this table, I've never seen such a long table. Where did you get it?"

A cabinetmaker friend of mine, Norm, made it for me. I told him I wanted it to seat sixteen people comfortably and it would be outside. He made it out of recycled teak and prefabricated the whole thing, then brought all the parts over and assembled it right here on the deck. He designed it so it can be disassembled in case I want to move it. It's been exposed to the weather out here for almost fifteen years and still looks like new."

"I love the idea of eating outside in your own little private paradise. Of course, having a first class cook on board doesn't hurt. Thank you, Jacques for that excellent breakfast. I'm starting to feel much better now."

"Thanks for the compliment Erik the pleasure is mine. This is a great location too. We can walk to the boat, downtown, Maury's, and to our local market, Fausto's."

"The weather's great, most of the time," I said, "and what we like best is the laid back, Key West lifestyle. What more could you want?"

"I'm a little jealous. I could see myself settling here."

"You couldn't go wrong," I said.

"Erik, how did your cousin know there were gold coins in the cylinders?" asked Jacques. "Also, was he a Nazi?"

"I've got a couple of questions too. How old were you when you came to America? And why did your parents decide to come here?"

"Let me tell you about my parents first. After the First World War things were pretty bad in Germany and the future didn't look too promising. My parents were looking for a better life, and they were fortunate to have the chance to come to America in 1919. My father a master machinist easily arranged a job in advance. In 1921 I came along. We lived in a German Community in New York City, where German was a second language for everyone, at home. Of course, I spoke English in the street playing with the other kids and in school, so I grew up able to speak both languages without an accent.

"My father had to learn English because he wanted to eventually start his own machine shop. My mother never did quite learn it; she always depended on my father or me as translators.

"My grandparents on my fathers' side in Germany were to celebrate their fiftieth wedding anniversary on November 5, 1938. For years my parents were planning to be there. We never traveled anywhere and for our first trip we were excited to be going to Germany on a luxury liner. We would have our own cabin and eat all our meals in a fancy dining room. That's all we talked about for the several weeks leading up to the departure date.

"I looked forward to seeing my fathers' parents and relatives for the first time. Also, the places they both described with such pride ever since I could remember.

"The day finally arrived and on a crisp October morning, we boarded the SS Bremen, a beautiful German cruise ship. Tugboats pushed the big ship into the channel and once on her own, she picked up speed and headed for the open sea.

Sailing by the Statue of Liberty in New York harbor, my parents 'God blessed her' and reminisced about their arrival in America, when they saw her for the first time so many years before.

"Crossing the Atlantic, they joyfully described their Homeland, saying how much I would love it there.

"The day we arrived in Germany the weather cooperated with a beautiful clear cool day. It seemed that everyone wore some kind of uniform. Also, the ubiquitous swastika claimed a place on flags, banners, buttons, armbands etc. My father said it was just a fad.

"We claimed our luggage and went through customs. One of my uncles, Karl Von Hurlich, an important General in the German Army, met us. A tall imposing figure in his uniform with a chest full of medals, he swaggered around and had all the personnel nervously trying to please him. With him as our escort, our passports were quickly stamped, and we were waved on through. He had an official car and driver waiting which took us directly to my grandparents' home.

"My father was joy stricken when he saw his parents for the first time in almost twenty years. Tears, laughter, hugs, and kisses were the order of the day. I especially loved my grand parents; they were so kind to me. I lost count of all the relatives I met that day.

"One of my cousins, Gerhard Wagner introduced himself to me. We both were seventeen and we got along very well. We both were the same height with blonde wavy hair. He proudly wore the uniform of the Nazi Youth Corps. He started to tell me about the Youth Corps, politics, and Hitler. That's when we began to argue, so we agreed to change the subject and avoid it in the future. We did have many of the same interests, so after our agreement everything was fine between us. We spent a lot of time boating, fishing, and hiking. We became good friends.

"On November fifth, my beautiful grandparents celebrated their golden wedding anniversary with a grand party. They looked so cute dressed up in their local traditional German costumes. All the women and girls wore the local traditional Dirndls and the men and boys wore their lederhosen. Gerhard let me borrow one of his costumes to wear and tried to teach me some of the dance steps. German music and singing filled the air with plenty of good German food, beer, schnapps, costumes, and folk dancing. Little did any of us know how treasured and longed for those happy days would soon become.

"We spent several days in Berlin. I'll never forget the sights and sounds I experienced at that time. The euphoria of the people transcended all reason. It seemed like a band played on every corner. The uniforms, the slogans, the swastikas were all steeped thoroughly into everyday life.

"Suddenly, a great amount of commotion stirred up the crowded sidewalks. He is coming! He is coming! Everyone stopped what they were doing and gathered at the curbs, as some official cars approached. In the third open car, with flags bearing the swastika, a uniformed man with a little moustache stood with his arm outstretched, greeting the people. It was Adolph Hitler. The adoring crowd electrified, returned the gesture shouting Heil Hitler. They were ecstatic with joy. I will never forget that scene.

"I noticed many of the store windows had the Star of David displayed. I found out that they were required to do this by law.

"Several days later on the night of November ninth, forever after, known as Kristallnacht, a nightmare began, not only for the Jewish race, but also for the human race. They waited until dark to carry out their grim mission of smashing every windowpane marked with the Star of David. The millions of glass shards glistened like crystal in the light of the street lamps and torches of the Nazi mobs carrying out their destructive anti-Semitism. Synagogues were burned down and dozens of Jews were murdered and injured that night.

"Seeing the aftermath of such madness, my parents were stunned and saddened to see the Germany they loved sink so low... We were glad to be leaving for America.

"A day before we were to leave, General Von Hurlich came to visit my father to ask a favor. A very close friend of his, whom he could never associate with again because he happened to be Jewish, had a granddaughter who's mother and father were murdered on Kristallnacht.

"Good friends were hiding her because they were fearful of what would happen to her, in this climate of hate, if the authorities found her. She was ten years old, heartbroken, and scared. The General had a plan to have my parents take her back to America; she would just pretend to be their daughter. Because of his status and connections, he would have everything arranged. My parents looked at each other and nodded agreement without a second thought.

"The next day we said our goodbyes. I had to force my goodbye to Gerhard, because I suspected that he might have participated in Kristallnacht. I wished him luck, but he said he didn't need luck. The Third Reich would last for a thousand years.

"The Generals' car came and took us to the ship. We went through customs and boarded. I was puzzled about the whereabouts of the little girl. But, when we entered our stateroom, there on a small suitcase sat a beautiful child with long blonde hair and blue eyes.

"Because of all the secrecy, we knew nothing about her, not even her name.

"My mother went over to her and saw a frightened and trembling little girl. She knelt down beside her and gently took her hand then asked her name.

'My name is Iris.'

"My mother introduced my father and me to her, and she stood up and politely curtsied to us.

"How anxious she must have been, waiting alone in that cabin, hearing footsteps in the hallway, and staring at the door latch. And of course the poor little dear still grieved for her parents.

"My mother motioned to us to leave, so my father and I went up to the lounge.

"Pinned inside her coat were official stamped adoption papers, making my parents her legal guardians. A note instructed them where to place their signatures to complete the documents. Also, included a visa from the American Embassy to enter the United States and a ticket to sail on the SS Bremen. All the documents had her full name as Iris Marlene Von Hurlich.

"We thought it best to have her stay in the cabin for the first day, for safety, until the ship was well out to sea. We needn't have worried; no one questioned her presence throughout the entire trip.

"The next morning my mother brought out a suitcase and called Iris over.

"This was a gift for you, Iris, from the brave women who sheltered you from the Nazis." When she opened it, Iris' eyes lit up and we saw her smile for the first time. Then, as they started to unpack the wardrobe of new clothing in her size, including shoes, Iris started to cry and she allowed my mother to hold her in her arms. Again, we were beckoned to leave the cabin.

"About an hour later, my mother joined us, with a smiling Iris next to her. She looked so pretty in a new pink dress with matching purse and shoes. I'll never know what went on in that hour, but Iris left that cabin a happy little girl.

"My father took her by the hand and brought her to the little flower shop on board and bought her a tiny corsage. She beamed, when the lady pinned it on her. She later pressed it in a book and still has it today.

"By the time we got home, Iris had become a cherished part of the family. She had my father wrapped around her little finger, he couldn't say no to her. I started thinking like a big brother watching out for a little sister. And of course, my mother couldn't wait to spoil her.

I haven't lost you, have I?"

"On the contrary it's a fascinating story, please continue," I said.

"I want to hear more too," said Jacques, "but give me a couple of minutes to make some more coffee. I made some corn muffins earlier while you two were snoring."

"So, your parents adopted your sister?"

"Yes, and she's been a welcome addition to our little family, especially for my mother. That reminds me, I told Iris that I would call her today."

"Use my phone; it's in the kitchen, there."

"Thank you, I'll reverse the charges. I won't be long."

Jacques placed a pot of fresh coffee on the table along with a plate of corn muffins, saying, "I added a little TABASCO to perk them up a bit."

"I knew you would!"

Erik coming back to the table, said, "She's coming down here. She'll fly into Miami late this afternoon and tomorrow rent a car and drive down the Keys. She's looking forward to that drive and meeting both of you. Hey, Jacques these muffins are good. Wait a minute! Do I detect a little TABASCO sauce? Where's the water?"

"I just put in a little, honest."

"I'm only kidding. They're delicious."

"You can't escape getting a dose of that TABASCO sauce, when Jacques is cooking," I said. "Go on with your story, Erik."

"Less than a year later Germany invaded Poland and that started the war in Europe. Being German, we all followed it closely so a couple of years later when America entered the war, it didn't come as a surprise. When I told my parents that I wanted to enlist in the Army that didn't come as a surprise either, in fact they were proud of me. Iris was only thirteen and hated to see me go, but she was old enough to know that my country needed me, and it was my duty.

'Hitler and his minions have enslaved our people,' my father told me. 'Defeat them, so they can take back their Country.'

"Because, I spoke fluent German I wanted to join the OSS. I managed to survive the intensive training and graduated. We infiltrated enemy lines and played as much havoc as possible. Many a time I put on a German uniform and impersonated enlisted men or officers. I often think back about the chances I took and the consequences if caught, but I have to admit, probably because of my youth, I enjoyed the risk taking and the excitement. I liked the Army so much I stayed in after the war and made it a career. I retired after twenty years.

"In the meantime, my father did his part to help the war effort. His business grew quickly, because his specialty of precision machining reached record demand. He started getting military orders from all over the country. He made parts for airplanes, ships, tanks, guns etc. He had a gift for organizing and delegating and over night his little shop became a series of large factories. After the war he sold the business to a large Corporation. He invested most of his fortune in commercial real estate in Manhattan, which turned out to be a fantastic investment. An international real estate firm manages all the properties, so we haven't much to do. As they say in New York, we're comfortable.

"My mother and father still enjoy traveling back and forth to West Germany. They still have friends and relatives there.

"Yes, Jacques, Gerhard was a full-fledged Nazi and a member of the dreaded SS assigned to one of the many concentration camps that were springing up everywhere.

"On a cold overcast day, one of the more notorious officers summoned Gerhard and ordered him to shoot a prisoner, a frightened old man, raggedly dressed, wearing a yellow star.

'Shoot, damn you,' the officer shouted. 'I command you in the name of the Fuhrer.'

"Gerhard slowly raised his rifle and pointed it at the old man, who calmly knelt down and holding his hands over his face he spoke something in Hebrew.

'I ordered you to shoot, damn you!' screamed the Officer into Gerhard's ear.

"Gerhard pulled the trigger. The loudness of the shot startled him, as it harshly echoed off the surrounding buildings. The old man slumped over onto the street. Looking down, he noticed that even though the old man's suit and vest were threadbare, somehow he managed to be clean-shaven and made sure his tie was neatly knotted.

"A screaming elderly woman also wearing a yellow star ran to the old man lying in the street. She picked up his hand and held it to her lips and sobbed saying the same Hebrew phrase over and over. Gerhard noticed again, even though her clothes were shabby and worn, she too had her silver hair done up as perfect as can be. Somehow, they found strength to keep their dignity even as barbarians tore their world apart. In that moment, he realized that's exactly what he had become, a barbarian."

"The officer putting his hand on Gerhard's shoulder said, 'That wasn't so difficult now, the next one will be easier and soon it will be fun.'

"Then with a grin, he pulled out his pistol and shot the old woman.

"That shot sickened Gerhard as he looked down at the pathetic old couple, their blood commingling onto the cobblestones. He wondered, could they have been husband and wife, brother and sister or just close friends? The Officer, returning the pistol to its holster, swaggered off with an air of accomplishment. Gerhard lifted his rifle and aimed between the shoulders of the officer. But, he couldn't do it. Disgusted with himself, he lowered the gun.

"You will pay for this someday," he muttered at the officer.

"Gerhard told me he has relived that scene in minute detail every night since, especially the face of that frightened old man and his last words in Hebrew, which he learned later meant, 'Blessed is the True Judge'. It was a Jewish blessing that has been passed down for thousands of years in response to death and tragedy.

He didn't want to have to kill another one of those poor people. It's one thing to kill on the battlefield and another to commit murder. Misery and death were everywhere in that evil place. He had to get away.

"He noticed a plea for volunteers in the submarine service on the bulletin board in the barracks. He applied and within a week he had orders to report to submariner school. He couldn't wait to leave that hellish concentration camp; well knowing his chances of survival in a submarine were small.

"Gerhard's first mission in a U-Boat happened to be to Key West to deliver the first of some top-secret articles to various destinations. The water around the keys being shallow required they go in on the surface, so it had to be a night mission to deliver a heavy wooden box. As luck would have it, they ran aground and it took several hours to finally get free. The mission had to be scratched, and they needed to get a move on to reach deep water before daylight. A lookout spotted an American patrol boat steadily gaining. Anticipating gunfire the Captain submerged his boat just enough to protect the fragile hull from damage. Of course this caused a drop in speed.

"A World War Two submarine was basically a surface ship capable of submerging. It traveled on the surface most of the time so had the shape of most ships to cut through the water and be stable on the ocean. The means of propulsion were diesel engines and/or batteries. The batteries could be used when submerged, but had limited useful life before needing a recharge. Running at full speed would use up the batteries in and hour or so. Therefore when running underwater they would use a very slow speed to conserve the battery life, sometimes only two to five knots. This could give them up to twenty hours underwater, which was about the limit of the air supply for the crew.

"The diesels could only be used on the surface, because they needed air to run, but they were limited only by the fuel supply, so they could travel on the surface seven to eight thousand miles or more. Also, while they were running they recharged the batteries. The diesels could be used while partially submerged with the aid of a snorkel tube to supply air to the engines. However, it could only be used down to periscope depth, and it produced an exhaust noise on the surface.

"So, because of the underwater limitations, you can understand why the submarine had to be designed mainly for the surface and used underwater just for stealth. And unfortunately, that shape created a lot of drag when running submerged.

"The eastern horizon started glowing red, outlining the tiny silhouette of an enemy destroyer putting out lots of smoke. The American patrol boat closed in and their gunner chased his gunnery crew away from their deck gun, wounding two who were brought below. They retreated to the cover of the conning tower and returned fire with small arms.

"The Captain, certain that they were about to be captured, ordered all the top-secret items jettisoned.

"Gerhard took part in that task at one of the rear torpedo tubes. One by one they lifted the small extremely heavy wooden boxes into the torpedo tube and pushed it as far forward in the tube as possible, then closed the breech and using compressed air, blew it out of the sub. They repeated this over and over. When lifting the last box it got away and crashed to the deck splitting open and spilling its contents, bronze cylinders. The chief ordered the cylinders put into the torpedo tube, and they were expelled from the sub. Because it would float, they kept the wood on board.

"Then, they had a stroke of luck. The patrol boat caught fire and came to a stop. They soon left it behind and finding deep water were able to dive and escape.

"The chief told Gerhard to clean up the wood. That's when he noticed that they missed one of the cylinders. When he picked it up he was surprised how much it weighed for its small size. He turned to tell the chief, but he found himself alone. Then, he did a daring thing, he found a place where he could conceal the cylinder and decided to say nothing."

"So that's why they were in shallow water so close to dawn," I said. "They ran aground and lost three or four hours. The mission should have only lasted a couple of hours. Also, we weren't on fire, mostly steam and some oil smoke from the overheated engine. We thought we hit just one of their guys not two. It's interesting to hear the other side's description of the skirmish. Sorry to interrupt, Erik, please continue."

"That's okay, break in any time.

"When the sub returned to Germany, Gerhard got a week's leave. He waited until one of his friends had the watch at the gangway and then took the cylinder off the U-Boat hidden in his sea bag. He went directly home to his parents' house in the country. They were happy to see him and celebrated with a little welcome home party with some friends and neighbors.

"Later, when alone in his room, he sat down at his desk and unscrewed the cover from the bronze cylinder. He had no idea what he might find. When he removed a tightly wadded piece of cotton, the sight of a gold coin made him gasp. He tipped the cylinder over and a stream of glistening coins slid out onto the desk with that noble clinking sound. Gleaming majestically, they seem to brighten the dimly lit room. Suddenly, his expression of delight changed to worry as he realized what he had done. If caught with this cylinder he imagined what would happen to him... and his family. He reluctantly replaced the coins into the cylinder and pressed the cotton as he found it and screwed the cover back on.

"He waited until late that night, when all was quiet and dug a hole at the base of an old apple tree. He put the cylinder in and covered it using water to compact the soil, then carefully replaced the sod over it.

"He took his secret back with him to the U-boat.

"After the war, he found out how widespread and massive the genocide had been. He turned himself in along with incriminating information on the SS officer to the authorities investigating war crimes. It turned out the officer had already been arrested for a long list of atrocities. He was given a dozen life sentences. Gerhard got a five-year sentence, but it was reduced to one year, because he turned himself in.

"While in prison he thought about the gold and what he could do with it, if and when recovered. He knew he would need help and in order to get that help, he would have to share it. Regardless, he decided to use whatever portion he did end up with to help the survivors of those awful concentration camps.

"For all these years he wrestled with the dilemma of trying to figure out how to find someone who could both fund and be trusted to retrieve the cylinders. When reading an article in National Geographic about underwater archeology, he noted the name of Iris Von Hurlich the woman diver featured. The name brought back the memory of my visit before the war and my grandparents' fiftieth anniversary party. He tracked down my address and sent me a letter, asking me if I knew of the Iris Von Hurlich in the article. I proudly let him know that the archeologist in the article was my sister. He wrote back begging me to come to West Germany as soon as possible to see him about something too serious to put in a letter. I kept stalling, but because of his persistence, I finally relented and took a trip to West Germany.

"He picked me up at the airport early in the morning, and he drove me to his deceased parent's home, which he inherited.

"I found a timid, almost sheepish Gerhard, completely different from the arrogant, overconfident one I remembered.

"We went into the kitchen and he took two bottles of beer out of the refrigerator, opened them and handed me one. We sat down and he told me the story about the cylinder. Of course, I became fascinated and asked if I could see it. As he got up, he pointed out the window to the apple tree where he hid the cylinder, then went in the other room, returned, and placed it on the table. He had polished it to make it look like the day he first saw it.

"It was a small cylinder with a hexagonal projection on each end. I could see that one end had a seam indicating a cover. I picked it up and it was surprisingly heavy for its size. Rotating it I noted the eagle clutching a swastika and serial number 1734 deeply engraved on the side. Having worked in my father's machine shop, I could appreciate the workmanship. All edges were carefully chamfered and the cylinder itself had a fine finish. The hex machined onto the cover and the base allowed for the use of wrenches. It measured about two inches in diameter by nine inches long. 'Now open it,' he said.

"I unscrewed the cover and saw the black rubber O-ring that made the cylinder watertight. I noticed that it wasn't quite full. I tilted the cylinder and let some of the coins slide into my shaking hand.

"Gerhard laughed, 'I had the same reaction.'

"He warned me to be careful, as the value can be greatly affected by the slightest scratches. The man at the pawnshop where he brought one of the coins chided him for carrying it in his pocket with other coins. He offered to buy the coin for 200 U.S. dollars. So, the numismatic value can be far greater than the actual gold itself depending on the date, mintmark, and condition. He admitted selling some of the coins at the pawnshop from time to time to supplement his income. Of the seventy-two coins originally in the cylinder, fifty-two remained.

"It gave me goose bumps to see the gold coins spread out on the kitchen table. He wanted to know if Iris could be persuaded to join in the search for the cylinders. I assured him that Iris would be very interested and I promptly agreed to join him in his quest for the cylinders.

"I asked him if he thought the pawnshop dealer gave him fair prices. He said a friend recommended him several years before, when he wanted to sell his Nazi SS ceremonial dagger. He felt the pawnbroker treated him fairly and trusted him. In fact, he had a helmet he wanted to sell and asked me to go with him, so I could meet him.

"Later that afternoon we drove to the pawnshop, and Gerhard introduced me to the owner. His name was Max Ehrlichmann, a grandfatherly old gentleman with a white beard, wearing rimless eyeglasses and suspenders. He could have played a great Santa Claus. He stood behind a long row of glass showcases displaying all kinds of coins, jewelry, watches, and military collectables. The rest of the shop contained the usual musical instruments, tools, china, and a vast collection of dust covered stuff. He greeted Gerhard by name and perked up when he saw the helmet. Gerhard introduced me as an American, and Max was surprised that I spoke German. We then had a long spirited conversation about the war and politics.

"Max made an offer for the helmet that seemed quite fair and pleased Gerhard. He then claimed he had connections and could get just about anything we wanted.

"I have to say that I liked Max and felt that he dealt honestly with Gerhard.

"Gerhard drove me around and gave me a tour of the area, and I took him to dinner at a fine restaurant. We went back to his house where I spent the night.

"He showed me the research he had conducted over the years. He learned about an Ensign William Baker who commanded the patrol boat on that early morning in Key West, but nothing else about that day.

"Some General and his staff came up with a global communications scheme they named 'Die Zylinder-Programm'. The cylinders could be buried or hidden in strategic locations all around the world, and their secret agents could send messages back and forth. The much-preferred inducement to betray one's country was gold. This explained why the cylinders were filled with gold coins to be used as seed money by their agents for bribery.

"The Cylinder Program proved to be an effective low tech, two-way communications system, especially in rural and primitive areas.

"He drove me to the airport the next day and when we were saying goodbye he gave me the Captains bible."

"I'm not a religious man, maybe you can make better use of it."

"That's a fascinating story, Erik," I said. "It makes me itchy to get out there and start looking for those cylinders."

"When I got back from West Germany, I was able to go over the whole story with Iris. There was no hesitation; she said she'd love to get involved with the search for the cylinders. Fortunately, she's between assignments and is home in New York.

"For the last fifteen years she's been on archaeological underwater dives all over the Mediterranean, locating Roman and Phoenician shipwrecks. That article in National Geographic surprised my parents and me as to how accomplished she had become in underwater exploration."

"With her experience," I said, "she sounds perfect for a project like this."

"Well, she'll be here tomorrow. I can't wait to see what she says about your place here. I know she's going to love it."

"She sounds like quite a gal," I said, "I'm looking forward to meeting her."

"Oh, you two are going to hit it off right away."

Jacques brought out some charts of the waters around Key West. We moved down to a clear part of the table and spread them out.

Pointing to one of the channels, I said, "That's right about where I first spotted the sub going in that direction heading for deep water there. This is about where the engine started heating up. Say, I just remembered, I had my crew toss over two heavy anchors to lighten up the boat just a few minutes before we sighted the sub. They're still there I'm sure, so that's a marker to be on the lookout for, I would guess right about here."

"Then that's the place to start looking, Right?" asked Erik.

"I don't know," I said. "That would give away the location, where we don't want anyone looking, especially our pal Joe. You know he's going to be watching us like a hawk. I'd say we throw them off by starting in a different location. In fact, we should be seen in several locations. That would really keep them guessing."

"It's an awful waste of time, but I guess we're forced to do it, Bill. How are we going to actually search for the cylinders? Do we just dive down and look around and then move to another site and do the same, until we find something? That will take us forever, unless we're very lucky."

"That's the sixty four thousand dollar question," I said. "We have to start looking somehow, but right now I have no idea."

"Maybe, we should neaten up the place here for Iris' visit?" said Jacques.

"Nah," said Erik. "She'll love it the way it is."

Looking around, Jacques said, "Okay, but I know one thing, women look at things different than men do."

"Anyway, we better start getting some equipment together," I said. "We can rent some scuba gear from a friend of mine, who owns a dive shop. Jacques and I have done a little bit of recreational diving, so we each have our own rigs. How about you, Erik are you a diver?"

"Yes, I had to learn in the OSS. Scuba was quite primitive then, but I've kept up to date with it."

"Okay, we'll need to rent two sets of equipment, one for you and one for Iris."

"Oh, Iris will have her own scuba gear. She always takes it with her that and her bicycle."

"Key West is a great place for a bike," said Jacques. "I'll have to go riding with her someday."

"She'd like that," said Erik.

"Alright, we'll get one scuba set up for you and some extra air tanks," I said. "Can you think of anything else?"

"We'll need an underwater metal detector," said Jacques.

"We may have to buy that," I said. "Off hand, I don't know anyone who has one we could borrow. White's Electronics makes one; we'll have to look into it."

The rest of the day we spent speculating about the gold and just taking it easy recuperating from the night before.

Erik checked out of his hotel and moved his things into my second floor bedroom. He also, sent his two bodyguards back to New York.

The three of us ended up at Maury's for a light dinner. We sat at the bar and planned to just have sandwiches and a couple of beers.

"I see you've got the place back together, Maury," I said. "Have you heard of any casualties?"

Maury laughing said, "Just the usual missing in action list, but the last one was accounted for at noon. There were a lot of hangovers in Key West this morning, speaking of which, how are you feeling?"

"I'm feeling fine, Jacques' recipe fixed us up this morning."

"I saw Jacques, like a drum major, marching you two down the street, if I only had a camera."

"I'm glad you didn't, you'd have that photo hanging up behind the bar there, ouch."

"That's a scary thought," said Erik, "a photo of us in action last night."

"You know, I'm going to get a camera today and keep it behind the bar here. It would be fun to take pictures of you guys."

"Please don't, Maury," I said.

"I'm only kidding; why, I'd lose half of my customers if I started taking pictures. By the way, I heard that Joe Stalker has been sending telegrams to West Germany and receiving some back. I can't tell you what they said, but these are the first telegrams he's ever sent since he's been here."

"Thanks for the information, Maury. Joe's up to something, we'll have to keep tabs on him. Let me know if you hear anything else."

When, Maury was well out of earshot, I said, "I have a feeling those telegrams are letting someone in West Germany know about the Nazi gold."

"It's no coincidence that Joe's sending those telegrams today," said Jacques. "I knew that little snitch, Slip heard everything last night,"

"I wonder who he's involved with in West Germany?" said Erik. "I hope it isn't who I think it is."

"Deep down, we both have a good idea who it is," I said.

We enjoyed our sandwiches and had a couple of more beers while we watched Jimmy singing. Then, we said good night to Maury and living up to our vow to behave went back to the house early and were in bed by ten o'clock.

Wednesday, January 12, 1966

The next day started off completely different from the morning before. We were having a lively conversation at 7:30 about the recovery of the cylinders over Jacques per usual, tasty breakfast. Iris was expected to arrive around noontime, so we were going to show Erik the boat and give him a water tour of the area and be back by 11:30.

Erik loved the boat and being out on the water. Like us he couldn't wait to get started with the search.

We returned to the house before noon and sat out on the front porch to spot Iris when she showed up. Jacques thoughtfully brought out a pitcher of iced tea.

We didn't have long to wait. A late model white Chevy station wagon pulled up in front of the house.

"Hi, Erik," she shouted, swinging open the door and hopping out of the car with a broad smile.

"Hi, Iris, welcome to Key West," he replied.

He ran out to greet her and holding her hands kissed her on the cheek.

"Did you enjoy the drive down the Keys?"

"I loved every mile," she said with a charming German accent, "It's a beautiful part of the world."

She wore a light blue dress that showed off a flawless athletic figure. Her blonde hair pulled back in a ponytail shone in the sun. Her blue eyes enhanced by her dress were striking. Erik's sister was a beautiful woman.

Jacques leaned over to me and whispered, "We should have cleaned up the house."

"Let me introduce you to my two new friends that I told you about," Erik said bringing her up to the porch. "This is Bill Baker, the charter boat Captain."

"Pleased to meet you, Bill," she said extending her hand. "I've heard some great things about you."

As we shook hands, I said, "Believe about half of what you heard. I'm very happy to meet you too, Iris."

"And this is Bill's mate, Jacques LaPort who, by the way, happens to be a great cook. I've gained three pounds in three days. I'm living proof."

She shook hands with Jacques, and said, "Erik's a fussy eater, so your cooking must be good. I don't need any pounds, though."

"He's just having fun with you. It's a pleasure to meet you, Iris. I see you have your bicycle with you. Maybe, we could take a ride sometime, so I can show you the island."

"Why, I'd love that, Jacques, maybe this afternoon. I'm itching for some exercise, after just sitting on that long plane ride and then the drive down here."

"I love your truck, Bill, it's so cute. What year is it?"

"Thank you, it's a 1940 Chevy. The original color black just didn't look right down here, I wanted something to suit Key West, so I had it painted key lime green."

"I like you're advertising slogan on the door, 'Bill Baker's Charters, we supply everything but the luck'."

"My first mate and partner, Tony and I dreamed that up one day when we first started. He had a gift for mechanics and kept that old truck running like a watch."

"Let's go inside, Iris, wait till you see this place," Erik said. "You're going to love it."

They went inside into the front living room.

Iris looked around and said, "What a dump! And what is that smell?"

"What a dump," shouted Ernie.

"Oh nice, they have a parrot and he agrees with me."

"Now, Iris," Erik pleaded, "isn't it cozy?"

"Cozy, like a cave!"

"Cozy, like a cave. Cozy, like a cave," repeated Ernie.

"Iris, how could you say that? This is Bill and Jacques home."

"They have my sympathies."

"My sympathies," repeated Ernie.

"Hello, Iris," she said peering into the cage.

"Hello Iris. Hello Iris," he chirped, tilting his head at her.

"You and I are going to get along just fine, aren't we, Ernie."

Jacques, discreetly picking up an ashtray full of cigar butts and hiding it behind his back, whispered to Bill, "I told you they think and see things different than we do."

She walked out into the bright sunlit kitchen and said, "This is better."

Then walking out onto the deck and seeing the bougainvillea and other plantings in bloom, said, "Now, this I like."

Jacques followed her and was relieved to see that she was smiling. He handed her an iced tea and invited her to sit down.

"I'll just come in the back way next time," she said.

Erik and I remained standing in the hallway looking into the front room.

He apologized to me saying, "Iris doesn't pull any punches, Bill. She tells it like it is. I guess she just doesn't like your front room."

Stunned by her comments, I said, "Those cigar butts are probably what she smelled. Maybe, Jacques was right; we should have had a field day and cleaned up the house. Do you think I should put up some curtains?"

"It couldn't hurt."

"My sympathies," stated Ernie.

"You traitor, you," I said, throwing the cover over his cage. "We should have cleaned up Ernie's cage too."

In the meantime, Iris noticed the charts spread out on the table and started to study them.

"Jacques, do you know the area where the cylinders might be?"

"Hey you guys, Iris wants to go over the charts."

Erik coaxed me to go out on the deck and look at the charts, trying to mitigate her blunt remarks.

"What did you want to know, Iris?" asked Erik. "I'm sure Bill will be glad to answer any of your questions."

"Where is the area we are interested in, Mr. Baker?"

I pointed to the chart and said, "This is approximately where I first encountered the U-Boat."

"Ah that is very good," she said. "The water is nice and shallow there. And, I can see that the sub was going in this direction."

"You're right, but how did you know that?"

"He needed the deep water over here to escape, Mr. Baker, so the Captain had no other choice but to take that course."

"So you can read these charts?" I asked.

She smiled and said, "I had plenty of experience reading them during my years in underwater archeology."

"Well, with all your experience!" I said sarcastically, still smarting from her earlier harsh remarks. "How do we cover all that area out there? We can't just keep doing exploratory dives here and there until we find something. That may take forever. How can we speed things up?"

"That is one way to approach the problem, Mr. Baker," she said looking straight at me, "However, a more efficient way would be to grid the whole area. Then, we scan each grid using a divers' sled."

"What's a divers' sled?" I asked humbly, seeing my comeuppance coming.

"A divers' sled is a special metal frame you trail behind your boat, allowing one or two divers to cling to it at a very slow speed, so they can observe the bottom. There are controls on the sled that allow the divers to steer it up and down and from side to side. The divers cause quite a drag on the boat, so when one or both divers drop off to investigate something interesting the operator of the boat can tell immediately. We can quickly cover a large area this way, if conditions are good. Who knows, maybe we will discover something else while we're out there looking for those cylinders."

That answer knocked my socks off. I was speechless.

"That's a terrific idea, Iris!" said Jacques. "Where can we get one of those sleds?"

"I'm a member in a divers club in Miami and they have a couple," she said. "I know some of their members. I'll give them a call and see if we can borrow one."

"That would be great, Iris," I said, very sheepishly.

"Did Erik show you the photos of the cylinders?" Mr. Baker.

"I forgot all about the photos, Iris. They're in my suitcase. I'll go get them."

"In the meantime, I'll make some more iced tea," said Jacques.

"While we're alone, Iris, I'd like to ask you, why are you calling me Mr. Baker?"

"I've known men like you. You aren't comfortable with women on your turf. I sensed it right away."

I was floored by that assertion!

I looked at her and thought isn't she something. I've never met a woman like her. Erik is right, she doesn't pull any punches and that one hit me in the old solar plexus. I hated to admit it, but there may be a little truth to it. Well, maybe a good deal of truth to it. I am used to being in charge, giving the orders not taking them. This gal shows up and starts to take over stealing my thunder, and I don't like it. Let's see, she has fantastic credentials as an archeological diver with a write up in National Geographic. Suggesting the use of that divers sled was brilliant. She's just the ticket for our search out there for those cylinders. She is obviously highly intelligent and on top of that a very good-looking woman.

If Tony were here what would he tell me to do? I can hear him now... 'What do you need all that thunder for, let her have some; why not let her have it all. Open your eyes and look at her; she's a beautiful woman.

You're momma didn't raise no fool. What else do you have to know?' emphasized with that wonderful laugh of his.

Thanks Tony.

Before I could answer her, Erik came out with the photos and Jacques with another pitcher of iced tea. Erik handed the photos to us.

"Look at all that gold," said Jacques.

"I'm getting gold fever," I said.

"Let's drink to that," said Erik. "Here's to gold fever."

Cheerfully, we all clinked our glasses of iced tea and repeated, "To gold fever."

"Iris," I said, "I'd like to show you some of the flowers out back here, let's take a little walk."

"That would be nice, Mr. Baker."

We went down a few steps and headed towards the centerpiece of the little yard, the delightful bougainvillea.

"What's that?" she asked. "It looks like someone just built a little roof on a foundation.

"That's an old cistern. Years ago before the Navy put in the pipeline from the mainland; people used these cisterns to collect rainwater from their roofs for their drinking water. They were covered like this to keep out leaves and critters that would spoil the water. This one is still working. Most of them in the Keys have been filled in, of course now I just use the water for the lawn and plants."

"Tomatoes, peppers and onions, I can see you're a gardener."

"I get that from my mother, she grew all of our vegetables up in New England. She canned everything, so we had home grown vegetables year round. We even had a root cellar. Her efforts made the depression years easier to cope with."

"That was hard work; she must have been a remarkable woman and I'm going to guess a marvelous cook."

"She still is on both counts, I wish you could meet her and taste some of that cooking. Actually, my parents come down here every February for a couple of weeks, so maybe you will get that chance."

"I'd like that."

"Listen, Iris, I'm just a stodgy old guy who has been doing the same thing here for nearly twenty years. I found something I really love to do. I've worked hard at it, and I've reached that stage where I can honestly say, without boasting, I'm good at it. I have a routine that some may call boring, but I like it. In fact, I love it. What I'm trying to say is, I'm pretty well set in my ways."

"You're not old and you're certainly not stodgy," she scolded. "Set in your ways isn't a bad thing. You're very fortunate to have found a career that you love and are happy with. I envy you; I wish I could say that I've found mine."

"Thank you, Iris, I appreciate that, but I'm surprised that you aren't happy with the underwater archeology. Erik tells me that you have been written up in National Geographic."

"I was, and I loved the notoriety it brought me and to what we were doing. I enjoy the underwater archeology, but I just don't feel like it's something I want to do the rest of my life. It's very serious business, in that you have to follow rigid, time-consuming procedures. Lately, its been getting monotonous. Being a German, I suppose I should like that. After fifteen years of it I recently started to realize that I was living the life of a nomad, moving from one site to another. I want to put down roots someplace and have a real life. When Erik told me about the search for the cylinders filled with gold coins; I jumped at the chance to team up with him. It sounded like fun to me. How could I resist a treasure hunt for gold in the Florida Keys?"

"It could be quite an adventure, Iris, especially if we could find those gold filled cylinders.

"But, getting back to you and me, Iris. I have to admit that you hit the nail on the head; I did feel threatened by you. This is my turf, as you said, and I'm not used to having someone, especially a woman, tell me what or how to do things. I am not inflexible. I'd like to work this out with you, but as I said, I'm set in my ways.

"I know every inch of the waterways around Key West, but just on the surface. You, on the other hand, have all that underwater knowledge and experience. What a combination we would make in this treasure hunt. We couldn't miss. What do you say we team up and have the fun you spoke of, locating that gold? I want to work with you on equal terms and if I back slide, you just give me a swift kick in the shins."

"Only a real man would say what you just did, Bill, I'm so happy we had this conversation and got everything out in the open. Let's go for it. I won't kick you in the shins, but I'll certainly let you know."

"Hey, you called me Bill. That's a good start."

We finished our little tour of the yard and then went back up onto the deck where Erik had four gold coins spread out on the table.

"They sure are beautiful," said Jacques. "Erik just explained how important it is to protect the coins from getting scratched. It can greatly affect their value."

"Can I pick one up?" I asked.

Oh sure," said Erik. "You just don't want to let them hit each other."

"Nothing in the world has the same heft and feel as gold," I said. "It actually has a warm feeling in your hand."

"I hope you're not upset, Iris, I know we promised not to show them to anyone, but I thought we could make an exception, here."

"Oh, I don't have a problem with that," then abruptly changing the subject. "You know I could go for something to eat, anyone else hungry?"

"How about some conch fritters?" I said.

"What are conch fritters?" asked Iris.

"They're made with ground conch, flour, eggs, milk, and a few different spices then deep fried," said Jacques. "You'll love them."

"They pronounce conch, 'conk' down here, Iris," said Erik.

"Okay, so 'conk' fritters are conch fritters, I get it now,"

"We'll go over to Bosun Jim's on the harbor," I said. "We can walk there."

I rolled up the charts and Erik carefully wrapped up the gold coins and slipped them into his pocket. Iris went and freshened up and we washed up in the kitchen sink.

A ten-minute walk down to the harbor brought us to the Fritter Boat. A jumbo double decked, pontoon boat transformed into a restaurant. As we crossed the gangplank onto the boat, Bosun Jim, a retired Navy Boatswain's mate and close friend of Maury Greer welcomed us aboard. They were stationed together for years.

"Hi Bill and Jacques," said Jim, shaking hands. "You need your conch fritter fix today? I had a grand time at that shindig the other night. I had a big head the next day till sundown, but it was worth it. I recognize him, from the party, but not this lovely young lady with you?"

"That's Erik and this is his sister, Iris," I said.

Jim shook hands with Erik and Iris, saying, "Hi Erik, and hello, Iris! I'm delighted to make your acquaintance; you are a breath of fresh air. Please, let me seat you. You missed the lunch hour crowd, so you can have the topside deck to yourselves."

He seated us, so we had a clear view of the harbor. He ran down to get some menus and came back with a little vase of flowers and placed it in front of Iris.

"Thank you, Jim," she said giving him a big smile.

Jim blushed and said, "My pleasure, Iris."

"They're chartering my boat for a few weeks," I said, "to explore the waters around the Keys."

"Oh, you're the one's looking for a Spanish treasure ship. It's all over town. Maury told me all about it. I wish you good luck in your adventure."

"I told Maury to keep that to himself," I said.

Jim started laughing and said, "You're not serious, Bill are you? They don't call him loose lips Maury for nothing."

"You're right. I should have known," I said with a grin.

"And what can I get for you, Iris? Oh, how I love that name!"

"Thank you, Jim. I hear the conch fritters are good here?"

"Good? Why they're outstanding! I make the best conch fritters in Key West and maybe in the whole world. I guarantee it! The only other one's as good are at Maury's," winking at Iris he said in a whisper. "I gave him the recipe."

"That settles it then. I'll have the conch fritters, with a glass of beer."

"A wise choice, my lady," said Jim with a bow. "I detected what I thought was a German accent and ordering a beer confirms it. Am I right?"

"You guessed it, Jim. I'm a Kraut."

"You know what I always say? Germans girls are God's gift to sailors. One time I met a girl in Bremen and she... Well that's for another time. Now, what do you mugs want?"

The three of us all ordered the same.

"The beer's cheaper if you get a pitcher, what do you say?"

"Why not?" said Iris.

The beer arrived and I told about some of the history of Key West, how when the Spanish discovered the island, human skeletons were strewn about. Apparently, the native inhabitants used it as a burial ground, or it could have been the aftermath of a war. They named it Cayo Hueso, which meant Bone Key. Being the western most key the Spanish Cayo Hueso gradually became in English, Key West.

The conch fritters arrived.

Jim hovered around the table waiting for Iris to try one.

Following Jacques example she dipped one into the dipping sauce and took a bite.

"Jim, you've got something here, this is delicious," she said sincerely.

"That dipping sauce is my own secret recipe," he said proudly.

"It's a secret? You mean you wouldn't tell anyone?" she asked.

"Well, maybe I'd tell you, Iris."

"You should feel pretty good, Jim," I said. "Iris tells it like it is. Trust me."

"I'm happy to hear that.

"I'll be down below, just holler if you need anything."

Silence prevailed, while everyone partook of the spicy little delicacies. Always, a sure sign, the chef has done his job well.

"That's quite a yacht pulling in," said Jacques.

A beautiful white yacht, flying an American flag, slowly navigated its way towards a nearby wharf. It made the other private yachts look like toys. She had to be one of the largest ever seen here in Key West.

"She's a beauty," I said, "I'll bet she's a hundred and thirty feet long,"

"Hundred and fifty feet," said Iris.

"No way, I don't think they make them that big."

"What the… That looks like Frank's yacht," said Erik standing up. "Can anyone read the name on the bow?"

"Not yet," I said. "I'll be able to in a couple of minutes. Why, do you recognize her?"

"I hope I'm wrong," he said, looking at Iris.

As the huge sleek pleasure craft inched toward the dock, the crew could be seen forward and aft readying the mooring lines. Their counterparts on the dock were standing by.

"I can read it now 'Princess Iris'," I said. "Iris, there's a boat named after you! What a coincidence."

"No coincidence, Bill. Iris what have you done?"

"That yacht is named after you, Iris?" I asked in surprise.

"Yes," answered Erik. "You told him everything, didn't you, about Bill Baker, the cylinders and the gold, everything. We weren't going to show the photos and the coins to anyone. What have you done, Iris? "

"I didn't see any harm in it. After all, he is a world-renowned numismatist. He promised he would keep it secret and not interfere with our search for the cylinders. He just wants to help us sell the gold coins for a small commission."

"Frank promised? And, you believed him? Why do you think he's here? Now you've done it. He'll start off just wanting to be a partner and before we know it he'll have everything."

"Who is this Frank?" I asked.

"We were engaged a couple of years ago," said Iris. "His name is Frank A. Lucre and he's not all that bad."

"Rattlesnakes aren't all that bad either," said Erik.

"He always treated me nice," she quipped.

"Well then, why didn't you marry him?"

"That's not fair!"

"Come on you two; settle down," I said. "There's nothing to be gained by bickering amongst ourselves?"

"I suggest we go back to the house and discuss all this there," said Jacques.

"Good idea," I said. "For all we know that little runt Slip may be lending an ear."

"Iris, we have to talk," said Erik.

"I didn't do anything wrong. You'll see it's all going to turn out fine, I'll talk to Frank."

"I wish you wouldn't."

We paid the check and thanked Jim for the great lunch and promised we'd be back soon. He gave Iris a container of his special dipping sauce. He appeared to be really smitten by her.

"Next time, Iris," he said, "you come alone and let me treat you to lunch."

"You're so sweet, Jim, thank you."

Jim watched her walk away, until she was out of sight.

We got back to the house, and Iris remembered that she had to check into the hotel. She told Jacques that she would be back for the bicycle ride around the island. She left the scuba equipment and the bike at the house and drove to the hotel.

After Iris left, we went into the house. Erik noticed that some of his things were out of place in his room. He mentioned it to Jacques and me. As we looked around, sure enough, we noticed more things out of place.

"Someone's definitely been searching the house," I said. "They did their best to hide it, but the cigars in my humidor are out of order from the way I like to keep them."

"The photos?" said Erik. "Did they get the photos?"

Jacques hurried into the kitchen and came back all smiles holding up the photos.

"They missed them. I put them in the phone book to protect them."

"Good job, Jacques," said Erik. "It's a good thing I took the gold coins with me."

"This smells of Joe Stalker," I said, " He didn't waste any time. He sent his flunky, Slip over here to poke around hoping to find something. That's probably why we didn't see him at the Fritter Boat. I don't think they found out anything, but we'll have to be careful of what we leave around here."

"I'll have to find a hiding place for the gold coins," said Erik.

"I have a safe deposit box; if you want you're welcome to use it."

"By all means that would be the safest place for them."

"We'll go to the bank tomorrow. Meanwhile, tell me more about this guy Frank."

"He's super rich for one thing and has a record of always coming out on top in all his dealings. He has a bevy of top-notch lawyers on his payroll, so he can grind down his opponents with all kinds of legal gymnastics until they run out of money or just give up, on his terms of course.

"On the other hand, he's extremely charming and sophisticated. He's been to all the best schools.

"That's why Iris fell for him. He dazzled her with his footwork. She finally came to her senses and realized that, the only thing he will ever love besides himself is his money. I thought that they ended their relationship, but unbeknownst to me she's been keeping in touch with him.

"He is an authority on rare coins and has one of the world's finest collections."

"We've got two outsiders that know about the gold now," I said. "Let's hope that's it."

"I'd better get my bicycle ready," said Jacques. "Iris will be along soon for our ride around the island. Should I mention the break-in?"

"No, let's keep it to ourselves for now," I said.

"I agree," said Erik "I don't think she has to know. No need for her to worry."

Iris walked back from the hotel and found Jacques checking out the bicycles for their ride. She now wore white shorts and a pink tank top and sneakers. Key West was in for a treat.

Jacques had oiled the chains and checked the brakes and tire pressure of the two bikes, so they were ready to go.

Iris gracefully boarded her bicycle and took a quick spin up and down the street displaying her mastery of the two-wheeled craft.

A few minutes later, with smiles and waves they peddled off on their grand tour of the island.

In the meantime Erik and I began working on a list of things we were going to need in the quest for the cylinders.

"Erik, how did Iris become interested in underwater archeology?"

"When in college she found out about an expedition to an ancient sunken shipwreck off the coast of Turkey. They were looking for interested students for a summer program, so she signed up and they accepted her. She had to learn scuba diving and the basics of underwater archeology. When they found a beautiful bronze statue at a wreck site she was hooked. She loved the experience and decided she wanted to pursue it."

"I'd like to get a copy of that National Geographic article sometime. I'd enjoy reading it."

"There were some great photos and a nice story; you'll be amazed. I know my parents and I were."

A couple of hours later Iris and Jacques returned to the yard.

"What a wonderful ride, Jacques," she said. "It's such a beautiful island. Thank you for showing it to me."

"My pleasure, Iris, I'd be happy to do it again anytime you say. Come on in for some lemonade."

"I am thirsty. That would be a treat."

You go on in Iris, "I'll take care of the bikes and meet you out on the deck."

"Thank you, Jacques. I think I'll go around the back way."

As she came up the back walkway she greeted Erik and me on the deck.

"So!" I asked, "how do you like Key West from the seat of a bicycle?"

"I love it. It's so beautiful. The weather, turquoise water, flowers and plenty of fun loving people, what more could anyone want?

"So, what are you two up to?"

"We made a list of equipment we're going to need," said Erik, "and we were just talking about how to get those cylinders into the boat unobserved, when we do find them."

"You're not going to like this, Erik, but I have an invitation from Frank. He's asking me to dine with him tomorrow night on his yacht. He wants me to bring my friends with me and to dress casual. When I checked in, the clerk at the front desk handed it to me."

"Absolutely not!" snarled Erik.

"Don't be so quick to decide, Erik," I said, "I think I would like to meet this fellow to see if he's as bad as you say he is. If so, he may have some weakness and one of us just might spot it."

"Don't forget, he'll be doing the same thing and, I'm afraid you'll find that he's far better at it then we are."

"You're giving Bill a preconceived notion of Frank," she said. "Let him meet Frank and then form his own opinion."

"Maybe you're right," turning to me, he said. "I'm curious to see what your impression of Frank will be. Very well, let's accept his invitation. I know one thing's for sure; he puts on a good spread. You'll be impressed."

"Speaking of food," I said, "how about going to Maury's tonight?"

"Good idea," said Erik. "You're going to like Maury's, Iris. You walked by it on the way from the hotel."

"I couldn't help notice the neon sign out front."

Jacques brought out a pitcher of iced lemonade and joined us.

"You should have seen Iris go on that bicycle of hers. I heard plenty of wolf whistles too."

"Oh, Jacques, they weren't whistling at me."

"Well they sure weren't whistling at me."

"Oh, I don't know, you're a good looking guy," I said with a grin. "And a snappy dresser."

Iris giggled and Erik started to laugh too.

"I'm a snappy dresser? Wearing shorts, sandals and an old tee shirt? You think that's a snappy dresser?"

"In Key West it is," I said.

"In Haiti, when I started to work, I spent half my salary every week at the haberdasher until I had a respectable wardrobe. Every Sunday morning, I used to put on a suit and tie. My shoes were polished, and I wore a derby hat, now that's what I call snappy dressing. The girls used to follow me around. That's how I met my wife…"

Jacques started to fill up. The unwitting mention of his wife stirred up a painful memory.

"Please. Excuse me. I'll be back in a while." as he left the deck and walked away.

"Is he all right, Bill?" asked Iris in a concerned voice.

"Will he be okay?" asked Erik.

"He hasn't mentioned his wife in a long time." I said. "He lost her about seven years ago. That's when I came to know him."

"What happened to her?" asked Iris.

"A Navy nurse friend of mine, Nathalie and I went over to Cuba for a few days. She volunteered her time and nursing skills at a Catholic free clinic for the poor run by nuns. We used to go over there every month or so. The Sister's always had a list for me that kept me busy making small repairs around the building.

"After putting in three twelve-hour days on her feet Nathalie earned the right to sleep on the trip back to Key West. When halfway across the Straits of Florida heading North, I thought I saw something off in the distance and changed course to check it out. As I came nearer, I could see through my binoculars the form of a man floating on the water.

"I woke up Nathalie and then pushed the throttle forward to maximum speed. Several minutes later, we pulled up alongside and found a black man clinging to a cabin door. It turned out to be Jacques. Delirious and semi-conscious, the poor man rambled on incoherently. We both struggled to get him up over the side of the boat. Nathalie checked his pulse and shook her head from side to side. She recognized the symptoms of extreme dehydration and didn't give much hope for survival. She mixed up a solution of a bit of salt, some sugar and water. We kept putting small amounts into his mouth until he swallowed it and then gave him more. This went on for the next four hours until we arrived at Key West. Her quick thinking and action saved his life.

"I radioed in to have an ambulance meet us at the dock. They put him on an I.V. solution immediately and rushed him to the Naval hospital.

"The next day, Nathalie then in uniform, was by his bedside when he regained consciousness.

'You gave us quite a scare, but you're going to be all right,' she told him.

"With tears in his eyes, he told her how the boat they were on sunk so quickly it took everything that could float down with it. A few minutes later, the cabin door came to the surface."

'It was a gift from God to save us,' he said, 'I retrieved the door and my wife and two little girls held on to it.'

"They drifted aimlessly for several days. Without food and water the children were the first to die, then his wife. One by one he watched them slip away. He couldn't remember anything after that."

'What is your name?'

'Jacques LaPort,' he told her. 'Why did God give us that door if he didn't want to save us? I want to die too.'

'Your wife and children are in heaven,' she told him, 'God sent the door, so you could live. You have to live. Who else will remember them?'

"That seemed to make sense to him. He nodded and fell back to sleep.

"Nathalie and I took a special interest in him. In addition to his physical condition a deep depression, understandably, had him in its clutches. Even with therapy, it looked like a long recuperation.

"I told her I never personally knew any black people, but Nathalie assured me not to worry, because we would have more in common than not. Fortunately, he spoke perfect English in addition to his native Haitian French. Without that obstacle, we were able to communicate easily, and I found out that Nathalie was right. I helped him with the immigration thing by becoming his sponsor and, I said I would employ him. I had a spare room so until he got better I let him stay with me. He quickly got his strength back and one afternoon after a charter, I opened the door to the aroma of bread baking. It brought me back to when I was a kid, and my mother used to bake bread every week. I went into the kitchen and Jacques had a first rate supper prepared. That's when he told me, he had been a professional chef in a restaurant in Haiti. Ever since he was a youngster, he always enjoyed cooking. I quickly made an agreement of room and board for cooking and KP; then later, he became my permanent Mate."

"Why did he leave Haiti," asked Iris.

"A rigged jury found him guilty of a crime he didn't commit, and they placed him under house arrest awaiting sentencing. Without him, his family would become impoverished, so he hatched a plan to escape.

"Relatives and friends helped by raising the bribery money, getting him the boat with supplies and seeing them off in the middle of the night."

"What a horror story," said Erik, "I'm glad you're splitting your share with him."

"He's been sending money regularly to repay his kinfolks in Haiti since he's been here. He's the kindest and gentlest man I've ever met."

"You're a pretty nice guy yourself, Bill," said Iris, "You saved his life and then stood by him until he recovered."

"Thank you, but I got much more out of it than I put in.

"I hope he'll be okay."

"He'll be fine, Iris."

"Will he be at Maury's tonight?"

"I'll make sure of it."

"I'd better go back to the hotel and get ready for tonight."

"You look fine the way you are," I said, "You don't have to get dressed up for Maury's. It's a pretty casual place."

"I'd feel better if I changed, though. I'll wear something casual. See you at seven."

She left by the back way and rode her bicycle over to the hotel.

Jacques returned a little later and the three of us took turns cleaning up and headed over to Maury's.

"Hey you guys," shouted Maury, "How's it going?"

We all acknowledged him and waved as we headed over to our usual booth.

Denise, from behind the bar, made eye contact with me and gave the pitcher sign and three fingers, which meant a pitcher of beer and three glasses. I returned an okay sign.

A few minutes later she delivered the goods.

"I saw you with a pretty girl today, Jacques?"

"That's Iris, Erik's sister. I was showing her the island."

"She just arrived today," said Erik. "She should be here any minute now."

"She's a very attractive woman. Is she married?"

"No, she's still single."

"I'll pass the word. A bunch of eligible bachelors hang out in here."
She scurried off and said something to Maury.

"Oh, oh!" I said, "Iris is in for a big surprise when she walks in here tonight."

A little later, Iris stepped through the doorway and looked around for us. She was wearing a custom fitted yellow dress, very modest, but not hiding any of her womanly attractiveness. Still sporting her ponytail and shod with a pair of Birkenstocks, she did not go unnoticed at Maury's. The whole bar grew silent, both men and women wondering, as she looked around, who the lucky guy might be.

Several young men, the eligible bachelors, greeted her by name and offered to buy her a drink. Spotting us, she started walking over to our booth, ignoring the pleading young men following her. We stood up and greeted her and invited her to sit down. She slid in beside me.

"Okay, boys," I said, "she's spoken for."

"Would you like to dance later, Iris," one of them asked.

"Maybe," she said with a smile.

"Yahoo! She said, maybe," he shouted, as they headed back to the bar.

"That's just their way of saying welcome," I said.

"How did they know my name?" she asked.

"You can thank Maury. The whole place knows your name and that you're single," said Erik. "I might add that there are a flock of eligible bachelors in here, Iris."

"I'm thrilled to know that, I suppose you gave them my room number at the hotel?"

"Of course not," said Erik. "By the way, what is your room number?"

"That, you're not going to know," she said.

Denise came by to meet Iris.

"Hello, Iris, my name is Denise. Welcome to Key West. That big Palooka behind the bar is my husband. Don't mind those fellows they were just being friendly."

"I'm beginning to feel right at home here," she said giving Erik a look.

"That's nice to hear," Denise said sincerely, "What can I get for you to drink, Iris?"

"I'd love a dry beefeater martini with a twist, please."

"A what?" Denise asked taken aback.

"Oh," catching the drift, "Make that a gin and tonic, Denise."

"Okay, coming right up. I have to tell you, Iris, I love your dress. And, where did you get those sandals? They look so comfortable.

"Thank you, Denise. I bought the sandals in West Germany. They're called Birkenstocks and are very comfortable; they conform to your feet. I've heard they're going to start selling them here in America soon."

"I'll be on the lookout for them. Anyway, Iris, you're just what this place needs, class."

"Class!" said Erik teasing. "I hope that doesn't go to your head."

"Oh please, Erik, you know me better than that."

"I think it's true, though," I said, "You do bring class to Maury's. You look very nice tonight, Iris and I'm very proud to be sitting next to you."

"Why, Bill," she said with a smile, "I didn't think you cared."

"Of course I care," I said, "In fact; I'd like to get to know you better. A friend of mine has a small sailboat I can borrow, maybe we can go out for a little sail sometime."

"I'd love that, I haven't been in a small sailboat since childhood. That would be a fun day."

"Great, I'll let you know when I can borrow the boat."

Denise brought the gin and tonic for Iris, along with silverware, napkins and a basket of rolls and butter.

"We've got some nice fresh dolphin tonight. Anyone interested?

"You eat dolphin?" asked Iris.

"I didn't know they were edible," said Erik, "Poor Flipper."

"No this is the fish," laughed Jacques, "Don't worry Flipper is not on the menu. Another name for it is mahi-mahi."

"I've had mahi-mahi," said Iris, "It's delicious. That's what I'll have, Denise."

"How would you like it cooked? Fried, baked stuffed, broiled or jerked, it comes with smashed potatoes and green beans."

"I'd like it broiled."

"Jerked," said Jacques.

Erik and I both opted for the baked stuffed.

"Jacques," said Iris, "it's good to see you laugh. Bill told us about how you lost your little family. I know it's been many years, but please accept my deepest sympathy."

"And mine also," said Erik.

"Thank you," he said, "It's an old wound that's still not quite healed. Knowing you care helps."

Maury left his sanctuary, behind the bar and came over to meet Iris.

"Hi Iris, I just came over to see if you're real. You sure brighten up the place. Can I get you anything?"

"I'm real all right. So far, I have everything I need, including some ardent local admirers, thank you."

"I see what you mean, they're just being neighborly, Iris. You let me know if anyone gets out of hand, I'll take care of them," his voice becoming stern.

"No that's okay; everyone's been very nice to me.

As a diver, I appreciate all the nautical things you have on display here."

"I'm happy to hear you say that, Iris. Denise reminds me every day to stop or we won't have room for the customers. Even so, if you want to add to the collection, feel free. Well, I've got to get back to my public. You let me know if I can do anything for you. And, remember, what I said about your admirers, Iris."

"I will, Maury, thank you so much."

The food arrived and the conversation slowed to a snails pace, a sure sign the food hit the spot. It didn't take long before four empty plates were staring up at the ceiling.

"I've never had a better fish dinner," said Iris, "It must be because of the ambience and of course the company."

"It could be that you were hungry," I said, "but the real reason is that the charter boat captains, including myself, catch and supply Maury with only the best and freshest fish daily; it's in our own interest because we all eat here as well."

"I really enjoyed that too," said Erik. "My hats off to you, Bill and all those other charter boat captains."

"Now you know why Jacques and I are regulars."

Denise swung by to clear the table.

"It looks like the mahi-mahi didn't disappoint."

"You did it again, Denise," I said.

"Would anyone like some dessert or coffee?"

"Coffee sounds good," said Iris.

"Coffee all around? Okay coming right up. By the way, Bill, Maury wants to see you."

I excused myself and went to see what Maury wanted.

"Bill," said Maury, "see those two muscle bound guys over in the corner, wearing navy blue tee shirts, you can't miss them. When one of them came over to get a pitcher of beer, I noticed the name Princess Iris embroidered on his jersey. They're off that big yacht that pulled in today. Is your Iris and the Princess Iris related?"

"They are one and the same. Iris and the owner were going to get married a couple of years ago, but they called it quits. I guess he decided to keep the name on the boat."

"There's more, Bill. He claimed that they're both former UDT's, and the owner hired them as mates with some possible underwater work. He said they weren't told what kind of work yet but didn't care because they were getting well paid. If I hear anything else, I'll let you know."

"Thanks Maury, I'd appreciate that."

This could be something serious. I think I'll keep it under wraps for now. I returned to the booth.

"What did Maury want?" asked Jacques.

"He wanted to know if there was a connection to the Princess Iris yacht that pulled in today and our Iris. I told him that you were engaged to the owner at one time, but called it off."

"I don't know why he didn't change the name of that boat," she said, "there's nothing between us anymore."

"In the meantime," I said, "we've got to come up with a plan on how we're going to bring up those cylinders on the sly. They need to know our progress of the recovery of the gold to time their theft, so Joe and his cohorts will be watching our every move out there."

"This is getting so complicated," said Iris, "Maybe we should just wait for a year or so, until he gives up and goes away."

"I don't think it would work," said Erik, "there's just too much money involved. He'd just wait us out, until we started looking again."

"We can figure it all out," said Jacques. "We're smarter than they are."

That's the spirit, Jacques," I said. "I'm with you."

One of the young men at the bar finally worked up enough courage to come over and asked Iris to dance. On the way over he put a nickel in the jukebox and selected a Chubby Checkers song 'Do the Twist'.

"Thank you, but I promised the first one to Bill."

"Oh, I can't dance to this music," I said, "I'm just a waltz kind a guy. Don't let me stop you, though. Go for it, Iris."

"Is that a dare, Bill?"

"Yes, let's see what you can do."

Iris hopped up and the proud young man politely escorted her to the little dance floor where they started to dance "The Twist". Her partner was a good dancer, and Iris was an excellent dancer. She cut quite a figure, had great rhythm, and knew all the moves. Everyone in the place started to watch her dance and began to applaud her talent. She became an instant hit in Maury's, especially with the eligible young bachelors. The coins started to drop into the jukebox and a line formed for the next dance with Iris. The first dance ended with a standing ovation, as the next in line took over. Iris, encouraged by everyone's approval, continued to treat all to a marvelous floorshow.

"I guess I forgot to tell you," said Erik, "Iris loves to dance."

"I can see that," I said, "And she's good at it too. She is a pleasure to watch."

After a dozen dances Iris told them she needed a breather. She thanked all the eligible bachelors.

"Let's do it again, sometime!"

She returned to the booth half out of breath, but smiling.

"I haven't had so much fun in a long time. These eligible bachelors are good dancers."

"You were great!" said Jacques.

"Thank you, I've always liked dancing."

"When I catch my breath, we'll dance to a waltz, Bill."

"Oh, I don't know," I said, "You're a professional."

"Get back, I dance for the fun of it and the exercise. You're not turning me down are you?"

"I'd never do that, Iris. It'll be a long wait to hear a waltz in here, so I better get over to that juke box and put one in the queue."

Denise brought over the coffee pot and topped off everyone's cup.

"You were marvelous," she said, "I wish I could dance like that."

"I could teach you, Denise."

"Oh, I'm beyond that now. And, besides, who would I dance with, my husband? I'll just enjoy watching you. Thanks for the offer, anyway, Iris."

Finally a waltz started to play.

"C'mon Bill, let's go, it's our turn. You picked out a nice song, Moon River. That will be our song."

"What do you mean our song?"

"The first song that a couple dances to, will always be their song. Everyone knows that, Bill."

We stepped out onto the empty little floor and started. No one ever saw me dance before, and to everyone's surprise, I waltzed very well with Iris. When the music ended we received several compliments.

"You dance really nice, Bill," she said, as we walked back to the booth. "I'm impressed."

"It's been a long time. I guess it's like riding a bicycle it comes back to you."

"We'll give it another try, soon," she said.

I had to admit that holding her hand with my arm around her little waist gave me a thrill. I actually got a little light headed in a most pleasant way as we waltzed around the little dance floor. The music ended all too soon.

We finished our coffee and agreed to call it a night. Erik escorted Iris back to her hotel, and Jacques and I went back to the house with a plan to get an early start in the morning.

Thursday, January 13, 1966

Next morning bright and early the three of us were having breakfast on the deck. Iris arrived on her bicycle and came up the back walk, wearing a blue chambray shirt, cut off blue jeans and sneakers. Even in work clothes she looked incredible.

"Good morning, boys," she said, with a beautiful smile."

The three of us greeted her and couldn't help but return that smile.

"Did you have breakfast, Iris?" Jacques asked.

"Yes, I went to a café on Duval Street and had a delicious ham and cheese pastry and coffee. It smelled so nice in there of fresh bread baking. I wouldn't mind having another cup though, Jacques."

"One coffee coming right up. That's one of the best bakeries in Key West. By the way please come here for breakfast, Iris, you're more than welcome. I'd enjoy cooking for you."

"Thank you Jacques, I'm going to take you up on that."

"Good, I'll be looking for you tomorrow morning."

"I think I have a solution to one of our problems, Bill," she said.

"Nice going, Iris, have a seat and tell us what you've got."

"First off, I called the diver's club in Miami and they agreed to let us use one of their sleds. I'll take a ride up and see if I can get a hitch for the wagon to tow it back with."

"That's good news," I said. "I'm looking forward to seeing how that thing works."

"Also, I thought of what you said about bringing up the cylinders without being seen. Would it be possible to install a small doorway into the side of the boat a little above the water line to pass the cylinders through? We could surface close to the boat and just put the cylinders through the door, instead of passing them over the side of the boat."

"That's a great idea, Iris!" I said. "Yes we can do that. It will have to be made somewhat watertight for when we're underway and not too noticeable when we're tied up at the dock. Now that's what I call using your noggin, Iris."

"I'm impressed, Iris," declared Erik.

"Way to go, Iris!" called Jacques from the kitchen.

"After breakfast," I said, "we'll go down to the boat and dope out how and where to install that little hatchway. Oh, what time is dinner on the Princess Iris?"

"He wants us there at four thirty for cocktails and to watch the sunset at about six. Dinner will be shortly afterwards."

"I don't think I should go," said Jacques. "I'm only the mate."

"I wish you would come," I said. "I'd like to see what you think of Frank. You have a much more common sense approach to things than I have. I tend to shoot from the hip. Between the two of us we'll be able to size this guy up. I value your opinion."

"Please come, Jacques," said Erik. "Remember you've got a stake in this adventure too. I don't trust that guy as far as I could throw this table, but like Bill said, you may see or hear something that we all miss."

"Oh, Erik, there you go again, I wish you wouldn't say things like that. Frank would never do anything devious. He's an honest man. I don't want Bill and Jacques to have any negative ideas before they meet him tonight."

"I'm not going to say another word about him," looking up at the ceiling. "But, you know how I feel."

"Won't you go for me, Jacques?" she said. "I'd feel bad if you didn't."

"Since you put it that way, Iris, I can't say no."

"You won't be sorry, I just know you'll have a good time."

"Well let's go down to the boat." I said.

"I've got to clean up the kitchen," said Jacques, "and go to Fausto's to stock up. Plan to come back here around one o'clock for lunch."

"Could I help you clean up?" asked Iris.

"This is how I earn my room and board around here. You go with Bill and Erik and get that pass through installed. You came up with a clever idea there."

"Thanks, Jacques, see you later for lunch."

Down at the boat we decided to put it on the port side near the stern. I suggested that we make a 3" square door hinged on the top, so it will tend to stay shut. We carefully made the opening with a saber saw and used the cut out for the door, so it wouldn't be too noticeable. In a couple of hours we had the door installed with a brass piano hinge. Using copper tacks we fastened a gasket around the perimeter of the door making it sort of watertight. A simple brass hook and eye on the inside kept it shut. Being almost a foot above the water line, it wouldn't be a problem.

As we were cleaning up, Jacques came running down to the boat with a telegram for Erik.

"This just came to the house. I thought it might be important, so I brought it right down. I hope it's nothing serious."

"Thank you, Jacques," he said, taking the telegram, "let's find out."

He opened it and after reading it, sat down on the edge of the boat and sadly said, "My cousin Gerhard is dead."

"What happened?" said Iris upset.

"Someone broke into his house and attacked him. He died later in the hospital. The wire is from my mother and father in West Germany. My poor parents just happened to be over there and are dealing with this tragedy. They included a phone number I can call."

"Let's go back to the house," I said, "you can use my phone."

Erik with Iris by his side, made the distressing call. Jacques and I went out on the deck to let them have their privacy, even though the conversation was all in German.

About fifteen minutes later Iris and Erik joined us on the deck.

Erik in an anxious voice said, "Someone severely assaulted Gerhard, ransacked his house, and left him for dead. He managed to crawl to the phone and call the police. My mother said he wanted me to know that he told them nothing, and he hid it again. She asked me what he meant by that, and I had to lie and say I didn't know. I couldn't tell her about the cylinder."

"You'll be able to explain everything to her later," I said, "she'll understand. I'm so sorry to the both of you for your loss. Is there anything I can do?"

"That goes for me too." said Jacques.

"No thank you. I think I'd like to go for a walk with Iris for a little while."

They headed down towards the water.

"You know, Jacques, I think someone tortured Gerhard to tell about the gold. They weren't able to get him to talk that's why they searched the house."

"You may be right, Bill. Erik's mother said they didn't get the cylinder. She also said he hid it again. I wonder if Erik knows what that means?"

"I hope so. Do you think that the pawnbroker is behind this?"

"He does seem like a prime suspect, Bill. He may have assumed that Gerhard had a hoard of gold coins in his house."

"On the other hand," I said, "it sounds like Gerhard has been selling the gold coins for years. Why try to rob him now?"

An hour later, Iris and Erik returned to the house, somewhat composed.

"We have both agreed that we will go to West Germany for Gerhard's services. We'll try and get a flight tomorrow afternoon from Miami. We were going to cancel tonight's affair with Frank, but decided to go ahead with it."

"I think you're doing the right thing on both accounts." I said. "Have you given any thought as to why or how this could have happened?"

"We just went over that," said Iris, "We suspect that the pawnbroker may have had a part in it."

"Jacques and I came to that same conclusion. But, Gerhard had known him for years. Why did the pawnbroker act now?"

"That's another one of the reasons we want to go to over there," said Erik. "I want to talk to him and see what he has to say. In any police investigation I think he should be included."

"We should only be gone a few days." said Iris. "On the way back from Miami, we'll pick up that sled. This tragic incident in no way discourages us from pursuing those cylinders. If and when we do find them, we would like Gerhard's share to go to the survivors of the death camps, as he wanted."

"I'm glad you both feel that way," I said. "I'm also more committed now than ever."

"Me too." said Jacques. "Nothing is going to stop us now."

"I'm glad to hear that," said Erik, "I'll make those airline reservations now."

"Let me finish that lunch I started," said Jacques.

In short order, he brought out to the deck cups of steaming fish chowder and a platter of tuna fish sandwiches.

"This chowder is delicious," said Erik, "I don't detect any TABASCO."

"It's in there," said Jacques, "I did cut back a little, just for you."

"I didn't realize how hungry I was," said Iris, "the chowder and sandwiches are scrumptious, Jacques."

"I'm happy that you like them that's my reward. I just put on a pot of coffee."

"After the coffee," I said, "we should start thinking about getting ready for the time on Frank's yacht."

"Will you pick me up at the La Concha," asked Iris, "on the way to the yacht, say around four fifteen? Remember it's casual."

"Of course, we'd be glad to," I said.

After the coffee and some of Jacques' cookies, Iris rode her bike to the hotel and the rest of us got ready to meet Frank on the Princess Iris. The three of us wore shorts, sandals, and pressed, starched short sleeve shirts with the top buttons open.

"I didn't tell you before," I said, on the way to the hotel, "Maury, informed me that Frank hired two former UDT divers recently. At some point tonight I'm going to ask him if he has any experienced divers on board. It will be interesting to see how he answers. If he lies about it, then we know he has something up his sleeve. If not, I think we may be able to trust him."

"Leave it to Maury to find that out." said Jacques. "That's a good idea Bill."

"I like that," said Erik. "It's a little test to check Frank's honesty. I'm betting that he fails it."

The three of us arrived at the hotel promptly at four fifteen to find Iris waiting out front. She had her hair done up in a twist in the back, held in place by an elegant tortoise shell comb. She looked charming in cream-colored Capri pants with embroidered tiny roses down the sides and a matching sleeveless top. A cream colored purse and sandals completed the ensemble.

"Iris," I said on impulse, "you look beautiful! I feel like we should go back and change into something nicer."

"Thank you, Bill. You all look fine the way you are. I guess I may have gotten a little carried away. I started off very casual, but kept adding things and this is what I ended up with."

"You look lovely, Iris," said Jacques, "we couldn't be more proud to be your escorts tonight."

"You've never looked nicer, Iris," said Erik.

"Thank you all for your compliments, and I'm proud to have three of the handsomest men in Key West for my escorts."

A ten-minute walk brought us to the impressive yacht, "Princess Iris." All white with plenty of beautiful mahogany trim. One hundred and fifty feet of pure luxury with natural teak decking, polished chrome everywhere, and lines neatly faked out. She couldn't have been more squared away. It appeared that Frank ran a tight ship.

"Good evening and welcome aboard," said one of the two neatly uniformed men stationed at the gangway. "Allow me to conduct you to the Captain."

He presented his arm to Iris and she took it with a smile. We followed them on board and then aft to a large promenade deck.

Just coming out of a doorway strode a tall, well-built, handsome man with a broad smile. He was all decked out in a navy blue sport jacket adorned with numerous shiny brass buttons, white shirt with a navy blue ascot tie, white shorts, socks and shoes. He stood under a white covered officer's hat that would make any dictator envious with its heavily encrusted gold braid, buttons, and golden oak leaf flourishes on the peak. As if that wasn't enough, it was flamboyantly adorned with a cap badge of oversized crossed anchors behind an enormous golden eagle.

"Good evening everyone and welcome to my humble boat," said Frank, "And of course it's wonderful to see my dearest Iris, again. You look positively gorgeous this evening, but of course you always do."

He gave her a hug and kissed her on the cheek.

"I thought you said casual and look at you all dressed up like a Fleet Admiral," said Iris.

He removed his hat revealing salt and pepper hair and said, "It is casual, Iris! But, I just love wearing this outfit when I'm on board, especially the hat, which I designed myself."

A steward promptly came over and took the extravagant hat. Frank removed the ascot tie and another steward stepped forward to help him off with the jacket.

"Voila, now I'm casual." then turning to Erik he extended his hand, saying, "It's good to see you again too, Erik. Now, Iris, please introduce me to your friends."

"Yes, of course. This is Bill Baker a charter boat captain here in Key West, whom we have engaged for a few weeks."

Frank reached out and gave me a hearty handshake, saying, "I'm very pleased to meet you, Bill. I've heard of your reputation of being a most successful trophy fisherman. I would like to engage you myself sometime for a fishing charter in the future."

"It's nice to meet you, Frank. I've been very fortunate, and I love what I do. I would enjoy that fishing trip sometime. Oh, this is my right hand man, Jacques. He's my mate and half the secret of my success."

Again, reaching out to Jacques he gave him a hearty handshake as well and said, "Welcome, Jacques, I heard that you are Haitian, is that true?"

"Yes, I was born and grew up there."

"When I graduated from college I spent a year in Haiti studying birds. I got to know your people well."

He then started speaking Haitian French with Jacques. They carried on a short conversation ending with both of them laughing.

"Please excuse our rudeness, but it brought back some happy memories. Of all the countries I've lived in all over the world, I've never felt more at home or welcome then in Haiti. One of the women on my staff here is from Haiti; she's a sous chef that's how I keep up my Haitian. I'll ask her to join us later."

"You may already know," I said, "that John Audubon lived in Key West for a while back in the early eighteen hundreds."

"That's something I didn't know, Bill. Do you have any more information about it?"

"As the story goes he lived aboard ship for the few weeks he stayed in Key West. He discovered more than a dozen local birds and spent many weeks visiting the Dry Tortugas and the upper Keys. A few years ago the Mitchell Wolfson Foundation restored the old Geiger house on Whitehead Street, which was originally built around the time of his visit and is now called the Audubon House. They have many of his drawings on display. He is purported to have drawn some of them in the gardens on that property."

"Thank you for sharing that with me, I can't wait to visit it."

"You never told me you studied birds," said Iris.

"You don't know everything about me, Iris. Maybe we needed a little more time to get to know each other better. I haven't given up hope."

Before she could answer him he announced, "May I offer you all a libation? Come on into the bar."

We went through a doorway and entered a small replica of an English Pub. Manning the dark mahogany bar, with several polished brass English beer taps, stood a bartender at the ready with a very impressive selection of spirits arrayed behind him.

In addition to a little buffet table laden with all kinds of goodies, a stewardess came through passing a variety of hors d'oeuvres.

"Wouldn't Maury love to see this?" I said.

"Who is Maury?" asked Frank.

"He owns Maury's Bar and Grill, the best bar in Key West. All the charter boat crews gather there every night. It's a fun place."

"I can vouch for that," said Erik.

"I can too," said Iris.

"Me too," said Jacques.

"Well, with endorsements like that, I'll have to visit Maury's."

"Please be our guest soon," I said.

"That sounds like an enjoyable evening."

"I'll have a dry Beefeater martini with a twist," said Iris.

"I think I'll try one of those English beers?" I said.

"Make it two," said Jacques.

"I'll make it unanimous," said Erik.

"I'll have my usual," said Frank.

"What's your usual?" I asked.

"Myer's Rum and ginger ale. I like rum when I'm in warm climates. They just seem to go together.

I'm sure that Iris told you I'm a numismatist, or as I like to think, just a coin collector. I'd like to show you a few of them. Please take your drinks with you."

He led us through a doorway into a handsome paneled office, carpeted with exquisite thick oriental rugs. Behind a large mahogany desk he stepped up to an oil painting that he swung aside revealing a wall safe. With a few quick turns he opened it and took out several trays and set them on the desk. Each tray held a dozen gold coins individually encased in a clear plastic box with a built in magnifying glass on each side, so both sides could be closely examined. Pertinent information imprinted on the edges told something about each coin such as the date, origin, and denomination

He spread the trays out and asked us all to please feel free to examine them.

I picked up a beautiful old one that had an inscription "Erculi Victori".

"I wonder what this one says?"

"That's a Roman coin and that means 'Hercules the Victor'," said Iris, "The Romans used abbreviations on their coins to save space.

"By the way, Bill," said Erik, "Iris can translate Latin and ancient Greek."

One by one we passed the old Roman and Greek coins to her for their translation. Some of the more modern coins had Latin too, which she also translated.

"I'm impressed, Iris I didn't realize you were so well informed about these ancient coins," said Frank.

"You don't know everything about me, Frank. That's an important part of archeology. Besides, you never showed me any of your coins."

"That would change, if you give us another chance," he said. "I have many more coins back in New York you could translate for me."

I'll bet he has some etchings too. I hope she doesn't fall for that line.

I noticed that Frank, very carefully made sure every tray had each compartment filled with a coin case, before he put them back into the safe.

"Now let's go back into the Pub," he said.

After refreshing our drinks, two beautiful women, each glowing with confidence, came into the Pub. One had flowing red hair simply parted in the middle, lovely green eyes, and fashionably attired in a peach colored summer dress fitted to show off her fabulous figure. Her name was Faith.

The other woman happened to be a stunning, rising young starlet on Broadway. In addition to confidence, she enjoyed a charismatic something that riveted all eyes on her whenever she walked into a room. Her light brown hair in a flip style, the current rage, looked elegant. She wore a snug fitting red satin outfit that emphasized her splendid figure. Her name was Liz; Frank's date.

"Hello everyone," said Faith. "I hope I didn't miss anything?"

"Hi, Faith," said Iris. "It's good to see you again."

They both hugged and kissed each other's cheek.

Frank introduced the two women to all and we all shook hands. The two new arrivals were quickly supplied with drinks and the little Pub began to buzz in pleasant conversation.

Frank spoke to one of the stewards who then withdrew. In short order, he returned to him with a message.

Frank approached Jacques and whispered, "It isn't fair, Jacques, there are three women here and four men, I just evened everything out. The woman I told you about earlier will be here shortly. Oh, you can help her with her English."

"That wasn't necessary, Frank," said Jacques, "but I will try and help her with her English."

"I just want everyone to enjoy this evening."

Erik got Iris aside and asked, "Who is this Faith? And, how do you know her?"

"She's Frank's late brother's wife. He died in a plane crash two years ago. I thought I told you about her. Why, do you like her?"

"Why, sure, I guess so." he managed to say.

"And you didn't want to come to Frank's party. C'mon, Erik, I'll introduce you."

She introduced Erik to Faith as her brother. They seem to hit it off and started chatting. Iris then started talking to Bill.

A petite Haitian woman appeared on the scene wearing a yellow sundress, with a beautiful smile. Her name was Nicole. She looked a little nervous joining her boss's party guests and not knowing anyone. Frank went over to her and putting her at ease escorted her to Jacques and introduced them. Soon, French filled the air like another instrument joining an orchestra. For the next hour, the bartender earned his keep, the banter and laughter increased, and happiness reigned in the little pub.

One of the stewards came through the pub tapping a three-note xylophone announcing dinner. The conversations wound down, and everyone headed out to the promenade deck, where an elegant table for eight greeted the delighted guests. Atop the white hand embroidered Irish linen lay a perfectly set table, boasting Frank's monogrammed silverware, china, and crystal. Two beautiful floral arrangements were centered on the table, along with three silver candelabras waiting the nearing sunset to be lit.

Several stewards stood at the ready to help the guests with their chairs. The presentation portrayed a beautiful and very impressive sight indeed.

Frank sat at the head of the table with his date at the opposite end. Iris was on his left, then Jacques and Nicole. Bill was on his right, then Erik and Faith.

Little menus were provided.

BILL-O-FARE

Appetizer: *Shrimp Cocktail or Fresh Fruit.*
Entrée: *Chicken Marsala, Baked Stuffed Grouper or Filet-Mignon.*
Dessert: *Baked Alaska, Assorted Cookies.*
Beverages: *Various Liqueurs, Coffee, Tea, etc.*
Wine: *Frank to recommend.*

Erik said it right, I thought, Frank puts on a good spread.

When all were seated, a small aperitif was placed before each guest. Then, on cue, we all turned and watched the sun slide into the ocean. Frank called for a toast, a beginning Key West tradition, to celebrate the sunset.

The stars were beginning to twinkle and the candles were lit. With an elegant meal in the offing anticipation was soaring. This promised to be a dining experience, never to be forgotten.

Frank took delight in recommending the proper wine for each guest as they ordered their entrées. He prided himself in having the finest wine cellar afloat. He had a steward running back and forth retrieving each wine as selected. His Wine Steward opened each bottle with a flourish, smelled the cork then poured a mouthful into a silver tasting cup attached to a silver chain around his neck. He tasted the wine and if satisfactory poured some into the guest's wine glass for his or her approval. All were delighted at this display and especially Frank's showboating performance describing the nuances of each wine.

The ambience, the excellent food and service generated a warm comradeship between the host and his guests.

After dessert, Frank announced that the men were going to go aft for Brandy and Cigars. The ladies were invited to go forward for an entertainment surprise, and he told them that the men would join them a little later.

The ladies went forward to find comfortable seats arranged in a semi-circle. A steward took their orders for beverages. They sat down waiting for the surprise.

Two men, one carrying a guitar, both casually dressed walked out. The guitar player sat on a stool that was provided and the other one introduced himself.

"Good evening ladies. My name is P.C. and I'd like to sing a few songs for you." The girls were amazed by the surprise and began to applaud the well-known singer.

The guitar player started to play and P.C. walked up to the seated ladies and began to sing several of his hit songs in his signature easy-going style.

Meanwhile, at the stern the four men sat in comfortable lounge chairs sipping Napoleon Brandy and smoking Cuban cigars. When everyone was settled, I raised the subject of the gold.

"How much do you know about the Nazi gold, Frank?" I asked.

"You are a man after my own heart, Bill, direct and to the point. I know that dozens of bronze cylinders supposedly filled with gold coins are strewn along the bottom somewhere off the coast here. And, you Bill are the only one who has the knowledge of where they might be."

"So, she told you everything. I knew it," said Erik showing his displeasure.

"Don't be upset with Iris. She thought I could help, and I think I could be of great assistance not only in recovering, but what's more important disposing of that gold if and when it's found."

"Sure, and how much are you going to want for that help?" said Erik caustically. "Twenty percent, forty per cent or why not all of it?"

"Erik, please calm down." I said, "Frank's in the know now and that's a fact. We can make him an adversary or an ally. Like Frank just said, we have to first find and recover the gold, then we have to dispose of it. Also, what about salvage rights, legal claims by the State of Florida and who knows who else, maybe West Germany, Israel and the Internal Revenue. We're going to need a ton of legal advice, and I think Frank may be able to help us in all those areas."

"I do have a premier legal team. I could handle that part of it."

"I'm beginning to get discouraged," said Erik. "I never thought about all those different agencies. You're right; those agencies will all have their hands out. I hope there'll be something left for us. I guess we will need legal advice, and I'm sure no one has a better legal team then Frank. And, like you say, it's better to have him on our side, then working against us."

"I can't believe how complicated this has suddenly become. Why can't we just sell the coins ourselves?" said Jacques.

"If you were talking a handful of coins, you could," said Frank, "however we're talking about possibly several thousand. It would be impossible to dispose of so many, without arousing the interest of those institutions that Bill just mentioned, needless to say, the dangerous criminal element, which would be certain to surface, wanting a piece of the action."

"Frank is absolutely right," I said, "it's too big to handle by ourselves; we are going to need professional help. Now, what do you want out of this, Frank?"

"To be honest with you, I would like to receive a ten percent commission for all of the gold coins I dispose of, probably through auction. I want the first pick of the rarest gold coins that must surely be in all those cylinders. I will pay the appraised value for each one I select less ten percent, which would have been the commission I would have received anyway. In return, I will handle all the legal matters and give any help I can in the retrieval of the coins."

"Do you have any diving capabilities on board here, now, Frank?"

"I never really have had any until a couple of weeks ago; I hired two former Navy divers as deck hands, and they seem quite capable. I thought they might be useful in the recovery effort if necessary. They're quite muscular; real fitness freaks, up before dawn, doing an hour of calisthenics before breakfast, and very fussy about what they eat. On the other hand they're known to be lusty drinkers."

"They may come in handy." I said. "But, I would keep them in the dark on this unless or until we do need them. So, what do you think, Erik?"

"Well, Frank, maybe I had you all wrong. I guess I owe you an apology. Your proposal sounds more than fair. Yes, Bill I think we should bring Frank into the fold."

"No apologies necessary, Erik. Thank you for your confidence. You won't be sorry."

"How about you, Jacques, what do you think?"

"If it all sounds good to you, Bill, I'm in."

"I guess that sums it up Frank. It looks like we have a deal."

We all stood up and shook hands on it with Frank.

"Very well, then let's join the girls," he said.

We went forward and were pleasantly surprised to see P.C. singing to the four women in an intimate setting. He had them charmed with his usual laid back easygoing style. We quietly took seats and were soon drawn into his spell. After a few more songs he started to talk to his small audience.

"Frank and I go way back. At first, when he asked me to come here and sing, I said no I didn't think I could make it. But, when he made a sizable donation to one of my favorite charities along with a few days on his beautiful yacht in Key West, on condition of anonymity, how could I refuse."

We all applauded Frank for his donation.

"Please let me introduce my wife to you. Normally, she stays in the background, but this is such a small audience, I don't think she'll mind."

She walked out and all applauded her as she took a seat with the women.

Frank stood up and said, "Thank you P.C. for coming. You've added so much to the evening. How about doing a few more songs and then we'll all retire to the pub for a night cap."

"That sounds good to me, Frank. You know one of the things I've enjoyed tonight is singing without a microphone. Now does anyone have any requests?"

He sang several more songs by request, then introduced his guitar accompanist and shaking his hand, thanked him. The small audience heartily applauded the both of them. P.C. pulled out a stack of his photos and a pen and personally autographed a photo to each one of the audience. Then, we all headed back into the pub.

The next hour we all spent socializing. Talking to a star like P.C. on a one to one basis was a thrill for us all, especially for the rising starlet, Liz.

The time finally came to call it a night, and we thanked Frank for a wonderful time. The three of us escorted Iris back to the La Concha Hotel.

Iris let Erik know that she would meet him at the house for breakfast with the car and her bag for the trip to West Germany the next morning. We said good night to her and headed back to the house.

Friday, January 14, 1966

The next morning, Jacques pleasantly awoke Erik and I with irresistible aromas from the preparation of a special going away breakfast.

Iris came up the back walk right on time, as usual.

Jacques sitting at the neatly set table on the deck arose to greet her.

"Good morning, Jacques, something smells good."

"Oh, I just whipped up something a little different today. I hope you like it? It's in the oven, just waiting until everyone is here."

"Well you haven't made anything yet I haven't liked. Where are the other two gents?"

"They'll be here any minute. I heard the shower running a little while ago. Have a seat."

Jacques poured her a cup of coffee from the pot on the table.

"How did you and Nicole hit it off last night? Did you like her?"

"Well, ah, yes." he answered, caught a little off guard, "I did like her, a lot!"

"I'm glad. She seems like a nice girl."

"Good morning, Iris. Erik will be down soon. He's just finishing his packing."

"Good morning, Bill."

I poured myself a coffee and sat next to her.

"That sure was a wonderful time last night," I said. "I've never experienced anything like it. I still can't believe it. It was like a dream. The yacht, the meal and meeting P.C., it was all unbelievable!"

"That's a good way to put it, like a dream," said Jacques.

"Frank really knows how to throw a party," she said.

"He sure does. Hey, something smells awful good, what's that you're cooking?"

"Oh, it's nothing, Bill. I just thought I'd make something special for Iris, where she's leaving today. Oh, and it's for you and Erik too."

"It smells good. What is it?"

"It's a surprise. You'll have to wait."

"Okay, but you're making me awful hungry. I'm sorry you have to leave on such a sad note, Iris. But, at least you'll get to see your parents."

"That's the only good part about it. The more I think about Gerhard's death, I can't help think that there's something sinister going on."

"I have to agree with you. I'm suspicious of the pawnbroker. I think he could have had a hand in it."

"Although, Erik did meet him and he seemed to be the nicest man."

"I guess the only way to find out, is to talk to him."

"Hi, Iris." said Erik coming out onto the deck. "Are you ready for our trip?"

"I'm ready. I was just going to say that I hate to leave this enchanting place. I'm beginning to like it here in Key West."

"I know what you mean. But, we'll be back in a few days. Those new 707's make flying to Europe so convenient now."

"Breakfast is served," said Jacques, using colorful mitts to bring out a hot pan brimming with rows of oven browned, steaming baked stuffed French toast.

"Oh, Jacques that looks so yummy." said Iris.

"And it smells fantastic." said Erik.

"This looks like special treatment, Jacques." I said, winking to Iris, "You never made this for me. What is it?"

"It's baked French Toast. Last night I cut some thick slices of Italian bread and stuffed them with apricot jam and cream cheese and a little nutmeg and put them in a pan. Then I whisked some eggs, milk, and vanilla and poured it over the bread then let it sit in the refrigerator overnight. This morning I put it in the oven and baked it."

"And, there's some orange sauce for a topping."

"Jacques, you outdid yourself this time," said Iris. "This is marvelous."

"It tastes like more," said Erik.

"You're the best," I said.

Jacques's sat down and helped us enjoy his handiwork, as we heaped well-deserved praise on him. He took genuine pleasure in making people happy with food.

After a second cup of coffee, the time came for them to leave. We all went through the front room and out to the front yard. Iris said goodbye to Ernie on the way and quickly glanced over at the windows. Unbeknownst to her, in the mirror next to the door, I saw her roll her eyes.

Outside, she shook hands with Jacques and came up to me and gave me a quick kiss on the cheek goodbye, then hopped in behind the wheel. The touch of her lips and the scent of her perfume was a pleasant surprise. Erik shook hands with Jacques and me and threw his bag in the back of the wagon, then got in next to Iris. Savoring the lingering perfume, I put my hand up to my cheek deeply moved by that kiss, as we both waved and watched them drive off.

"What do you say, we buy some curtains today?" I said.

"That would be a good start, Bill and let's clean up the place."

"I agree and this might be a good time, while they're gone, to pull the boat and have the bottom cleaned and repainted. I'll call and see when they can do it. While she's out of the water, we'll build a transom platform and attach it."

"It's been almost a year, Bill, since we last had it done, so it's due. I like the idea of that platform. I never liked using the ladder over the side."

I made the call and they were able to take it right away, so Jacques and I went down to the boat and ran it over to the boatyard. I've been using them since I first started here in Key West. They took over the boat and we walked home, stopping at Maury's on the way.

"What are you two doing in here at this time of day, playing hooky?" asked Maury.

"The boats getting her bottom cleaned and painted," I said, "so we have some time on our hands. We're going to build a full width transom platform, and attach it while she's in the boatyard. It'll make it easier for us to enter the water and get back into the boat when we're looking for that Spanish sunken treasure."

We sat up at the bar and ordered two beers. Maury asked if we wanted something to eat. We told him we just had a late breakfast.

"Where are Iris and Erik?"

"They had some sad news from West Germany. Erik has a cousin there, who was attacked in his home and later died. They went over to attend the funeral."

"That's terrible, I'm sorry to hear that. When are they coming back?"

"I'm not exactly sure. I think four or five days."

"It's a coincidence, I'm sure, but I heard that Joe Stalker went to Europe too, Holland. He left yesterday."

"That's strange. I wonder why Holland."

"I don't know, Bill, but that's what I heard. If I find out anything else, I'll let you know. Have you found any treasure out there yet?"

"We really haven't started, and we won't be going out until they get back.

Right now, we're off to get some curtains for our front room."

"I know from experience, Bill that's not a good area for a man to get mixed up in. Be forewarned."

"I think he may have a point there, Bill."

"There are only two windows. How tough can it be? Let's go, Jacques. See you later, Maury."

"See you, Maury. I think you're right on the curtains."

"I know I am. Good luck. You're going to need it."

We walked back to the house and took the truck over to Sears on Roosevelt Blvd.

On the way there, I wondered where we could buy one of those coin collector books that give the value of coins. Jacques thought maybe we could get one at Sears.

We found the curtain department and started looking at all the different window treatments. A woman came over and tried to help.

"Maybe we should ask Iris to pick out something, Bill."

"Look there's exactly what we want. The fish and fishing rods match the theme of the room. There are two different colors, which one do you think the green or the red?"

"I think we should wait."

"I want to surprise Iris. I think the green would be nice. Ernie is green."

"She'll be surprised alright. I'm afraid you will be too."

The sales woman helped us pick out the rods and hardware.

Before we left we did find the coin book we wanted.

We went right to work as soon as we got back to the house. It took a while to figure out how to install the hooks for the first curtain. Trying to hold and hammer the tiny nails, I hit my thumb, which necessitated using some of my limited Portuguese. The second one went a little easier.

I thought they looked great, but Jacques remained skeptical.

"I can't wait to see her reaction when she sees them."

"I told you before, Bill, women look at this stuff much differently than we do. Don't be disappointed if Iris doesn't like them."

"Of course she'll like them, just, look at them."

"What a dump," said Ernie.

"Aw, shut up, Ernie." I said.

The telephone rang and Frank wanted to know if we could get together. He said he'd come over to the house.

A half hour later, his car pulled up in front and Frank got out. The car drove off and he walked up to the front porch steps, where I greeted him.

"Hi, Bill, I hope I'm not putting you off schedule."

"Not at all, the boat is out of the water getting the bottom repainted, so we're grounded for a few days. Come on in."

As he entered the front room he said, "I like this room. It's a real man's room. I bet you can really unwind in here. Oh, hello Jacques how are you doing?"

"Hi Frank, I'm fine. Thank you for that wonderful treat last night, I really enjoyed it."

"I second that." I said. "I can't remember when I've had a better time."

"Thank you both. I think everyone had fun. I know I did."

"Let's go out on the deck. Have you had lunch? We were just going to have a late one."

"What have you got?"

"Cuban mix sandwiches and iced tea," said Jacques.

"What's a Cuban mix sandwich?"

"Roast pork, ham, cheese, mustard and pickles on Cuban bread pressed down in the pan to heat it up and melt the cheese. It's very good. They have them at Maury's."

"I've never had one, but I'm game, I'll try it."

Jacques with a big smile retreated to the kitchen to make up the sandwiches. Meanwhile, Frank and I went out onto the deck. Jacques was within earshot of our conversation.

"I have interests in businesses here and in Europe. Over the years I've acquired many contacts at all levels over there. Last night, Iris asked me to check out one of your competitors, Joe Stalker. We can't seem to find anything about him, so he may be using an alias. Can you give me any more information on him?"

"Joe's kind of a misfit here in Key West. He's about forty-five with a heavy German accent, but claims he grew up in South Africa. He does seem to be good at charter fishing, because he has brought in quite a few trophy fish. I've talked to some of his customers and they were quite satisfied and even thought him quite charming. However, that's a side of him we've never seen. The Joe we know is that of a loner and bully. I've mentioned him to the Police Chief and he's never been in any major trouble.

"Erik arrived in Key West on Monday and that night we got together at Maury's. He began to tell us how the Captain of the Nazi sub, thinking he was about to be captured, ordered some top-secret boxes to be jettisoned. He recently found out that those boxes were filled with gold and because I was the one that had the skirmish with him, I should know the approximate location where they might be. That's when we discovered Joe's stooge eavesdropping on us. We're certain he heard about the U-Boat, the gold, and how I'm the only one who knows where it could be. However, Erik told us later on about how his cousin Gerhard was aboard that sub and that the gold is coinage packed in bronze cylinders. So, at least, Joe's little bilge rat didn't hear that part.

"The next day on Tuesday, Maury told me Joe sent telegrams to West Germany and then on Wednesday he traveled to Holland. That's the first time he's left Key West since he came here, five years ago. Yesterday, Thursday, we found out that Erik's cousin, Gerhard had been murdered. All this leads me to think that Joe's somehow connected with the thugs in Germany who murdered Erik's cousin."

"You may have something there," said Frank. "He learns about Nazi gold in Key West, sends telegrams to West Germany, takes his first trip in five years to Holland, and then Gerhard is killed. It can't all be a coincidence; it has to be about the gold, but why go to Holland?"

"Maybe there's a reason he's afraid to enter West Germany?" said Jacques from the kitchen.

"I'll try and find out what it is. It sounds like Joe Stalker is in league with someone in West Germany who has a militant like authority over him."

"In the meantime, Frank, because Joe knows about the gold, I guess we'll just have to waste a lot of time moving around to different sites trying to conceal the real location of the cylinders."

"It is a waste of time, and it's going to prolong the whole enterprise, but I guess there's no other way."

Jacques brought out the sandwiches and the iced tea.

"You know what I think," he said, "they won't interfere with us searching and bringing up the cylinders. That would be foolish, it would be easier to just wait until we've done all the work and then simply steal them from us."

Frank and I looked at each other in one of those, "Why didn't I think of that." moments.

"You're absolutely right, Jacques," I said, "That makes so much more sense. They would be stupid to interfere with us finding the gold and bringing it in. Now, we can forget about going to different spots trying to throw them off."

"You're a genius!" said Frank, "and a good cook too. This sandwich is delicious!"

"I'm hardly a genius, but I am glad you like the sandwich."

"This is good news," I said. "Now, we can go directly to the site and start looking for those cylinders. They will be watching us to determine when we've salvaged all or at least most of the gold, so they can plan the robbery. We'll do our best to shield the salvage process as we bring in the cylinders, to keep them guessing. When the time comes we'll have to devise a way to trap them when they do make their move.

"I'm sure we'll think of something, Bill," said Jacques. "Like I said before, we're smarter than those guys."

"You're right there, Jacques." said Frank. "We'll just have to be one step ahead of them. Anyway, I have to get back to the Princess; there'll be a stack of messages for me. I'll look into getting more information on Joe Stalker and his trip to Holland."

As he stepped out onto the front porch his car pulled up in front of the house.

"How did he know when to come back and pick you up?" asked Jacques.

"He never left. He waited for me to come out."

"Oh, I could have brought him some iced tea."

"That's nice of you to think of that, Jacques. I'll tell him. Thanks again, for that Cuban sandwich. See you soon."

"There's a hardware store up in Marathon that has some underwater metal detectors, Jacques. Maybe, we should take a ride up there and check them out?"

The next three days, Saturday, Sunday and Monday were spent building the transom platform and getting ready for our underwater adventure.

We bought an underwater wand type metal detector up in Marathon and were anxious to try it out. We finished building the transom platform and attached it behind the stern so getting in and out of the water would be a lot easier. We were busy during the days and our evenings were spent talking about the cylinders filled with gold coins.

Iris and Erik were due back on Tuesday.

Saturday, Sunday and Monday (Maintenance)

Tuesday, January 18, 1966

Late in the afternoon, we heard Iris and Erik pull up in front of the house. Their flight arrived in the morning and they picked up the sled at the diving club in Miami, and then headed for Key West. We went out to greet the two weary travelers.

"Welcome home," I said as Iris and Erik got out of the wagon and stretched.

"You two must be tired. I've got a fresh pot of coffee going," said Jacques.

"That sounds wonderful," said Iris.

"Any cookies laying around back there?" asked Erik.

"Just a couple of dozen,"

"It's good to see you again, Iris," as I leaned over and returned that kiss on her cheek.

I meant it more than she knew.

"Thank you, Bill. We're both happy to be back."

"West Germany is a nice place to visit, but you can't beat the old U. S. of A.," said, Erik.

"So, this is a diver's sled," said Jacques, "there's much more to it than I thought."

"This is a more advanced model than the one's I've used in the Mediterranean, It's got a stick control to turn in all directions. I can't wait to use it."

"Come on in and tell us about the trip," I said, "Iris, I want to show you something. Come in the front door; it's in the front room."

"You know what I think of your front room, Bill."

"I made a change. Please come in and take a look."

As she entered the room, she said, "It doesn't smell so bad."

"We cleaned up the house and Ernie's cage," said Jacques, "and no more smoking cigars inside the house."

"What else is different?"

I pointed to the windows and said, "Ta Dah!"

"Oh, you put up curtains, with fishing rods and fish on them. Why green?"

"Ernie is green. I thought that would be a nice touch."

"Bill, I'm awful tired right now, so I don't care to comment on them, maybe tomorrow."

"It sounds as though you don't like them?"

"I didn't say that, but... I'll let you know tomorrow. Let's go outside."

We all went out on the deck and Jacques brought out the coffee and a big plate of his cookies.

I told them about the visit from Frank and the telegrams Joe sent to West Germany the day after the big party at Maury's. Then, how Joe took a sudden trip to Holland the following day. Frank said he'd try to get some information on Joe's trip and get back to us.

Also, I told them how Jacques had figured out that Joe wouldn't waste his time competing with us recovering the cylinders. He'd just wait until we did all the work finding them and then simply steal them from us. Now, we wouldn't have to waste our time going to bogus sites to throw them off. We could start the search right where I first spotted the U-Boat.

"Jacques, you're absolutely right," said Erik. "Why didn't we think of that?"

"Because we all jumped to a conclusion," said Iris, "Jacques thought deeper about the situation and figured it out. Nice going, Jacques."

"This just proves once again," I said, "that Jacques is the one with all the common sense."

"Thank you, but it just popped into my head."

"I'm glad it did, Jacques, it's going to save us all kinds of time and effort," I said.

"Tell us about your trip," said Jacques to change the subject away from him.

"The pawnbroker isn't a suspect," said Erik, "When we went to visit him at his shop, we were surprised to see him in a wheel chair. The two brutes that killed Gerhard paid him a visit first. The devils tried to make him talk too. They gave up after breaking his legs, and he became unconscious. They went through his files and found Gerhard's card and left the rest scattered all over the floor. The card had his name and address and a list of all the gold coins he sold. They left the old timer for dead and went directly to Gerhard's home. We know the rest."

"He felt terrible about Gerhard," said Iris, "and said he could identify them if he saw them again. The police had him look through hundreds of photos in vain.

"Not many were at the small burial service. Gerhard more than atoned for his past and didn't deserve to die like that. He told my mother, on his death bed, he rediscovered the God of his youth and was prepared to meet Him."

"We went to Gerhard's home," said Erik. "I had a good idea from his hint about hiding it again, he meant the apple tree he pointed out when I visited him. Sure enough when we dug around that old apple tree, we found the cylinder. We brought it back with us and I have it here in my carry on bag."

"I hope no one saw you digging it up." I said.

"I never thought of that, I can't say. I don't think so."

Erik brought out his carry on bag and pulled out the bronze cylinder.

He handed it to me and even though I knew it was going to be heavy, it still surprised me. It had the remaining forty-eight gold coins, so it would even have been heavier when full. The cylinder typified German craftsmanship.

I couldn't help wonder that there were seventy or eighty of these cylinders lying on the bottom just a few miles from here. Also, I thought about the possible dangers we faced. The people we were up against have shown that they would not stop at murder to get what they wanted. I didn't want to voice my opinion yet on who I thought they were until I had some proof.

"Here, Jacques heft this." I said, as I handed the cylinder to him.

"Wow, it's heavy and this one isn't even full."

Erik opened it and carefully spilled out the gold coins. Spellbound, we grew silent and just looked at them for a few moments. They were something to see.

"This sure is an incentive," I said, "to get out there and start looking for the rest of them. If you two are up to it, how about trying out that divers sled tomorrow afternoon. We'll let you sleep late tomorrow morning."

Iris and Erik agreed, especially about the extra sleep and said they weren't too tired to go to Maury's for a light dinner as long as we made it an early night. We agreed to meet Iris at Maury's in an hour.

Erik carefully replaced the coins into the cylinder and screwed on the cover and said, "Now, where can we hide this."

"There's a loose floorboard in the closet in your room Erik. I'll show you how to open it. While we're on the subject, where are we going to hide all those full cylinders as we find them? Everyone put your thinking caps on, we have to come up with an answer."

The diver's sled being constructed of aluminum sat on a small trailer. It only took one of us to easily move it by hand into the back yard next to the walkway.

Iris drove the wagon to the La Concha to check in.

Erik brought his suitcase into the house, and the three of us started to get ready for Maury's.

With the cylinder hidden safely in Erik's closet, we headed over to Maury's.

This happened to be the night that Bosun Jim gave free knot tying lessons. He did this every week and supplied the practice lines. He volunteered to teach anyone who wanted to learn how to tie some of the basic knots used by boaters. Competitive knot enthusiasts participated in Maury's Nautical Knot Night, which would be in another week or so. It has grown into a serious knot tying competition held semi-annually. Half of the entry fees were for a cash prize and the other half went to Toys for Tots. It's become such a popular event that contestants spilled out onto the sidewalk.

Iris arrived a little early and looked around for us.

Bosun Jim, delighted to see Iris, invited her to join the group while she waited for us. He supplied her with a couple of lengths of line from his old ditty bag. "On a ship we call it a line not a rope, Iris." he said. "Actually, onboard ship, a knot is considered a nautical mile. When a sailor fastens a line to something immovable, like a cleat, they call it a hitch. If it is attached to another line, they call it a bend. Since we're in Maury's and not at sea, we don't want to confuse people, so we'll call them knots."

"That's very interesting, my father may have told me that, but I can't remember. I haven't sailed the seven seas like you, Jim, but I've done a bit of sailing as a child in Germany. My father taught me how to sail and tie knots. That was a long time ago, so I don't know how many knots I can remember. He served as a sailor in the German Navy in World War One. He always boasted of his service as a common deck hand."

"That's how I started, when I enlisted. I loved the Navy and made it a career. In time, I worked my way up to Chief. Most people aren't aware of how vital knots are on board a ship. You know what I always say? A knot can save your life. I've seen it happen. Let me introduce you to my class tonight."

He brought her over to meet the Stanley twins, Christian and David and their wives Marlee and Allison. The twins stood up and shook hands with Iris and she then shook hands with their wives.

"Okay, young sailors, you too Iris, let's see you tie a bowline."

They all started to tie the knot except for Iris. "What's the matter, Iris; don't you remember how to tie a bowline? That's a common knot."

"I only know the German names for the knots."

Marlee finished first and held up the knot.

"Oh," she said, "a palstek knoten."

In the blink of an eye, she tied one and came in second.

"This is fun. Let's do another."

"I see you were taught by an expert, Iris. You know what I always say? Every knot has a secret that lets you tie it more quickly. I can see that your father knew those secrets. You didn't have to tell me he was a Navy man, I would have known."

"Thank you for telling me that, Jim, you and my father would have been kindred spirits."

"That's for sure, Iris, now we'll have to make a little change here."

He turned around and secretly tied a knot. Then he held it up and announced,

"Tie a figure eight knot."

"Acht knoten," she said and in a flash held up the finished knot to the surprise of the others.

"Okay this last one is for a free draft. Again, he secretly tied the knot and held it up. "Tie a sheet bend."

"Schotstek knoten." And, in a jiffy, she held up the finished knot beating the others.

"Iris please tie that knot again, slowly. I've never seen it tied like that before. It's much faster than I've ever seen."

They all gathered around her as she went through the steps of tying the knot. She patiently repeated it over and over until they all had it mastered.

"That's the first time one of my students showed me a better way to tie a knot."

"I guess my father taught me well."

"Like you said, Iris, your father and I would have been kindred spirits. You won the beer fair and square."

"It looks like I had an unfair advantage though, so please allow me to buy you all a round."

The knot-tying students thanked Iris and promised that they would practice for the next time.

"That's it for tonight young sailors, and you know what I always say? If you find yourself at the end of your rope, tie a knot and hang on.

"Iris, you're very good at knot tying, I hope you can make it next time. It's an incentive for the others. Now they have a reason to learn, they'll want to beat Iris. In fact I think you should enter my contest. It's coming up a week from Saturday on the thirtieth."

"I would love to enter if you think I'm good enough. I'll try to learn the English names of the knots by then. Thank you for helping me by letting me see the knots."

"That was only fair Iris, and I think you would make a good showing in the contest. I suppose now, you'll be joining the three Herren over there."

"Oh, you speak German?"

"Just a few words that a German lady friend taught me years ago."

"Hi Iris," said Denise, "Watch out for this guy he's a lady killer."

"Iris is perfectly safe with me, Denise, you know that. My wayward days are behind me, but I lived life to the full when I could and have no regrets, except one."

"What is that, Jim?"

"I have a daughter who just turned eighteen the last time I saw her, over twenty years ago. She had blonde hair and blue eyes just like you, Iris. When I first saw you, on the Fritter Boat, I thought that she had come to visit me. You reminded me of what I think she would look like today."

"Do you know where she lives? Why don't you write her?"

"I've been trying to get him to do that for years," said Denise.

"Let sleeping dogs lie. We had a nasty argument. I didn't like the company she kept. I struck her. I didn't mean it; it just happened. Every morning, when I look in the mirror, I can hear that slap and it breaks my heart. She hates me and with good reason."

"I have a feeling that she will forgive you, if she hasn't already." said Iris, "You really should contact her and tell her you're sorry. Both of you are letting your pride get in the way. It's up to you to make the first move."

"Do you think so? I'd give the world if you were right."

"The best way to find out Jim," said Denise, "is to write that long overdue letter."

"Would you help me write the letter, Iris?"

"I'd be more than happy to. You work on it for a couple of days, then we'll go over it and between us, we'll get you two back together again. By the way what's her name?"

"Her name is Kristin. Thanks, Iris your swell."

"Thanks to you Jim, for letting me join your class tonight, I look forward to the next one. I guess I better go join the herren."

"Auf Wiedersehen, Iris."

She brought her draft beer with her and joined us at our usual booth.

"We didn't want to interrupt you," I said. "It looked like you were having a good time with the knot tying."

"Oh, I was. Bosun Jim is performing a good service, teaching how to tie knots. You know it's true that in an emergency a knot could save a life, especially at sea. My father told me that."

"He's a good sport to give his time like that. Everyone appreciates it. I sit in once in awhile myself for a refresher course."

Having just eaten a few of Jacques cookies at the house, we decided to order assorted appetizers and share.

Iris and Erik were so tired they didn't eat much. They started yawning, and I suggested that Erik escort Iris back to the hotel, and Jacques and I would meet him at the house a little later.

"I won't argue with that," said Iris, "let's go Erik."

Jacques and I settled the tab with Denise, and she put the leftovers in a bag for us to take home. We got to the house just before Erik came in. He couldn't wait to hit the hay, so we said goodnight.

Jacques and I went out on the deck and lit up cigars and talked about where to hide those heavy bronze cylinders when we found them.

Wednesday, January 19, 1966

After breakfast we went down to the boat early with all the diving gear and rigged up a towing line for the diver's sled.

Around noontime we went back to the house. We could hear the shower running, so we knew Erik was up. Jacques put on the coffee and started to whip up a breakfast for him and a lunch for us. I went out on the deck and spread out the charts.

Right on schedule, Iris came up the back walk with her bike. She had a couple of packages in her basket. I was dying to ask her about the curtains, but I thought better of it. I hated to admit it, but I guess, Maury knew what he was talking about.

"Good afternoon to you guys, this is the big day!"

She wore her chambray shirt, this time tied in the front and her cut off dungaree shorts and sneakers. Again, she proved she could look good in anything.

"Could I get you something to eat?" asked Jacques from the kitchen.

"Thank you Jacques, just coffee, I went to that cafe again. I brought you some goodies, this time."

She handed him two loaves of fresh baked bread.

"Thank you Iris, nothing like fresh bread, have a seat and I'll bring you that coffee."

Erik walked out onto the deck wearing shorts, a tee shirt, and sandals.

"Good morning everybody, or make that good afternoon. Something smells good. What's cooking Jacques?"

"How do buckwheat pancakes, sausages and coffee sound?"

"I've become your greatest admirer chef Jacques. That sounds great."

I gave Iris directions to the most convenient boat ramp to launch the diver's sled.

"It's a really nice sled," she said, "it has a wind shield or I should say a water shield. It floats, so we just tow it to the site. I can't wait to try it out and to get underwater again."

"I'm looking forward to it too," I said. "Jacques and I brought all the gear down to the boat this morning. We went out the other day and found where I think the anchors should be, if memory serves me correct. So, that's where we'll begin the search.

I hope you didn't forget that Jacques and I have a charter tomorrow. You and Erik will have the day off."

The fishing charter that was scheduled had become an annual affair over the years. We became good friends with him, so I couldn't give it off to one of my fellow Captains. Besides, Jacques and I really looked forward to his hilarious company each year.

"I know what Erik will do tomorrow," said Iris, "he'll sleep till after noon."

"I bet I know what you'll do?" he said back to her, "you'll go shopping all day."

"So what if I do?"

"So what if I sleep all day."

"You two sound like a couple of kids." I said, "Listen up, we're taking next Tuesday off too, so I can take Iris on that sailing trip I promised. Would that be okay, Iris?"

"I'd like that very much Bill. I'll be looking forward to it."

"Good, I already arranged with my friend to have the sailboat available."

We all turned to and helped Jacques clear the table and clean up the kitchen.

Iris and Erik drove the sled to the boat ramp, and Jacques and I took the truck to the boat. We arrived at the boat ramp in time to see Iris back down the trailer like a pro. Erik tossed us the line, and we pulled the sled off the trailer. She parked the wagon and trailer, and they met us at the nearby floating dock.

"Nice job of backing the trailer down the ramp, Iris." I said. "Many people have trouble doing that. In fact, when it's busy, that's a local sport watching the funny predicaments inexperienced people get themselves into."

"I used to be one of them," she said.

It felt good to have everyone on board and finally be heading out to the site to begin our search for the gold. Where to hide the cylinders, when we brought them in, still weighed on my mind.

"I like the platform you added, Bill." said Iris, "I was a little worried about trying to climb over the side of the boat."

"Jacques and I installed it for that reason. Let's face it, there's no way to gracefully climb over the side of a boat like this, even with a ladder, especially with scuba equipment."

We arrived at the approximate area, where I ordered the two anchors thrown overboard so many years ago. They should be fairly easy to spot, because they were bulky and probably wouldn't be buried in the sand. If we could find them that would be a good starting point for our search.

Iris removed her shirt and stepped out of her shorts revealing her blue two-piece bathing suit. She sure did look nice.

Iris wanted me to be the first one to ride the sled with her. She and Erik stepped over onto the transom platform where he helped her on with her gear and did the safety check. I followed their lead, and Jacques helped me don my gear and did the safety check as well. We sat down and put on our swim fins, then slid into the water together, swam to the sled, and climbed on.

Jacques started ahead very slowly pulling us along. It took a while to get the right towing speed. Iris at the control stick knew exactly how to control the sled and maneuvered us below the surface. It was a marvelous sensation, as we glided along, like being in an airplane, looking down watching the landscape slip by, of course in this case the ocean bottom. We could see very well, thanks to the clear waters of the Keys. Iris really knew her stuff. I never would have thought of using a diver's sled to search for the cylinders. In fact, I never knew there was such a thing as a diver's sled. It's a magnificent way to search a huge amount of area very quickly.

She shouted to me to hold on. Then, she made the sled do a 360-degree barrel roll. I had to admit it was fun and I realized that being with Iris was fun too.

She signaled me to leave the sled. Our clinging to the sled created a heavy drag on the Rose Maria. As soon as we let go, Jacques could feel right away that we had left the sled, so he made a big turn and came back to the same spot, putting it in neutral to stop the propeller. We surfaced and swam to the boat. She wanted Jacques to be the next to try the sled and then Erik.

Later on while Iris and Erik were underwater Jacques confided in me that, even though they just met, he started to have feelings for Nicole.

"I can't help but feel guilty," he said, "I still love the memory of my wife and children even after all of these years and I miss them. God knows I've been true to my wife, but as the years go by I find the void in my life from their passing can't be filled by just their memories. The urge to have a close relationship with a living woman gets stronger.

What do you think, Bill, is it wrong for me to get involved with Nicole?"

"You know, Jacques, I never told you this; I made a vow on Rose's grave that I'd be true to her forever. However, I've been haunted by that vow over the years, especially now, since Iris has come on the scene.

"A couple of days ago, I mentioned the vow to a priest friend and told him about how Rose and Billy died. He drew me into a conversation about my life from that day up to the present. He concluded that because of the trauma of loss, I blocked out all past and future close relationships to prevent that pain of loss from happening again. That's why I made the vow. He told me that all close relationships carry risks, but the rewards and ultimately the memories far outweigh them. Finally, he told me that you can't make a valid vow with the dead."

"I never made a vow," said Jacques, "but I just didn't have any desire to, you know, get involved again until now, because of Nicole. It feels good to talk about this, Bill."

"You're right, it does feel good to talk about it. I guess it always seemed too painful a subject to bring up. I think we both know that we've suppressed our emotions way too long. Nicole and Iris coming into our lives brought all this to the surface, gently forcing us to face the issue.

"Come to think about it," Jacques, "we just saved ourselves a bundle on psychiatric therapy."

He started laughing and got me going too. The laughter brought relief and made talking about that dreaded subject easier.

"So, you like Iris?"

"Well, who wouldn't like Iris? I don't think she'd ever go for me though. I'm just a poor charter boat guy; I couldn't afford to make her happy. She's used to nice things, expensive things. She's also very intelligent, maybe too much so for a guy like me."

"Sometimes opposites attract, Bill. I think she does like you. I noticed little things, like the way she slides into the booth next to you, at Maury's."

"Do you think so, Jacques? Don't kid me now."

"I wouldn't kid about something like that."

"So you like Nicole?"

"Very much so, she's so easy to talk to. She loves cooking too! I know it's early in our relationship, but I have a fantasy scenario of us opening a little restaurant together here in Key West."

"That's a great idea. I know that's what you were meant to do, Jacques. I have a good feeling about finding this gold and there will be enough for you and Nicole to make that dream come true. You two are going to open that restaurant."

Just then we felt the boat surge signaling that Iris and Erik left the sled, and we came around. Sure enough the two heads bobbed up and they started swimming to the boat.

Holding on to the sled and enduring the push of the water was both exhilarating and tiring. Even though the water seemed warm, riding on the sled tended to drain the body heat more rapidly. So, after Erik's lesson on the sled, Iris came up onto the transom platform all tuckered out ready for a well-deserved rest.

"We found your anchors, Bill!" she said.

"Iris, you're shivering," I said. "Get that gear off. Jacques get a blanket from below."

Erik helped her off with the equipment and over the transom.

"The anchors are right below about fifty meters apart."

"Never mind the anchors. Wrap this blanket around you and get warm. We'll have to wear wetsuits from now on. Let's call it a day.

"But we still have some time left, Bill."

"We've done enough today, Iris. Jacques, do a triangulation on this spot, so we can start here on Friday morning."

Jacques with a trained eye lined up several landmarks and jotted them down. He's done this so many times to relocate a good fishing spot that he's become quite good at it.

"Should we bring up those anchors on Friday?" asked Erik.

"Maybe it would be best to leave them there for now," I said, "as a future reference point just in case. By the way, has anyone noticed anyone spying on us?"

"Actually," said Jacques, "there's a small skiff anchored about a half mile off to the East. I checked with binoculars through a window inside, and it looks just like slick Slip watching us with binoculars. Not many people wear a sailor's hat turned down. He's got a fishing pole, but I think that's just for show."

"That little buzzard," I said. "We know who's behind him. Let's give him a little scare."

We stowed all the gear and I pushed the throttle full forward. The Rose Maria reared up and sped straight for the little skiff.

"Jacques, I want to make sure it's our buddy slacker Slip so get those binoculars and let me know when you can make a positive ID. I don't want to shake up some innocent fisherman."

As we closed in on the skiff, we could see the man trying desperately to haul in the anchor.

"That's an affirmative on slimy Slip, Bill."

"Okay, you little canary," I said. "Pay back time."

I watched him stare at us in disbelief as we bore down on him. He let go of the anchor line and made a panicky dive out of the boat. I turned the wheel and missed the skiff by several feet. I slowed and made a wide three hundred and sixty degree turn pulling up alongside just as the saturated Slip climbed back into the boat.

"That was close!" I shouted, "I hope you're okay. What a coincidence you being out here, I didn't see you until the last minute. Any luck fishing?"

Clearly frightened, he shook his head no. I waved and gave a long drawn out sorry, and we headed for the boat ramp.

I turned to Iris and asked her how she was doing?

"I can't believe you did that Bill. That seems so out of character for you. I think you actually got angry."

"I wanted to get even with that little stoolie and send a message that we are on to them. Slip that little Judas, will be a little more careful from now on how he spies on us. He'll have a good tale to tell his boss tonight. The farther away they stay to spy on us the harder it'll be to see what we're doing.

"How are you feeling, Iris? Are you getting warmed up yet?"

"I'm getting there."

"Here, Iris," said Jacques, "I heated up some coffee and put a little something in it."

"Be careful, Iris," said Erik, "That TABASCO is lethal."

"Don't be silly, Erik. I put a little dark rum and sugar in it."

"Mm, it tastes good, Jacques. I'm feeling warmer already. I like all the attention I'm getting. You guys are spoiling me."

We put Erik ashore and after several entertaining attempts he managed to back the trailer down into the water. Our heckling didn't help. He pulled the sled on, hauled it out and drove it back to the house. Iris came with us, and we headed back to the dock. Jacques said he'd take care of the boat, so I could drive Iris back to the house. I told him, I'd pick him up later and get the gear.

Erik was waiting at the house for us.

"How are you doing, Iris?" he asked.

"Oh, I'm fine now. I should have known better. I've always worn a wetsuit before on extended dives, especially on the sled. Is there a place in Key West where Erik and I can buy them?"

"I have a friend who owns a dive shop here. He has a good selection of them on display. Jacques and I already have ours, but if you feel up to it we could take a ride over there later on?"

"Sure, I feel fine now, whenever you want to go."

I drove to the boat and got Jacques and the equipment.

When we got back, we put everything in the house, except a couple of tanks that needed to be refilled.

Jacques asked if anyone would like something to eat? We suddenly realized how hungry we were, especially Iris. We all said yes.

"Give me a couple of minutes and I'll fix up something."

Leave it to Jacques; within a half hour he had a platter of BLT sandwiches made up using the fresh bread Iris brought earlier. Those sandwiches sure hit the spot and yes, Jacques did put a touch of TABASCO in the mayonnaise.

After our late afternoon lunch, the three of us got into the truck and headed to the dive shop. Jacques stayed at the house. It was a nice feeling having Iris sitting next to me.

"I thought of an idea, Bill," said Iris, "about what to do with those cylinders when we bring them in. What if we sneaked them into that old cistern in the backyard? What do you think?"

"You know, I like that, Iris! That would be a terrific hiding place. All the downspouts flow into one pipe that's just a few inches underground, and it runs under the deck out to the cistern. I could uncover it and cut into it under the deck and then slide the cylinders into the cistern unseen. There's even a trap door in the deck to get down there."

"Not to get technical," said Erik, "How do you push them through that pipe into the cistern?"

"We'll just use an old bamboo fishing pole, I've got a few of them laying around. We can put a piece of tin over the cutout and replace the dirt to hide it. The pipe enters the cistern below the water line so there'll be no splashing sound. And the water certainly won't hurt the cylinders."

"We need a red herring," said Erik, "we have to convince them that we're hiding them somewhere else. Someplace they think they can easily rob at the right time. Otherwise, they will eventually figure out what we're doing. They're not stupid."

"You're right there," I said, "we do need your red herring. Well so far, at least, we have half the problem solved."

We pulled into the parking lot at Jake's Dive Shop.

Jake and I go way back to when I started here with Tony. In fact, he gave me my first lessons in Scuba diving.

"How goes the battle, Jake?" I said.

"Not bad, I hear you're looking for sunken treasure."

"Who told you that?"

"Maury Greer told me."

"I told him not to tell anyone about it."

"I hate to be the one to inform you," he said, with a chuckle, "but Maury Greer is the Hedda Hopper of Key West. He's the salt of the earth, but just don't tell him to keep a secret."

"I guess I should have known. The word would have gotten out eventually."

"Well, if you do find any, keep it to yourself. Two guys were in here yesterday asking if I knew of anyone looking for gold."

"Oh really, are they locals?"

"No. I never saw them before. One of them spoke with a German accent and the other one, with the shaved head, kept silent. I fought those Krauts during the war. I don't mind telling you I have no use for them. Present company excluded of course, as he tipped his hat to Iris and nodded to Erik.

"Well, I guess what I really mean is that I didn't like the Nazi troops I fought during the war. They were real, shall we say… tenacious. I served as a private under Patton and we lost many a good man prying them out of their bunkers. As far as the German civilians go, I'll never forget the looks on their faces as we pushed through their bombed out towns and villages. They were hungry and scared. You can't hate people in that situation. You pity them."

"I don't blame you Jake," said Iris, "I hate the Nazis too, because they killed my parents. And, Erik here, he fought them like you did in the war. There were good Germans too, some of them, at great risk saved me from those Nazis."

Then she said something to him in Yiddish. His eyes lit up and they stepped aside and carried on an animated conversation.

"By the way, Bill," said Erik. "Iris speaks Yiddish."

"I guess she does."

After several minutes, Iris and Jake apologized and assured us we were not in any way mentioned negatively in their conversation. He reached out and shook hands with Erik.

"Iris told me you were OSS in the war, Erik. I personally saw the aftermath of one of their missions. That sure helped take the heat off us grunts. Iris took me by surprise when she spoke Yiddish. I don't use it that often anymore and I'm a little rusty, but it was fun. She's quite a young lady. She wants to look at wet suits, c'mon in."

We went into his shop and Iris and Erik started to look over the suits on display. He showed them his stock in the back room and told them to help themselves.

Jake and I went around back to fill the tanks.

"So, did those two characters have anything else to say? I asked.

"I didn't let on that you were treasure hunting. It's none of their business. I filled up their air tanks and carried a couple out to their car. As the silent one lifted up one of the tanks to put it into the trunk, his sleeve pulled back, and I saw a swastika tattoo. I pretended I didn't see it. Like I said, I don't like those guys."

"Do they have their own boat or are they chartering?"

"They said they're chartering Joe Stalker's boat for some pleasure diving on the reefs and big game fishing. As you know he's the same ilk."

We put the tanks into the back of the truck and joined Iris and Erik. They both found what they needed and Jake gave them a hefty discount.

Iris said something in Yiddish and waved goodbye. He smiled and tipped his hat to her.

"Thanks Jake," I said, "I'll take your advice. If we find any treasure I'll remember not to tell Maury."

On the way back to the house we talked about what we had just heard from Jake. Joe Stalker being involved didn't surprise us, but Jake seeing that swastika tattoo was disturbing, especially for Iris.

"I'm worried," said Erik, "I think that those two men could have had a hand in my cousin Gerhard's murder?"

"Oh, Erik, I hope you're wrong." said Iris.

"I hate to say it, but I think Erik may be right. We ought to assume they were involved.

"By the way, Iris, how did you learn to speak Yiddish?"

"That goes back to my childhood in Germany and then in New York. It's my heritage, you know."

"You were talking to him a long time, what did you say?"

"I first asked him if he spoke Yiddish. He said he hasn't used it very much since he left the Bronx and moved here right after the war. I told him how close friends of my parents saved me from the Nazis, and Erik's parents sneaked me out of Germany and adopted me as their own. He described some of the horrible things he saw when they captured some of the concentration camps and thanked God that I escaped. I also asked him about the Temple here, and he told me their schedule. The day after tomorrow is Saturday, and I would like to go."

"Of course, Iris, what time is the service?

"It's at 9:30 in the morning, and Jake said he and his wife would pick me up at the hotel."

"That's good of him and it's nice that you keep that up. Jacques and I are both Catholic, and we go to Mass on Sundays. What about you Erik?"

"Erik's a bad boy," said Iris, "he says his prayers in bed on Sunday morning. At least that's what he tells me."

"Honest! I really do say my prayers in bed."

"We'll let you sleep then." I said.

"If you don't mind Bill, I'd like to go with you and Jacques to the Mass on Sunday. I don't want to go every week, just this once to see the church."

"Of course I wouldn't mind! I'd be proud to take you. Have you ever gone to a Mass before?"

"Yes, I liked it when they said the Mass in Latin, but they just changed it to the language of each country."

"I kind of like it better now, because I never understood the Latin, I had to follow it in the English translation in the prayer book. By the way, how did you know Jake was Jewish?"

"I saw his name under the Dive Shop sign, 'Jacob Rosengart, Prop.' and just took a chance. He's a really nice man and told me to tell you to remember him, if we need any help."

"You're right he is a good man, and I know he means it with his offer to help. I hope we won't need it.

"We'll plan on going out early on Friday for a full day, then on Saturday and Sunday just in the afternoon, if that's okay Iris."

That would be fine with me Bill."

Jacques had his feet up on the railing sitting on the front porch, reading the newspaper, as we drove in.

"Did you get everything you needed?"

"Yes, we're all set for a full day on Friday," I answered. "Jake gave us some interesting information. Let's go out back and we'll talk about it."

As usual, Jacques had a treat for us; some iced tea and pineapple scones with key lime zest were waiting for us out on the deck.

"Jacques, you make the best scones. You're going to make me fat."

"My scones are made with love, Iris. They don't have any calories. So, enjoy."

"No calories? I'm in," said Erik.

"So, what did Jake have to say?"

We filled him in with the news we learned from Jake.

"It sounds to me," said Jacques, "that Joe Stalker informed someone over there about the gold and the Nazi submarine here in Key West. They must have had other information that led them to Gerhard, a submariner who sold some gold coins to the pawnbroker. I'm sure, while trying to get him to talk, they thought they killed him. That's why they searched his house. It's got to be some kind of international organization and Joe Stalker is part of a cell here in Key West. Do you think it could be some kind of mafia based in West Germany?"

"That's the big question," I said, "and I fear that swastika may be a clue. Erik, try and remember back, when you and Gerhard went to the pawnshop together to sell that helmet. Was there anyone else there, who could have overheard your conversation?"

"What a dummkopf I am. Yes, a man about our age happened to be there and asked Gerhard if the helmet belonged to him. They had a brief conversation about their war experiences. I remembered Gerhard told him that he served on a U-Boat. Gerhard introduced him to me and I shook hands with him. He asked Max to show him a watch from the showcase. That's all I can remember right now."

"So, he got your name. Was there any mention of the gold coins?" I asked.

"Actually, when we were leaving, the pawnbroker, looking up from haggling over the price of a watch with that fellow, asked Gerhard if he had any more gold coins to sell. Gerhard said he might have a few more in the future, so I know he heard it."

"I have a feeling," I said, "that Joe is involved with a group of former Nazis in West Germany. Of course, I don't have any proof right now, but that fellow you met in the pawnshop could have passed the information about Gerhard along with your name to that group. They knew about his duty in the submarine service so when they got Joe's telegraph messages from Key West about the Nazi gold, the U-Boat, your name, and mine that triggered the visit to Gerhard. If true, it would explain everything."

"It sounds plausible," said Erik, "that could be why they went after the pawnbroker to get Gerhard's address, assuming he knew the location of the gold in Key West. Poor Gerhard being inside the submarine throughout the whole incident had no idea where they were. Also, it accounts for these two Germans who just happened to show up in Key West to charter Joe's boat for 'Pleasure Diving and Big Game Fishing'."

"After the funeral," said Iris, "my parents held a small reception and being German Americans everyone wanted to talk to us. We both mentioned we were vacationing in Key West, Florida. There were several men there who said they knew Gerhard during the war, but they could have been there for information. We probably shouldn't have mentioned Key West."

"You're right, Iris," said Erik, "we should have been more careful. I guess we just weren't thinking."

"It's water over the dam now. They're here and we can't change that. I believe they're only interested in the gold and won't want to attract attention to themselves, for now. However, we can't assume they will wait until all the gold is retrieved to make their move."

The phone rang and to my surprise it was Frank. He just arrived from New York, in his private plane. He wanted to get together later to share some important information. I suggested Maury's at seven and he agreed saying that he would be buying.

On hearing the news Iris looked at her watch and said she had better go back to the hotel and change. She would meet us later at Maury's.

We took turns getting cleaned up and changed, then headed to our favorite bar.

I told Denise of our expected VIP guest, and she set us up with a corner booth for the five of us.

We just finished our first round, when Iris walked in casually dressed, looking great as usual, returning greetings from the gang as she headed to our booth.

Shortly after, our eminent host arrived. We waved to him, and he joined us. Denise came over, welcomed him to Maury's, and took the order for drinks.

"How's everything in New York?" I asked.

"It's okay now! Every time I go away for more than a few days, things start to unravel and it takes a while to straighten it all out. How's it going down here?"

"Very good, we had the divers sled out today, and Iris gave us all a lesson on how to use it. She spotted the anchors I threw overboard when I started chasing that sub."

Denise arrived with the drinks and a basket of conch fritters.

"Here's something to munch on while you're deciding what to order. The special tonight is prime rib with mashed potatoes, butternut squash, and green beans. I'll check back in a bit."

"What are these?" asked Frank.

"They're conch fritters," said Iris, "It's pronounced conk down here, but it's spelled conch. You're in for a treat. Dip them in that sauce, like this."

"Oh, I see. In Key West it's conk."

Frank picked up one and following Iris's demonstration took a bite.

"Hey, they are good. I never heard of them before. I guess I've lived a sheltered life."

We all laughed and toasted Frank's happy epicurean adventure as Maury came over to say hello.

"I'm glad to see everyone is having a good time tonight."

"Hi, Maury," I said, "I'd like you to meet Frank Lucre. He's the owner of the Princess Iris in the harbor."

As they shook hands, Maury complimented Frank on the beautiful yacht, and Frank reciprocated by praising Maury's unique establishment with all the nautical artifacts on display.

"I've met your lovely wife Denise, and she's been taking very good care of us."

"Thank you and if there's anything I can do, don't hesitate to ask. By the way, I've heard you have your own pub on board. I'd like to see it some time."

"Consider yourself invited. I'll be here for a few days, so you and Denise will have lunch with me. Name the time."

"That would be swell. I'll check with Denise and let you know. Well, I have to get back to the bar, nice meeting you, Frank."

"Same goes for me Maury. I'll talk to you later.

He's a big guy. How tall is he?"

"He's six foot six," I answered. "He's a good man and a good friend."

We all decided to order the prime rib.

After a little small talk, while we were waiting for our meals, I raised the subject of our gathering.

"So, tell us what new information you've come across."

"I told you that I would try and find out something about Joe Stalker. Through my sources, I've found out that's not his real name; it's Hermann Schmidt. As we suspected there's a warrant out for his arrest in West Germany for assault and attempted murder. When he flew to Holland he had to use his real passport, not the alias papers he uses here in Key West. From that, I learned that he did prison time in West Germany for war crimes. After his release, he got in trouble for starting a fight in a bar and almost killing a man. He fled West Germany and lived in Cuba for many years before coming here. While in Cuba he acquired his boat and picked up his running mate, Slip. That's about all they could find out about him."

Iris asked, "Do you know what his war crimes were?"

"Yes, he was an SS guard in one of the concentration camps who delighted in brutally beating up defenseless prisoners. There were dozens of witnesses who testified against him."

"I know it's a long shot," Erik asked, "Do you think he knew Gerhard, my cousin? He also served as an SS guard,"

"Iris told me about him, I'm sorry to hear about his death. As of now, there's no connection, but that would be interesting to find out."

"How did you get this information?" I asked.

"I can't tell you my exact sources, but I can tell you that some of the help is from Israel. They are the most active country pursuing former Nazi war criminals worldwide with very good results. They are most agreeable to share what they have if it helps to further their goals."

"I thought the war ended in 1945." said Jacques. "Weren't the really bad Nazis all rounded up and dealt with?"

"Not all of them," said Frank, "many escaped capture and went into hiding all over the world. Some disguised themselves and are hiding in plain sight now living respectable lives. In other cases, underground groups have formed hoping to someday regain their former greatness."

"I think one of those groups is behind Gerhard's murder," said Erik.

"Why don't they arrest Joe Stalker if he's still a Nazi?" asked Iris.

"In America, it's not illegal to be a Nazi," Frank said. "As far as the U. S. is concerned, he's paid his debt for his war crimes. As long as he stays out of trouble, he's a free man."

"Do you know who Joe met in Holland?" I asked.

"Unfortunately, all we know is the date and time he went through customs at the airport in Holland and when he checked in for the return flight home. My hunch is, like Erik said, he met with an underground Nazi group who summoned him there. Whoever they are, they put all the pieces together and found out about the lost Nazi gold here. I'm sure they feel it rightfully belongs to them and are salivating to get their hands on it. All that gold could go a long way in advancing their dark agenda."

"I'm sure you're right," said Erik. "I think we're all convinced now, the final piece of the puzzle came from the information passed along by Joe Stalker."

I told Frank of our conversation with Jake today, about the two Germans supposedly pleasure diving and big game fishing with Joe. I let it be known that I was convinced they were part of that Nazi group he mentioned and were directly involved with Gerhard's murder and the attempted murder of the pawnbroker. The clincher being the glimpse Jake got of the swastika tattoo.

Denise arrived with the meals and we all settled down to enjoy the hearty prime rib feast. As usual the conversation declined until we nearly finished.

"The prime rib was excellent," said Frank.

Denise happened by in time to hear that.

"We get our beef from my sister, a lady rancher near Ocala. All her cattle are grass-fed. You can't beat the taste and quality."

We all agreed and the empty plates backed it up.

"How about some dessert and coffee?"

As she talked she never missed a beat efficiently loading up her tray.

"By all means," said Frank, "What have you got?"

"Tonight it's bread pudding and Indian pudding."

"Indian pudding! I haven't had that in years. That's what I'd like."

Iris decided against dessert. Erik and I ordered the Indian pudding, and Jacques went for the bread pudding with coffee all around.

"So, you found the anchors, Iris!" said Frank.

"Yes, they were sitting right where they landed all those years ago. Except for some barnacles and coral they look as good as new. They will give us a good reference point to start our search on Friday. Bill's sure that we can now follow the exact course of the sub."

"There's Bosun Jim," said Iris. "Please excuse me, I have to talk to him about something."

As she walked across towards the bar several men and women hailed "Hello, Iris" to whom she happily smiled and returned the greeting. She put her hand on Bosun Jim's shoulder, sat down next to him, and started a conversation. He produced a piece of paper that she read and then using his pen made some notations on it. She returned it, patted him on the back, and headed to our booth.

"Is there something going on with you and Bosun Jim?" I asked.

"Don't be silly. I'm just helping him with a personal problem and I want to keep it private."

"I was a little worried too, Iris," said Frank. "You know I haven't given up hope for us."

I flinched a little at that remark and watched closely for Iris' reaction. I felt better when she seemed to let it go over her head.

Enjoying the dessert and coffee we speculated about the Nazis, Joe Stalker, and the bronze cylinders out there filled with gold.

Jacques periodically, checked for any signs of the shifty Slip.

Frank, true to his word took care of the bill and left a generous tip for Denise. We all left Maury's and thanked him for his generosity as his car pulled up to the curb.

The chauffeur hopped out, ran around, and opened the door. Frank got in, and we all wished him a good night.

Erik escorted Iris back to her hotel, and Jacques and I headed for the house.

Thursday, January 20, 1966

The next day, Jacques and I had the boat all ready to go when our charter showed up right on time.

The first thing he said when he arrived was, "I've got all new material this year."

A natural born comedian, he had us in stitches with his jokes and funny stories from start to finish. He also could see humor in everything and had a one liner to prove it. I told him we should be paying him for all the entertainment.

"Where do you get all these jokes," I asked.

"From the prisoners!" he said. "They keep me well supplied. Humor is one of the ways they try to break the monotony."

You would never have guessed that he ran a prison. Being a warden was a serious responsibility; he had to be careful about what he said on the job and in public. There wasn't much room for his comedy except with the prisoners themselves. Emotions would get bottled up and he needed a way to periodically blow off steam.

He would laugh and say, "Every once in a while, I have to escape from that prison."

If he caught a good size fish he would pose for a picture with it and then tell us to release it.

"I don't need any trophies on my walls, although, I have a couple of prisoners, I'd like to see… Well, some things are better left unsaid."

This annual trip ranked number one of all his favorite therapeutic escapes. Jacques and I did everything we could to make every trip better than the last one. He loved fine food, and Jacques always pleased him with a gourmet luncheon on the boat complete with a select wine. By the end of the day our sides were sore from laughing. He ranked number one by far as our favorite charter.

Friday, January 21, 1966

The next day at eight o'clock, Iris came up the back walk all dressed for a full day on the water.

"Hi Iris, breakfast is almost ready," greeted Jacques, "I'm making up a mess of ham and scrambled eggs with peppers from Bill's garden. Have a seat, there's some juice and coffee on the table."

"That sounds good to me. You're a wonder Jacques."

Erik and I were reading the newspaper and drinking coffee.

"Another perfect day in paradise," I said. "A nice day to find a cylinder full of gold coins."

"If we don't find one, we can't blame the weather. Key West is blest with this beautiful climate."

Jacques brought out a plate stacked high with toast, followed up with a platter of ham, and a big bowl of scrambled eggs with peppers.

"That's a picture, Jacques," said Erik. "Will you marry me?"

"Sorry, Erik, you're not my type. Be warned, I put a little TABASCO sauce in those eggs."

Jacques sat down and joined us in polishing off his tasty offering.

"I won't need any weights today," said Iris, "with all your good cooking I'm going to sink like a stone."

"We'll just have a light lunch on the boat. I'm bringing the fixings for grilled cheese and tomato sandwiches."

"You're the greatest, Jacques," said Erik.

"I have to say, it's much more fun cooking for a bunch of people, the more the better."

We helped him clean up the kitchen and an hour later we were on the site where Iris found the anchors. Jacques observing the landmarks he had chosen the day before put us almost exactly over them.

Iris and Erik, sporting their new wet suits, took the first turn on the sled. Even in a wet suit, Iris looked amazing. We all agreed that about thirty minutes should be the maximum for each turn. They left the sled several times to investigate promising formations. Each time we would stop, our adrenaline rose until they surfaced and gave the thumbs down sign. Then, they would get back on the sled and resume the search. We all took our turns on the sled in the six sessions we were able to get in during that second day, unfortunately with no results.

We headed to the boat ramp and dropped off Iris and Erik with the sled. Erik deferred the backing down of the trailer to Iris. Jacques and I brought the boat back to our slip, cleaned her up, and we all met back at the house.

Jacques had a date with Nicole and Erik had a date with Faith. I asked Iris for a date and she readily agreed. I walked her to the hotel and told her I'd pick her up later at seven.

I figured the shower would be tied up for a while, so I stopped in at Maury's and sat up at the bar.

"Hi, Bill, what'll you have?" asked Maury.

"I'll just have a draft. Hey, I'm taking Iris out to dinner tonight, and I'd like to take her someplace nice, any ideas?"

"You mean nicer than here?"

"I've got nothing against Maury's Bar and Grill. I just think she would like table cloths and candles for a change."

"I know what you mean, just pulling your leg. That's Denise's department, let me go ask her."

After a few minutes I heard some yelling from the kitchen and the sound of some dishes breaking. A little while later, Maury came back with a big smile on his face.

"What happened out there?"

"I just asked her where there's a romantic restaurant in Key West with tablecloths and candles a guy could take his girlfriend. She must have been having a bad day. To save my life, I told her it was for us, I wanted a nice place to take her sometime soon. She then apologized for throwing the dishes at me, and said she would make it up to me. She then gave me a kiss. She said, the best place in Key West that's very romantic is the Casa Marina Hotel restaurant. They serve outside on the water and they have tablecloths and candles. We'll be going there next week. I didn't let on that you were the one that wanted to know."

"So, I didn't get you in trouble then?"

"No, on the contrary, she's all lovey-dovey. We haven't been out together since I don't know when. She's a good kid and I'm long overdue taking her out to a nice place. I'll enjoy seeing her all dressed up and having fun for a change. I'm counting on you not to give me away, Bill."

"Don't worry, Maury. Mum's the word!

"So that's where I'll take Iris. It's kind of ritzy for me, but I want to treat her to something special tonight. I'll let you know how it is. I better get going, I told her I'd pick her up at seven."

"Don't forget your wallet," he said with a grin.

I walked back to the house, where Jacques and Erik were all dressed up and ready to go. I wished them a good time and took my shower, shaved and put on a white shirt, navy shorts, and my best sandals. I topped it all off with a rarely worn beige sport jacket.

I walked into the La Concha lobby at exactly seven and went to the concierge and ordered a cab. I turned around just in time to see Iris step out of the elevator looking so cute in a beautiful pink and white floral dress. She had her hair up in a twist again with the tortoise comb, which I really liked. With matching pink high heels and purse she looked elegant. I started to get that pleasant light-headed feeling again.

"Don't you look handsome with the jacket Bill," she said with a smile.

"Thank you Iris and don't you look charming as usual."

"Thank you Bill. Where are you taking me tonight?"

"It's a surprise. I just called a cab; it should be here shortly."

We went outside and didn't have to wait too long for the cab to show up. I opened the door for Iris and she hopped in. I slid in beside her and told the cabbie where to go. A few minutes later the cab pulled up to the Casa Marina, I got out and helped Iris alight, then paid and tipped the cabbie. On the way through the lobby to the restaurant, I noticed the admiring looks Iris received that made me feel privileged to be her escort. I had reservations, so we were promptly brought outside to a nicely set table boasting the important white linen tablecloth. I was doubly pleased to see a flickering candle under an hourglass hurricane sleeve. A panoramic view of the ocean, with baby waves breaking on the shore and the low clatter of palms, created a romantic movie like setting.

"Oh, this is so pretty here. Key West holds so many surprises."

"It is nice, isn't it; I wanted to do something special for you tonight."

"Thank you, Bill this is special, and you've made me very happy. I didn't expect this."

"This is a fancy place, I hope the menu isn't in French?"

"That's okay, Bill, I speak a little French."

"Why am I not surprised at that?"

"Have no fear, it's in English. Everything looks good. What are you going to get?"

I opened the menu and of course the first thing I looked at were the prices. This is going to hit my pocketbook hard, but no matter, it's for Iris and she's worth it.

"I'm not sure yet, let's order after we have a drink," I said.

The waiter came over and took our order for cocktails. He mentioned a couple of specials.

"I don't know what I want," she said. "I'm going to wait until you pick something."

"I don't think I'll get seafood, because Maury's has the best, so I'll probably go for either beef or chicken. Does that help?"

"You're right about the seafood. That tropical chicken special he mentioned sounds wonderful, maybe I'll go for that."

The waiter returned with our drinks and brought a little tray of hors d'oeuvres.

We decided to order that tropical chicken special and then sat back, sipped our drinks, nibbled on the tasty snacks, and basked in the tropical ambience.

The waiter came by to see how we were doing, and we placed our order.

"Do you ever go back to that town where you grew up?"

"Oh, Scituate. Yes, I visit my parents every year in July or August and they come down here and visit me every February. In fact they'll be coming down in another month. I'd like you to meet them."

"I'm looking forward to it, Bill."

"I wish you could see the town; it's right on the coast. I think you would like it there. I'm sort of a history buff today, because of my mother, who loved American history and especially that of Scituate. She made sure I knew all about the history of our town, like the old Stockbridge Grist Mill, built in 1650 by John Stockbridge. I think it might be the oldest in the country that still works. It was in business until 1922. Now it's preserved as an historic site. Samuel Woodworth another Scituate native mentioned it in his poem 'The Old Oaken Bucket'."

"It sounds charming. Maybe someday I will go there. My family used to go to Cape Cod every summer for a couple of weeks. We rented a cottage in Provincetown. One year we did go up to Plymouth for the day and saw the famous rock that the pilgrims stepped on when they arrived. I remember asking Erik why it was so small."

"In Plymouth you were only twenty miles from Scituate."

"My father did drive all around the area. He loved the style of the old houses. Maybe we did drive through Scituate, Erik might know."

"Who knows, Iris, we could have been like two ships passing in the night."

The waiter brought us our garden salads, refreshed our drinks, and told us the entree would be served in about fifteen minutes.

"My parents wanted me to learn the history of my new homeland, America, so they explained how the Pilgrims founded Plymouth to escape religious persecution. Also, how the Indians were friendly to them and taught them to plant corn with the squash and beans using fish as fertilizer. The big leaves of the squash shaded the ground helping to keep it from drying out and keep the weeds down. The beans would climb up the stocks of the corn so they didn't need beanpoles. Those Indians were quite clever weren't they?

"My father also said they tried a communal form of government the first year 1621, where everyone would work the land and put the crops in a common storehouse to be issued as needed. Laziness prevailed and it turned out to be a disaster. Many starved and died that winter and the next. Governor Bradford then gave everyone their own land to work and be on their own, in other words free enterprise. That year, God gave them plenty, prompting the first Thanksgiving to celebrate an abundant harvest in 1623. There's quite a bit of history there, I'd like to go back again sometime. I still love going to Cape Cod whenever I can. It's a wonderful place to unwind and find peace."

"Without the help of those Indians," I said, "the Pilgrims never would have made it. They did have a fairly good relationship for many years. Then, as more and more Europeans came they started to push the Indians off their land, which prompted them to push back. Soon, fighting began and led to the King Phillip War in New England in 1675-76. A lot of people were killed on both sides, especially among the Indians, until their leader, King Phillip was killed, and they were forced into the background of history.

"Communism isn't the answer. When the government controls things, individuals lose incentive. When people are left to their own devices they become very creative and come up with innovative ways of doing things. Imagine all the inventions that wouldn't have been created, if that experiment of Bradford's worked?" I bet we'd still be using horses for transportation. Look at me, coming down here with Tony and starting a fishing charter business. It would be very difficult to do that under Communism. I believe the Pilgrims sowed the seeds of Capitalism in America."

Our meals arrived and were served in a small casserole dish piping hot from the oven. Chunks of chicken were mixed with pineapple, mango, plantains and rice with spices. It tasted wonderful and put a damper on our conversation while we nodded to each other how good it tasted.

"I'll have to tell Jacques about this dish, he's always looking for new recipes."

"Knowing Jacques," she said, "I'm sure he will come up with his own version of it."

"You're right. And I wouldn't be surprised if he worked in a little TABASCO sauce," I said jokingly.

"Even if he does, I know it will taste good.

That was delicious, Bill. I'm stuffed. No dessert tonight, just coffee."

"You took the words right out of my mouth. Coffee sounds great."

We lingered over a couple of cups of coffee, and we were getting ready to leave, when we heard some nice music start up from inside. Iris wanted to check it out, so we went into their bar where an older woman dressed in a beige cocktail dress with sequins sat at a baby grand piano playing and singing. When she saw the dance floor, Iris looked at me, and I knew what she had in mind. She went over and spoke to the pianist who nodded. A few moments later she started playing and singing Moon River, our song. We danced together and I felt goose bumps as I held her so close to me. I knew then that I was falling in love with Iris.

We danced a few more songs and then decided to leave because Jake would be picking her up at 8:30 in the morning for Temple. I thanked the pianist and slipped a dollar into her tip jar.

The night was made for walking with a light breeze and a sky crammed full of stars, so we decided to forego the taxi. She stopped and started to take off her shoes. I suggested that she keep them on. Against my advice she took them off. Just then one of our jumbo cockroaches scurried across the sidewalk, and she jumped out of the way.

"I hope that wasn't a mouse, Bill," she said startled and putting her shoes back on.

"No," I laughed, "that's just a Palmetto bug, which sounds a little nicer then a cockroach. They come out at night and are harmless, but you wouldn't want to step on one with bare feet."

"Are they all that big? I'm not too fond of bugs."

"Yes, that's about the average size. Have you noticed some wild roosters and chicken running around?"

"I've heard the roosters and I saw a mother hen with her chicks behind the Hotel."

"They help curb the population of these Palmetto bugs."

"Next time I'll wear more comfortable shoes."

We laughed about it and started to count them on the way back to the Hotel and gave up after a quick dozen.

"That's one of the nice things I like about Key West, Bill, in spite of those Palmetto bugs, is that it is a walkable city."

We entered the Hotel lobby and she reminded me again that she had to get up early, because Jake and his wife were picking her up in the morning. I hated to say goodnight to her, but she suddenly put her arms around my neck and gave me a kiss and thanked me for the happiest evening she's had in a long time. That took me by surprise and I managed to stumble out something about how it was my pleasure. Then the elevator door opened, she stepped in, the doors closed, and just like that I found myself alone.

I stood there a few moments and then smiled. Iris has become a part of my life now. I walked back to the house savoring that warm kiss and the nearness of her while we were dancing. She fanned a cold ember inside me back to a flame and it felt good.

Saturday, January 22, 1966

We had the next morning off, so we all slept late for a change. As usual, Jacques was the first one up and sent those irresistible aromas through the house coaxing Erik and I from our beds. We talked about our dates the night before, over stacks of pecan pancakes with maple syrup, bacon, and coffee.

Around noon, when we heard Iris coming up the back walk whistling, Erik and Jacques both looked at me with a smile, no words were needed. Jacques shooed us out of his kitchen telling me to bring the pot of coffee out to the deck.

"Good morning boys," she said.

"You sound chipper this morning, Iris," said Erik, "that guy you went out with last night must have shown you a good time."

"He did, indeed. We went to a fancy restaurant on the beach and had the most delicious meal. Then we went dancing."

"That guy," I said, "enjoyed it too."

"How about you and Jacques did you both have a good time?"

"Faith and I did. We went bar hopping and ended up at Maury's for something to eat. We danced a little and she mostly wanted to talk about me."

"Nicole and I had dinner on the Fritter Boat, then we walked all around the whole island just talking. I had a great time and I think she did too."

"I'm sure she did, Jacques," said Iris, "it was a beautiful night for walking. Did you see any of those icky Palmetto bugs?"

"Of course, but Nicole and I grew up with them."

He brought out the rest of the pineapple scones he made on Thursday. It didn't take long for us to make them disappear. We talked about the day ahead and the hope of finding that first cylinder. We all helped Jacques clear the table and clean up the kitchen.

We spent the afternoon seeking the hidden cylinders. We had three sessions on the sled with no luck.

Sunday, January 23, 1966

The next morning Jacques and I met Iris at the hotel and continued walking to Saint Mary's Star of the Sea for an early Mass. She looked like a doll all dressed up in a pale blue dress with a little straw hat.

She was no stranger to the ceremony. She genuflected like a good Catholic and followed along with us through the whole Mass. She did not receive Communion. She said that wouldn't be proper.

When we came back to the house, Iris and I went out on the deck and shared the Sunday paper while Jacques started making some breakfast. With the aromas of coffee and minute steaks frying it wasn't long before we heard the shower running. Erik arrived just in time to join the three of us in partaking of Jacques' hearty breakfast of steak, eggs, home fries, and whole-wheat toast.

Iris started to give us a primer on Yiddish humor. However, Erik chimed in with his limited use of the language, and it didn't take long for it to degenerate into some pretty risqué double entendre, causing Iris to blush.

"For some reason, Erik only remembers the naughty words," she said, "and here it is Sunday morning. I hope you said your prayers in bed this morning, while we were at Mass."

"Honest, I did say my prayers and you're trying to change the subject."

I came to her rescue and said, "I think we ought to get going, so we can get in two or three sled cycles."

We did get in the three sled cycles, but again without success. We needed something to get the excitement back. Watching all those thumbs down signs started to get to all of us. No one said it, but discouragement was building.

Back at the house Jacques made up a wonderful spaghetti dinner with his special meatballs and Caribbean tomato sauce a la TABASCO. With a couple of bottles of Chianti thrown in, we were soon laughing and boasting on how we were going to track down every one of those damn cylinders.

Monday, January 24, 1966

The next day, we spent the morning, again without finding any cylinders.

We were starting to get a little down, except for Iris. She had been through this many times before on those archeological endeavors. She told us what we didn't want to hear that it could take time, a lot of time.

What we did find were several really old bottles, some dating back to the seventeen hundred's and an early Evinrude one cylinder outboard motor. Tony would have called it a one lunger. We were impressed how mostly bronze, brass, and copper were used in its construction. We later gave the bottles and the motor to Maury. He loved the outboard and hoped to get it restored. The antique bottles he proudly placed with dozens of others that found their way into his glass display case next to the cigarette machine.

We spent the afternoon taking turns on the sled, ending another disappointing day. With heavy hearts we came in and after putting everything away, Erik suggested we go over to Maury's for a drink on him. How could we pass that up?

We walked over to Maury's and sat up at the bar. None of us knew what to get for a drink, so we asked Maury to help us out. He started down the list and came to "Sailor in the Shade".

"What's in that," asked, Iris.

"It's an iced tea with a shot of Gosling's dark rum and a wedge of lime with a little umbrella. We're fresh out of umbrellas."

"Does that mean the sailor won't be in the shade?"

"You guessed it, Iris."

"That's what I'll have, it sounds good," she said.

Iris took a sip and approved, then Erik, Jacques and I ordered the same.

Of course, one led to a second and why not, thanks to Erik. Jacques wisely switched to a draft beer.

Maury suggested something to eat, especially for Iris, who showed signs of getting a bit frisky.

"Is anyone else hungry?" I said. "How about getting a booth and having something to eat?"

"That's a good idea," said Erik, "now that you mention it I am hungry. What are we waiting for?"

The four of us went over to our regular booth and Denise came by to tell us the special of the night.

"We don't have it that often, but tonight it's Roast turkey with all the fixings, we're celebrating Thanksgiving early."

Jacques said he never heard of Thanksgiving until he came to America, but really enjoyed the traditional dinner especially with the cranberry sauce.

Thanksgiving in January sounded pretty good, so we all ordered the special. Those "Sailor not in the Shade" drinks were taking their toll on us, so we decide on a pitcher of plain Iced Tea with limes.

Denise took the order; nodded and said, "Smart move."

"Is it true that President Harry Truman use to come here?" asked Iris.

"Yes, but he wasn't the first president," I said. "President Taft stopped here on his way to inspect the progress on the construction of the Panama Canal way back in 1912. The house that Harry Truman stayed in became known as the Little White House. He loved Key West and spent a good deal of time here; he was also quite a fisherman. They renamed Division Street to Truman Avenue on November 20, 1948. I remember the month and day, because it's my birthday and it was the year before Tony and I moved here. Then, Eisenhower and Kennedy came; I saw them both on their visits. Not many people know that Thomas Edison stayed in the house during World War One, donating his time for the war effort. He lived here for six months improving all kinds of weapons."

"Key West has quite a tale to tell, doesn't it, Bill," she said.

"It sure does, I'm always learning new things about its history."

The thanksgiving meal arrived and it didn't take long for us to dispatch it. All conversation ceased for the duration of the meal. It tasted so good, we all cleaned our plates and just like the turkey, we were all pleasantly stuffed.

No dessert, no coffee and no leftovers. For health reasons, we all agreed it would be best to finish off the evening by taking a long walk, to burn up some of those calories.

Tuesday, January 25, 1966

The next morning, our sailing day, Iris came over to the house promptly at ten for a late breakfast at Jacques invitation. He couldn't wait to serve her a breakfast fit for a queen. He made the most delicious crepe suzettes with a hot sauce of caramelized sugar, orange juice, and Grand Marnier. He ignited the Grand Marnier, which made quite a show, as he elegantly served it and then departed leaving us alone on the deck to enjoy the little feast. I didn't expect that and it pleased me.

Iris was delighted and sang his praises.

"I've got to admit, Jacques outdid himself again," she said. "When he finds out, Erik is going to regret sleeping late.

"Erik always did enjoy sleeping late. If we had to be somewhere he took pride in being the first one up ready and waiting for the rest of us. But, give him a day off and he will sleep until afternoon."

I liked being alone with Iris and I hoped she like being with me.

We enjoyed Jacques efforts and told him so afterwards.

As we were leaving for our sailing jaunt, Jacques had another surprise for us, a picnic basket of sandwiches, fruit and a bottle of wine.

"We're only going out for a couple of hours."

"Well, now you can make a day of it," he said with a wink.

"Jacques is right. We will make a day of it," she said.

We took the truck and drove down to the marina. I took the picnic basket, and we walked down to the slip where we found the beautiful little twelve-foot lapstrake dinghy tied up. A wooden boat, left natural and finished with several coats of clear spar varnish. The removable mast was rigged with a boomless spritsail.

Iris said her father's boat, the one in which he taught her how to sail, was built the same way, but a little longer and had a boom and a jib.

This one was a beautiful display of workmanship by a Key West local, built on molds using steam bent ribs and cedar planks fastened with copper nails and roves. He's been very generous to let me use it several times, and I found it a joy to sail and row alone.

Iris in her haste to get started hopped in.

I untied the lines and joined her. I thought I'd give her some pointers on sailing. I barley sat down when she unfurled the sail and let the wind take us away. Working the rudder and sail like an old salt she meandered us through a maze of boats out into open water. I realized I'd best sit back and watch, unless needed.

She wanted to know what they called the line to the clew of the sail. I told her we call it a sheet.

"In German we say schot."

She pointed to the head, the luff, the tack and so forth. I would tell her the English and she would tell me the German. She made me test her to make sure she had it all memorized. She was a German all right.

It took about an hour and a half to reach the island. We pulled into a little secluded beach I had discovered years ago. I enjoyed visiting the little haven so much I brought out some tools a few years back and built a crude table and seats out of driftwood. I made it very primitive and heavy so no one would even think about stealing it. I even planted a couple of palm trees to compliment the Austrian pines. I put up a little sign inviting all to use it, just keep it tidy. The evidence of use without a sign of litter, made me proud of the residents of Key West. It presented a perfect place for our picnic today.

"You put all this together by yourself? It looks so natural like it belongs here. And this place, it's so beautiful and peaceful."

"I like to come out here occasionally to get away from it all. It helps me put things back into proper perspective. There are times, when we all need a place of refuge."

"And, you're sharing it with me, Bill. Thank you."

We didn't feel like eating, so we set Jacques basket on the table and went for a walk to explore the little island. Iris found some pretty shells and driftwood and said she wanted to make a little wall hanging. An hour or so went by and we ended up back at the table with an appetite.

Iris opened up Jacques basket and set the table with the plates, sandwiches and the bottle of wine and she smiled when she saw the little vase of flowers he included.

"Isn't he nice to do that for me, Bill?"

"Why do you assume they are for you? I think he may have put them in there for me."

She didn't know what to say. And she looked at me in a most peculiar way. I couldn't keep a straight face and started to smile.

"Oh, you're joking with me. For a minute I thought... Never mind what I thought. I have to remember to thank him for the flowers."

"You're right. He is a very thoughtful caring man. I don't know what I'd do without him. You know he's been getting serious with Nicole?"

"I kind of thought that. Nicole seems like such a nice woman. I hope it works out for them, the poor man losing his little family that way, how tragic."

"In fact, with his share of the treasure he wants to open a little restaurant here in Key West with her."

"That would be so perfect for them. He loves cooking, and he's so good at it too, and she's a sous chef. I hope that's what happens to them.

"Oh, and I've got news for you. Erik has been getting serious with Faith."

"That's been getting pretty obvious," I said, "because he's been missing more and more. Good for him. I hope it works out for them too."

"As you know he was in the Army for twenty years and traveled all over the world. He had lots of girlfriends, but never found that special one. Maybe it will be Faith."

The next logical subject would have been me getting serious with her, but I couldn't muster the courage to say it.

"Jacques roast beef sandwiches with the horseradish are delicious," she said, " he even included a bag of potato chips and the red wine is a perfect compliment."

"What about you, Iris. In your Yiddish conversation with Jake you told him what happened to your mother and father when you were a little girl. Erik told us some of the story of how his parents helped you escape Nazi Germany, saving your life. You've endured tragedy as well."

"And, they lovingly adopted me as their own. I owe them so much.

"I'll never forget that morning of terror. The women I was staying with took me to a General, who I found out later was a relative of the Von Hurlich's. They didn't tell me what was going to happen, so I thought the worse. I realize now that they knew the less I was told the safer I would be. Two very stern uniformed men with those dreadful swastikas on their arms, took me to an awaiting official car and drove me to the ship. They brought me on board and put me in the Von Hurlich's cabin, hours before they started boarding. They told me not to move an inch. Those swastikas made me weak with fear. My world had collapsed around me. I didn't know what to expect.

"I didn't move that inch for what seemed like forever. Then, I heard the key turning in the door. I was petrified.

"Sitting on my little suitcase I froze, as Erik and his parents entered the cabin. Erik's mother came over and knelt down beside me and speaking to me in German, asked me my name. I just managed to say it. She introduced Erik and his father to me and then told them to leave. She had the kindest eyes I had seen since I last saw my parents, which instantly dispelled my fear.

"In those horrible days, I learned how people's eyes revealed what lurked in their hearts. I became very good at it. I could recognize love, despair, and hate like that in the eyes of those two Nazi soldiers who brought me to the ship. Looking into Mrs. Von Hurlich's beautiful, loving eyes was a heaven sent moment. She talked to me openly and calmly, and I seemed to hear, as in a dream, my own dear mother's voice saying, 'Listen to her, Iris and do as she says'."

"I can't imagine going through something so awful at ten years old," I said. "I hate to think of some of the things you must have witnessed."

"I'm most vulnerable, in the middle of the night sometimes, when those specters appear as real as yesterday, even after all these years. I guess I'll never be free from their visits. If it wasn't for the Von Hurlich's, I don't know what would have become of me."

"Terrible things have happened in Germany," she told me, "your parents have been killed by the Nazis just because they were Jewish and if they find you, they may do the same to you. Thankfully, there are still good Germans. Several close friends of your parents risked their own lives to save yours. You owe it to them and your mother and father to grow up and become the woman you were meant to be. Your parents will always be with you. Those evil Nazis can never take away your memories of them, or their love. I cannot replace your mother, and I don't want to. I would like us to become best friends, so we'll just work at that. My husband and my son Erik want to be your friends too. We will always be here to help and support you.

"And they were. They treated me as their own unconditionally. Dear Erik has always been and still is my big, protective brother.

"I'll always remember and revere my real parents. I think of them every day and try to be a credit to them.

"Mr. and Mrs. Von Hurlich have been wonderful to me and it didn't take long for me to love them both dearly, and I proudly became their daughter. In time, I was happy to call them mom and dad. I can never repay them for what they did for me."

"What about your religion? You were Jewish in your childhood. Your new parents weren't Jewish."

"Shortly after we arrived in New York my new mother took me to visit the local synagogue and we talked to the Rabbi. He was very nice and spoke to me in German. I was enrolled in the Hebrew school and every Saturday I had to go to Temple. I'm a non-Orthodox Jew like most American Jews. On Sunday the rest of the family went to the Lutheran church. I didn't like staying at home alone, so I went with them. At first I was a little nervous, but after a while I began to feel comfortable. In fact, I felt kind of special in both places. I hope you don't think I'm sacrilegious, but I like to think I'm Jewish with a little Lutheran thrown in. Of course, I wouldn't tell just anyone that. Does that shock you?"

"Of course not, I'm quite impressed that you can be active in two religions. Most people have trouble with one. When you came to Mass with Jacques and me last Sunday, were you thinking of adding a third religion?"

"Now you're joshing with me, Bill, it's mostly curiosity about what the church looked like inside, I've reached my limit, on religions. I have to admit though, there are times when it's an advantage to be one or the other."

"I've told you all about me. What about you? How did you end up here in Key West?"

I told her about growing up in Scituate, my girlfriend, my Navy days, getting married, my son, the car accident, and Tony Sousa. She listened attentively to my long chronicle.

"Well, you asked for it, that's my whole life's story in a nutshell."

"You've had some tragedy too, I'm sorry to hear. But, it sounds like you've had an enjoyable life here in Key West. What a wonderful man, Tony must have been. You must miss him?"

"I do miss him and think about him every day. He would have loved you, Iris. Tony had a saying that, 'The only thing better than a beautiful boat, is a beautiful woman'. He treated every day as a gift and lived his life with passion. Right up until the end he never let his age get in the way."

"I wish I could have known him. And, thank you for the compliment."

"Well it's true. You are a beautiful woman, Iris."

"I know."

I looked a little perplexed by what she just said.

She laughed and said, "I'm only kidding. But seriously, you, Jacques, and I have similar heartbreaks in our past. I lost my parents, and you and Jacques both lost your little families. Last year, I went to a psychiatrist, and he seemed to think I resist deep relationships because I don't want to be hurt again. Also, he thought I tend to be a perfectionist to compensate. Maybe that's why I couldn't go through with marrying Frank.

"If he's correct, I'm guilty for a long history of ending relationships that were becoming serious. Who knows, I may have gotten married years ago if I didn't tragically lose my parents. Those poor fellows, I'm sure when we broke up, they all thought they were to blame. I wonder why I'm telling you all this private stuff? It must be this little oasis of yours."

"You're not the only one with baggage. You won't believe this, Iris, but the other day, when you were giving Erik his lesson on the diver's sled, Jacques and I had that same conversation. We both, after all these years, were able to talk freely to each other about the painful experience of losing our loved ones. As a result, we have resisted close relationships with women. We came to the same conclusion as your psychiatrist and laughed about how we save a big psychiatric bill. However, we didn't figure out the perfectionist angle. I'll have to tell him."

I opened up to her and told her how I made a vow on my wife's grave and how my priest friend told me that I couldn't make a vow with the dead. Iris and I put each other at ease and freely shared some personal details of our lives. It felt so nice being alone with her like this. I knew now that I was in love with Iris.

The sound of thunder off in the distance abruptly turned our attention to some of the inkiest black clouds I had ever seen. Spewing spikes of lightning, the dark tempest was speeding our way.

"Some of these squalls can be nasty, Iris," I said, trying to sound calm. "Let's pull the boat up here and turn it over and lean it on the table for a shelter."

I removed the sail and folded it up. I unstepped the mast and detached the rudder. The two of us easily pulled the little boat up to the heavy table and Iris lashed it down securely. Meanwhile, I put the stopper on the wine and the dishes back in the basket and put it under the boat along with the folded sail for us to sit on.

We both got under and were ready for whatever happened.

"I'm kind of excited and afraid," she said.

"Tony impressed on me to take any storm serious, especially at sea. This happens occasionally, but that's one of the reasons I like it here. You never quite know what to expect. One minute it's a beautiful sunny day and the next... Here we go!"

Large noisy drops began to fall here and there, bringing the sweet smell of the rain. Then, the gusty wind whipped up the sand and it rudely invaded our hiding place. The boat lurched from side to side but held in place. The booming thunder, coming simultaneously with each bolt of lightning, told us the strikes were alarmingly close and extremely dangerous. Added to that, we had to endure the incessant drumming of the torrential rain on our improvised shelter. It was by far the worse squall I've experienced in all my years in Key West. The storm became so violent, it scared me, and I had genuine concerned for Iris. She moved close to me, and I could feel her trembling. I put my arms around her and held her tightly.

A pine tree nearby took a direct hit. The bright bolt of lightning, the ear-splitting clap of thunder, and the grinding sound of splitting wood all happening in the same instant had to be the most terrifying experience of my life. Iris stiffened in fear and buried her face in my chest. The time between the lightning flashes and the thunder started to increase as the swiftly moving storm past over us and rumbled off into the distance. Embracing her in such an intimate manner, I regretted the rapid departure of the violent storm. I didn't want to let go of her, so I told her we should wait a while to be sure. The sun came back out and it became eerily still and quiet. Her eyes were shut and her beautiful face and lips beguiled me to lean down and kiss her. She started to kiss me back and then quickly pulled away.

We got out from under the boat and marveled at the damaged pine tree all charred black and the smell of burned wood. Then, as we looked at each other covered in damp sand, we started to laugh.

"I'll never get this sand out of my hair," she said.

We took off the sandy clothes down to our bathing suits and raced each other into the water. It was a delight to see her laugh as she tried to rinse the sand out of her hair. We desanded our clothing in the water and draped it over the table to dry.

"Well, I hope we don't see another storm like that for awhile, Bill. Thanks to your quick action you probably saved our lives. I never would have thought of using the boat for a shelter."

"I have to confess that's the worse squall I've ever been through here, but I'm glad we were on land instead of out on the water. Don't forget you tied down the boat, so we'll have to tell Bosun Jim your knots saved our lives."

The thunderstorm that had just menaced us raced away across the water out to sea, still flashing and booming like a child throwing a tantrum. Amazingly, the weather returned to the way it was before, as though nothing had ever happened.

The sand found its way into the picnic basket, but fortunately we had eaten the sandwiches. The plates and glasses were sandy, but we rinsed them off in the water. I reopened the half finished bottle of wine and we toasted to our survival of the storm.

"I'm so glad we ate Jacques sandwiches. It would have been a shame if they got ruined. I liked the horseradish he put on them. You're so lucky to have him doing your cooking."

"Don't I know it? When he told me that he and Nicole were thinking of starting a restaurant, I realized I might lose him. I'd miss him, but at the same time I'd be happy for him too."

"He'd still be here in Key West, and I know you would be most welcome in his restaurant whenever you missed his cooking."

"That's true and we could still get together at Maury's every once in awhile."

"What are you going to do with your share of the treasure, Bill?"

"That's a good question. I really don't need anything, although the boat is getting old. If there's enough money, I might get a new boat. A fiberglass one would be nice. The maintenance of a wooden boat is starting to get to me."

We easily and openly talked to each other until to my dismay, we realized how close to the horizon the sun was getting.

We righted the boat, stepped the mast, rigged the sail, and stowed our gear. As we pushed off from our secret little island, Iris got us underway heading for home. She had to tack most of the way back, which she did on autopilot. She became silent and seemed to be a million miles away. She gripped the tiller firmly with both hands under the fair wind. I sat mesmerized watching her, as she looked intently forward. Her stunning features and damp blonde hair tussled by the wind, aroused feelings long dormant. I wanted to preserve this picture and store it in my memory bank forever.

I wondered what she was thinking. Did she regret that she told me too much about herself? She needn't worry because everything she told me I locked in my heart. I kept thinking of that kiss. Did she think of it too? Maybe she's upset about that kiss? Although, she did kiss me back. So many questions, I'm getting confused. I'm acting like a teenager. I should just talk to her and tell her I love her, but I'm afraid to hear what she might say. Who do I think I am? She'd never go for me. I wish I knew her thoughts. No, maybe I'm better off not knowing. I wish Tony were here.

Mercifully she broke the silence.

"You know, Bill, I love Key West. I've lived in all kinds of places all over the world and although I've only been here two weeks, I've never been happier anywhere else. The people here are real. They live their lives the way they want, without pretense. What you see is what you get. I feel very comfortable and accepted. I've made more true friends here in those two weeks then I have in my whole life."

"I'm happy to hear that Iris. I hope I'm privileged to be counted in that lucky group."

"Of course, Bill. You're right at the top."

My heart soared when she said that. But, what kind of friend did she mean? At least, I'm at the top of a list.

We arrived back at the slip just as Old Sol was sinking into the sea. I secured the boat and we gave it a thorough cleaning to get all the sand out. We left her like we found her.

"Thank you for an adventurous day, Bill. I'll always remember it, especially that squall. Thank you for letting me take charge of sailing the boat, it brought back many pleasant memories for me. I'd like to do this again sometime."

"Anytime, Iris, just say the word. Would you like to meet at Maury's tonight for dinner?"

"I'd like that. Say about seven?"

I dropped her off at the hotel and then drove back to an empty house. I took a shower and put on the Key West uniform, shorts, tee shirt and sandals and headed for Maury's.

I walked into the bar at about six thirty and I sat down on a bar stool, Maury put a cold draft beer in front of me.

"Tell me how did you make out at the Casa Marina restaurant, Bill?"

"We really enjoyed it, Maury. Make sure you eat out on their patio overlooking the water. You and Denise will love the atmosphere. It's a little pricey, but Iris loved it and the food couldn't have been better, so I think it was worth it. Denise sure knows how to pick them. Don't forget your dancing shoes for after dinner in their bar."

"I'm glad you both enjoyed it, I'm looking forward to going. I don't know about the dancing, though."

"I'm meeting Iris here for dinner at seven. What are the specials tonight?"

"First try Denise's new appetizer fish dip and crackers. She's putting it out free tonight to find out if it's a keeper. Here, try some."

"Hey that's good. I bet Iris will like it."

"The big special tonight is the king mackerel steak with a tomato mushroom sauce. I just had it and it's really good."

"That's all I need to know.

"Hey, look who's coming in. It's Erik and is that the same girl I saw him with the other night? She's gorgeous."

Faith looked charming with her flowing red hair simply parted in the middle wearing a beautiful green embroidered Chinese silk dress with modest slits up the sides. She widened many eyes of both men and women, in Maury's.

"Yes that's the same girl, Faith; she was married to Frank's brother who died in a plane crash a couple of years ago."

"Oh, what a shame. The poor kid," he said sympathetically.

"Frank told Erik that since they started dating he's seen a change in her for the better. That's why he talked her into coming down here hoping she could break out of her malaise. It's been two years and he thought it was about time for her to get back into the game. Erik seems to be the perfect medicine so far."

"Speaking of Frank, Denise and I are invited to lunch on board the Princess tomorrow. I'm a little nervous. I'd like to bring him something, any suggestions?"

"I know he's partial to dark rum, like Myer's Rum."

"Say, I have a special bottle of Myer's Rum, the liquor salesman gave me last Christmas. It's a limited edition made for gifts for their best customers. I bet he hasn't seen it. I'll give it to him tomorrow. Thanks, Bill."

"Always happy to help, have a great time tomorrow. You'll love his pub."

I went over to Faith and Erik to let them know I expected Iris any minute, and invited them to join us for dinner, which they happily agreed to.

Denise came by and set us up with a corner booth.

"That's a beautiful outfit, Faith," said Denise, "I wish I could wear something like that."

"Thank you, but I'm afraid I'm a bit overdressed."

"Maybe, but just think of all the men you're making happy, and all the women you're making jealous, don't you love it?"

I looked over and saw Iris walk in. I went up to her and told her Faith and Erik would be joining us. She was delighted and happy to see them together and waved.

"Oh, Bill I have to talk to Bosun Jim at the bar," she said. "I'll join you in a minute."

She went over and they talked a bit and then shook hands. She headed back to our table greeting several friends on the way. In her readily adopted Key West style of dress she looked terrific in a sleeveless white blouse, khaki shorts, and sandals.

"What's this foreign intrigue going on with Bosun Jim?" I asked. "I saw you shake hands with him."

"I just congratulated him for something he did a few days ago and it's a secret, I told you. You'll find out about it in good time if it all works out as planned."

"It looks like I'm a little overdressed tonight," said Faith, looking at Iris' outfit, "Erik should have told me we were coming to Maury's."

"I don't think she's overdressed, do you, Iris?" said Erik.

"You look fine, Faith. Just be glad you're with a gentleman friend, there are a flock of hungry eligible bachelors in here, take my word for it. Although, I'll say this for them, they are good dancers."

Denise arrived with what was becoming a tradition with us, a basket of conch fritters. She said hello to Iris and took the order for drinks. She told us about the king mackerel steak special for the night and highly recommended it. We all ordered it with great anticipation.

"I've been telling Faith a little about our treasure hunt for that sunken Spanish treasure ship," said Erik, "Of course so far all we've found are some real old liquor bottles that we donated to Maury's collection over there."

"If treasure were easy to find," said Faith, "There wouldn't be any left."

"That's right, Faith," said Iris, "Men are so impatient."

"Are you a scuba diver, Faith?" I asked.

"Oh, heavens no, I barely know how to swim. I like land sports like skiing, hunting, and freshwater fishing. My late husband and I enjoyed things like that. In fact, even in Frank's big beautiful yacht, I can't relax until we're tied up at the dock."

"I thought maybe you could give us a hand looking for the treasure, but that's okay I understand."

"I certainly wish I could. Maybe there will be some other way in which I could help. Maybe you'll think of something."

"Hunting! You never told me you liked hunting," said Erik. "With a gun?"

"Naturally with a gun, but I also like archery season. My father has always been an avid hunter since childhood, like his own father. He went on several safaris in Africa and took me on his last one, when I was only seventeen. The home I grew up in looked like a museum with all kinds of mounted heads and African native paraphernalia."

"You mean you actually shoot animals?" asked Erik in disbelief.

"Of course, that's what hunting is. Unlike my father, I just kill what I will use. He hunted for trophies, although I did have my first deer head mounted, but I used the meat. I like venison and some birds, so I really only hunt deer, turkeys, pheasant, and quail."

"Wow, just when you think you know someone."

"Oh, stop it Erik. It's something I grew up with. It's natural to me."

"Do you dress the animal after you kill it?"

"Of course, you can't eat it the fur and the bones. What's your problem? You must know how we get that steak you're so fond of? I just do the same thing for my venison."

"The deep sea fishing I do is hunting." I said, "You have to know your prey's habitat, season, feeding habits etc."

"You're right Bill. I use the same techniques on land. It's not as easy as it looks. There's a lot of preparation, equipment, and many hours stalking. Don't forget the times you come home empty handed."

"What kind of guns do you have?" I asked.

"For the deer I use a Winchester 270 with a scope, which my father gave me. I have a twelve-gauge double barrel shotgun for the birds. I also have a modern muzzleloader flintlock rifle and archery equipment for those seasons. It's great sport."

"I'd like to see your guns sometime. I have a German Luger and a reproduction western style lever action Winchester Model 1873 rifle like the one John Wayne uses to defend himself in the movies, the gun that won the west. I keep them in Maury's vault out back here. I don't suppose you have them with you down here?"

"No, the only gun I have when I travel is in my purse. I'd like to shoot that John Wayne rifle sometime though, Bill."

"You have a gun in your purse!" asked an incredulous Erik.

She opened her purse and pulled out a small black thirty eight-caliber revolver.

"I'm licensed to carry and I know how to use it."

"Is it loaded? And, have you ever used it?" asked Erik sheepishly.

"Now, why would I carry an empty gun? Of course it's loaded. No, I haven't shot anyone, so far. I've had to show it a couple of times and that did the job, so I don't have any notches on the handle... yet."

"I guess I better behave myself when I'm around you."

"That's right; I'd hate to have to shoot you."

"Don't even kid about that, Faith."

"Oh, don't worry, I wouldn't shoot to kill. I know all the vitals, the heart, liver, kidneys etc. I wouldn't ventilate you there; like in the movies when the good guy gets shot it's always a flesh wound. That's what I'd give you."

"I feel much better now, knowing you won't ventilate my vitals."

"Enough you two, let's change the subject," said Iris, "How come Maury has a vault? And I didn't know you had guns, Bill."

"I bought them during the war. I used to bring them out on the patrol boat.

"This used to be a bank many years ago, and they built the building around the vault. It would have been too expensive to remove, so Maury got a free vault when he bought the building. It's huge. He'd be happy to show it to you any time."

Denise brought the dinners and made sure we had everything we needed. It was a well-known fact at Maury's that the conversation tapered off when the food arrived.

"I didn't think I would finish it," said Faith, "but I managed to eat the whole thing."

"I know what you mean," I said. "We rarely walk out of here with a doggy bag."

Denise came by and cleared the table and asked about dessert and coffee. The girls both ordered coffee and said they couldn't eat another thing, but asked what the desserts were.

She said the two desserts tonight were a pineapple upside down cake and their usual Indian pudding. The girls decided to split the pineapple upside down cake and Erik and I ordered the Indian pudding with coffee.

Afterwards, we walked the girls over to the La Concha Hotel and Erik continued on with Faith to the Princess.

In front of the elevator, we quickly kissed good night, and she said she would see me in the morning. I headed back to the house with a little spring in my step. As I approached the house, I noticed someone on the porch. It turned out to be Nicole.

In her broken English and panicky voice, "Oh, Bill thank God you came home. I didn't know who else to turn to. I'm so worried about Jacques. He told me he would be at the yacht at seven, but he never showed up. I looked in at Maury's thinking he may be with you. I didn't want to disturb you with your friends."

"You should have, Nicole. You know Jacques is my closest friend, and I would do anything for him. I didn't see him at the house earlier, so I just assumed he was with you. The only other place I can think of is down at the boat, but why?"

"I did walk down there, but I didn't go on the boat. I called his name but no one answered."

"Let's take a walk and see. Let me get the keys and a flashlight."

While in the house I checked his room just to make sure. We headed down to the boat and from a distance, everything looked normal. But when we went on board, I noticed right away the unlocked door, so I knew something was wrong. I shone the light into the cabin and there to my dread, I saw Jacques lying on a bunk, tied up with a piece of tape over his mouth. He wasn't moving, and I feared the worse, until he turned his head.

Nicole let out a sob and ran to his side, and she carefully removed the tape. It took us quite a bit of time untying the intricate knots.

"Are you okay? You can thank Nicole for us finding you."

"Thank you, Nicole. I'm glad to see both of you. I'm fine, just stiff from being in this position so long. I've been tied up here since six thirty. I heard you calling me, Nicole, but I couldn't answer because of the tape."

"It's about eleven now. You're lucky you had a date with Nicole; otherwise you'd be here until morning. Erik and I would have gone to bed assuming you were still out with her. So, tell us what happened?"

"I came down to do a quick check on the boat, and they surprised me. There were two of them with masks on. They sure knew their knots. They trussed me up tight like a turkey, I couldn't move and with that tape I couldn't yell for help. When I saw how big and strong they were, I thought for sure they were going to work me over. They hustled me into the cabin and to my relief they were very gentle with me. Neither one of them spoke all the time they were here."

"Why did they do this to you?" asked Nicole.

He held out his hand showing a piece of paper with fifty percent printed in large letters.

"They shoved this into my hand as they left."

"This is a warning," I said, "letting us know, what they're capable of. Did you notice anything about them that would help to identify them such as a ring, a scar or tattoo?"

"They took me by surprise, Bill. They scared me; I can't remember anything unusual about them."

"I know, Jacques, forget it for now, maybe tomorrow you'll think of something."

I reached under the sink and found the bottle of rum and offered it to him. He took a good swig and handed it back.

"Thanks, Bill I guess I needed that. I'm sorry to have you see me like this, Nicole."

"I don't care about that, I'm just glad you're safe."

They delivered their notice, and they want half of what we find. I wish I knew who they were. I don't think it could have been Joe Stalker and his Nazi friends. They wouldn't have been so gentle. It has to be someone else who found out about the cylinders.

"As far as tomorrow is concerned, you can take the day off and stay at the house."

"Oh no, I'm not staying at the house alone. They may call on me again."

"I don't think so. They put their message across, loud and clear; no one gets hurt if we cooperate. They'll be in contact with us, at some point, to arrange how to transfer the goods to them. Anyway, wait until tomorrow and see how you feel."

"You must be hungry," said Nicole, "Let's get you back to the house and I'll fix you something."

"That would be really nice, Nicole. Now that you mention it, I am quite hungry and thirsty. Let's go."

By the time we reached the house Jacques had worked out the stiffness of being in one position for so long. He downed two glasses of water and sat down. Nicole made him a sandwich and put on a pot of coffee.

Erik came in and was surprised to see Nicole. When we explained what had happened. He became upset and started to blame himself for bringing all this trouble on us.

"I'd never forgive myself if something happened to Jacques."

I interrupted Erik and excused myself and asked him to step into the front room with me. When we got there I motioned to keep his voice down.

"I'm sorry to interrupt you, Erik, but I was afraid you may mention the Nazi gold in front of Nicole."

"You're right," he said in a lowered voice. "I was going to do just that. Thanks, Bill.

"Poor Gerhard died because of it and that kindly old pawnbroker ended up in a wheelchair. I wish I never heard about those cylinders."

"Now listen," I said quietly. "We're all grownups here. None of us are blind to the fact that there's an element of danger in an undertaking like this, with so much gold involved. We're all aware about the die-hard Nazi group determined to grab it for their cause and now it looks like someone else is out there looking to deal themselves in. We've got to keep this project under wraps or there'll be more incidents like this.

"Erik, you didn't cause any of this, it's just plain old fashioned greed bringing out the worst in people."

"I guess you're right, Bill. But, this event tonight with Jacques has me worried. It could have been serious. What are we going to do to protect ourselves?"

"Well, for starters, I'm going down to Maury's tomorrow and pick up my Luger. I don't like having it around, but this thing with Jacques, like you say, could have turned out very different. If they want to play rough, we'll show them how rough is played in Key West.

"Now let's join Nicole and Jacques."

Wednesday, January 26, 1966

The next morning, brought a cold front down from up North with the temperature dropping down into the mid fifties; I thought it would be too cold for scuba diving, so I called it until the next good day. It worked out well, because after the threatening ordeal Jacques just went through, we needed to get together and discuss our options. Also, Iris needed time to practice for the knot-tying contest coming up. So, the four of us spent the morning at the house talking things over. Jacques remembered something about the two assailants.

"I distinctly recall the strong smell of sauerkraut from one of them and beer from both of them."

"That could mean," said Iris, "That one of them is German or he just likes sauerkraut. How can that help us?"

"The other thing is they were good at tying knots," said Erik.

"That's for sure," I said, "Nicole and I had a hard time untying those knots. Some of them were quite unusual."

"I wish I could have seen those knots," said Iris, "They must have been trained in some branch of the military where knots are very important, maybe on board a naval ship like Bosun Jim. He's good with knots."

"Or commando training," said Erik, "we used all kinds of knots in the OSS. On missions we used ropes to scale and rappel walls and buildings. Frank has two former U. S. Navy UDT's working on his yacht."

"That's right," said Jacques, "Bill told us about them that night on the way to the yacht. But Frank owned up to them when you asked him if he had any divers aboard. I'm sure he's not involved in this."

"I agree with you, but remember how he said they were quite muscular?"

"I see where you're going." said Jacques, "I wonder... did they serve sauerkraut in the yacht's galley yesterday? I'll call Nicole and find out."

Jacques called Nicole and found out that they did indeed serve sauerkraut.

"Somehow, they got wind of our project," I said. "I don't suppose that sauerkraut is enough proof. We've got to get them to admit they are blackmailing us."

"They're good at tying knots," said Iris, "Maury's Nautical Knot Night is coming up. I bet they couldn't resist entering the contest, if they knew about it. Maybe, Maury could serve some kind of sauerkraut special."

"That's a great idea, Iris," I said, "They're known to be big drinkers. If we were nice to them and bought a few rounds, maybe we could cajole them into spilling the beans. I'll talk to Maury and see if we can make it an Oktoberfest Nautical Knot Night. Try saying that three times fast. We'll make sure the Princess Iris gets plenty of printed flyers."

"I'll have Nicole give them each their personal copy," said Jacques.

The next two days Thursday and Friday, weather wise were the same. I took advantage of the time off to get to know Iris better. I gave her a Cook's tour of the island, and I introduced her to just about everyone I knew. She was aware that Key West allowed people to be their own unique selves, but a couple of them we met were real space shots. Anywhere else in the country, they would probably be locked up, like the fellow who still wore a funnel on his head to protect his brain from the Russian Sputnik that orbited the earth back in 1957. It burned up a few months later as it fell from orbit, but that didn't convince him. He claimed he could see it every night traveling across the sky. Most were just a little quirky, but all were kind and gentle folks just doing their thing. She marveled at all of them and made me realize what a rare gift Key West was.

Thursday and Friday (Cold Weather)

Again, I felt it too cold to go out on the water. Jacques took advantage of the time and baked plenty of cookies for the freezer and tried out some new recipes on us. Iris practiced her knot tying. Erik caught up on his sleep and I got to read my fishing magazines that were piling up. Both evenings we ended up at Maury's for a nightcap.

Saturday, January 29, 1966

The morning of Maury's Oktoberfest Nautical Knot Night, being a Saturday, Iris went to Temple. Around noon Faith came to the house as prearranged to help Iris pick out her handgun. Faith tried to talk Erik into buying a gun, but he wouldn't hear of it. He said he had seen enough of guns during the war. Iris on the other hand became quite interested. I agreed to drive them up to a gun shop in Marathon. Erik and Jacques passed on the offer to come with us.

Iris soon came up the back walk, all ready to become an armed citizen. We hopped into the old Chevy truck and headed up A1A. Iris suggested we stop and get something to eat on the way. Faith said she felt like a hot dog. I knew a place that had foot long hotdogs, about halfway to the gun shop. That sounded good to them, so twenty minutes later we pulled into Otto's Hotdog Heaven. A big sign stated "Hotdogs every Which-a-Way".

"With a name like Otto," said Iris, "he has to have good frankfurters."

"He sure does," I said, "wait till you see this place. He's got a hundred ways to fix a hotdog."

The girls had never seen anything like Otto's. You get your foot long hot dog and decorate it yourself at a huge toppings bar. He had chili, cheese, onions, a huge selection of mustards and relishes, sauerkraut, jalapenos, catsup, mayo, pickled peppers, and on and on. I got a kick out of watching the girls go through the line putting a little of this and a little of that, until the hot dog disappeared. We went outside and sat at a picnic table equipped with rolls of paper towels, which soon became obvious why.

"How am I going to eat this?" asked Iris, "My mouth isn't big enough."

"I'll show you how," said Faith.

She picked it up with both hands and took a big bite, with some of the toppings sliding down her chin. She grabbed for a paper towel wiped it away and went in for another bite.

"It's delicious, Iris! Go for it," she managed to say with her mouth full.

Faith and I laughed at Iris daintily nibbling at it to avoid getting messy. She finally gave up and dove in. I handed her some paper towels and we all had fun eating the sloppy dogs.

After a visit to the rest rooms we were all cleaned up like nothing ever happened. We hit the road again and in a half hour pulled into the gun shop parking lot.

With Faith's expertise on guns I left them on their own. I looked around and bought some gun oil and shells. They spent quite a while trying to decide on the kind of pocket gun for Iris. They narrowed it down to a small 22-caliber snub-nosed chrome plated revolver. Faith recommended a revolver for a first gun because of its simplicity of use and easy maintenance.

The shop owner took us all out back and gave her a quick course on using it. Iris was a natural and in only a couple of reloads started to hit the target like a pro.

On the way back to Key West, Faith captivated us with her description of the safari to Africa with her father. She detailed how she stalked a tiger and as it was charging directly at her shot it. The heavy caliber bullet did its job, but that didn't prevent the momentum of the oncoming cat from slamming into her knocking her down. Unharmed, she untangled herself and stood looking down at the magnificent animal. Her father congratulated her on the fine shot she had just made. She dropped the rifle and looked at him ashamed and began to cry for ending the life of such a splendid, wild, and free animal. It resulted in a confrontation with her father over the senseless killing of wild animals just for trophies and leaving their carcasses to rot. From that day on, she vowed never to hunt and kill an animal unless she used the meat herself or gave it away to someone who needed it.

Iris and I both heartily agreed with her.

We stopped at the police station and saw the chief. After asking her a few very serious questions, he gave Iris a license to carry.

I dropped Faith off at the yacht and Iris at the hotel then drove to the house to get ready for the big contest.

A good two hours before the contest all six of us arrived at Maury's. People were arriving early to get good seats so the place was nearly filled up for the big event.

Maury had his organizing hat on running around setting up everything for the contest. They had a total of thirty-four entrants at ten dollars each. Nine of them were women. The grand prize turned out to be one hundred and seventy dollars with the same amount going to Toys for Tots.

A four piece German band including, of course a big tuba began setting up with all four musicians decked out in their lederhosen. It looked like another memorable night at Maury's.

The rules of the contest were quite simple. A tied knot would be held up and its name announced. Everyone would be given plenty of time to complete the knot. Bosun Jim would then inspect each knot and if someone tied it incorrectly they would be eliminated. After several times with each knot getting progressively harder eliminations would take their toll and the group would be down to just a handful of serious contenders. Then the format would change and a time limit of three minutes would be introduced to correctly tie a knot to Bosun Jim's approval. When the three minutes were up, anyone with an improperly tied or unfinished knot would be eliminated. This would go on until we had a winner.

"Hi Maury," I said, "Looks like a big night tonight. Oh, how did you make out with your lunch on Frank's yacht?"

"I have to tell you, Denise and I were treated like royalty; everything from soup to nuts. We had an elegant time. And that English Pub, I couldn't believe it. You'd swear you were in England. I told him next time he comes to Maury's everything's on the house. Oh, and he loved the special edition Myers's Rum I gave him. Thanks for the suggestion, Bill."

"I'm glad to hear it, he seems like a regular guy in spite of all his money."

"I agree, Bill. He doesn't talk down to you."

"Lets face it Maury, no one talks down to you!"

"Oh, I get it because of my height. That's a good one, Bill.

"Hi everybody, how are you doing? Iris are you ready for the contest?"

"I'm a little nervous, Maury, but I'm as ready as I'll ever be."

"Oh, you'll be fine. Bill had a great idea to make tonight a German Oktoberfest. I brought in six kegs of German Draft beer and lots of pretzels. A German cook friend of mine from a Key Largo restaurant agreed to do the meal tonight, and he brought along an oompah band. The special tonight is Beef Sauerbraten with Sauerkraut and Spaetzle. Oh, by the way those two UDT's, you asked me about, one of them signed up for the contest. Yes sir, this is going to be a big night. Again, good luck Iris. I'm rooting for you."

"Thank you, Maury; I'll do the best I can."

Denise all smiles greeted the six of us and led us to our reserved regular booth, where a large bowl of pretzels greeted us.

Being Nicole's first time in Maury's, Jacques pointed out some of the salvaged objects and how they came to be here. She was impressed with the fun ambience and the building excitement ahead of the contest.

Bosun Jim put up a display of dozens of knots next to "Old Mariah", some of them quite intricate.

Maury arranged to have benches put out on the sidewalk to accommodate the growing numbers.

Iris, anticipating the contest, couldn't eat anything. We all ordered the German draft beer except for Iris, who opted for a Coke and everyone agreed to wait until after the contest to enjoy the German Special.

"I see our two suspects are here," I said. "Maury told me just one of them entered the contest. We'll keep tabs on them and wait until they're well oiled up before we try to get them to talk."

Bosun Jim came by to wish Iris luck and showed her an unopened letter.

"I got it today, Iris and I'm afraid to open it before I host the contest tonight. Afterwards, I'd appreciate it if you would be with me when I do."

"Of course, Bosun Jim I'd be glad to. I just know it will be good news."

"I hope so, Iris, I hope so. Well, good luck tonight. Try and relax and be yourself, you'll do well."

"Thanks, Bosun Jim."

"What did he mean by all that?" I asked.

"I told you before; it's a secret between Jim and me. I'll let you know all about it later."

The time finally arrived to start the contest, and Bosun Jim rang Old Mariah a couple of times to quiet the jovial gathering.

"Maury asked me to tell you that everyone who drops out gets a genuine German draft beer on the house as a consolation prize. So, there are really are no losers here tonight. Okay, let's get started. Is everyone ready?"

The entrants all let him know that they were.

He held up a sample and announced the first knot. It's a square knot. Everyone in Maury's fell silent as thirty-four pairs of hands busily began tying the simple knot then proudly held it up for Jim's careful scrutiny. He patiently meandered through the crowded bar and out onto the sidewalk inspecting each held up knot.

"Well, that's a new one. Pat yourselves on the back. That's the first time everyone got the first knot right. I see you've been practicing. I think these knot enthusiasts deserve a round of applause."

A burst of applause and cheers encouraged the contestants as they prepared for their next challenge.

Bosun Jim announced the next knot, a clove hitch. This knot took a little longer for everyone to tie. Again, he verified each contestant's attempt and had to reluctantly disqualify several knots. Sympathetic sighs were heard as he announced each incorrectly tied knot.

The third, fourth and fifth knots resulted in reducing the number of entries down to sixteen. He called a fifteen minute intermission, and the finalists were asked to all assemble on the dance floor where chairs were provided. The oompah band started up and the sound level in Maury's returned to almost normal.

The former UDT being amongst the sixteen used the timeout to go to the bar and have a beer along with his running mate.

This prompted Bosun Jim to say to him, "Better go easy on that, you're going to need a clear head for the next round of knots."

"I can tie anything you can come up with, drunk or sober," he wisecracked.

"Oh, is that so?" Bosun Jim coolly replied, "We'll see."

His partner quickly said, "He's just kidding, Boats. Ain't that right?" nudging his partner.

"Yeah, sure, just kidding," he said sarcastically.

Bosun Jim walked away without responding.

"So far so good, Iris," I said.

"Those were the easy ones, Bill. I'm worried about the ones coming up next. I guess I better go up and take a seat."

"Good luck, Iris," we all said in unison.

She smiled and headed for the dance floor.

Bosun Jim signaled the band to wind down and then rang "Old Mariah" to get everyone's attention again. He gave each participant a dowel, a metal ring and an extra length of line to use in tying the next series of knots.

"Now, we start the timed part of the competition. I will hold up a sample of the knot, announce the name, and then ring the bell to start. Each contestant will have three minutes to complete his or her knot. I'll let you know when there is one minute left and then when the time is up, I'll ring the bell. Is everyone ready?"

All sixteen hopefuls gave a sign of their readiness.

Holding up a sample he announced, "The first knot is a Bowline," and rang the bell.

At the end of two minutes he announced, "one minute left."

A minute later he rang the bell.

"Let's see how you did."

He checked each knot and disqualified three.

"I tied that knot a dozen times last night," said one of them with a laugh, "my mind just went blank tonight."

As the three left the floor and headed to the bar for their German draft, they received a round of applause. The three empty chairs were removed.

Bosun Jim announced the next knot and when the times up bell rang, four more chairs were removed. Six men and three women remained.

These nine really knew their knots, and it took a dozen more bells to whittle them down to the last two, Iris and the surly UDT.

Bosun Jim announced another fifteen-minute intermission, and the band started up and the excitement and noise level reached record levels.

Iris came over to the booth and sat down. She looked exhausted.

"Congratulations, Iris," I said.

"I haven't won yet."

Denise came over with a glass of ice water.

"Here, Iris have a drink of water, it will make you feel better. Your opponent is over at the bar drinking and bragging how he's going to win. My money's on you, Iris"

"Money, what do you mean money? You're not actually betting money on me?"

"Of course, I am. That's why half of the people are here tonight. There's a slew of side bets going on in here. I heard that you are the favorite."

"That's just what I need, more pressure. I hope I can live up to your expectations."

"Just do the best you can. You're a winner either way, I really mean that."

"Thanks, Denise. That means a lot to me. I better get back."

When the two remaining chairs were filled, Bosun Jim went over to the UDT and asked him his name.

The band stopped and Bosun Jim rang the bell quieting the crowd, "We're down to the last two contestants, Iris and Bob. Good luck to the both of you."

He held up a sample knot and said, "A double-fisherman's knot," and rang the bell.

At the one-minute warning, Iris held up the finished knot.

Seeing her finished knot, Bob became all thumbs as he frantically fumbled and finished his knot just in time as the final bell rang.

Bosun Jim carefully inspected Iris's knot and pronounced it good. He then looked at Bob's knot and shaking his head declared the knot tied incorrectly. Bob jumped up defiantly and questioned the decision. Bosun Jim simply rotated the knot and compared it to the sample to reveal that he tied one side of the knot backwards from the other. Red faced, Bob threw the knot down and said with disgust, "I lost to a girl."

A little sigh went around the bar followed by silence.

Bosun Jim, cupping his hand over Bob's ear, authoritatively whispered, "No, you didn't, you ass! you lost to a better knotswoman. Now suck it up and don't embarrass yourself here. Congratulate her and shake hands. Be a man for God's sake!"

All eyes were on him as he politely shook hands with Iris, saying in a loud clear voice, "Congratulations, Iris, you won fair and square."

At that, Bosun Jim held up Iris's arm and declared her the winner and the crowd went wild. Bob sheepishly headed for the bar and to his amazement he started to get pats on the back and handshakes over how good and gracious a loser he turned out to be. He couldn't believe all this sincere sudden attention. For the first time since he had been coming into Maury's, people treated him like a regular. His hard flinty veneer began to soften as he joined his sidekick, Ray, at the bar.

Maury personally served him his consolation German draft beer and shook his hand saying, "You're a real sportsman, Bob. The next best thing to a winner is a good loser."

Bosun Jim came by and shaking his hand said, "I had you all wrong, Bob. Thanks for being a good sport. I'd like you to come up and be there while I present the cash prize to Iris."

Bob agreed and the three of them assembled in front of the old bell. Bosun Jim rang it a couple of times to quiet down the bar.

"It's time to award the grand prize. But, before I do I want you all to recognize Bob here for making it a close competition. Even though he came in second, he's a great knotsman and a really good sport about losing to Iris."

A hearty round of applause brought a broad smile to Bob's face as he basked in the unforeseen praise.

"And now with great pleasure I present this trophy and the cash prize of one hundred and seventy dollars to Iris for being the new champion knotswoman of Key West. And I might add the first woman to ever do so."

Everyone especially the women were on their feet to cheer Iris. It went on for several minutes. One woman yelled, "Way to go, Iris." Someone else yelled "Speech."

Iris stepped forward and said, "Thank you, thank you. I owe this moment to my dear late father, who many years ago taught me how to tie knots. I'd like to thank Bosun Jim for his encouragement and that of all my friends here.

Now, I'm going to give back seventy dollars to Bosun Jim for Toys for Tots and with this hundred-dollars I want Maury to ring "Old Mariah" for drinks on the house."

The place came unglued.

Jacques leaned over to Bill and said, "Here we go again. It's going to be another typical night at Maury's."

"Does this mean another Key West Shindig?" asked Erik.

"It sure does look that way, Erik," I said.

Maury accepted the money and stepped up to the grand old bell and sounded the traditional eight bells and then came that hallowed ninth toll, heralding, "Drinks are on the house." Of course the special preordained rules kicked in; happy hour prices in effect for hard liquor and bottled beer until closing, whenever that was, private party signs were put out, draft beer on the house until the money ran out, and reuse your glasses.

The band started playing and the dance floor filled up. All the eligible bachelors, young and old, wanted to dance the polka with Iris before she could get back to our booth.

"By the way, Bill," said Erik. "Iris can dance the polka."

"She sure can and she's quite good at it. But, I think I better come to her aid after a few dances."

She did her best to oblige several of them, until I came to her rescue and escorted her back to our booth. On the way back I congratulated her on winning.

Erik gave her a hug and hearty handshakes were forthcoming from Faith, Nicole, and Jacques.

"Gee, Iris you were wonderful," said Faith, "I couldn't even tie my shoes correctly in front of all those people."

"I have trouble tying my necktie and that's when I'm alone," said Erik.

"Your father must have been a wonderful man to have spent so much time with you," said Nicole.

"I only wish he could have been here to see me win this contest tonight."

"I believe he does know you won tonight, Iris, and I also believe he may have helped you win," said Jacques.

"I'm sure you're right, Jacques. I thought of him with every knot I tied."

Maury's may have been in a party mode already, but Iris's donation of the free beer fueled the loud conversations, jokes, laughter, music, dancing and fun to a higher degree both in decibel level and joy. Cares and worries left the building, at least for the night. It was a beautiful thing to see.

Denise brought a glass of German draft beer for a thirsty and hungry Iris. We finally got to order the special of the night, Beef Sauerbraten with Sauerkraut and Spaetzle all around. Denise had all she could do to keep up, even with the extra help brought in for the night.

She squeezed in next to Iris and said, "I sure picked the wrong day to break in a new pair of shoes. Let me just get off my dogs for a minute and congratulate Iris. You're winning meant so much to us women and that was very generous of you to put back part your winnings for Toys for Tots and the beer. I made forty bucks on my wager on you. I'm donating twenty back to Toys for Tots."

"Thanks Denise. I'm happy you didn't lose money on me. I'm glad to give back something for all those who have been so nice to me since I came here."

"From the looks of it, they sure do appreciate it, especially the ones that bet on you. Well, I better get a move on before Maury catches me sitting down on the job. Your food will be coming right out."

The police chief arrived and took up residence on his reserved stool next to Old Mariah. Maury saw to it he received the red carpet treatment, including access to his private bottle under the bar. It was shaping up to be another memorable night in Key West.

Our meals arrived and we were all pretty hungry. Iris and Erik both pronounce the meal authentic German Cuisine. The rest of us just knew it tasted good.

Iris excused herself to go see Bosun Jim about that letter. We could see them from our booth leave Maury's and walk over to a bench under a street light. Bosun Jim opened the letter and read it. He then put his head down and Iris put her hand on his shoulder. Then, they stood up, and started back to Maury's.

Iris came back to the booth and sat down.

"Tell us about that letter, Iris," asked Erik, "I hope it wasn't bad news?"

"Now, can you tell us what's been going on with you and Bosun Jim?" I asked.

"That letter did bring him good news. Bosun Jim, hasn't seen his daughter in over twenty years. They had a nasty quarrel over a boyfriend when she was just a teenager. At his request, I helped him write an overdue apology letter. He received her response today and with apprehension waited until after the contest to open it. As it turned out, she's been longing to get back together too, so the letter was timely.

She told him that her husband left her right after the birth of their son. It was a shock to Bosun Jim to learn that he was a grandfather and that his grandson just turned twenty-one. Of course that delighted him, but at the same time he felt terrible knowing the hardship she must have endured raising him as a single parent. The saddest part for him was all the missed years of watching the boy grow up. He could have been helping her financially, even if from afar.

Bosun Jim is all excited because she will be coming down to Key West for the reunion along with her son."

"He must be very happy," said Jacques, "You did a good thing, Iris, helping him write that letter."

Interrupting us was Bob, three sheets to the wind and a little unsteady on his pins.

Sloshing his words, he spoke directly to Jacques, "I've got something to say to you. I tied you up, me and Ray and we're sorry. We heard you found some treasure and we wanted half of it. We made a lot of friends here. We love Key West and want to live here. If we stole your money we'd have to leave. We don't want to leave. Did I tell you we love Key West? We both talked it over and we're both sorry, really sorry. Can you forgive us, Jacques? Oh, and thank you Iris for the free beer."

Jacques caught off guard, didn't know what to say and perplexed looked over at me. I suggested since no one really got hurt it might be a good idea to forgive them.

Jacques readily agreed, saying, "I forgive you, Bob and Ray too. No hard feelings."

"I'm a little drunk right now, so I want to talk to you guys tomorrow or whenever on about how we can make up for our bad behavior. Sorry for the intrusion."

He walked away with a starboard list, towards the bar. We all looked at each other in disbelief.

"What just happened?" asked Faith.

"I'm not sure," I said. "It looks like the trap we set worked, only instead of having them run out of Key West, it looks like we just acquired two new friends."

"I know he had a couple of beers," said Iris, "but he did sound sincere."

"A couple of beers," said Erik. "How about a couple of dozen."

"I still think he sounded sincere, though," said Iris.

"We have to wait until he's sober and then find out for sure, if he remembers," said Jacques.

"I agree with Jacques," I said. "They are trained scuba divers and they also have other skills that may be of use to us at some time in the future. Let's hope he means it."

If the women weren't with us, this would have been a repeat of the night Erik arrived in Key West. The presence of the girls tempered our drinking and had us all sipping coffee after dessert, just as the revelry started to peak.

We escorted the girls back to their abodes and reluctantly started walking back to the house. We could hear the ruckus from Maury's two blocks away. We walked by and could see that there was one hell of a good time going on in there. Erik and I were being drawn in like a couple of moths to a flame. Jacques dutifully reminded me that we had to go to the 7:30 Mass in the morning, because Iris was coming to the house at ten for breakfast. Erik flipped a coin to decide whether he would go or stay. He never did tell us if he picked heads or tails. He just said he lost.

The three of us walked silently back to the house and were all tucked in well before eleven o'clock.

Sunday, January 30, 1966

The next morning, Jacques woke me up early, and we went to Mass. When we got back and changed, Jacques took charge of the kitchen and soon the aroma of coffee and frying bacon got the slumbering Erik's attention.

Breakfast was all ready when Iris came up the back walk promptly at ten. Jacques made an outstanding omelet filled with cheese, bacon and onions with flattened Cuban bread toast on the side. The four of us sat down and put away his classic breakfast. We were well fortified for an afternoon of treasure hunting. Jacques refused any help cleaning up and insisted we enjoy another cup of coffee before we go.

"I don't miss the hangover we might have had this morning," said Erik, "and Jacques' cure for it."

"What's the cure," asked Iris. "Is it a home remedy?"

"I wonder? Hey Jacques, is it a Voodoo thing?"

"I don't believe in Voodoo," said Jacques from the kitchen, "but some Haitian people do. No that's a cure I made up myself and perfected it on Bill."

"Please, leave me out of it."

Jacques coming out on the deck said, "I needed a… I almost said victim, anyway I needed someone to test it on to get the right proportion of tomato juice, lemon and TABASCO and a couple of secret ingredients. It took a little time, but we finally got it perfected. Right, Bill?"

"Isn't there something else we can talk about?"

"No, I'm interested," said Iris, "It sounds like hangovers are common around here. You must be big party guys?"

"Not me," said Jacques, "I'm not the big party guy around here, I never have hangovers."

"That was years ago." I said, "We better get ready to go."

"But, we just got the final recipe perfected a few weeks ago."

"You're not helping me here, Jacques." I said feeling my face getting red.

"All I know, Iris don't ever try it," said Erik, "Its strong medicine, maybe even worse than the ailment."

"Oh, so you've had need for it?"

"Well ah, just once, the night I arrived in Key West, I helped Bill celebrate with Jacques the day he got the big tip."

"There you go again, bringing me into it. Let's get going."

"So, it sounds like you're the big party animal, Bill."

"I can't deny I like a good time, but I wouldn't say I'm a party animal. Look at last night, Erik and I behaved ourselves, and we woke up this morning without the need for the cure."

"That's true," she said, "and I'm sure there are dozens of hangovers in Key West this morning."

"That's for sure," said Jacques. "That fellow Bob who tied me up is having a beauty right now. If he remembers what he said last night and we do become friends, I'll give him the recipe."

"So, what do you say, we get this show on the road," I pleaded.

Iris and Erik left first and drove the sled to the boat ramp.

Jacques and I took the truck and brought all the gear down to the boat, shoved off and picked up the sled at the boat ramp and then picked up Iris and Erik on the adjacent floating dock. The weather turned beautiful again and we were all in good spirits. An hour later, Iris and I were being towed along on the diver's sled, scanning the bottom.

"I think I saw something!" Iris shouted leaving the sled.

I followed, wondering what she saw. She swam back to a sandy area, which I couldn't see anything unusual about. She waved the metal detector over it and waved me on. My heart started beating faster. We both started scooping the sand away revealing several cylinders. We kept digging and found a total of nine. Gerhard thought there were nine in each box.

The boat circled around and waited overhead. I surfaced with one of the cylinders out of sight and gave the thumbs down sign for any onlookers. Then I told them to unhook Iris' little door. I submerged and came up on that side of the boat and slipped the heavy cylinder through. Iris and I, elated by the discovery, happily made the four more trips for the elusive gold-filled cylinders and slid them through the little hatchway unseen.

"You found them all!" said Erik in a low voice as we surfaced.

We pulled ourselves up onto the transom platform. Jacques helped us off with our gear and we stepped over the transom trying to look dejected. I picked up one of the heavy cylinders, holding it down and out of sight. It was a beautiful verdigris color with that despised Nazi symbol of the eagle holding a swastika above a serial number clearly engraved on the side. As I held it in my hand, my thoughts drifted back to that day during the war. Who could have imagined, on that wild morning long ago when bullets were flying, these cylinders worth a fortune were secretly being sent to the bottom.

"You can thank Iris for spotting them. I don't know how she knew they were there. I would have kept on going."

"You'll spot the next one, Bill. I've just had a little more experience than you."

I couldn't resist the urge to open one. I asked Jacques to get a couple of wrenches and I took the heavy prize into the cabin. As we all gathered around, Jacques held the cylinder and I placed the wrenches and twisted. Surprisingly, the cover loosened more easily than I thought it would after all those years on the bottom, and I unscrewed it the rest of the way by hand. The neoprene O-ring still retained its resiliency, keeping the threads of the cover and the interior of the cylinder dry. Inside a wad of cotton kept the coins stationary like in the one Gerhard smuggled home. I pulled out the cotton exposing a gleaming gold coin that left us all speechless. Iris then summed it up for all of us.

"Es ist ein wunderbarer Anblick!" (It is a wonderful sight!)

"Those Germans really knew how to make things," said Erik. "My father would love to see one of these cylinders."

"Yes, dad would appreciate the workmanship," said Iris, "but not the reason they were made."

We all went back out and Jacques being the last one got our attention from inside the hatchway to show us a bottle of champagne. He disappeared and a couple of minutes later we heard the cork pop and waited with anticipation. Carrying a tray with a coffee pot and some mugs he came out and gave us each a mug, then in plain sight poured the champagne from the coffee pot. There the four of us pretending to be drinking hot coffee on this beautiful Sunday afternoon in Key West, discreetly toasted our good fortune and sipped champagne. I looked into Iris's blue eyes made even bluer by the turquois water surrounding us, and told her I loved her, to myself.

It was four o'clock, so we called it a day and excitedly headed in with our treasure. We each would take two cylinders and I would carry three back to the house. I emphasized the need to keep this find to ourselves. We discussed secrecy at great length all the way back. We all agreed to absolutely not tell a living soul. We dropped Erik and Iris off at the boat ramp with the sled and proceeded to the dock. Jacques and I cleaned up the boat and loaded all the gear onto the truck. We stopped off to have the empty tanks filled at Jake's. We got back to the house around 6:00 o'clock. We saw the trailer with the diver's sled in the back yard, but the wagon was gone. Iris and Erik weren't in the house so we wondered where they were.

Around seven o'clock, we heard the wagon pull in.

"What happened?" I said, "Where have you been?"

"When we got back here, I called the yacht," she said, "and found out that Frank had just arrived this morning. I told him about the cylinders and he wanted to see them. We brought a couple of them over and he looked at all the coins. He said one of them could bring two thousand dollars at auction."

"What the hell happened to the secrecy we all pledged to?" I said angrily, "Who else did you tell?"

"Well," said Erik hesitantly, "I showed them to Faith, but she won't tell anyone."

Iris filled up and said, "I only tried to help! I didn't think you meant Frank. He won't ever say anything."

"I thought we agreed to keep it to ourselves until we retrieved all the cylinders. It may be a long time before we find the rest of them. Now, there are six people that have to keep a secret."

"Seven," said Jacques, "You know, when we were at Jake's and I went over to the grocery store to get a few things? I ran into Nicole and I couldn't help but tell her."

"Oh, great!" I said my voice rising, "Let's go down and tell Maury, and then tell him not to say anything. You don't understand what's going to happen. It's just too much to ask of someone, not to talk about something this monumental. You all just did it, and you have the most to lose. All of Key West is going to know. We'll surely have company out there now."

"Well, you won't have my company out there," said Iris tears starting, "I quit! Keep your old cylinders."

She marched through the front room and stormed out the door, jumped into the wagon and drove off.

"That's just what we need now, fighting amongst ourselves. Erik, go after her and try to get her to come back. She's a crucial part of this thing and may be the only one who can spot those cylinders out there."

"I'll try, but I have to tell you, once she digs in her heels, that's it. She really knows how to hold a grudge."

Erik headed for the La Concha to try and catch up with her.

In the meantime Jacques and I went about hiding the cylinders in the cistern like we had planned. We went under the deck through the floor hatch and probing around located the main drain just a few inches below the surface. The clay pipe broke easily with a hammer to make an opening. Jacques put a cylinder in and, using an old bamboo fishing pole, I pushed it into the cistern. We repeated that eight more times. I formed a piece of tin to tightly wrap around the hole in the pipe and covered it all up with dirt. We then went back up through the hatch onto the deck.

Jacques put on some coffee and we waited anxiously for Erik to come back.

"She's not at the hotel. I saw the wagon over near the yacht. She must have gone to see Frank."

"All we can do now is wait and see what happens." I said.

An hour later, Frank called us saying he had Iris there all upset. He calmed her down and talked her into going back to renew the search for the cylinders. She would be there at eight in the morning. He told me to try and act like nothing had happened. I thanked him for helping and explained briefly our side of the story.

Erik and Jacques, listening, got the gist of the conversation.

"Frank must be pretty persuasive," said, Erik, "I wonder what he promised, to get her to change her mind so quickly. It must have been something big."

"He didn't go into that on the phone. If so, we'll find out soon enough. At least she's going to continue working with us. I guess I mucked up things between us."

"She'll forget about it, Bill," said Jacques, "Just say you're sorry."

"I don't know. I have a feeling it went deeper than that."

We went over to Maury's hoping maybe she would walk in. We sat at the bar and had several drafts and kept an eye on the door, but she was a no show.

Instead of a big meal we just had sandwiches at the bar and then headed back to the house.

Monday, January 31, 1966

The next morning at eight o'clock, we were all anxiously watching for Iris. Right on time as usual, she came up the back walk pretending that nothing happened. We were all walking on eggs, afraid to say the wrong thing. It was obvious though; there were still strained relations between Iris and me. Jacques had breakfast prepared, but she said she had eaten already, so she went out to hook up the trailer. Erik grabbed some French toast and a mug of coffee and followed her outside.

"We'll meet you at the boat ramp," he said.

I looked at Jacques and said, "I don't think sorry is going to cut it."

Later, on the boat, Erik whispered to me, "You're right, Iris is mad at you."

She emphasized the shunning when she said she didn't want to go on the sled with me, so I took a turn with Erik and then Jacques. She went with Erik on the first underwater quest, then alternated with Jacques. I knew there was nothing I could say that would change things, so I kept silent.

"Look at those two boats," said Jacques, "they look like they're following us."

I wanted to say, I told you so, but again I kept it to myself.

On the third rotation, Iris and Erik came up with another batch of cylinders, which they carefully slipped unseen through the little hatch. Still, she wouldn't budge on her feelings. The cold shoulder was payback for my outburst the day before, a clear declaration that "no one talks to her like that". Erik knew his sister well; carrying a grudge was simply another skill she honed with perfection.

We ended the day as usual only she went straight to the hotel, and we went on to the house. Again, Jacques and I deposited the new cylinders into the cistern as before.

We went over to Maury's and sat up at the bar. Maury asked for Iris and Erik said she had some things to do.

He leaned across the bar and whispered to me, "I heard you guys found a big brass box filled with Spanish gold doubloons from a shipwreck. Is it true?"

"Who told you that," I asked.

"It's all over the grapevine. Everyone heard it. Is it true?"

"We found a couple of gold coins, but that's all." I lied.

"I thought so; it would be pretty hard to keep any big find like that a secret, especially here in Key West. Anyways, what's your pleasure tonight?"

"I think I'd like a double scotch on the boulders."

"Make it two," said Erik.

"This sounds serious," said Maury, "want to tell me what's going on? I won't say a word."

"Let me think about it, Maury," I said, unable to keep from smiling.

"I'll just have a draft," said Jacques.

Denise came over and said, "Hey what am I? Chopped liver? How come you're eating at the bar? Last night you avoided me too."

"We're not avoiding you, Denise," said Erik, "It's just that Iris and Bill have had a falling out. He's feeling a little down."

"I'm sorry to hear that," said Denise. "Is there anything I can do? Want me to talk to her?"

"No, I don't think it would help right now," I said. "We just need a little time to let things settle down. Thanks, anyway, Denise."

"Okay, I'll leave you alone. Let me know if you need anything."

I could tell she wanted to help, but I thought it best to leave Iris alone for now. We sat at the bar for a couple of hours and had snacks with our drinks. Jacques suggested coffee would be a wise choice, and we agreed. Erik and I each ordered Irish coffee to his chagrin. I knew I was trying to drown my sorrows, but it dawned on me to ask why Erik was keeping up with me. He said that he felt bad about the whole thing. He should have talked Iris out of calling Frank, but he had to admit he couldn't resist telling Faith. In short he blamed himself for everything.

I couldn't let him take the fall. That wouldn't be fair when we all knew I caused it by opening my big mouth, and I told him so. I never should have yelled at Iris, that's what started it all. Poor Iris, I hurt her feelings, and she'll never speak to me again.

Jacques pleaded with us that it was time to go.

"We've got to get up early tomorrow," he said, "Iris will be there at eight o'clock."

"You're right Jacques," I said, "You're a true friend. And Erik here, he's a true friend too. We're all three true friends. We're the Three Amigos. Let's go home my Amigos."

We ambled back to the house and Jacques made us as comfortable as he could on the couch and chair in the front room. We said good night to Jacques.

Ernie, out of the blue, said, "My sympathies!"

Tuesday, February 1, 1966

The next morning after a shot of Jacques famous cure, Erik and I put on a good show of being normal. Iris came up the back walk right on time looking bright eyed and beautiful.

"What's for breakfast, Jacques? I'm really hungry this morning."

"Flapjacks, how many do you want?"

"Sounds wonderful, give me a big stack of them, please."

Erik and I were nursing our coffee, wondering why she was so chipper this morning. We watched as she waded into those flapjacks like a long shoreman.

"No one else eating this morning?" she asked.

"I ate earlier and these two Amigos were whooping it up last night at Maury's."

"Amigos! Where'd that come from? And what excuse did they have for celebrating?"

"Last night Bill had an epiphany and christened us the Three Amigos. The night of the Three Amigos that's what we're calling it. Those two don't need an excuse to celebrate. When they feel like celebrating, they celebrate. Anyway, that's why they're a little under the weather this morning."

"I like that, the Three Amigos; I'll have to remember it. I'm sorry you two don't feel well; do you want to cancel today?" she asked with a little hint of sarcasm and a lovely smile.

Erik and I looked at each other's bloodshot eyes and holding our coffee mugs with both hands, agreed that we were fine and could hardly wait to get out there and resume the search.

"That's good, because I have a feeling we're going to do well again today."

Iris and Erik drove the sled to the ramp while Jacques and I loaded up the boat and headed over there to pick them up.

On the way, I asked Jacques, "I wonder why Iris is so happy today. Do you think she's gotten over everything?"

"I don't know about you, but I learned early on to get nervous when a woman suddenly changes from being angry at you to being nice. In fact, an English playwright made mention of it in one of his plays over two hundred years ago. It usually means something expensive or painful is on the way."

"I don't believe that, she's just come to realize that I was right that's all."

"You're setting yourself up for a big surprise."

We backed the boat up to the ramp and hooked the towing line to the sled. They parked the wagon and came back out onto the floating dock to where we were waiting. Jacques helped them come aboard.

I headed out towards our last successful location. There were four boats waiting for us. Jacques lined up the three landmarks he had established to get us to the exact spot. He became so good at this he usually placed us within a hundred feet of a site.

Iris asked Jacques to join her on the sled for the first session and within twenty minutes she sighted the third cache of cylinders. She had a talent for spotting those subtle clues that told her that something man made was underneath. I concluded that she alone could see them and the rest of us were just going along for the ride.

They surfaced and gave exaggerated thumbs down signs and then softly called for the little hatch to be opened. Then one by one the nine cylinders were slid through the little door unseen by our encroaching spectators.

Iris and Jacques came aboard to our subdued hearty congratulations and a well-deserved rest.

"So far, Iris," I said, "You're the only one who has been successful at locating these cylinders. We may have missed cylinders in all those areas we've already covered without you. I hate to say it, but you'll have to be on that sled for every session from now on, and we may have to go back over areas we've already done."

"That's okay, I don't mind. I really enjoy this."

"I'm glad you feel that way, but this puts a big burden on you. I don't want you to overdo it, so we'll limit your underwater time to four thirty-minute sessions per day with at least an hour of rest in between. Do you think that would be too much?"

"I think that would be okay, I may be able to do more."

"We'll try it and see how it works out and adjust it to suit you. I want you to be safe."

"We've found three clusters of cylinders so far," said Erik. "Gerhard told us he thought there were about ten in all. That could mean anywhere between eight and twelve. How will we know?"

"We'll probably never know." said Jacques. "If we find eight I think we should be happy."

"I agree," I said. "After eight, we should call it quits. What do you think?"

We all agreed with the hope that we would find at least eight.

When Iris had her rest, Erik went with her on the next shift. I was getting a little apprehensive as to whether I was going to be asked. After a half hour they came aboard empty, and we waited an hour while she rested. I was relieved to hear her asked me to join her on the third and final turn of the day. About twenty minutes later, she shouted to me and left the sled. I follow right behind her and again, she found another clump of cylinders. She was amazing; she made it look so easy. We owed the success of this whole quest to her.

I went up and gave the thumbs down sign for the sake of the growing number of uninvited guests, then quietly asked for the hatch to be opened again. As before, Jacques discreetly maneuvered the boat so Iris's little hatch was hidden from our nosey guests. We happily made the trips up and down, until all the cylinders were aboard. We all celebrated, this time with a tot of rum, from the coffee pot.

On the way back, Iris informed us that Frank planned a little party on his yacht that night and the Three Amigos were invited.

"What's the big occasion?" asked Erik.

"Oh, he just wants to see all you guys again and talk things over. It should be a nice quiet informal dinner party at five o'clock. I'm sure we'll all have a good time. As Erik said, Frank knows how to throw a party."

We had the routine down now of dropping Iris and Erik off with the sled, and Jacques and I bringing the boat to the dock. This time, they had eight cylinders and we had ten, to bring back to the house. What a magnificent feeling.

Back at the house, Jacques and I made the largest deposit yet, into our cistern bank. We were confident that they were safely hidden.

Iris left to get ready for the time on the yacht. We had some iced tea on the deck and talked until the time came to get ready ourselves.

Erik hit the shower first, and Jacques and I continued to talk.

"I think Iris is coming around, she almost seemed her old self today."

"I don't know, Bill. I have a feeling that something's up. Remember what I said about a woman going from angry to nice too quick."

"Oh, you're just imagining things; I bet everything will be back to normal tomorrow. She saw those boats out there today. She knows I was right, and I don't care if she doesn't apologize. I'll let it go."

"Just be on guard, Bill. I don't want to see you get hurt."

"Get hurt? What can go wrong?"

Erik came out onto the deck looking spiffy. Jacques said he wanted to square away the kitchen so he let me be the next to use the shower. A little later Jacques took his turn.

At quarter of five we headed over to the yacht.

A block away we could hear live country music. As we got closer, we could see the band in their straw cowboy hats on board the yacht making the pleasing music.

On duty at the gangway were the two UDT's, Bob and Ray. They greeted us like long lost cousins. Bob specifically repeated to us that they wanted to make up for the terrible way they treated Jacques.

He held up a big fist with a smile and stated, "You call on us if you ever need our kind of help. We owe you big time."

"That's a generous offer," I said, "we just might take you up on that. We'll be in touch."

We all shook hands and went on board, where we were greeted by Faith and Nicole both wearing pretty sundresses, Nicole in pink and Faith in a multi-colored Hawaiian print. Frank came over and welcomed us and brought us all into his now famous English Pub.

Erik and Faith got together as did Jacques and Nicole, leaving me with Frank. He asked me what I would like from the bar and I said whatever he's drinking would be okay. A minute later I had a Myer's Rum and ginger ale in my hand. We sat up at the bar.

"Iris tells me you had quite a successful day."

Out of earshot of the bartender, I said quietly, "Yes, we've been lucky the last three days. We've come up with a total of twenty seven cylinders so far."

I figured I'd give him the correct number, since he probably knew already.

"You do have them in a secure place I hope?" He asked.

Evidently, Iris kept that secret, which made me feel good.

"Yes, I think they're quite safe. Now that you mention it, we have to come up with a plan of what to do with those cylinders when we recover them all. There may be seventy at least. They will be difficult to move because of how heavy they are."

"You're right," he said, in a low voice. "We do need a way to transport them secretly to a safe location, maybe just a few at time, so we can open each one and inventory the contents."

I sensed that he had something else on his mind, as he talked to me about the gold. He kept avoiding eye contact, which wasn't like him. I wrote it off as his excitement about the gold.

Just then Iris made her grand entrance. She looked stunning in a white shift with matching sandals. A beautiful new, heavy gold necklace adorned her neck.

She came over and said hello to me and stood next to Frank. I started to get a sinking feeling.

"Hello, Bill. Look at the beautiful necklace Frank gave me tonight."

I managed to say, "It's beautiful, Iris, and it looks very nice on you."

I took a big sip of my drink and thought; this doesn't look like it's going to be a good night for me. I suddenly became the odd man out here and the word ambush flashed before me. I had that feeling the condemned man must have, just before his last appointment. To say the least, it was an uncomfortable moment for me; if she wanted me to squirm? I was squirming.

I was at a loss for words and thankfully, at that awkward moment, Frank called us all to dinner. I brought up the rear, as we all funneled out the doorway onto the promenade deck. The band continued to play, but at a lower volume for dining. In spite of my situation, I noted the sun nearing the horizon and the heat of the day being supplanted by a light sea breeze picking up. We could look across to Mallory Square and see the crowd starting to turn west, in anticipation of a beginning ritual for tourists.

The sun methodically inched its way into the ocean releasing a burst of color on the scattered clouds. The small gathering on Mallory Square gave a cheer of approval and we, led by Frank, toasted another beautiful sunset in Key West.

Like the last time we dined here the table was lavishly set with fine white linen and his personnel china and silverware. Silver candelabras were waiting for darkness to be lit. The main course consisted of our delicious, fresh local lobster and grouper. Frank proudly declared that two of his crewmembers, Bob and Ray actually caught the lobsters and speared the grouper a few hours ago.

Everything was first class and delicious from start to finish. Fine food and wine and good conversation made the time pass in a most pleasing way for everyone, except me. Frank knew how to throw a party.

As we were waiting for dessert, two bottles of chilled champagne were uncorked and the appropriate glasses filled in front of each guest.

I started twitching, feeling the tip of Iris' knife in my back.

Frank stood up from his seat at the head of the table and stated that he had an announcement to make.

I could see it coming. I braced myself, grasping at the straws of hope.

"It gives me great pleasure to make this announcement to you our closest and dearest friends. Iris and I have agreed to renew our engagement. In front of all of you here, I return my engagement ring and my love to her."

Her imaginary knife plunged in up to the hilt. There was no blood, but the pain was real.

Iris stood up beside him and smiling put out her hand to accept the ring, a three-carat perfect white diamond in a platinum setting from Tiffany's of New York.

He slipped it on her finger. They embraced and kissed each other to the applause of all the guests.

Frank picked up his glass and asked everyone to toast his future bride. We all toasted Iris and wished the two of them the best.

The girls couldn't wait to see the gorgeous diamond, which Iris flaunted with panache. I had to admit it was quite a rock.

Dessert and coffee came next. The mini banana splits were a big hit. A tiny scoop each of strawberry, chocolate, and vanilla ice cream between a split baby banana. All topped with strawberry syrup, chocolate syrup, and pineapple topping. A sprinkle of nuts, whipped cream, and a cherry on top completed the cute finish to an elegant evening.

I felt like the banana.

The band started playing slow country dance music. Frank and Iris were the first out on the dance floor, joined by Faith and Erik, then Nicole and Jacques. It was unbearable sitting at the table by myself watching them all dancing. I finally got up and walked over and asked to cut in and dance with Iris. Frank graciously stepped aside and returned to the table.

As we danced, I said, "I hope you didn't do this just to get back at me."

"Of course not. I just realized that I might have broken up with Frank because of being afraid of close relationships, like we talked about. I have to find out."

"Well in that case, I sincerely wish you and Frank all the happiness that's possible for two people to have in this life."

I never told a bigger lie in my life and I prayed that she had just told me a whopper too.

"Thank you Bill, I appreciate that."

The dance ended, and I returned to my seat and painfully watched them all dancing. A steward asked if I'd like anything and I ordered a double scotch on the rocks. When it arrived I got up and went over to the rail and looked out over the lights of Key West. I'll just go back to where I belong, I thought.

After an hour or so and a second double scotch, Jacques and Erik came over and said they were ready to leave. The three of us said good night to everyone and thanked Frank for the superb meal and of course wished the newly engaged couple all the best.

I just experienced a very low point in my life, but as Tony would say you can't unsink a boat. What's done is done and laughter is the best medicine. So Erik and Jacques agreed to come with me to Maury's as the Three Amigos and have a few laughs.

On the way over there, I asked Jacques what that Englishman said about a woman going from angry to nice suddenly?

"That was the playwright William Congreve and he wrote, 'Hell hath no fury, like a woman scorned'."

"He got that right," I said.

The place had a pretty good crowd for a weeknight. Jimmy up on his little stage was singing and strumming with a few couples dancing. From over in the corner waving us to their table were Bob and Ray. We went over and joined them.

They were delighted to see us and bought us a round.

"I want to thank you all proper," said Ray, "For letting us off the hook like you did. Bob and I could have gotten jail time for what we did. We certainly owe you big and we won't hesitate to honor that debt any time you say."

"Well if the occasion arises," I said, "I'll let you know. What do you say, Jacques, should we consider it by the boards?"

"Absolutely," he said, "its water over the dam. We enjoyed the lobster and grouper you supplied for the dinner tonight."

They both said it was their pleasure and promised to get us some next time they went out.

"By the way would you be interested in a good recipe for a hangover?"

"Where were you Sunday morning?" said Bob, pulling out a pencil, "I had a big head all day. Yes, please give us that recipe. Does it really work?"

"Ask Bill and Erik here."

"It works for me," I said.

"It will straighten you right out," said Erik. "You've got to chug-a-lug it down quick, though."

Jacques used the pencil and wrote out the recipe on a napkin.

"So what are you doing tonight for excitement?" I asked.

"You're seeing it. We're just enjoying Maury's and making new friends. They're a good bunch in here. By the way your money's no good here tonight. We're picking up the tab."

"So, you guys were UDT's?" asked Erik.

"Yes," answered Ray. "Although, they just changed it from Underwater Demolition Teams to Seal Teams."

"I was OSS in the War."

"You were! They both said in awe. We learned all about you guys. You set a lot of the standards for our training today. I bet you were in on some serious stuff."

Erik, after a few drinks, opened up and described some of his adventures during the War in Europe. He commanded a three-man special operations Jedburgh team or Jeds for short. They parachuted behind enemy lines on sabotage missions, collaborating with local resistance forces. We were all ears and couldn't get enough. Erik captivated us all with his real life adventures behind enemy lines. He stood up and showed us how he swaggered when he impersonated a German officer. He sounded so authoritative when he barked orders in German at us that I would have obeyed him, if I knew what he said. He had us all spellbound with some of the missions he carried out with his men. Jacques and I were amazed at the extent of the wartime experiences of the mild mannered Erik that we thought we knew. He received all kinds of medals and commendations including two purple hearts. The camaraderie with Bob and Ray encouraged Erik to let his hair down and talk freely in depth about experiences that had long been suppressed.

As the hours went by, the place started to empty out. Maury came over and pulled up a chair and joined the conversation. He had a couple of stories that went back to World War One. We were all going strong, when Denise came over and told us to wrap it up.

We all stood up and looked around and were surprised to see the place was empty. We all shook hands and said good night to Denise and Maury and headed for the door.

Out on the sidewalk we said good night to our two new friends, Bob and Ray. They headed for the yacht and we headed for the house.

The Three Amigos meeting up with Bob and Ray did wonders for me. It got me off to a good start on the long process ahead of getting over Iris.

Wednesday, February 2, 1966

The next morning, it surprised me at how good I felt after such a late night. In spite of all the drinking, I didn't need Jacques cure.

Iris came up the walk right on time as usual, bringing her appetite for Jacques' good cooking.

"Good morning fellas," she said with that pretty smile of hers.

We all greeted her as Jacques handed her a cup of coffee and politely pulled out the chair for her.

"Where's your ring, Iris?" Erik quipped, "Don't tell me the engagements off again."

"Erik, don't be so dumb. You don't think I'd risk losing it out there, do you? I left it on the yacht in Franks safe.

Oh, by the way, I'm checking out of the hotel and moving over to the yacht. Frank and I discussed it last night. No sense spending all that extra money. And that hotel room was becoming claustrophobic."

Go ahead Iris; give that knife in my back a twist. I can take it.

"That's a good idea," said Jacques, "you'll save some money and it'll sure be more comfortable."

Oh please Jacques, don't you get in on the knife twisting too.

We finished up breakfast then following our routine plan of the day and thanks to Jacques reckoning, we were soon over the site of our last successful dive. This time there were five other boats in the area. We checked them out with the binoculars and recognized three but not the other two. As I had predicted the word about us finding treasure resulted in unwanted company. So far they were keeping their distance watching us through binoculars. We had to keep up the charade, or we'd have divers down below, looking over our shoulders.

"Well, Iris," I said, "that little door idea you had certainly has come in handy, along with giving the thumbs down sign and Jacques coffee pot, so far it has them hoodwinked."

"I guess I owe you an apology, Bill, I can see now that we should have kept the cylinders a secret with just the four of us."

"Forget it, Iris; so far there's been no harm done. I'm sorry I lost my temper and raised my voice to you."

"Maybe, I deserved it, but thanks anyway for not rubbing my nose in it."

"What do you say, we find some more cylinders."

Her sincere apology moved me. I started thinking that maybe she truly believed in the reason for renewing the engagement with Frank. Maybe, I had a chance after all; if she found out she honestly didn't love him and then broke up with him again.

What am I doing? What have I got to offer her? I'm just setting myself up for another big disappointment. Don't forget that knife sticking out of your back. But I do love her, and I don't want to lose her. All she'd be to Frank is just another trophy.

Erik went with her on the first shift. I noticed the boats were keeping pace with us, as we traveled along pulling the sled. I wondered how many more were going to be joining the party.

"Erik impressed me last night," said Jacques, "He has quite a war record. He really opened up with Bob and Ray."

"He's such a quiet refined man. It's hard to picture him doing all those things he described, and I'm sure he left out a lot, too."

The half hour went by and Iris and Erik came back aboard without any luck. We had some lunch and coffee and Iris went below to rest awhile. When she turned out again, I joined her for the next ride on the sled with the same results.

After another intermission, Jacques took his turn on the sled with Iris. Within minutes we felt them leave the sled. We circled around and put the engine in neutral. I unhooked the little door and sure enough a cylinder came sliding through, then another. They each brought one at a time to the side of the boat and secretly slid them through the little door. After the ninth one they surfaced to the rear of the boat, gave the thumbs down sign and came up to the transom platform empty handed.

When they were aboard, Erik filling in for Jacques had the coffee pot all ready to pour. After our celebratory libation, we stowed all the gear and headed back to the ramp. It looked like the ruse worked because the five boats went off in different directions.

"It looks like your little door worked again, Iris," said Jacques.

"So far so good, by the way, I didn't tell Frank where we were hiding the cylinders, even though he asked me. I almost did, I held back because you got so angry with us showing him those two cylinders. I'm glad I didn't now, after seeing those five boats today."

"Again, I'm sorry I blew up about that, Iris. I didn't mean anything personal."

"I deserved it. I admit I was foolish not to see what could happen. I wish I could undo it somehow."

"Don't be too hard on yourself. The next big thing now, is to start thinking about how we're going to move all those cylinders. That's going to be really difficult to keep secret."

"I'm sure we'll figure it out, Bill."

I like the way she said my name. I'm glad we're talking again.

We did the end of the day routine again, without incident. Jacques and I made another deposit to the cistern bank.

Erik produced a bottle of Bacardi white rum and announced he would make up a pitcher of rum swizzles.

"Could you have one, Iris before heading back to the yacht?" he asked.

"Oh, sure," she said, "Frank had to go back to New York for a few days, so I'm in no hurry."

"The cat's away, eh Iris?" he said jokingly.

"Please, Erik, you know me better than that."

"What do you need to make those rum swizzles?" asked Jacques.

"I'll need a pitcher, some pineapple juice, orange juice, lime and Grenadine syrup, also, a shaker and some ice."

"I think I can fix you up. I have some Myers rum you may want to add to it."

"Thanks, Jacques. Now you go sit down for a change while I demonstrate my mixology skills."

In no time at all, we were toasting our luck with a delicious rum swizzle.

"Erik," I said, "You should have been a bartender. This is a very good drink."

"Actually, I worked as a bartender my last year of college.

The first round led to a second and we all toasted again to our success so far. Then someone mentioned food. Jacques said he could whip up something.

"You deserve a night off," I said. "We're practically millionaires, let's spend some of that money, we haven't got yet. I suggest we go out and eat."

"I agree," said Erik, "That's something I've always wanted to do. Spend money I haven't got."

"If we haven't got it, how can we spend it?" asked Jacques.

"I'll show you how," said Iris, "Let's go to Maury's."

"I hope we don't end up washing dishes," said Jacques.

Off we went to the best bar in Key West. On the way Iris realized that we hadn't cleaned up and changed from being on the boat all day. She was quite concerned about how she looked. We convinced her that she looked more like a local that way. That logic seemed to satisfy her, and she suddenly felt proud of the way she looked.

As we walked into Maury's, Jimmy was singing one of his own songs and several couples were dancing. Bob and Ray waved to us from their now usual corner table. Denise greeted us and brought us to our own familiar booth.

"Can I get you anything from the bar?"

"We just had a couple of rum swizzles," said Iris, "I'd guess I'll have another one Denise."

"You guys want the same?"

"I think I'll switch to a draft," I said.

Erik and Jacques both went the same route.

"A pitcher makes more sense, boys," she said.

We all agreed and went for it.

Jacques jaw dropped as he said, "I don't believe it. Look who just walked in?"

We all looked over and there they stood bold as brass, Joe Stalker, Slip, and two other men. Maury went right over to them and a lively discussion ensued. The conversation ended, and we could hear the words, "Okay, but I'm warning you not to start any trouble."

Denise showed them to a booth as far away from us as possible. The two strangers were big men too. One had a shaved head like Joe. The other had salt and pepper colored hair neatly cut. Slip had on his usual chambray shirt with the arms torn off and the other three wore long sleeve shirts, in spite of the warm weather. Denise returned to them with a pitcher of beer and four glasses.

She brought Iris her rum swizzle and our pitcher of draft beer with three glasses.

"I supposed you noticed Joe and his buddies over there. Maury said they could stay if they behaved themselves. I hope he didn't make a mistake. I brought them their beer first, so maybe it will calm them down before they can cause trouble."

"We noticed, Denise," I said. "Do you recognize those other two men?"

"No, but the one with the hair speaks with a German accent. The bald one didn't say anything."

"Thanks, Denise; we'll keep an eye on them."

"Okay, let me know if you need anything."

She headed off toward the bar to talk to Maury.

"Those are the two men that Jake told us about," I said. "They supposedly, are chartering Joe's boat. Jake got a glimpse of a swastika on the bald guys forearm. I wonder why they came in here tonight?"

"I bet they know that we found some cylinders," said Jacques.

"How could they have found out?" asked Iris. "Surely, Frank wouldn't have told them. And I know that Faith and Nicole would never say anything."

"Maybe they don't know anything," said Erik. "I bet their curiosity drove them to the point that they had to come in here tonight just to try and find out something. That one with the hair looks familiar. If, I'm not mistaken he was the man that talked to Gerhard in the pawnshop in West Germany. I'm not a hundred percent sure though."

"If that's the case," I said, "he could have been one of the men who attacked the pawnbroker and Gerhard."

"Like I said, though I'm not sure."

"It's nice to see tricky Slip is with them," said Jacques, "we don't have to worry about him being under one of these benches."

"You've got that right," I said. "If you can't see that little scummy rat, he's probably creeped within earshot of us."

We tried to change the subject, but it kept coming back to them. Jimmy took a break and the jukebox started to play.

"Oh, Bill they're playing our song." said Iris. "That's the song we first danced to, 'Moon River'. Let's dance."

She stood up and put out her hand.

"I don't know, Iris. You're engaged."

"Hurry up before it's over."

I got up and we went out to the dance floor and started to waltz to the music. It became obvious to me that the rum swizzles were catching up to Iris. As we were dancing I got a tap on my shoulder. It was the stranger with the hair.

"May I cut in, Sir," he said politely.

I looked at Iris and she nodded okay to me. Caught off guard by his friendly manner and against my better judgment, I stepped aside as he took her right hand with his left, put his right hand around her waist, then expertly waltzed her away to the music. I walked back to the booth in disbelief and waited for what seemed ages for the music to stop.

They were talking while they were dancing, and we all were dying to know what about. She appeared to be having a grand time out there with him. The music stopped, and they stood there waiting for the next song. It wasn't a waltz, but they got right into it.

"Like I said before that sister of mine loves to dance."

"I don't like who she's dancing with, though," I said.

One of the young fellows, she had danced with before on another occasion decided to cut in. We watched as he tapped the man on the shoulder. The poor lad was pushed away so hard that he lost his balance and fell down.

"I'm going to put a stop to this," I said.

I went over and firmly tapped his shoulder and again he turned and tried to push me. I pulled his arm down and let him have it to the cheers from the irate crowd. He went down, but not for long. I told a frightened Iris to get back to the booth. Erik showed up by her side and escorted her away.

He jumped back on his feet and came at me with a vengeance, but my old boxing instincts kicked in. He charged at me with his head down and like a matador dodging a bull, I sidestepped and gave him a chop with the edge of my hand on the back of his neck that brought him down on all fours with a groan. He staggered to his feet and turned around looking for me.

"I'm right here where you left me. Do you want some more?"

I was being cockier than I probably should have been, but he got my dander up. Instead of charging me again, he walked over slowly with a purpose, putting up his fists. We faced each other, and we went around sparring and then he caught me on the side of the head. It hurt, but I managed to stay on my feet and took a swing back at him that he easily blocked. My boxing skills were pretty rusty, but one of the old tricks came to mind. I faked a right to his jaw, which he put up his hand to deflect and then I quickly faked a left to his stomach to which he instinctively lowered his both hands to evade. My right hand with everything I had, connected solidly with the lower left side of his jaw. I saw his eyes roll upward and he went down for the count.

I started walking back to the booth to an uproar of approval, when Joe Stalker tackled me from behind. At long last, we were going to settle the mutual bitterness between us. We both went down, and I managed to separate myself from him. We got up on our feet facing each other. I swung at him and he ducked. We went around sparring with each other and then he got me good on the chin. I staggered back against the bar with arms outstretched to steady myself. Seeing stars, I turned around and put both hands on the bar and as quick as a wink unseen, Maury shoved a roll of nickels into my right hand. I closed my fist on them, but then I pushed them back to him, and he quickly covered them with his big hand.

"I want to fight him fair, Maury, thanks anyway," I whispered.

A little unsteady, I walked back and the sparring began again. I felt my jaw beginning to swell up and starting to hurt. It was obvious that he was a student in the art of fisticuffs. Adrenalin kicked in, and I got a burst of needed energy. I threw a punch and tagged him on the side of the face, but that just cause him to smile at me. I managed another blow to the breadbasket, which felt like hitting a sand filled punching bag. He looked at me and again smiled with contempt. I was in trouble here, and started wishing I were somewhere else. Those nickels were beginning to sound like a pretty good idea. Giving me that big smile he faked a right jab at my head and I regretfully put both hands up to block it. He instantly followed through with a body blow with his left that took the starch out of me and sent me back against the bar again. I turned around and put my forehead down on the bar shaking my head, and I could see that Maury still had the nickels under his hand.

"I'm too old for fair, Maury."

I slid my hand under his and took hold of the roll of coins. I turned and faced my opponent. He had a smirk on his face and looked at me with scorn. He toyed with me again, jabbing and faking punches. It became a cat and mouse game to him and I was the mouse. The only thing in my favor could be his over confidence. The nickels were an edge, but I took very serious his statement that he wanted to put my lights out. I tried to keep up the bravado.

"You don't have what it takes to put me away."

Me talking back with arrogance sidetracked Joe just a little, so when his pal with the hair gave out a groan trying to get up off the floor, he mistakenly turned his head. I put the nickels to work and tagged him square on the jaw. Amazed, he reeled backwards losing his balance and fell on one knee. He quickly got back up a little wobbly on his feet. At last I had that edge, I thought.

Joe reached into his pocket and pulled out a large gold ring and placed it on his right hand finger.

"Now, I will put my mark on you, Bill Baker, the greatest charter boat captain in Key West."

He brandished the ring in my face and my stomach turned, when I got a good look at it. Prominently raised on it was that most dreaded symbol, the swastika. I couldn't let him plant that thing on me. We started to spar around, and I could tell that he was a little more cautious now; knowing if he got careless I could hurt him. I concentrated on that swastika ring and had to avoid it at all costs.

He managed to manoeuver me up against the wall. He put his left hand on my chest and holding me at arms length, threw a wild and powerful punch at my face, which I just managed to dodge causing him to put his fist into the wooden wall. He pulled his hand back in pain and shook it. I didn't waste that precious second he gave me, and I let him have it square on the jaw again. He staggered back and almost fell, but caught his balance and looked at me and to my amazement smiled again. He was one tough Nazi.

"Now, I'm going to make you pay for that," he said.

"You mean I should have stood there and let you hit me? I might be crazy, Joe, but I'm not stupid."

I'm not too smart either, to be in this fix. Then I got a wild and possibly absurd idea, hoping and praying it would work. I carefully transferred the roll of nickels into my left hand unseen, then suddenly stood at attention, raised and straightened my right arm and hand up saying, "Heil Hitler."

Joe immediately stood at attention and raising his right hand repeated, "Heil Hi…"

Before he could finish that awful greeting, my left arm and shoulder were propelling a fist full of Tom Jefferson's straight into his jutting jaw. I felt something crack and it wasn't my weighted reinforced left hand. He went down on all fours and attempted to get up. I secreted the nickels into my pocket, went to his side and lifting him up by the collar and belt dragged him stumbling across the floor ramming his head into Old Mariah. The heavy old bell made a dull gong sound, and I let go of Joe Stalker, watching as he collapsed in a heap on the floor.

Dazed, out of breath, and experiencing a little tunnel vision, I started back to the booth for the second time. The man with the hair suddenly, roughly grabbed me from behind and expertly locked my arms. He then turned me around to face the chuckling bald headed man, who calmly walked up in front of me with a broad smile and shook his big fist in my face saying something in German that didn't need any translation. He then slowly started to pull it back in delighted anticipation of putting me on the moon. Clearly, this tactic from their playbook had been used many times before. I braced myself for the coup de grace. I could feel the powerful blow coming my way. The excruciating pain would only last a few seconds and then the numbing relief of shock would set in. I knew about these things, and I was ready to accept them. The thing I regretted most was tomorrow, looking into a mirror at myself with missing front teeth. I tried with all my might to spin the two of us around to miss the blow, but his feet were too well planted.

Unbeknownst to me over in the corner the two UDT boys had been watching everything with keen interest. As soon as they saw me being grabbed from behind, they looked at each other with Cheshire catlike grins and said, "Fight!"

They were off like a couple of jackrabbits. A bigger fist suddenly covered the big fist en route my way. Bob spun him around and clocked him once, causing him to do a pirouette sending him out onto the dance floor to face Ray who planted a ham of a fist into his face knocking him flat on his back.

At the same time, Erik came to my rescue and put an arm around the neck of the man holding me, making him let go of my arms. He then let the brute go and turning him around, pushed him back. Enraged the man stepped forward with his fists at the ready. In the blink of an eye, Erik brought his left foot up and caught him under the chin causing him to stagger uncontrollably backwards across the floor and onto a table scattering those sitting around it. Seeing him stumbling backwards their way, they all managed to save their drinks and get out of the way as he indignantly planted himself flat on his back on their table. It wasn't over yet; the bald headed one with the help of the back of a chair, amazingly got up and holding a knife in his right hand staggered towards me.

Erik stepping between us, said. "Knives are my specialty, Bill."

In another swift move up came that educated foot striking his hand with such force that the knife was flung straight up, embedding its blade deeply into the wooden ceiling.

Disarmed, holding the limp hand with his left, grimacing in pain and facing Erik, the man looked around for an escape, but there was none. By now, a wall of angry people had surrounded us and started to egg on Erik.

"Give him that foot," yelled someone.

The outcome for the bald headed man was certain.

"Ich gebe auf," he glumly said, meaning, 'I give up'.

"Eine gute entscheidung," said Erik, meaning, 'A good decision'.

The silent crowded bar erupted in unbridled cheering.

"Hey, you handled yourself pretty good," said Bob, "for an old guy. It looks like Erik hasn't lost his edge either."

"Watch that old guy stuff, but I thank you for your help," I said. "You probably saved their lives. I had them right where I wanted them."

"You could have fooled us, but we don't tolerate that two against one fighting," said Ray, "I got a feeling this ain't over between you and them, so remember to call on us when they want that show down and let us in on the fun."

"And thanks, Erik," I said putting my hand on his shoulder, "I was in deep doo-doo there."

"What are friends for, I kind of enjoyed it. It's been a long time."

The police showed up with the paddy wagon and Maury, holding Slip up by the back of his shirt so his toes were barely touching the floor, stated, "They started it, and this one belongs to them."

Dozens of witnesses came forward, to corroborate the story.

"That big fellow may need medical attention," I said to one of the policemen, "I think he has a broken jaw. The bald guy has a broken wrist and the one on the table should be okay when he comes to."

"Are you all right?" he asked.

"I'm good; they got the worst of it," I said

"That's an understatement, we'll swing by the hospital first and have them all checked out."

Another policeman getting Joe up off the floor, asked, "What's this mark on top of his head?"

Maury and I went over and there clearly imprinted on Joe's head was the reverse image of Mariah transferred from the old bell.

"Well, every time he looks in the mirror from now on," said Maury, "he's going to see Mariah looking back at him. He won't ever be able to forget this day."

Then someone noticed the swastika where Joe punched the wall, and the knife protruding from the ceiling.

"Maybe we should remove them, Maury," said Denise.

"Hell no!" he said. "As time goes by they will be great reminders of the magnificent fight we saw here today."

I went back to the booth and there as neat as you please was Iris, snuggled up against the wall sound asleep.

"She's been there since I brought her back from the dance floor," said Erik.

"You really showed them, Bill," said Jacques, "You really packed a punch."

"I surprised myself, Jacques," patting the appreciated roll of nickels in my pocket.

I kept the nickel trick to myself hoping that maybe Maury would too. We all lost our appetite and decided to call it a night, especially me. Everyone in Maury's was talking about and describing the fight they just saw. With each telling it grew in stature and became known as "The Night of the Big Fight at Maury's."

Erik woke Iris and she was really upset that the "Big Fight" was over. She wanted me to tell her everything that she'd missed.

"It will have to wait until morning," I said. "Right now I need to tend to my cuts and bruises and get an ice pack on this jaw."

Erik escorted his groggy and inquisitive sister back to the yacht.

As we headed back to the house, I began to lean on Jacques heavier and heavier. I don't think I would have made it back if it weren't for him. As the adrenaline subsided, I really began hurting.

He helped me into the kitchen, sat me in a chair, and gave me a couple of aspirins with a glass of water. I found several new bruises besides the ones I knew of and my jaw and left eye were swelling up big time. That eye will be black tomorrow, I thought. Fortunately, I still had all my teeth and no broken bones. I just had a couple of days of soreness ahead of me. Jacques made up a big icepack, and I put it on my jaw and eye for a half hour. I rubbed some Bengay on all the aching spots and he doctored all my cuts with Mercurochrome and Band-Aids. Finally he gently helped me into my bed.

Thursday, February 3, 1966

The next morning, the aroma of coffee woke me from a deep restorative sleep. As, I relived the night before; I shuddered at what could have gone wrong. I could still see that fist poised ready to strike. I owe Bob and Ray big time for keeping that from happening.

As I started to get out of bed, I thought of how Bob called me an old guy. I denied it last night, but there's no denying it this morning.

Jacques came in with a cup of coffee and to see how I slept. I tried to put a good face on it, but he knew I was hurting.

"Can you manage or do you need a little help," he asked.

"I'm a little stiff. Maybe you better help me take the first few steps, just in case."

He helped me get dressed and said I looked and sounded like I had a golf ball in my mouth.

"That's just what it feels like too."

Once I started to move around; I felt a little better. I looked in the mirror and winced, but I still had a toothy smile. I went out onto the deck and sat down. Jacques handed me a glass of water and a couple of aspirins.

A few minutes later Iris showed up itching to hear about the big fight the night before.

"You look terrible, Bill, you've got a black eye and your mouth is all swollen."

"Thanks, Iris, but you should see the other guy. I think your limit on rum swizzles is two. You slept through the whole thing."

"I'm sorry, Bill, those drinks just went right to my head."

"Do you remember dancing with that man who came in with Joe Stalker?"

"Yes, he knew how to dance really well. I talked with him in German. He seemed so nice. He said he was surprised to see such a pretty German girl here in Key West. He asked me if I found any gold yet. I had sense enough to tell him no and that we were looking for a sunken Spanish ship without any luck so far. That's when you stepped in and rescued me. I remember Erik walking me back to the booth and then the next thing I knew he wanted me to wake up to leave."

I described the whole fight blow by blow. I left out the detail about the roll of nickels. That would be a secret between Maury and me. Wait a minute that's an oxymoron. Oh well, we'll see what happens; maybe this will be the first secret he keeps. Although, I have a feeling he's going to want that roll of nickels to put on display. Regardless, I have to return them to him with my thanks.

"You're so lucky that you didn't end up in the hospital. I saw Bob this morning and he said you knew how to take care of yourself. He thinks the world of you."

"I think the world of him too. If it weren't for him and Ray, I would be in the hospital today, or worse."

"Bob said he heard they kept Joe Stalker overnight to have his jaw wired up today. He'll be like that for several weeks until it's mended."

Erik and Jacques came out onto the deck, just in time to hear that.

"Isn't that a shame," said Erik, "My heart bleeds for him."

"I know he isn't going to let this slide. He'll be gunning for me to get even, but that's okay, I'll be ready for him."

"Hi Iris," said Jacques. "How about a coffee? Are you hungry?"

"Wait a minute, I still have some rum swizzle left, Iris."

"Erik, I'll never let you mix me another drink again. You slipped me a Michael Finn last night."

"You mean a Mickey Finn," he laughed, "I followed the recipe exactly."

"I don't feel good and have a headache, because of you."

"This is your lucky day, Iris."

"What do you mean?"

"Jacques, we need a dose of the Cure for Iris."

"Coming right up," he replied.

"I don't know," she said hesitantly, "you said it was strong medicine."

"Go ahead, Iris, it will fix you right up," I said.

Jacques came out with a glass of the now famous Cure.

"You have to get it down quick Iris for it to work," he said sincerely, "then you'll feel like a million bucks."

"Okay," she said taking the glass and sniffing it.

She brought it up to her lips and then tossed it back, down the hatch. Her eyes widened and she let out a yell that could be heard a block away.

The three Amigos started laughing. I had to put my hand up to my mouth because it hurt when I laughed.

She made a grimace that told us we had crossed the line. The laughter abruptly ended.

"You're trying to kill me. Water," she begged.

Jacques had a glass at the ready, and she quickly gulped it down. "Don't ever do that to me again."

"But how do you feel now, Iris?" asked Erik

Thinking for a moment, she said, "You know, I think I do feel better. Yes I feel much better! But, not a million bucks better. You're right Erik, its strong medicine."

We all laughed again, and Jacques asked if he could get her something to eat?

"I'd love a cup of coffee," she said. "What have you got that's ready?"

"All I have ready are some eggs Benedict, would that be okay?"

"You're an angel, Jacques that sounds wonderful."

We were all glad to see Iris back to her old self and that she survived the Cure.

We all sat down and enjoyed Jacques coffee and eggs Benedict and told him so.

"I talked to Bosun Jim and he told me his daughter and grandson are due to arrive the day after tomorrow, Saturday at six PM. He asked me to go with him to the airport. He's so nervous about meeting her and doesn't want anything to go wrong. Later at seven he's having a little time at Maury's. We're all invited."

"I'd love to go." I said.

Erik and Jacques both agreed that they would like to go too.

"I'm excited to see his daughter and grandson," she said. "I'm sure everything will be fine."

"You were very nice, Iris," I said, "to help him reconcile with his daughter. I know, Bosun Jim will always be grateful."

"He didn't know what to say in that letter and he dreaded the answer. I only gave him some ideas to get him to start. Once he did, the words just naturally came to him."

"You got him to finally do it, where everyone else failed.

"Well let's go find some more cylinders. I felt good enough to go out, but just for the ride. I suggested we leave a little late this morning and plan to do just a couple of sessions on the sled."

Erik mentioned that we've now got a total of thirty-six cylinders. He wondered if we should leave two batches out there just in case something unforeseen happens. At least, we would have something to fall back on to show for our efforts.

We all agreed that it sounded like a good plan. No one else has any idea how many cylinders there are out there, so whatever number we choose to bring in that would be it.

"I know I've mentioned this before," I said, "But we do have to come up with a plan on how to move these cylinders secretly from our cistern bank. Eventually we may have seventy or eighty and they are very heavy. Anyone got any ideas?"

We all came up empty on that question, so we would have to wait and hope for the best. The one thing we knew for sure, we had to keep the cylinders and their whereabouts secret until we retrieved them all. So far, by trickery, we had been unhindered in our search and recovery of them.

We all agreed that Joe Stalker and his pals were the most likely suspects to try and steal the cylinders from us. At some point we were sure they were going to make a move. So far, they didn't know about the cylinders; only that a lot of gold was out there. They didn't know how much if any, we had recovered. They needed that information to time the heist. I'm sure they wouldn't care if they got all of it or just most of it. That's why they came to Maury's last night, hoping they could find out at what stage of the recovery we were at. They got a little more than they bargained for.

"What if," said Iris, "we made up some replica cylinders out of wood and painted them a verdigris color and weighted them with lead. Somehow, we could trick them into stealing those. As long as we can keep them from actually picking one up or looking too close, they wouldn't know the difference."

"You may have something there," I said, "Of course we'd have to let them know that there are cylinders and that they contain gold coins. Remember that night when Erik first told us about the Nazi gold and seedy Slip heard it; he took off before Erik told us the gold was in coinage contained in cylinders. If they never saw a cylinder up close, they wouldn't know what the wooden ones were. They would want to inspect them closely before accepting them. We'll have to figure out how we can subtly let them know about the real bronze cylinders filled with the gold coins. Then, we have to come up with a plan to have them try and steal the phony ones, which I'm sure we could figure out. I like that idea, Iris."

"How are we going to make the fake ones?" asked Jacques.

"That isn't too difficult," said Iris. "All I need is access to a decent woodworking shop with a wood lathe, and I could make as many as we needed. We'd have to keep it a secret, though. See, Bill, I've learned my lesson."

"I'm proud of you, Iris and I think we all appreciate the reason for secrecy now.

"I know just the place where you can make those cylinders, Iris. I have a good friend that lets me use his little shop in his garage once in a while, to make something for the boat or the house. In fact, Jacques and I made the transom platform there, while you and Erik were in West Germany. He's been talking about going hunting up in Georgia one of these days. If I can encourage him to go on that trip, then we could use his shop without any questions about what we're making."

"Maybe," she said, "you could get him to go on that hunting trip soon, so we can get those wooden cylinders made. Speaking of going, we'd better get going ourselves, it's almost eleven, and we'll have just enough time to do a couple of shifts on the sled."

There were seven boats hovering around us keeping their distance for the short but very profitable few hours we were out there.

Later that evening, Jacques and I made another deposit into our backyard bank. Thanks to Iris's know how, she found two more stashes of cylinders. That brought the total up to fifty-four. She spotted a third and we all decided to leave it out there as a retirement fund. Jacques did a triangulation on it and recorded it for future reference. We made the decision to harvest just two more caches and leave the rest out there as insurance.

Friday, February 4, 1966

The next day, we were on site early. I felt much better, the swelling went down on my face and I took the first shift with Iris. We were going to try and do four. It was getting ridiculous out there with eight boats shadowing us.

When Iris and I finished and got back into the boat, Jacques saw a ninth one heading towards us.

"It looks like Joe's boat," he said.

As it came closer, we could see it was Joe Stalker's boat.

He came up alongside and shook his fist defiantly trying to say something through his wired down teeth.

"How's the jaw?" I hollered to him. "I notice you're wearing a hat.

"You'll have to speak up a little, Joe, I can't hear you!"

"He said he's going to get even with you," shouted the man with the hair.

"Hey Joe, do us all a favor and take the gas pipe." I returned.

I noticed that the bald man had a small cast on his right wrist.

He started to come closer and closer with his boat. I pulled out my German Luger and aimed at him. If looks could kill I would be dead. He turned the boat away and sped off. We didn't see him for the rest of that day.

"Why do you antagonize him so?" asked Iris.

"I couldn't let him ram my boat. And besides, the madder he gets the more apt he'll be to make a mistake, like giving that salute and sticking his jaw out for me the other night."

"I hope your right, Bill."

"We've got other things to worry about, Iris."

Erik took the next turn with Iris and she spotted another cache of cylinders. One by one the nine gold filled cylinders were sent through the little door.

They came aboard and Iris went in to rest up for the last tour of the day.

An hour later Iris and Jacques were scanning the bottom.

Jacques shouted to Iris that he saw something and left the sled. Iris followed and what appeared to be an old bottle was a cylinder. They waved the metal detector around, but couldn't find any more. They surfaced and slid it through the hatch and climbed onto the transom platform.

"It's strange," said Iris, "there was only one cylinder down there."

"It was sticking out of the sand," said Jacques. "At first I thought it was a bottle, but I figured I'd better check it out."

"That's the last batch then," said Erik. "Gerhard said that the last box of cylinders dropped and broke open. They just jettisoned the loose cylinders and remember he hijacked one, so there will be just eight. They are down there, but spread around."

"That means," I said, "this is the end of the line."

Iris and Jacques went back down and using the metal detector quickly found the remaining seven scattered cylinders.

The end of the day saw us bringing in seventeen more cylinders and the knowledge that there were at least two more caches left out there for our golden years. Those two reserves, the four of us swore to secrecy. This secret, I knew would be kept.

When we got back to the house we found the front door ajar.

"Looks like we had visitors, again," I said, "And I bet I know who they were."

We went in and sure enough the place had been thoroughly searched. This time they didn't attempt to hide their rummaging from us. It looked like a cyclone ran through the house. Drawers emptied out on the floor, closets ransacked, and even my cigars were tossed on the floor and stepped on.

I took the cover off Ernie's cage and he said, "What a dump!"

"You can say that again, Ernie."

"What a dump!" he complied.

I anxiously ran out to the cistern to check the access hatch and thankfully the padlock hadn't been tampered with. I opened the floor hatch on the deck and looked under. I had taken the precaution of setting a few stones in a little pattern to be able to visually check if our bank deposit pipe was disturbed. Again I was relieved to see that none of the stones were out of place.

Erik remembered the cylinder hidden in his bedroom closet and ran up to check. He came back down holding the floorboard.

"They took that cylinder," he said dejectedly, "there were forty-eight coins in it."

"I can't believe it," I said, "I never thought anyone would ever find that hiding place."

"But that solves the problem of letting them know about the cylinders and the gold coins," said Jacques. "Now, when they see the wooden cylinders, they will be more apt to accept them as real."

"That's right!" said Erik. "When you think about it, we couldn't have come up with a better plan to let them know about the cylinders and the gold coins without making them suspicious? By stealing that cylinder, they found out on their own and have an actual sample. And, those forty-eight gold coins will be the clincher."

It took a couple of hours to put everything back together. Jacques and I made the last deposit to our bank, bringing the total to seventy-one. Then we all gathered on the deck for a celebratory drink.

"Why don't you call the police, Bill?" asked Iris.

"We can't prove who did it and we really don't want to draw attention to ourselves. They must be pretty anxious though, coming to Maury's the other night and then breaking in here like this. Someone higher up must be putting pressure on them for results. If they knew for sure we had the goods; they would hit us right away. That's good news for now, but we have to keep them guessing a little longer so you can get those wooden cylinders made.

"I'm going to see my woodworking friend, Norm, tomorrow. If I can talk him into going hunting you could start making them right away. I have a feeling we're going to need them pretty soon."

"What's that you've got there, Erik?" asked Iris.

"It's the U-Boat Captain's personal bible," he answered, "Those intruders threw it on the floor. I quickly looked at it before and didn't notice that he made some notations here and there. I did know about the small key tied to the page marker ribbon. Here, take a look."

Erik handed her the bible and she looked at the key then started leafing through it. Something got her attention; she started to study it intensely.

"What's caught your eye there, Iris," I asked.

"I think the Captain may have something to tell us in his bible. On the back page there are rows of numbers that look like some kind of code."

Being in German, Jacques and I couldn't make any sense out of it. Iris became fascinated by it and kept studying it, trying to figure it out. To our surprise, she actually went into the front room so she could concentrate. Since we stopped smoking cigars in there, maybe the smell didn't offend her any more. We all went out on the deck and speculated as to what the Captain had stowed away in his personal bible.

In the meantime Jacques put on some coffee and made up some sandwiches. Iris said she wasn't hungry and asked us to leave her alone.

We decided to play poker while we waited for her to solve the mystery. Jacques as usual had us on the run. He became a different person when he played cards, the epitome of a riverboat gambler. In two hours he managed to end up with almost all the chips. Erik finally said "Uncle" and to my relief, Iris came walking out with a big grin.

"I've solved the puzzle. Where the longitude and the latitude mentioned intersects, is in this area. Let's see your chart of the Keys."

We spread out the chart and sure enough we plotted the location to a tiny island very close to Key West.

"I don't believe it," I said, "You know where that is. Iris? That's the secret little island, where we had our picnic."

"Well, according to the Captain's code it looks like something of importance is hidden there. Also, three tree stumps are noted."

"I hope we all realize the need of secrecy," I said, "If we all go out there they would follow us. If Iris and I went out there in that sailboat again, I don't think anyone would take notice. What do you say, Iris, how about tomorrow, if I can get the boat."

"I can't wait, Bill. I wonder what's out there. I have to go to Temple tomorrow, but I can be here at noon. Is that okay?"

"Of course, Iris. We've got a date."

Saturday, February 5, 1966

The next morning, the Three Amigos slept late. Then as usual, Jacques hit the deck first, sending his magical aromas wafting through the house enticing Erik and me to his kitchen.

Iris came up the back walk at twelve o'clock sharp. She had on a blouse and shorts over her bathing suit and sandals. I had the same except for a tee shirt. We both wore ball caps.

Jacques fixed us another picnic basket and we took the old Chevy truck down to the marina.

When we got to the boat, Iris took over and I just waited to get the order to cast off. When it came, I untied the lines and hopped in; I sat back and admired her as she skillfully worked the mainsail of the little craft, gracefully weaving through the maze of moored boats. She and the boat became as one. She was constantly in motion until we reached the channel and then she got to sit back and relax with me in the stern. A clear blue sky, calm turquoise water, and a light breeze all came together to give us a perfect day for sailing in the Keys.

We came in site of the little island and Iris said, "I hope we don't have another one of those storms today."

"Oh, I don't know, I didn't mind it," thinking of our embrace under the boat and that kiss.

"Well I did, it really frightened me."

"You can relax, according to the forecast, if you can believe them, there's no rain for the next few days."

We pulled into the pretty little island and fortunately we had it to ourselves again. We were both so excited, as soon as I secured the boat; we started looking for stumps. We came to a clearing and there they were, the three stumps in a rough circle. We both concluded that the point in the middle of the stumps marked the spot where to dig. I brought with us an Army surplus entrenching tool and started digging. Scooping out the soft sand went quickly and down about eighteen inches I felt something. I didn't know what it could be so I took care not to do any damage. Soon, I had the top of a rectangular box uncovered. My hands were shaking as I loosened it from its resting place of over twenty years.

Iris urged me on, and tried to guess what could be in it. We were both anxious, when I pulled it out and set it on the ground.

"Oh, Bill hurry up and open it. Let's see what's in it."

"Let me fill in the hole first."

I had to get some sand to replace the volume of the box and carefully filled in the hole and smoothed out the surface to hide any trace of our digging.

"What if it's a bomb?" I said.

Iris gave me a frightened look.

"Only kidding, let's take our time on this. It isn't heavy enough to be gold, but it must be something valuable. Let's bring it out to the table and give it a good cleaning first."

I dusted off the caked on sand and we could see that it was made of brass. It had turned the same verdigris color as the cylinders. I carried it out to the table and set it down.

A sudden thought of secrecy ran through my mind.

"I hope no one is watching us," I said.

I grabbed the binoculars and scanned the water in all directions and couldn't see any boats lurking out there.

I guess we were right about them not caring about us coming out here for an innocent picnic. Little do they know?

We washed off the box and then Iris made out some German wording engraved on the top along with that familiar Eagle clutching a swastika.

"It says, 'Property of the German Third Reich, Top Secret'. There must be something very important in there, Bill."

It didn't have a lock, just two latches. Evidently they assumed the words "Top Secret" would be enough to scare anyone from being curious. I opened the latches and with a little effort lifted the lid. A rubber seal had kept the interior dry. A black briefcase with the symbol of the Reich, embossed in gold, was perfectly preserved as the day someone placed it there, along with the aroma of leather. I lifted out the briefcase and we saw the attached chain with a handcuff.

"We'll need a key to open it. Iris, did you bring the Captain's bible with you?"

"Yes, it's right here," reaching into her beach bag.

Sure enough, the key unlocked the briefcase. Inside we found hundreds of pages of documents all typed on official German Third Reich stationery. I handed some of them to Iris and she started to scan them.

After quickly leafing through the pages, she looked at me and said, "Bill, one of these sets of documents outline the whole Cylinder Program in detail with those responsible for its inception and how it would be implemented. Included are all the cities around the world where they were to be placed with the actual names of the spies to contact. There are dozens of other documents here that will take a lot more time to study. Erik should take a look at these also."

"They're of no value now," I said, "but back during the war this information would have been very useful to the Allies. Thankfully, we managed to win the war anyway. Can you think of any idea why the Captain hid the briefcase? I assume he wanted Gerhard to have it."

"I have no idea why he buried the briefcase, Bill, he must have been ordered to do so with the intention of it being picked up on a future campaign. I'm sure the Captain just wanted Gerhard to have his personal bible and that's all. The war ended so the need for secrecy ended too. I like to think that the Captain planned to tell Gerhard about it. But, of course he died before they had a chance to meet."

We unpacked Jacques lunch and again when she saw the little bouquet of flowers he included for her, she smiled.

"He's so thoughtful."

I uncorked the wine and we toasted our treasure hunt that turned to mush.

"I wouldn't be surprised if the contents of the briefcase had some historical value." I said, "I'm sure there are researchers who would love to have access to these papers."

"You're right, Bill. We should make sure they all get back to the West German government for that reason."

As we ate Jacques tasty sliced chicken sandwiches with lettuce, tomato and mayo, I decided to let Iris know my feelings for her.

"I know," she said, "And I have feelings for you too, Bill. But, I'm afraid that I broke up with Frank for all the wrong reasons. I have to find out if I really love him and if he loves me. I have to do this; otherwise it would always be there."

At least, she said she has feelings for me. I'll cling to that for now, but I hope it's not just her pride making her go through with this.

We talked for an hour or so and enjoyed the last of the white wine.

"How about a swim," I said, "Last one in is a rotten egg."

Stripping down to our bathing suits, we raced across the warm sand and ran out to waist deep water.

"I won!" she said.

"It was a tie."

"Was not."

"Let's have a race to settle it." I said.

I went back to the table and got the empty wine bottle and pushed the cork back in. I came back and tossed it out as far as I could.

"Whoever gets to it first is the winner."

"Okay, do you want a head start?" she asked smugly.

"I'll give you one."

"On your mark, get set, go," she shouted.

We both dove in and started swimming toward the bottle. I figured I'd let her win, but when I looked her way I couldn't believe seeing her kicking feet in front of me. I tried my best to catch up to her, but she held up the bottle while I still had at least ten feet to go. As we were treading water I thought to myself, "Is there anything she isn't good at?"

"You cheated," I lied, "you got a head start."

"Like fun, I offered to give you a head start. You're just a sore loser."

"I'm only kidding, Iris. Where did you learn to swim like that? Let me guess, you won a gold medal for swimming in the Olympics.

"No, I just won a bronze."

"You're kidding me, Iris."

"Yes, I'm kidding you. I like to swim on the surface as well as underwater. When's the last time you swam like this? I bet it's been a while."

"You're right; I guess I just need to practice more. That makes me feel better about losing… to a girl."

She splashed water at me and I splashed back and before we knew it we were embracing and we kissed.

"We shouldn't have done that," she said, "I feel like I've done something wrong, but I did like it."

"I did too, please don't blame yourself. It just happened and I can't say I'm sorry."

"I guess we better head back. I did have fun today, Bill, but I still have to go through with this thing with Frank. I hope you understand."

"I think I do, Iris. And don't worry no one will ever know about this, not even Maury."

She splashed water at me and laughed.

We swam back to shore and sat on the bench and talked until our suits dried out a little, then we picked up our gear and stowed it in the boat. Iris got in and I slid the little boat off the soft sand into deeper water and hopped in. I took my seat again and delighted in watching her manipulate the little sailboat.

We arrived back at the slip at four-thirty and cleaned up the boat. I put a towel over the box and carried it to the truck. On the way back to the house, Iris reminded me of the gathering Bosun Jim was having for his daughter and grandson at seven. She had to get ready to drive Bosun Jim to the airport and pick them up at six.

I dropped her off at the yacht, and I went to see my woodworking friend Norm about the use of his shop. It turned out that he needed a hundred-dollars to be able to go hunting, so I struck a deal for the use of his shop while he was gone, for that amount. All excited, he planned to leave early the next morning.

Jacques and Erik were all ready for the time at Maury's when I got back to the house. I took the briefcase out of the box and opened it and handed it to Erik and asked him to see what he thought. I ran up and took a quick shower and changed. When I came down Erik said pretty much what Iris said about the Cylinder Program. He thought that it could have been a diplomat's briefcase, because of the handcuff and would like to spend more time going over the many documents.

"We better get going, "I said, "We don't want to be late."

We walked into Maury's and joined the dozen or so guests and friends waiting for Bosun Jim, his daughter and grandson.

Faith was already there and Erik joined her.

Maury had arranged a corner area for the private party. Denise took orders for drinks and passed appetizers.

I got Maury aside and handed him the roll of nickels.

"These saved my bacon the other night, Maury. I owe you."

He took the roll and opened the cash register draw and broke it into the tray.

"Forget it, Bill. I have."

I thanked Maury and went over and joined Jacques and Erik.

Someone said, "Here they come!"

Bosun Jim walked in as proud as a peacock with his daughter and grandson to the applause of all. Iris came over and sat with us.

Bosun Jim proudly introduced his daughter Kristin and her son Samuel and asked everyone to please welcome them to Key West. She was a very attractive woman in her late thirties with blonde hair. I could see why Bosun Jim may have mistaken Iris for his daughter when he first saw her from a distance. Samuel was a fine looking young man who just turned twenty-one. I could see a little of Bosun Jim in him.

"I have to thank my good friend Iris," he said, "for helping an old sailor write a long overdue letter that made this night possible. You know what I always say, if at first you don't succeed try, try again. Well, I did try off and on for years to write that letter myself, but the words just wouldn't come. Then, Iris came along and in no time at all, I sent a letter that brought my dear Kristin and my grandson Sam back to me again. Thank you, Iris."

We all applauded Iris and toasted the new arrivals.

Iris told us about their touching meeting at the airport, "Bosun Jim and Kristin hugged each other and got so choked up, neither one could speak. They just started crying with joy. Poor Samuel didn't know what to do, so I told him to let them have a few minutes to themselves, and we walked away a bit, and I told him about Key West.

"Later Bosun Jim, after composing himself, gave Samuel a hearty handshake and a big hug, welcoming him to Key West.

"I drove them to the fritter boat and Bosun Jim proudly showed them his little place of business. Then we went to his cute little Conch house nearby and, as soon as we entered the front door, we knew we were in the home of a U. S. Navy man. Nautical souvenirs from his thirty years of service were everywhere. They each would have their own room and after they freshened up, we all headed for Maury's."

"I'm glad everything went well for him," I said.

"He's so happy; I have to admit I cried along with them at the airport too. She seems like a wonderful girl and a good mother too. Her son is a handsome young gentleman. Maybe you could take them out on the boat while they're here."

"That's a great idea, Iris. I bet Bosun Jim would get a kick out of it too. He's never been on my boat. We'll all go out fishing and then have a big fish cookout back at the house. It would be good for Jacques and me; we've been getting rusty not doing any charters. Maybe, you could find out what's a good day for them."

"Are you sure we'll catch some fish or will we have to stop off at the fish market?"

"I'm not even going to answer that, Iris."

"Okay, I'll set it up with Bosun Jim."

I got to talk to Kristin and found out that she's never been to Key West. I told her a little about the place and she seemed to be quite interested in the weather we have here. I had the feeling we may have a new resident soon.

I also met Samuel or Sam, the handle he prefers and Iris pegged him, an intelligent clean-cut young man his mother could be proud of. He told me that she loved to entertain and sang at weddings and nightclubs. I asked him if she would mind singing a couple of songs here, now.

"Are you kidding? I'm surprised she hasn't started already. You won't have to ask her twice."

I went over and spoke to her about it and told her I could play the guitar for her. Sam wasn't kidding she didn't need a bit of coaxing.

"How about 'Boogie woogie bugle boy'?"

"Sure, I'm game," I said.

We went up on Jimmy's little stage and I turned on the mike and picked up his guitar. I've long ago obtained his permission to use it. We spent a few minutes running through some chords to get the right key. Then she took the mike and started to sing. Wow! Could she belt out a song! She got everyone's attention, including people passing by who started to gather on the sidewalk to listen. Then they started to come in and sit down. "Boogie Woogie Bugle Boy" I remembered from World War Two as an iconic hit song by the Andrew sisters. No veteran walking by could resist coming in to hear it and reminisce.

Faith dragged a reluctant Erik to the dance floor and started jitterbugging, but once there he actually danced quite well. An eligible bachelor asked Iris to dance and she instantly accepted and soon several other jitterbuggers joined them.

When she finished, the crowded bar demanded more and she happily obliged. The next song was "Coming in on a wing and a prayer" and then a dozen more songs that were popular during the War to the delight of the nostalgic crowd.

Maury had to shanghai a couple of off duty bartenders to help out with the sudden increase in business.

I was happy to see Jimmy show up and take over for me. He accompanied her with the guitar on a couple of songs and then they did a duet that brought the house down. The invited guests and the gathering crowd wanted more. After a few songs with Jimmy, she had to take a break and she came back and joined the party. Everyone recognized Kristin's talent, especially Denise and Maury who offered her a job on the spot.

Jacques asked Erik where he learned to dance? He confessed that Iris taught him how to dance when she was a teenager.

On his break, Jimmy came over and wanted to know more about Kristin and if she wanted to team up with him.

Of course, Bosun Jim could hardly contain himself.

"That's my daughter," he boastfully said, several times.

The party ended on a happy note with, Kristin and Sam well accepted and visually more relaxed than when they first walked into Maury's. That's what Key West does to people.

The Three Amigos saw Iris to the yacht and then headed for the house.

As soon as we arrived, Erik took the stack of official papers from the briefcase and went into the front room to examine them.

Jacques made a pot of coffee and brought a cup into Erik. We went out on the deck with ours.

"Kristin is quite a singer, isn't she," said Jacques.

"You can say that again. I wish I played a better guitar backing her up."

"You did very well, Bill."

"Nice try. She had such a strong voice she really didn't even need me. I felt relieved handing the guitar over to Jimmy when he showed up. They seemed to hit it off together. That duet they sang was fantastic. It's hard to believe they just met a few minutes before and did that song without any rehearsal."

"Guess what I found?" shouted Erik from the front room, "You won't believe it."

"Come on out and tell us," I said.

He walked out holding up a stack of papers, all smiles and shaking his head.

"Those Germans are something else. Here is a complete manifest of all the cylinders, including the serial numbers of each one and its contents. It must have been made out by a numismatist because each coin is described with the date, mintmark and condition. I wonder why they went to all that trouble because these coins were going to be just put back into circulation and lost forever. I guess it's a German thing."

"Does it say how many cylinders there are?" I asked.

"Let's see, they are listed by serial number starting with 1700 to 1789. That would be eighty-nine. There's one missing, because there are nine in each box. There should be ninety."

"You didn't count the first one," said Jacques, "The first one ends in zero not one."

"I don't understand?"

"If the numbers were zero, one and two how many would you have?" using his fingers to count.

"You're right, Jacques, "I see it now. I didn't count the first one, which ends in zero. I should have paid more attention in math class."

"That means there's still eighteen out there," I said in a lowered voice, "and only Iris and you Jacques, know where they are. That will remain our little secret.

You know who'd love to get hold of that manifest?"

"Frank," Jacques and I said together.

"Iris told me," said Erik, "she thinks he's coming down here the day after tomorrow. He could give us a good idea of what the value of all those coins will be. Although, I just realized we never kept track of the serial numbers. We don't know which ones we have and which ones are missing. At least we'll know what the whole shebang would be worth."

"I just thought of something else," I said, "if we show him that manifest of the cylinders, the actual total of cylinders will be known. That will spoil our plan of leaving a few out there for the future."

"That's right," said Jacques, "maybe we shouldn't be so quick to give out that information."

"I agree with Jacques," said Erik, "let's keep this under our hat until we see how everything pans out."

"That's settled then," I said, "we'll keep it a secret and put that manifest into my safe deposit box as soon as we can."

Sunday, February 6, 1966

The next morning Sunday, Jacques and I went to the 7:30 Mass. When we came back we heard the shower running, so Erik was on deck. Iris arrived at about ten o'clock with her usual appetite, which Jacques eagerly wanted to satisfy.

"How are the Three Amigos this morning?"

The Three Amigos nodded and returned the question.

"I'm good, what's up for today?"

"I think we'll go out today without the sled. We'll find those two anchors and bring them in. I'm sure Maury could work them into his décor."

"I bet Jacques will put us right over them," she said.

"I'll do my best," handing her a cup of coffee.

"I talked to Bosun Jim and he loved the idea of a fishing trip and the fish barbecue afterwards. He said he'd be happy to supply the shrimp, conch fritters, and the beer. Also, do you need another grill? And, would the day after tomorrow be too soon?"

"That would be okay with the Three Amigos," getting the nods from Jacques and Erik.

"Let me use your phone and I'll give him a call and let him know right away."

"You don't have to ask, Iris, you know where it is. Afterwards, let's go over what you need to make up those dummy cylinders. Norm said we can use his woodworking shop for the next five days."

"Oh, Iris," said Jacques, "tell him that we could use that extra grill. I've got plenty of charcoal."

She made the call and told us that Bosun Jim was delighted.

"He's going to bring the extra grill over sometime today and leave it in the back yard."

"That's going to be a fun day." I said, "Let's go over what you're going to need to make those wooden cylinders."

"How many do you think we should make?" she asked.

"That's a good question," I said. "No one knows how many there are, so it's pretty much up to us to decide on a number."

"Making those cylinder up is going to be a lot of work for Iris," said Erik, "so what's the least amount that we need? I don't think we need seventy-one."

"You're right there," I said.

"All we need is enough to make a good showing," said Jacques, "a pile of thirty or forty would be impressive."

"Let's make up forty," said Iris.

We all agreed that would be plenty to satisfy our Nazi foes.

"The size of the cylinders, are a little less than two inches in diameter by nine inches long. I think a hardwood like maple would be a good choice. It has a tight grain and when painted will look like metal. I wonder if we could get some two-inch dowel stock in maple or birch. Then we wouldn't have to spend time trimming off the corners on square stock."

"I'll get on the phone and see what I can do."

I made a call to Strunk Lumber, and I talked to a fellow who said they didn't have dowels but they had some two-inch full round maple railing stock. Iris said that would be perfect and they had the forty feet we needed ready for delivery.

We finished breakfast, helped Jacques clean up, and headed out to find the anchors.

When we got out to the site we found a dozen boats waiting for us.

Jacques demonstrated his locating skill by putting us almost on top of the anchors. We used our fish boom with the motorize winch to haul in the hefty anchors. When we started to hoist up the first one, all the boats moved in closer to see what we were bringing up. They were visibly disappointed when they saw the anchors. I hollered over that they could get a better look at them when Maury puts them on display. Half of them gave up and left the area.

The heavily galvanized anchors had to be cleaned up, but they looked pretty good after more than twenty years under water. We brought them in and dropped them off in back of Maury's. He was thrilled and said he had a perfect spot for them.

Monday, February 7, 1966

The next morning, after one of Jacques' ample breakfasts, Iris and I headed over to Norm's shop. I unlocked the side door and we walked in. I punched in the code to the alarm system, which went directly to the police station, so security wasn't a problem. It's a two-car garage that Norm converted into a very compact and efficient woodworking shop complete with air conditioning. There were two windows, so we decided to cover them in case our pal snoopy Slip came prowling around.

Iris felt right at home in the well equipped and maintained little shop. A big sign on the wall stated 'A place for everything and everything in its place'. It certainly held true here.

"I think Norm might be German," said Iris, "I hate to have to disturb anything here; it's so neat and clean."

"Actually he's Scottish descent, but don't worry we'll clean it all up before we leave. That's the only reason he lets me use it, because he knows I'll leave it the way I found it."

She checked out the wood lathe and the table saw. She looked around at some of his home made fixtures and found an indexing one that she could adapt to machine the wrench hex flats.

The truck from Strunk Lumber pulled up with the two-inch railing stock. I opened the garage door and helped the driver bring it in. There was enough to make well over forty cylinders. Any extra stock we'd leave for Norm.

First off, Iris wanted to make up a couple of samples to see how they would look all finished. She cut three pieces of the stock a half-inch longer than needed and found the center on the ends. She mounted one in the lathe and then with a skew, turned off a very thin shaving to get a nice smooth finish. She turned a groove about three quarters of an inch from one end to simulate a cover. Then, with a handful of lathe shavings burnished the cylinder while it was spinning on the lathe. This was repeated for the other two. She put a three-jaw chuck on the lathe and used it to face off an eighth of an inch on the cover end of the cylinder then flipped it end for end and trimmed it to the finished size.

For the next step, she used that fixture of Norm's on the table saw to make the hex flats on the simulated cover and the base. The cylinder was clamped into the fixture and run across the dado cutter on the table saw to make the first side of the three eighths inch deep hex flat. She then indexed the fixture to make the next cut and repeated this to complete the six sides. This was done again on the base and then finally she bored a one-inch diameter hole up through the bottom to be later filled with lead and plugged. The finished cylinder looked pretty good to me, and I thought it would fool anyone when sprayed a verdigris color.

I gave Iris the green light on the cylinders and asked if she needed any help. She told me she worked best alone.

I had to get some verdigris colored lacquer, so I'd have to leave her alone for a couple of hours.

"That's okay, as long as you bring me a coffee when you come back, Bill."

I told her to bolt the door behind me and not to let anyone in. Norm had a phone in the shop, so if she needed anything I told her to call the house. I left the number next to the phone.

I went back to the house and Jacques helped me fish one of the cylinders out of our secret bank through the access hatch built into the roof. I brought a toolbox out and pretended to be repairing the hatch in order to throw off anyone who might be watching us, namely, the wily Slip.

I needed it to get a color match for the lacquer we needed. Also, we could compare the coins in that cylinder with the list Erik found in the Nazi briefcase.

I took just the cover with me into the auto body shop and left the empty cylinder in the truck. They were able to come up with a very close match. I figured a gallon would be enough; I also got a gallon of lacquer primer. I picked up some coffee and doughnuts for us and headed over to Norm's.

Iris had quite a bit of work done on the cylinders. She cut up enough for forty and was half way through the task of trimming with the skew and turning the simulated cover. She took a break and I smeared a little of the paint sample on a scrap piece of maple, which she approved. We sat down at Hanks desk and enjoyed the coffee and doughnuts together.

Afterwards, I used Norm's little spray booth to give Iris's sample a coat of primer and then a coat of the verdigris lacquer. It looked pretty good until we compared it to the real cylinder. It appeared to be too perfect. We realized that it needed some stains and streaks. I tinkered around and came up with a paint mixture that I carefully applied with a crumpled up newspaper that looked like the real thing.

She continued finishing the rest of the forty cylinders and then started facing off the ends. Next would be machining the hex flats on each end with Norm's fixture on the table saw.

I spent the rest of the day with the diligent Iris. She had a particular way of working in a very efficient manner and once when I tried to suggest something, she gave me a look that without words told me I was on thin ice. After that, I got the message not to interrupt or try and help unless she specifically asked. I sprayed them, as they were completed, except for the finish coat on the bottoms. By the end of the day she had just a dozen left to machine the hex flats on, then lastly to bore the one-inch hole in the base to install the lead. We called it a day, set the alarm and locked up.

As I drove up next to the yacht to drop her off, I said, "You really know your stuff, Iris and I'm very proud of you, and I enjoyed working with you today. You must be tired?"

"Thank you, Bill. I really like woodworking, but I am a little tired. I'm looking forward to the big fishing trip with Bosun Jim tomorrow. That will be a fun day, and I'll be able to take it easy and rejuvenate."

"It will be a fun day, and I'll make sure you do relax and rest up. I never thought to ask, what time is Bosun Jim coming to the boat?"

"I told him about nine o'clock."

"That's perfect; I'll see you at the house in the morning then. If Frank show's up bring him along."

She waved and I headed back to the house. Those cylinders were coming out nice. Now, we had to figure out how to use them.

Jacques was preparing the fixings for both the lunch for the next day's excursion and the big fish barbecue after. Erik made himself comfortable in the front room going through the German documents.

"What kind of fish are you planning to go for tomorrow, Bill?" asked Jacques.

"I'd like them to experience going after the big game fish, especially Bosun Jim. We've got to get a photo of him in the chair. Everyone who wants to can have a try at it. Unless we catch a real trophy, we'll just catch and release. Then, we'll go to one of our spots for grouper and dolphin, they're a nice fish for a cookout."

"That sounds good to me. I'll be ready, to cook whatever we catch"

I went into the front room to see if Erik learned anything worthwhile from all those papers.

"So, have you found anything new, Erik?"

"I searched through the briefcase and did find a tightly folded piece of paper hidden under a leather flap, which could mean a little hanky-panky. It's a list of very unique coins that are in a special cylinder without a serial number. I know we checked all the cylinders we brought in and they all had serial numbers, so the cylinder is not in with the ones we recovered. There is a chance that it could be still out there with ones we've decided to retrieve at a later date. The dates of the coins in this one are all very old and the condition of all of them is excellent. For some reason there are only sixty-eight coins instead of seventy-two.

"All the rest of the documents in the briefcase are just boring pages of correspondence.

"When I looked at the Captain's bible after Iris decoded the location of the briefcase, on the next line I noticed a reference to a quote from 2 Chronicles 15:7 'But as for you, be strong and don't give up, for your work will be rewarded.' Any idea about what that could mean?"

"That certainly is a special cylinder," I said, "and probably worth a fortune by itself. I'm sure it wouldn't be thrown in with all the others. That missing serial number tells it all. Someone had a plan to divert it to make his future years comfortable, whether the Third Reich worked out or not. I wonder if it was the Captain? Like you said a little hanky-panky. Let's show that biblical quote to Jacques."

"That means to persevere and not give up, like when you start doing some kind of good work don't stop," said Jacques.

"You're right, Jacques, don't stop," I said. "Don't stop digging that's what he meant. When we found the briefcase I just assumed that was the treasure. The Captain is telling us not to stop digging. I might be wrong, but I believe that there's something else out there."

"I wonder what it could be," said Erik.

"There's only one way to find out. The only thing is, if Iris and I go out again in the sailboat that's sure to arouse suspicion. We'll have to figure another way to get out there."

"If you wait a week or so," said Jacques, "I don't think anyone would question that."

"That's true; I guess we'll just have to wait, although, I don't know if I can stand the suspense."

"How did Iris make out with the replica cylinders?" asked Erik.

"Very well, one more day and they'll be finished. She's doing a fantastic job. She really knows her way around a woodworking shop."

"That's nothing; you should see her in a machine shop, making those big complicated machines cut through solid steel like butter. She really knows her stuff, there's nothing she can't make once she sets her mind to it."

"She really is something," I said, "I never knew a woman like her. I wonder where she gets all that energy."

"I don't know where it comes from, but that's how I always remember her. She always seemed to garner more energy as the day went on, while everyone else's tapered off."

"If you find out what it is," said Jacques, "we could bottle it and sell it. I could use a shot of it about this time of day."

"What's the matter with that TABASCO cure of yours?" asked Erik, teasing.

"That only works for hangovers. Supper's ready."

We went out to the deck where Jacques had a big turkey potpie with homemade piecrust ready to be served. He roasted a turkey and sliced it up for sandwiches for the big fishing trip. The rest of the meat went into the potpie and with the carcass he planned to make a turkey soup.

"Delicious, Jacques," said Erik. "This is the best turkey pot pie I've ever had. Please accept my compliments and fair warning, I'm going to have seconds."

"Your compliments are accepted and appreciated. Having seconds always flatters a cook."

"I second the seconds," I said.

After the meal and of course the dessert we had coffee and talked about the next day's fishing trip. As usual we came back to talking about the cylinders. I told Erik about the one we fished out of the cistern and asked him to check it with the manifest and the coin book we bought at Sears.

Jacques went and got the book and Erik called out the date, mintmark, and the condition of the first coin from the manifest. Jacques found the coin in the book and it had a value of one hundred and sixty dollars.

It took an hour to come up with a very rough total of almost ten thousand dollars for the coins in that one cylinder. Multiplying that number by seventy-one came to about 700,000 dollars. Having the actual coins and the quotes from the book were tangible proof that we were going to be much richer than we thought. We fell silent and then decided to try and not think about it.

"How are we going to use Iris's wooden cylinders to trick the bad guys?" asked Erik.

We all drew a blank. The plan would have to be devised on the fly as things developed. We had no idea when they would make their move.

We broke out a deck of cards and played poker for a couple of hours until Jacques ended up with all the money, then we hit the sack.

Tuesday, February 8, 1966

Next morning, the smell of coffee and something baking, pleasantly woke me from a sound sleep. I got up, showered, and shaved. I then hollered up to Erik to rise and shine. Surprisingly, he slept through Jacques tempting aromas.

I walked out onto the deck and there, Iris and Frank were having their coffee.

"Good morning, Bill," they said together.

"Good morning, Iris and you too, Frank, I'm glad you could make it today for our big fishing trip."

"Thank you for inviting me. It's a real treat, and I'm looking forward to the fish barbecue afterwards.

"By the way I heard about the big fight at Maury's. I wish I was there, it must have been something."

"It sure was. It didn't look to good towards the end, but I got some much appreciated help from your UDT mates and Erik, so I managed to come out on top."

"I fell asleep and missed the whole thing, but everyone said you were wonderful, Bill. You're too modest to tell what really happened."

Hearing her say it that way made my heart swell with joy and bolstered my outlook.

"Thanks, Iris, but I didn't look too good the next day. When you saw me, you said so yourself, remember?"

"Still you came out as the winner," said Frank, "that's all that matters.

"As you know, Faith isn't too fond of boating, and Nicole decided to keep her company, so they passed on the fishing trip, but they can't wait to come later for the cookout."

"That's okay," I said, "we'll all be together at the barbecue; it's going to be a fun day for sure."

Jacques poured me a cup of coffee and I joined them.

A few minutes later, Jacques presented a big basket of bran muffins hot out of the oven, which soon began to disappear.

"Now that's a bran muffin," said Frank, "with bran, raisins, nuts, molasses and even some chocolate bits. I wish I could have one of these every morning."

"You can. I'll give Nicole the recipe," said Jacques proudly.

"Je vous remercie beaucoup, mon ami," said Frank, Thank you very much, my friend.

"Votre plus que bienvenue, Frank." You're more than welcome.

Erik came on the scene in time to hear the French spoken.

"Good morning, everyone. It's amazing how different French is from German," said Erik, "The countries neighbor each other and German is so guttural and harsh sounding, and French is so refined and graceful. I wonder why the two languages didn't blend together."

"Because they were always at war with each other." said Iris.

"I guess that's the reason. But the blending of the two would have been a beautiful thing, don't you think?"

"All it would have done is soften the German and ruin the French making both languages uninteresting," said Iris.

"Without starting an argument, I would just like to say I disagree," said Erik.

"Without starting an argument, I would just like to say that you don't know what you're talking about. I like both languages the way they are." retorted Iris.

"I just stated a hypothetical thought, Iris. Don't make a Federal case out of it."

"What time did you say that Bosun Jim is meeting us at the boat, Iris?" I asked hoping to change the subject.

"He said about nine o'clock," she then said in a whisper to Erik, "You don't make sense."

"See, she always has to get in the last word."

"No, I don't."

"I give up, Iris you win."

"Do I get a prize?"

"Enough you two," I said, "We've got to get a move on if we're going to be at the boat at nine."

"I'll help Jacques clean up," said Iris.

"Good, Erik and I will load up the truck. C'mon Frank you can help too."

I drove with Jacques and Iris in the cab and Erik and Frank climbed into the back with the gear. It's only a few blocks to the boat, but I think Frank got a kick out of riding in the open truck.

We transferred everything to the boat, and I started the engine to warm it up. Every now and then, when I start the engine, I smile and remember the first time Tony started up his Maria that day long ago in Scituate Harbor.

A few minutes later Bosun Jim, Kristin and Sam came aboard. Jacques cast off the lines and we were off. It was another picture perfect day in Key West, with a calm sea, and the usual light breeze. We headed out to deep water to try our luck.

We put Bosun Jim in the chair first. Jacques fixed a Ballyhoo baitfish in his special way, so it would appear to be swimming when being trolled. Now it became a waiting game. Jacques got the camera and took his picture.

We didn't have to wait long when he got a strike to the cheers of all. Jacques by his side coached him as he reeled in the first catch of the day. It was a good size king mackerel.

"That's a keeper, Bosun Jim," I said, from the upper controls, "They're good eating. We're off to a good start for our fish barbecue this afternoon."

Jacques put Sam in the chair next. He had never been deep-sea fishing before, so Jacques explained everything to him. I got a kick out of Sam so excited and full of anticipation. After several times reeling in to check the bait, poor Sam began to lose heart. At least a half hour had gone by. Then, something took the bait, something big. He forgot everything, but Jacques came to the rescue determined that Sam would bring that fish in. He stood next to Sam talking him through every move. After a while he started catching on. Jacques let him play that fish on his own and before long we had a fifteen-pound dolphin on board. Jacques took a photo of Sam holding up the handsome fish.

"Good job Sam," I hollered down, "That's another good eating fish."

Jacques put Frank in the chair for his turn. He posed as Jacques took his picture. Frank no stranger to deep-sea fishing, to be sure, had plenty of trophies on his walls. Within fifteen minutes, Frank had another deep-sea battle on his hands. Jacques discreetly looked up at me and mouthed the word 'shark'. Frank continued fighting the fish and finally brought him alongside. Iris gave Frank the bad news that it looked like a big shark.

"We have to cut him loose, Frank," said Jacques, "We can't take him onboard."

"That's okay, Jacques, he gave us a little excitement, by all means let him go."

"How about you, Iris," said Jacques, "do you want to try your luck?"

"No, thanks, Jacques, I'll save my turn for another time."

Jacques chose a reluctant Kristin next to take the chair.

"Maybe someone else should go; I've never done this before."

"Well, that's all the more reason you should try it," said Jacques encouragingly.

"Okay, I'll try. You're right, Jacques, I want to be able to tell my friends back home I did this."

"That's the spirit, good luck. I'll get a picture of you in the chair as proof," as he set her up with the big rod and reel.

Jacques took the photo and then patiently showed her how to pay out the baited line and how the reel worked. He told her he would be near to guide her when needed.

We all patiently waited and waited. She reeled in several times so Jacques could check the bait.

"I guess I'm not lucky."

As soon as she said that, something took the bait. Jacques told her how to set the hook and then the fun began. It turned out to be a sailfish and a nice one. He put on a marvelous show for all of us, leaping out of the water twisting and flapping trying desperately to shake the hook. It took her forty-five minutes to bring that fish alongside. It was a real trophy fish that would make any serious fisherman proud.

"Nice going, mom," said an excited Sam.

Kristin looked down at the exhausted fish.

"Do we have to take him; can we let him go?"

"That's up to you Kristin," I said, "We can release him and in an hour or so he'll be his old self."

"That's what I want to do, Bill."

Jacques grabbed the fish by the bill with a gloved hand and pulled him up enough to remove the hook with pliers and then lifted the big tired fish up in his arms.

"He's at least forty pounds, Kristin," he said, "a nice fish."

Erik took a quick photo with Jacques holding the sailfish and Kristin holding up its sail. Jacques then gently lowered him back into the water and let him go. We watched as he started to regenerate some of his energy and then a very lucky sailfish slowly swam away.

We all congratulated Kristin on her catch and release of the majestic fish. Now, when she went home she had something to show and tell her friends.

"Let's go inshore," I said, "We'll have lunch and then we'll try to catch some grouper to round out the menu."

We went in to more shallow water, to a spot we knew usually had plenty of grouper. Everyone felt very relaxed now and hungry. We dropped anchor and Jacques brought out the turkey sandwiches with potato chips and choice of ice-cold beer or Cokes. There's something about being on the water that makes food taste doubly good.

Bosun Jim started telling some tall tales about his Navy days. He had a gift as a storyteller and entertained us while we were eating. Almost two enjoyable hours were whiled away before we knew it.

"Who wants to try fishing?" asked Jacques. "How about you, Iris?"

"Okay, I'll give it a try."

A half hour went by and nothing. She reeled in several times to see the bait untouched.

"I guess the fish don't like me today," she said. "Maybe someone else should try."

"Be patient, Iris," I said. "Hey Jacques, let's try a different bait."

"Good idea," he said, "I'll try a nice piece of that mackerel we caught."

He baited the hook and Iris started letting the line out and suddenly she got a hit. She set the hook and the rod bent down as she started to reel in.

"You've got something big there, Iris," said Frank.

It took her fifteen minutes to get the fish up so we could see what she had.

"It's a grouper," said Jacques, "He's big enough for two cookouts."

Jacques used the gaff to get it up, so he could grab it by the gills and haul it in. He held it up with the scale and read eighteen pounds.

"We won't have to go to the fish market today, Iris," I said.

I asked everyone if they were ready to call it a day and all agreed. We stowed all the fishing gear, hauled in the anchor, and headed for the dock. On the way back Jacques gave a professional demonstration on how to clean and filet fish. A flock of seagulls and a few pelicans followed us, diving for the treats that Jacques tossed over the side. The dolphin and grouper he filleted and the Mackerel he cut into steaks. All the fish was prepared for the grill and on ice before we reached the harbor.

With all the help it didn't take long to wash down the boat and load up the truck. Bosun Jim, Kristin, and Sam would meet us at the house. The rest of us got into the truck and followed.

When we pulled up, Faith and Nicole were sitting on the front porch waiting for us.

"Have you been waiting long," I asked.

"Not too long we didn't want to be late," answered Faith.

We all gathered on the deck, and one by one took turns to freshen up. Jacques had everything prepared ahead of time, a big garden salad, potato salad and coleslaw along with cheese and crackers and condiments. Even the grills were all ready to be lit, which he did upon arrival.

I brought out several carafes of white wine and set them on the table.

A delivery of cooked chilled shrimp, conch fritters and ice-cold beer arrived right on schedule.

"I just have to heat up the conch fritters, Jacques," said Bosun Jim, "Show me where the oven is."

"I'll take care of that for you," said Nicole, "I'm helping out Jacques today."

"Why thank you, Nicole, I appreciate that."

"If you don't mind?" said Jacques to Bosun Jim. "I could use some help on the two grills with the fish."

"You just try and stop me. I'll get out there right now and stoke the fires."

Jacques welcomed Nicole's help and in no time at all, hot conch fritters and cold shrimp were being passed around.

It started to get dark, so I went around and lit the Tiki torches, which gave a South Seas touch to the event.

"Don't forget to try my dipping sauce," said Bosun Jim.

Jacques brought out the fish to the grills. The extra grill came in handy and both were in the best of hands, as the two men worked together doing what they both loved best.

"Jacques had rubs and coatings for the dolphin and grouper. For the mackerel steaks he made up something with a mayonnaise base. He delighted in doing all this. Bosun Jim taking it all in, openly said, he was picking Jacques brains for new recipes. They were both having fun, sharing their common love of cooking.

Kristin told Iris how ironic it seemed that her father owned a little seafood restaurant, because she worked in a restaurant as a waitress for ten years.

"That's how I had to make a living for myself and my newborn son, Sam. One slow night, I started singing and the customers liked it, and my tips got bigger. That became part of the job and one night a local nightclub owner offered me a full time job with a lot more money.

"My husband wanted out right after I had Sam, so we filed for a divorce. I never heard from him again.

"My father could see what I couldn't, and I recently admitted it to him. We never should have stayed separated so long. Pride stole away all those years from us. Now, I understand why it's one of the seven deadly sins."

As Jacques and Bosun Jim worked their magic, the aromas wafting from the grills had everyone's attention. In the meantime, Nicole put out the salad and the side dishes on the buffet table with a stack of plates, silverware and napkins.

After about ten minutes, Jacques announced, "The fish is just about ready, so everyone get a plate and start filling it with your sides. We'll be bringing the fish over to the table family style."

When all were seated and at the ready, Jacques and Bosun Jim placed several platters piled high with the hot off the grill fish on the table, within reach of everyone. Some were blackened, some poached in aluminum pouches with sliced lemon and spices, and of course just plain grilled. Several sauces and chutneys were served as well.

Everyone, including the chefs du jour were able to be seated at the long table where the clinking of silverware being put to good use and the polite human purring of pleasure told all.

"I have to tell you, Bill," said Bosun Jim breaking the silence, "My hat's off to you, this table is a great idea. I've been to times like this where you have to sit with a plate on your lap. Look, all of us are sitting at the same table."

"Thank you, I know what you mean. That's what got me thinking about having a long table. I can sit twenty guests. It's made of teak, so, as you know, it gets better with age."

"Everything is delicious, Bill," said Kristin, "Thank you for a wonderful day. I'll never forget it."

"My pleasure, but don't forget our fine Chef Jacques here, along with being a first rate mate, he's also a darned good cook."

"Thank you," said Jacques, "And don't forget Bosun Jim, he brought the appetizers and made me look good with all his work."

"Oh, I didn't do much. You know what I always say, when you're having fun doing a job it isn't work."

"Iris tells me you're graduating from college soon, Sam," asked Frank, "what are you majoring in?"

"I'm majoring in economics, sir. I really like the stock market."

"My favorite subject, we have to talk. I'm always on the lookout for new talent. Could you come over to my yacht tomorrow say around ten o'clock?"

"Why... yes, sir," as he looked for his mother's nod, "I'll be there."

"Good. Until tomorrow then."

"What kind of work do you do, Faith," asked Kristin innocently.

"Well right now I'm sponging on my brother in law, Frank."

"I heard that," said Frank, "I wish you wouldn't put it that way, Faith. You know that you're welcome as long as you want to stay."

"I know, Frank, I guess what I really mean is that I'm taking advantage of your hospitality. The first week or so, you could call me a guest, but after that I feel like I've become a freeloader. I like it so much here in Key West I hate to leave, but I feel kind of guilty living on your yacht."

"Well don't, because you're like a real sister to me, and I want you to feel at home. We're family."

"Thank you Frank, you're most generous. What I'm really thinking about is buying a house and making Key West my home."

"You never told me about a house, Faith," said Erik.

"You want to know something funny," said Iris, "I thought about buying a house here too. I'm hooked on this place."

"Here's something funnier, I've only been here for a couple of days," said Kristin, "And I would love to live here for a while to see if it's for real, especially where Maury offered me a job."

"How does this sound, Iris," said Faith, "What if you and I bought a house together, we could have Kristin stay with us until she decides what she wants to do."

"How about you, Nicole," said Iris, "If Faith and I bought a house would you come and live with us too and make it a foursome?"

"I have a good job working on Mr. Lucre's yacht. And I have to go where the yacht goes. But, if things change, I'd love to be able to stay with you and Faith."

"Hey, what about me, Iris, I'm your brother. Can I stay with you?"

"You're not serious, Erik," said Iris, "The only people living in the house would be all us women."

"I wouldn't hold that against you."

"You're incorrigible, Erik, the answer is no and that's final."

"Well, Iris what do you think?" asked Faith, "Shall we go house hunting?"

"It wouldn't hurt to look."

The women took over one end of the table and the men the other. Both engaged in lively and animated conversation punctuated with plenty of laughter. This went on for some time and then Jacques tactfully announced coffee and one of his specialties, Key Lime Pie for dessert.

Every one lined up for the coffee and pie and went back to their seats. The praises for Jacques Key Lime pie started coming. Jacques all smiles modestly accepted the well-deserved compliments.

Then the conversations started up again as before.

Bosun Jim thanked me for inviting his daughter and grandson and for one of the happiest days of his life.

Frank got up and said, "It's not the company, it's the hour. I've got some early telephone conference calls in the morning and as much as I hate to leave such a great time, I really must go. Thank you Bill for being so generous, sharing your boat and home. And thank you Jacques for the wonderful food you worked so hard preparing. Iris, Faith, and Nicole, why don't you stay, if you'd like."

"I better go, too," said Iris, "I have to get up early. Good night everyone. Thank you Bill and Jacques."

We all wished them goodnight.

"I'll stay," said Faith, "If Erik will walk me home later."

"I'd be happy to," said Erik.

"I'll walk Nicole home," said Jacques.

Frank and Iris both left together, which put my nose out of joint, but I tried not to let it show.

We all just sat at the table and talked for a while and then Bosun Jim said that they should go too. They thanked Jacques and me for an elegant day. Kristin and Sam said their good byes and thanks as well, on the way out. Everyone took home enough for another meal.

The rest of us turned to and helped Jacques clean up and do the dishes and put every thing away.

I suggested that Nicole take some of the fish for the yacht's galley.

I decided to call it a night myself and said good night to the girls and Erik and a hearty well done to Jacques. I left the two couples to enjoy the rest of the evening alone.

Wednesday, February 9, 1966

The next morning, Iris and I went to Norm's woodworking shop to continue working on the replica cylinders. She finished up indexing the ends and then started boring the holes up through the bottom for the lead weight. I started to do the newspaper treatment on them in batches as she finished boring the holes. We would paint the bottoms later when they were weighted, plugged and trimmed.

I thought of melting lead and pouring it into each hole. Iris disliked that idea saying that the hot lead would burn the area around the hole and ruin the surface. We decided to get some lead shot to use instead. I called the gun shop in Marathon where Iris bought her gun, and they had it in twenty-five pound bags. I had to admit it would be easier and safer than melting and pouring hot lead.

I went out to get some coffee and when I got back we sat down and talked.

"Are you and Faith serious about buying a house here?"

"Yes, like I told you before, I've fallen in love with Key West with its ease of making friends, tolerance of unique lifestyles, the weather and all kinds of other things. It's a fun place to be."

"It is a unique place for sure.

"Faith seems like an easygoing girl, and I think she would be a good partner in buying a house. What does Frank think about all this?"

"He knows, and is a little uncertain about it."

"Kristin seems like a nice girl too, and her son is a credit to her. Bosun Jim's tickled pink that they all got back together, thanks to you. He said he's got his fingers crossed in anticipation of her moving to Key West. When Maury offered her that job, he couldn't contain himself."

"Kristin hasn't had it easy, being left with a newborn with no family to fall back on. I don't know how she did it. Not knowing about Sam bothers Bosun Jim more than anything. He laments all those years he didn't know what she was going through alone. He could have been helping her out financially if nothing else. Even so, Sam turned out to be a fine young man. Frank is talking to him this morning about an internship with his company."

"That's very generous of Frank, I hope it works out for Sam."

"Frank is a good judge of character and doesn't make an offer like that without being sure he will get his money's worth. When it comes to business, Frank is all business."

Did I detect a veiled criticism of Frank there; if so that would be a first. It gave me some needed encouragement that my chances were improving.

"He's flying back to New York today and will be back Tuesday night."

We talked about the fishing trip and the barbecue the night before and what a great time we all had.

"Well what do you say, shall we get back to work?" she said, "I'll bore the rest of those holes and then I'll make up some wooden plugs to seal in the lead shot. How much shot do you think we need?"

"I have no idea. Could you drill an inch diameter hole in a piece of wood the same depth you'll drill in the cylinders. I'll bring it with me and see if they can figure it out at the gun shop."

"Maybe I'll take a ride up there now. Hey, do you feel like taking a ride? We could stop and get something to eat along the way. We'll be back in two or three hours. C'mon, let's take a break."

"Maybe another one of those messy hot dogs?"

"I had in mind a nice hamburger and a Coke."

"You talked me into it, Bill. Let me drill that hole in a block of wood to take with us and shake the sawdust out of my hair."

"You look fine; we look like a couple of workers."

"Would that mean I look like a local?"

"Very much so, Iris."

In her blue chambray shirt and cut off blue jeans and sneakers, she looked like a local and a beautiful one at that.

Every time I looked at her, I thought about those kisses we shared. I wanted to hold her in my arms and tell her how much I loved her, but Frank's big diamond ring, which she isn't wearing for safety reasons today, is like a big red stop sign staring me in the face.

On the hour or so drive to Marathon, by being a good listener and easy to talk to, with a probing question here and there, I unwittingly told her more details of my life's story than I ever told anyone. For some reason I couldn't hold anything back. She would have made a good interrogator. As we pulled into the gun shop parking lot, I vowed to hear her life's story on the way back.

The shop owner poured some lead shot into the hole in the wood and allowing room for the plug it amounted to about one and a quarter pounds. One and a quarter times forty cylinders called for fifty pounds of shot.

With the fifty pounds of shot in the back of the truck, we headed back down A1A. We stopped at a little hamburger place I liked in Big Pine, Bertha's Big Burgers. It overlooked the water with tables outside under some palm trees.

I told Iris to get a table and I'd go in and get her a hamburger. They had a special called, "The Kitchen Sink". I got two of those with an order of fries to split and a couple of Cokes.

"It's so pretty here, Bill. I wish I could just sit here for the rest of the day."

"Well maybe someday, but we really do have to get back and finish those cylinders."

When she took a bite of her hamburger, juices and sauce ran down her chin.

"Oh, not again, Bill, what's with you and messy food?"

I laughed and handed her some napkins.

"They're messy, but they do taste good," she said, laughing. "Next time you take me out to lunch, I'll remember to bring a bib."

I hoped there would be a next time and many times after that. I felt so good when she laughed.

After our teenager lunch, we started back to Key West. She tried to translate a long German joke into English. She had me in stitches, not because it was funny, but because it became so complicated and made no sense when translated literally. She thought I was laughing at the joke. I didn't have the heart to tell her. I never did get to hear her life's story, which I vowed I would on the way back.

I carried the heavy bags into the shop and opened one. I filled a cylinder with the lead pellets and she glued in a plug. After a while when the glue set up, she trimmed it flush. I sprayed the bottom of the cylinder with the verdigris lacquer. After my newspaper treatment, it looked fantastic. As long as they were not actually picked up and handled, they looked real. But, how are we going to use them?

Another day in the shop and they should be finished. Then we had the problem of moving and hiding them. I could back the truck up into the shop, and we could load them up and cover them with a tarp, but where do we take them?

We called it a day and locked up, set the alarm, and went back to the house. The two Amigos were there, and we all went out on the deck and over some of Jacques' iced tea and a piece of leftover Key Lime Pie, we discussed the problem of what to do with the fake cylinders.

"In a war movie I saw one time," said Jacques, a Japanese Officer stated, 'Take the obvious and reverse it'."

"What does that mean," asked Erik.

"It means," said Jacques, "Do the opposite of what everyone thinks. We're trying to hide the cylinders. What if we did the opposite and let everyone see them."

"That doesn't make sense," said Erik, "We'd be letting the cat out of the bag."

"Wait a minute," I said, "That would let the bad guys know we recovered the treasure and they would then try to rob us. But they would be going after the fake cylinders. Maybe we could catch them in the act. We wouldn't be risking the real cylinders."

"I see what you're saying," said Erik, "We may be able to make them try and rob us at the place we choose. We could guard it and be ready when they hit."

"Something like that," I said, "Now where could we set that up. We don't want it to be here. Where would be the logical place for us to put the cylinders for safe keeping?"

"How about a bank vault?" said Iris.

"I don't think that would work out," said Erik, "There would be all kinds of paper work. And they would want to know what they are and so forth."

"Not if it happened to be Maury's bank vault," she said.

"That's an excellent idea, Iris," I said. "We could transfer the dummy cylinders into his vault quietly some night after hours and get Maury to vow not to tell anyone. Within twenty-four hours all of Key West would know. Then, we'll keep watch on the place and nab whoever tries to break in. I'll talk to him and see if he'll go along with it."

"I like the fact," said Jacques, "that the real cylinders aren't at risk."

"By the way Iris," I said, "Erik found a clue in the Captain's personal bible. It's a biblical quote we think means that we should have kept digging after we found the briefcase. We'll have to make another trip out there to see if it's true."

Erik went and got the bible and showed the note to Iris. She did notice the quote before, but didn't relate it to the digging.

"Now that you put it that way it does seem to have that meaning. I wonder what could be out there. I can't wait to see, let's go out there now," she said.

"That's the problem; we've just been out there. If we go back too soon, our friends may get suspicious and follow us. We'll have to wait for a few more days. I'm curious too."

"I suppose we have to wait," looking at Jacques, "I did so want another one of your wonderful lunch baskets. Unless... we go out at night."

"That's and idea. We could take my little skiff with the outboard. It's all ready to go next to the Rose Maria. We could sneak out after nine o'clock and be back by midnight."

"Let's go tonight, Bill," she said, "I can't wait to see what's out there."

"It will be dark enough in a couple of hours, why not, let's go for it. I'll get a flashlight, the shovel, and make sure we have a full tank of gas."

Jacques prepared a great supper with some of the leftover fish from the cookout, fishcakes, black beans and his version of Boston brown bread.

Around eight thirty, Iris and I started to get ready to leave. Jacques pleasantly surprised us with a thermos of coffee and a good supply of his cookies. We walked out the back way and went a round about route to my skiff, to make sure no one followed us. We got in the little boat and rowed out a good distance, before we started the motor. An hour later we pulled up onto the beach of the little island. I took the shovel and handed the flashlight to Iris. From memory we found the three stumps very quickly and I started to dig. We were both excited as to what we would find. I dug down almost three feet when I felt something with the little shovel.

"What is it, Bill?"

"It's a cylinder."

I reached down and pulled it out. I dug deeper and widened the hole to make sure there weren't any more.

I filled in the hole and like before carefully smoothed out the area. We went back to the boat and I washed the cylinder in the water. Iris held the flashlight on it and we could see the eagle clutching the swastika but no serial number. I tried to open it by hand, but we'd need wrenches to loosen it.

We got into the boat and headed back. I opened the thermos and we shared a cup of coffee and a few of Jacques "you can't eat just one" cookies. I told Iris about the paper Erik found hidden in a fold in the briefcase with the contents of a cylinder that didn't have a serial number. All the coins mentioned were very old, rare, and in excellent condition. This could be it, but we'd have to wait until we got back to the house to get some wrenches to find out.

Several times I wanted to tell her that I loved her, and Frank was not the right man for her, but I knew she had to go through with her scheme. Like Erik said, once she digs in her heels, that's it.

At midnight we pulled into the dock. I secured the skiff and we walked back to the house. We weren't surprised to see Erik and Jacques up waiting for us.

"What did you find," they both said together.

We showed them the cylinder and Erik noticed right away it didn't have a serial number.

"That's it," he said, "that's the cylinder mentioned in the hidden manifest. These coins are probably more valuable then all the others put together. Let's open it and see if the coins match that manifest."

I found a couple of wrenches and when I loosened the cover I unscrewed it the rest of the way by hand. I removed the wad of cotton and the first coin appeared on the list.

I asked Jacques to get the coin book from Sears. When he came back with it, Erik gave him the year, the mintmark, and condition of the twenty dollar gold piece from the list.

"There must be some mistake," said Jacques, "the book said it's worth five thousand dollars."

"Let me see," said Erik. "No mistake that's the coin right there. Only a few hundred were minted."

Iris had to sit down.

"You could buy a house in Key West," I said, "for that one coin. What are we going to do with this cylinder? It doesn't seem right to just throw it in with the others?"

Look!" said Erik, "there's a thin pad of cotton between each coin. That's to keep them from touching each other to prevent damage. That explains why there's only sixty eight coins in this cylinder."

"I think we should put this one aside," said Iris, "We don't know how all this is going to turn out, with all the agencies, legal fees and commissions, then splitting it three ways. It doesn't sound like we'll have much left to show for our efforts. Let's make this one private stock."

"I couldn't agree more, Iris," I said, "what do you think, Jacques?"

"It would be like having an insurance policy, especially with the two caches of cylinders still out there."

"My sentiments, exactly," said Erik.

"Okay, let's all shake on it and promise to keep it secret," I said.

We all shook hands and agreed to let me put it in my safe deposit box at the bank.

I drove Iris to the yacht and on the way we decided to meet at the house about ten in the morning. Bob, on duty at the gangway, saw her to her cabin.

Thursday, February 10, 1966

Iris arrived right at ten o'clock and Jacques as usual handed her a mug of coffee and served up a hearty late breakfast. She was his favorite customer.

I told her that I talked to Maury this morning, and he would be glad to go along with the plan. To whet his gossip appetite, I showed him the cylinder we retrieved from the cistern. I opened it and spilled out the gold coins. He became very excited, and I knew he couldn't wait for me to leave, so he could get started.

If we finished up the cylinders today, we could move them into the vault later tonight.

"Things should start to get interesting," I said.

"But, what if Maury keeps the secret and doesn't tell anyone," she said.

Jacques and I burst out laughing.

"Did you hear that, Bill?" said Jacques, "Loose lips Maury keeping a secret."

"Oh, Iris, Forgive us for laughing," I said, "You don't know Maury. He will swear on a stack of bibles to keep it a secret, but it just won't happen. It's like telling a leaky boat not to leak. In fact, after showing him the gold coins, I know he's telling people as we speak."

Iris and I went to Norm's woodworking shop and worked on the cylinders. As she bored the holes up through the bottom I filled them with the lead shot and glued in a plug. When she finished the boring she started trimming the plugs flush on the lathe. I then started painting the bottoms and doing the newspaper treatment. At last they were finished.

As we were making the plans to move them later that night, we realized that it wouldn't be good if Maury saw them. He would know right away that they were wood and of course that would be broadcast as well. Iris came up with the answer to make simple plywood boxes for them and nail the lids on.

We decided to put eight cylinders in a box so we would need five boxes.

"While we're at it," she said, "Let's make four extra boxes to make it look better."

"I like that idea, Iris. We'll mark them so we know which is which."

A bronze cylinder full of gold coins weighed about six pounds. Our wooden ones even with the lead shot were just two pounds. We needed more weight in the boxes. I suggested using some red bricks at six pounds apiece. To get the boxes to weigh about fifty pounds we figured five bricks would do the trick. Eight bricks would go into each of the extra four boxes. The inside dimensions of the boxes would have to be about twelve by twelve inches and thirteen and quarter inches high. We would need nine boxes for the forty cylinders including the extra four with just bricks.

I went over to Strunk lumber with the list she gave me. She suggested I have them rip the plywood to width for us, so we wouldn't have to manhandle the four by eight foot sheets in the small shop. Iris stayed behind to make up a finished drawing with the actual dimensions.

I brought back the plywood and bricks we needed along with some sandwiches and cokes. We sat down and ate and talked about some of the fun things we've done over the last few weeks. Sitting there with her hair and rumpled clothes all dusty, holding a sandwich in one hand and a coke in the other, only heightened my respect and love for this remarkable woman. I just wished that I knew, what was going on in that little head of hers.

As soon as she finished eating, Iris went right back to work milling up the parts for the boxes and spacers to keep the cylinders apart and upright. She handled Norm's pneumatic staple gun like a pro to make short work of the assembly of the boxes. We placed four bricks in the bottom of a box, then a piece of plywood, and the extra brick. We inserted the spacers, the eight wooden cylinders, and then Iris stapled the lids on. The boxes with just bricks were packed with sawdust. We repeated that eight more times and at last we were done.

I made arrangements with Maury that Erik and I would bring them over later that night.

Iris looked tired, so I suggested we wait until the next day to clean up the shop, which she welcomed. We locked up the place and set the alarm. I dropped her off at the yacht, and she said she'd be at the house around ten in the morning.

I proceeded on home and after dark; Erik and I went back to the shop. I was concerned about the weight of all the boxes in the old truck, so we decided to make two trips. Erik suggested taking four for the first trip and put those on the deck, then get the last five and leave them in the truck covered over with a tarp. I agreed with him and when we finished, I backed the truck up into the yard in front of the deck, so we could keep an eye on them. Then we patiently waited until closing time to bring them to Maury's.

Around one A.M., we made the two trips to Maury's. We drove around in back, where he met us with a two-wheeler. We moved in the heavy boxes one at a time until they were all safely ensconced in the enormous vault. I shook hands with Maury and he solemnly swore to keep our secret.

"In a couple of days, if not sooner," I said to Erik on the way back to the house, "our friends will be aware that the cylinders are in Maury's vault."

"That's a really massive vault," said Erik, "They're going to need dynamite to get into it."

"You're right! Erik! I never thought of that, I hope they don't destroy Maury's bar. Maybe this wasn't such a good idea. Well, we'll be on guard to stop them before they can set off any blast. Starting tomorrow night, we'll be standing watch at Maury's."

Friday, February 11, 1966

True to form Iris came up the back walk at exactly ten o'clock.

Jacques as usual had a steaming mug of coffee and a tasty offering for his special regular.

After breakfast we drove over to Norm's shop and spent a couple of hours cleaning up. Iris sharpened the turning tools she used and the saw blades as well. We left it like we found it, with everything in its place, like the sign said.

"It feels so good to be finished with this project," said Iris, "no more pressure. Although, I loved the thrill of searching for those cylinders and coming up with solutions to the problems as they arose. Now that it's all over, and we've found the gold it feels anticlimactic. I guess all the fun was in the chase."

"We still have a few more obstacles to overcome. But, you're right about all the fun being in the chase. I experience that every time we catch a trophy fish. All the pleasure is in tempting the fish to bite, hooking him up, playing him and finally landing him. After that, the fun is over and I feel sorry for the fish. I always have a good feeling when we release a catch."

"I hope and pray this scheme works out for us, Bill. I don't want anyone to get hurt."

"We'll all be careful and do what's right. Try not to worry about it.

"What are you going to do with the rest of your day?"

"I'm going to meet Faith and have a late lunch and do some house hunting."

"Good for you, Iris. I hope you find something you both like. I know you'll be happy living here in Key West."

I drove her to the yacht and reluctantly watched her go aboard, then went back to the house.

Jacques made up some sandwiches and iced tea and we, the Three Amigos, enjoyed lunch out on the comfortable deck. We talked for a while about what Iris said, and we all agreed that once we found the gold the excitement ended. Like the build up to a horse race, then the race itself, then the finish. Once it's over, there seems to be a little feeling of disappointment.

"Especially when you're holding a bunch of losing ticket stubs," said Erik.

We laughed and then speculated about what the next few days would bring, as we confronted our four unsavory opponents.

That night, Erik and I became night owls pulling surveillance duty, fully armed, inside Maury's. We showed up at the back door around eleven P.M. and stayed in Maury's office until closing time. Maury locked us in and we sat in the dark, waiting for our friends to show up, until seven in the morning. That's when Maury opened up for cleaning and prep work.

Saturday, February 12, 1966

The next morning, Iris came over at noon after Temple.

"I guess Maury didn't waste any time getting the word out. Bob told me about the treasure in Maury's vault this morning. He told me not to say anything about it, because it's supposed to be a secret."

"I knew Maury wouldn't disappoint us," I said.

That night and the following three nights, Sunday, Monday and Tuesday, Erik and I performed guard duty at Maury's.

We needn't have bothered, because what they had in mind was unexpected, personal and low, even for them.

Sunday, Monday and Tuesday

(Stakeout)

Wednesday, February 16, 1966

At seven A.M. Frank called all in a panic.

"I'm sorry to bother you so early, Bill," he said in a shaky voice, "but is Iris there?"

"No she isn't. What's wrong, Frank?"

"I flew in late last night and just assumed that she had turned into her cabin early. Nicole woke me this morning saying that she never came in last night. Her bed hasn't been slept in."

"How about Faith is she there? Maybe she's with her?"

"Faith is right here and she's worried too."

"Let me call you right back, I'll ask Erik and Jacques if they know anything."

Jacques standing next to me in the kitchen took in the conversation and he had no idea where she could be. I woke up Erik and he didn't know anything. He leaped out of bed, very concerned about his sister and hurriedly dressed. I called Frank back and told him that Erik and Jacques didn't know either. He said he would be right over.

"I'm afraid we have to assume kidnapping," I said.

"If they harm Iris in any way," said Erik, "there isn't anywhere on earth they can hide from me."

"You don't think those people would do anything to hurt Iris, do you Bill?" asked Jacques.

"If they do, I'm with Erik. We'll make them pay dearly for it. That I swear."

Frank came in full of questions. We calmed him down and I told him what I felt, that Iris had been abducted for ransom, which of course, would be the cylinders.

"We should have known that they would do something like this. We should have been more careful. We should have foreseen that Iris would be a target for kidnapping. If anything happens to her, I'll never forgive myself."

"Settle down, Frank," I said. "That's the last thing any of us thought they would do. In fact, Erik and I have been guarding the cylinders in Maury's vault to keep Joe Stalker and company from stealing them.

"We're at their mercy now, and we'll have to wait until we hear from them. Of course we'll do anything necessary to get Iris back."

"I heard that the cylinders are in Maury's vault. No one's supposed to know. So that's true then, Bill?

"Yes it's true, Frank. We thought that would be the safest place to store them. Somehow the secret got leaked."

"Yes we'll give them whatever they want. I have resources, if it's money they want I can get it."

"I think they'll want the cylinders."

"C'mon, Erik, let's go pay Joe Stalker a visit," I said.

I checked my Luger and tucked it into my belt then we headed over to Joe's apartment. We knocked on his door and as I expected no one answered. One of the neighbors heard us and came out and told us that he and his comrade moved out the day before.

We went down to charter boat row and found out the same story. Joe's boat was gone.

"They must have spent the night moored off shore, somewhere," I said. "There are a hundred places they could be hiding. I hate the thoughts of Iris being on that boat with those four lowlifes."

"I wish I could get my hands on them," said Erik angrily.

"That goes double for me, Erik, but all we can do is wait until they contact us."

We didn't have to wait very long. It came in the morning mail in a manila envelope addressed in block letters to disguise the writer. Sure enough, they wanted all of the cylinders hidden in the vault at Maury's. Iris was safe and would remain safe unless we did something foolish, like notifying the police.

A crudely drawn map of Key West with the 24-degree latitude and the 82-degree longitude intersecting about forty miles south west of Key West marked with a red X. The red X indicated the spot where we were to be at 1300 hours on Thursday the seventeenth. We were to have all the cylinders visible in an open skiff ready to be exchanged for an open skiff with Iris in it. Both skiffs were to have two 150-foot lines each, one fastened to the bow and the other to the stern. There should be no other boats within sight. Each skiff will be set adrift bow first being held back by the stern line. A swimmer will be allowed from each vessel to retrieve the ends of the bowlines and then each party for the exchange will pull both skiffs simultaneously. Remember, dire consequences for deviation from this procedure will be promptly carried out.

"I know from firsthand experience with these animals," said Erik, "they will follow through with their threat without the slightest hesitation. We have to cooperate with them until we know that Iris is safe and then it will be our turn to deal with them. They're dead men if they harm, Iris."

"Here are the facts so far as I see it." I said. "They want to meet out there because it will be easier to see any threat to them. They will be in International Waters and have Joe Stalker's boat with a full tank of gas for their getaway trip to Cuba. They will be well armed and ready to eliminate any witnesses. Can anyone think of anything else?"

"It's very deep out there," said Jacques, "about three thousand feet. That's a good spot to get rid of evidence, like a boat and witnesses."

"We should call the coast guard," said Frank.

"Frank," I said. "We can't forget about Iris. We're dealing with some really bad people here. They are Nazis, and they want to bring back the Third Reich. If they even think we're talking to the authorities they will kill Iris without a thought. Remember what I said, after they get what they want they won't be leaving any witnesses. That's why they stated no other boats in sight and picked that deep water location."

"Won't they be happy to just get the cylinders?" said Frank.

"Just try and imagine what Hitler would do."

"You're right Bill, they plan to kill us all. I never thought of that, I don't feel so good. I have a migraine. I better go back to the yacht and lie down."

"That's okay," I said. "We'll work out all the details. I'll give you a call tomorrow morning."

Jacques put on some more coffee and started to get something ready for lunch. Erik and I went out on the deck and a few minutes later Faith came walking up the back path, wearing a white short sleeve blouse, khaki shorts and sandals.

"Faith, what are you doing here?" asked Erik.

"I'm worried about Iris."

We told her that Iris was kidnapped and showed her the ransom letter.

"I was afraid it was something like that. Well, I'm here to help. Since I've come to know Iris better, she has become one of my best friends. I want to help get her back safe and sound. Do you think they would hurt a wonderful person like Iris, Bill?"

Hearing it spoken like that turned my stomach, as many tender images of Iris flooded through my mind. I became enraged at her kidnappers, but I had to force myself to keep a clear head.

"Yes, Faith, I hate to tell you, we're quite sure they were responsible for the death of Erik's cousin, Gerhard Wagner in West Germany. I don't think they would think twice about carrying out their threats.

"We're going to exchange the cylinders for Iris, tomorrow," I said, "about forty miles out to sea. After they get the cylinders, we think they will try and eliminate us and sink the boat, then flee to Cuba. There's no doubt in my mind that they are capable of such a heinous act."

"I'm going with you tomorrow. I didn't want to boast before but I've won plenty of trophies for sharp shooting. I even went up against some Army snipers and won. I hit what I aim at, and I have no qualms about shooting to kill if my friend Iris's life is at stake."

"I won't deny that we could use your talent," I said, "but it's going to be dangerous out there."

"There's going to be shooting out there," said Erik. "I don't want anything to happen to you, Faith."

"Listen, those low down S.O.B's have Iris and no one's stopping me from going out there to shoot their Asses off! I'm not too crazy about going out on the ocean, but I am the most qualified one here to shoot and hit a target from a moving deck.

"Who knows, Erik, I may pick up a notch or two tomorrow," she said coolly.

Erik had that look of being proud of his girlfriend and scared of her at the same time.

"Sit down with us Faith," I said, "and help us come up with a plan to outwit these vermin."

I filled her in on the plan we were working on and how we were going to comply with their demands.

Jacques came out with the coffee and said hello to Faith.

"I heard you telling about all those trophies you won, I'm sure glad you're on our side."

"I just want Iris back in one piece, Jacques that's all, and I'll do what it takes."

We spent the next several hours finalizing the plan to rescue Iris. Everything had to be geared toward her safety and had to be coordinated around that one o'clock deadline.

The news about Iris spread quickly and many people wanted to help. We knew, if left to act on their own, they could create a problem and might endanger Iris. Erik with his experience knew how to organize an operation like this. Once the general plan had been agreed upon, he took over and came up with contingency plans none of us would have thought of. A couple of examples were to have on hand some incendiary rounds to shoot into their boat in several places to set it on fire. They would have to stop shooting at us to fight the fires. Also, to get some heavy sheet metal to line the cockpit of the Rose Maria, so we could duck behind for protection when they started shooting at us.

After a quick lunch, Erik and I took the truck and dropped Faith off at the yacht, then went and picked up some one eighth inch thick sheet metal and used it to lined the boat cockpit.

I had an old skiff in storage that Erik and I dragged out and put in the back of the Chevy truck along with about a 150 pounds of old scrape iron and some canvas to hide it. We brought the skiff back to the house and put it in the back yard. Because it had been in storage it had dried out, so we filled it with water to swell up the seams. It would be watertight by morning.

We had to have them see the skiff loaded with the cylinders sink before they could pull it to their boat. That way, they would report back to their superiors the loss of the gold in that extremely deep water, ending all future interest in us. However, the main reason was so they wouldn't be able to pick up one of the cylinders and find out they were fake. To insure that it would sink on cue, we bored a couple of two-inch diameter holes into the lowest part of the transom. We fitted the holes with two wooden plugs with screw eyes attached to thin wires, which we could pull at the appropriate time. Lead weights were attached to the two plugs to make sure they would sink undetected when pulled. To help things along, the scrap iron added to the weight of the replica cylinders ensuring the skiff would sink quickly.

We topped off the gas tanks and I checked the engine. The old Rose Maria had to earn her keep tomorrow. We figured it would take at least two and a half hours to travel the forty miles to the red X site. We planned to leave at ten A. M.

We managed to get all that done before eight PM.

When we got back to the house, Faith had come by and was waiting for us. Jacques had some sandwiches made and we all sat out on the deck to eat and go over the plan again, to make sure we hadn't forgotten anything. Jacques reminded me to bring a pry bar with us to open the boxes of cylinders, which would have been a problem out there without it. I went and got the flat bar right then, so I wouldn't forget, and placed it with my guns.

Being close to midnight, we decided to call it quits. Even though Faith carried her personal weapon, I told Erik to take my Luger with him while he drove her back to the yacht. Ray was on duty, also carrying a side arm and he personally saw her to her cabin.

Thursday, February 17, 1966

The Three Amigos were up at daybreak. After a quick breakfast we started getting everything together. I packed my guns and some extra ammunition. We had a long day ahead of us on the boat, so Jacques made up a bunch of sandwiches for everyone. Erik made up a detailed checklist to make sure we didn't forget anything.

I asked Jacques to stay onshore, but he felt insulted to think I would ask him such a thing. I apologized, shook his hand and welcomed him.

At eight o'clock, Faith showed up with her pistol and an M-16 with a half a dozen clips, one of which had red tape wrapped around it to denote incendiary rounds. She wore a long sleeve shirt, jeans, and sneakers with her hair pulled back in a ponytail

"Where did you get the M-16 and the incendiary rounds?" I asked.

"You'd be surprised what Bob and Ray have access to. They're useful guys to have around. And they told me to tell you that they're in, and they're coming equipped. They'll meet us at the boat at nine thirty."

"That's good, I knew I could count on them and thank you again Faith, for throwing in with us.

Bob and Ray, when they see all the wooden cylinders, are going to have a few questions. I suggest that we take them into our confidence and decide on some type of compensation. There will be a need for security later on when we start to move the real cylinders, and I think I'd feel better having them around."

"I go along with that Bill," said Jacques, "we could give them a random cylinder to split."

"I like that idea," said Erik, "If they're lucky they may make out really well."

I agreed with them and felt that Iris would too, if she were here. On the boat trip out to the showdown, I told Jacques and Erik that I would make the proposal to them.

Faith and Jacques left for the boat at nine to double check everything, so we'd have extra time in case we forgot something.

Erik and I went to Maury's and moved the boxes of cylinders to the boat.

Knowing what the cylinders look like, they should be happy when they see the skiff full of them.

We went back to the house to get the little boat. It was swelled up and still had a few inches of water left in it, which we dumped out. We put it in the truck, brought it down to the dock, and set her in the water behind the Rose Maria. We carefully placed the iron into the ill-fated craft and concealed it with the canvas.

I called Frank and found that he was distraught and still suffering with his migraine. He apologized for not coming with us and wished us luck.

I talked to my friends in the Coast Guard, and they agreed to keep out of the way until needed. Maury and Bosun Jim had their assignments as well.

At ten o'clock the Three Amigos along with Faith, Bob, and Ray were all on board. The two UDT's brought a small arsenal of guns, grenades, and ammunition. We were ready for battle.

We left the dock, towing the iron-laden skiff behind us. A half hour later we were out in the open ocean heading for the agreed rendezvous.

I talked to Bob and Ray and let them in on the secret of the wooden cylinders and gave them our proposal. They both said that they were there because they owed us and for the fun. Regardless, I said we wanted to give them one of the real cylinders and contents for their help today and for the next few weeks.

Faith started to get a little seasick and needed help. I asked Jacques to get her a sleeve of Saltines from the galley and told her to look out at the horizon and munch on them.

I asked Erik to open a couple of boxes of cylinders so we could quickly load up the skiff when we got there.

Ray agreed to be our swimmer to retrieve the line from the skiff that would carry Iris.

When we were halfway there, Faith said the Saltines did the trick and wanted to try out the M-16. Jacques tossed an empty wine bottle into the water behind the boat. It filled halfway and then stood upright bobbing as we sped ahead. Faith watched as it got smaller and smaller. We all wondered what she was waiting for. Jacques got out the binoculars to keep an eye on the diminishing target. Finally she lifted the M-16 and almost instantly fired one shot.

"She hit it!" shouted Jacques.

I could just barely see the green pieces of glass flung into the air.

We were all impressed by her eyesight and marksmanship.

"Nice shooting, Faith," I said. "Jacques, what else do you have she can shoot at?"

Jacques found some empty beer bottles and asked Faith how she wanted to shoot at them.

"Toss one up in the air behind the boat."

Jacques threw it as high as he could and just before it hit the water a bullet shattered it.

"Try two this time, Jacques."

Jacques asked Bob to throw one with him. They counted to three and threw the bottles high in the air. Bob's went much higher than Jacques. Again, two shots rang out and the flying glass from the two bottles fell into the ocean.

"Thanks, I'm all set now. I'll have to get me one of these, I like it."

Within an hour we sighted the enemy's boat through binoculars heading for the same place. Everyone got below except Jacques and me. It looked like they would be there a little ahead of us. Within an hour we were within shouting distance.

At last we were face to face with our adversaries, all four of them. Joe Stalker, his two compatriots, and peering through a window, we could see the little ratfink Slip.

Joe remained incommunicado because of his wired jaw.

"Where are the cylinders?" demanded the man with the hair, looking at the empty skiff.

"Where is Iris?" I countered back.

They let Iris stand up. A feeling of relief and fear gripped me as I waved to her knowing I was powerless to do anything... for now. She was wearing navy blue shorts and a white short sleeve blouse. With her hands tied behind her back, she managed a nod to us with a feeble smile.

I held up an open box of the cylinders and started loading them into the skiff. I couldn't resist putting a couple aside as souvenirs for Iris. Erik started to pry open the other boxes, saving the ones with just the bricks for last.

Bob and Ray came out and started to help us.

"You should have done that before you came out here, and we told you to come alone," shouted the one with hair, angrily, seeing Erik, Bob, and Ray.

"And if the skiff capsized would you have believed us? We needed help moving all this gold," I snarled back.

They conferred back and forth then he shouted to us to hurry and to my relief, not to bother opening the rest of the boxes. The skiff sunk low in the water, as we added the rest of the heavy boxes. I tossed the bowline out as far as I could and Erik pushed on the stern to set it on its way. Being so low in the water it didn't go very far.

In the mean time they placed Iris into their skiff, tossed the line out, and likewise sent the little boat toward us. The German with the hair pulled off his shirt revealing several swastikas and dove in to retrieve the bowline of our skiff. Bob dove in and swam for the bowline of theirs. When both sides were in possession of the lines we each began pulling the precious cargos towards each other. I pulled the one with Iris and the man with the hair kept me from pulling too fast. Joe and the bald man were pulling the overloaded skiff against Jacques and Bob.

"Be careful!" I yelled. "That skiff is way overloaded with all that gold. Don't pull too hard or you'll swamp it."

When the skiffs were side by side I quietly gave Bob the word to pull one of the plugs on our skiff. Bob discreetly gave a yank on one of the wires that were threaded through Iris' little door and we saw it pop out and sink undetected. I started to pull on Iris' line a little more firmly getting a complaint from the man with the hair paying out the stern line.

"You've got your gold let me pull in Iris," I pleaded.

In a huff, he tossed away the line and relieved the bald man who was having trouble trying to help Joe, because of the cast on his wrist. They both began to pull in the loaded skiff, which got harder as it started sinking deeper.

Erik helped me quickly pull in Iris. As soon as she came alongside she stood up and stepped forward to let us unceremoniously get her on board and whisked below, to join Faith who had been patiently waiting clutching the M-16.

Erik gave Iris a hug and said, "I'm so grateful you're safe. I've been terribly worried about you, Iris."

"Are you all right, Iris? Did they hurt you?" I asked.

"I'm okay. They didn't harm me at all, honest. But, those swine took my brand new pistol away from me."

"After you untie her Faith get ready," I said, "things are going to start happening. You stay below Iris. That's an order."

I quietly told Bob to pull the other plug. He reached down and pulled the remaining wire. The second plug followed its mate on the long journey to the bottom.

I reached for the radio and called the Coast Guard and gave them the word to come on as fast as possible. Maury was holding back several boats each full of Key Westers, all volunteers wanting to help us. When they saw the Coast Guard move that was their signal to move out too.

"Hey, go easy with that line you're getting water into the skiff." I shouted.

They still had about thirty feet to go, and I could see the skiff sinking perilously lower getting harder to pull. The frustration and anxiety started to build as they all pulled on the line. They were so focused that they didn't notice the Coast Guard cutter heading our way with the armada of smaller boats following.

The three of them started pulling on the line and suddenly it broke. They panicked and started yelling at each other. They got another line, and the German with the hair dove into the water again. He tied the new line to the bow ring of the skiff and swam back and climbed on board. This time Joe wrapped the line around his waist and marched with all his strength backward pulling his own boat toward the skiff as well. He then moved forward taking up the slack around his waist and marched backward again even as the water started lapping over the gunwales of the doomed skiff.

"Joe, get that line off you!" I shouted. "That skiff is sinking and it will pull you down with it."

The other two goons under Joe's orders picked up their rifles and started to shoot at us. The bald one because of the cast on his right wrist, had to use his left hand and rest the rifle on his right arm. We all got down and could hear bullets as they penetrated the side of the boat making bumps in the sheet metal. Ray jumped up and fired a few rounds back at them. Surprised by the returned shots, they ducked down and held their fire.

The skiff finally started sinking pulling Joe with ever strengthening force and he couldn't untangle himself. Panic stricken, he started screaming in German through his wired teeth as he was being inextricably pulled from the boat. The two horrified men put down their weapons and tried desperately to untie him, but as the skiff started slowly going down the line tightened even more. I will never forget the terrified look on Joe's face as he strained mightily in his losing effort to keep from being drawn down into the abyss.

I shouted to Faith to come out and try to shoot the taut line that had its death grip on Joe. She raised the M-16 and quickly fired a shot. The line parted and Joe was flung violently backward, but safely into the boat. The two astonished men watched the weighted skiff disappear with what they were convinced was all that Nazi gold.

The thought occurred to me that they were going to have a lot of explaining to do, to their overseers. The reward for this failure may not be very pleasant. They may have to seek another safe haven other than Cuba.

The two angry men started to pick up their rifles again.

"Faith," I said, "I think they need a demonstration of your marksmanship. Show them what you can do."

"I'd be delighted, Bill. Watch this."

Before they could fire their weapons, Faith stood up and calmly fired two quick shots in succession and continued to aim the M-16 at them. Instantly both men clutched their right ears, the bald man had to use his left hand. In an exhibition of shooting that would have pleased Annie Oakley, Faith had clipped each man's right ear. Looking at each other's bloodied ears, they realized the superb marksmanship that had just been achieved. Then, seeing Faith still drawing a bead on them, they set their guns down PDQ and put the available other hands up in surrender.

"Yes sir, I've got to get me one of these M-16's."

"That's shooting I'd pay money to see," said Bob, "Faith, consider that piece yours."

"Why thank you, Bob."

"If I didn't see it with my own eyes, I never would have believed it," said Ray.

Then a familiar face appeared. The cowering Slip, with a wary eye on Faith, cautiously came out with a couple of rags for the two men's ears.

"Do you want me to clip him too, Bill?"

"No, I think you've done enough clipping for today, they've got the message loud and clear. Well done, Faith!"

"Awe Bill, you're a spoilsport," said Bob.

The Coast Guard cutter arrived first, and they sent an armed team onto Joe's boat. I hollered over that the chrome plated pistol belonged to us. It was found and returned, but the several other weapons and ammunition on board were accidently dropped over board. They photographed the three men and then a corpsman stitched up the two ears and declared them okay. The sheepish and silent Joe received some ice for the large bump on the back of his head, suffered when he fell backward into the boat.

The Captain said he had no right to detain them out here, but let them know that there will be wanted posters, on each one of them for kidnapping, in all U. S. Ports.

Then, six charter boats and a shrimper arrived on the scene, all of them crowded with gun toting passengers. One of them came up close with Maury and Bosun Jim both wearing their 1911 forty-fives. Maury easily heard, hailed us.

"You guys need any help out here?"

"We're okay, now!" using my megaphone, "You missed all the fun. Faith gave Joe Stalker and his fellow Nazis a lesson in sharpshooting. They won't be giving us any more trouble."

Standing next to them was Nicole waving to Jacques and next to her were Kristin, Sam, and Jake carrying his World War Two, M-1 rifle.

"Thanks for backing us up," I said with Iris by my side.

The Coast Guard Captain said, "You sure are a lucky guy to have all these friends come way out here to help you, Bill."

"Key West friendship runs deep, Captain, and thank you for your help as well."

With that he gave me an informal salute and the order to his crew to return to base. The slipshod Slip, taking the wheel of Joe's boat, didn't waste any time heading south for Cuba with the three dispirited Nazis. As they navigated the gauntlet of Key West boats, they were pummeled with a variety of unvarnished taunts and jeers.

"Thank God you're safe, Iris," I said, "Are you sure they didn't hurt you?"

"If they did, Iris," said Faith, holding up the red clip. "Let me know, I can still spray them with a clip full of incendiary rounds."

"No, I have to say they treated me okay. Let them go. Where's Frank?"

"He suddenly got a headache," said Faith, "when he heard there might be shooting out here and a chance he could get killed. The big coward is back on his yacht lying down. Don't tell him I said that!"

Oh, Faith, Thank you so much. I love your delivery; it has a much keener edge to it, then if I said it. I never would have used the word coward. I watched Iris' face for the effect.

She calmly asked to use my megaphone. She climbed up onto the tower and made an announcement to all the boats gathered around us.

"Big Shindig at Maury's tonight and you're all invited. We're going to celebrate our friendship the Key West way... Did you hear me?"

Cheers, horns, whistles and gunshots sent a clear message that they did.

"Frank's paying for this party, every penny of it," she shouted down to us angrily, "This is going to be an un-engagement party for him and me. He's getting his ring back tonight, this time for good."

She climbed down from the tower, and it was evident that she was ripping mad. If Frank was within reach, she would have laid him out in lavender.

She started pacing up and down, I knew the best thing for me to do, was to keep silent. Jacques handed her the open bottle of rum, and she grabbed it and took a healthy swig.

"Thank you, Jacques, keep it handy!"

She looked out at the horizon deep breathing for a few minutes and then turned to me and smiled.

"By the way, Bill," she said, in her usual tone of voice, "it's a good thing they never searched me. Look what I've got."

She reached into her pocket and pulled out four gold doubloons and placed them in my hand.

"These are real, Iris! Where did you get them?"

"On one of the dives a while back, I saw the outline of a shipwreck. I waved the metal detector around, and there were hundreds of coins just a few inches under the sand. I just took four to show you at some later date, because we had enough going on at the time. I had Jacques triangulate the spot as interesting. I put them in my pocket to show you just before they kidnapped me."

"Here we go again!" said Jacques.

"Does this un-engagement party mean you're not engaged any more, Iris?"

"You got that right, Bill. It's officially over between Frank and me."

I pulled her to me and held her in my arms and kissed her. She put her arms around me and kissed me back. This time she didn't pull away. The eight boats surrounding us started up again with the loud cheers, horns, whistle, gunshots and even a couple of signal rockets, like a fourth of July celebration. They knew; everyone in Key West knew; we belonged together.